To all the dreamers who are stubbornly following their hearts:

I see you.

Keep going.

You've got this.

"Hope is the thing with feathers
That perches in the soul
And sings the tune without the words
And never stops at all."

—EMILY DICKINSON

Reality With You

A NOVEL

CHAPTER 1

Lennon

Lennon Young moved like a ghost through the current of strangers, her mind stuck replaying the meeting she'd left minutes ago in a Manhattan high-rise.

"It isn't working for us," the Goldrush Records executive said, hands folded over a polished mahogany desk. She'd noticed how weak they looked—like they'd never experienced labor or made anything besides deals he was willing to break. "The label wants to go in a different direction."

"So … you want me to rework the music? Again?"

They'd been down this road a few times. The sound's not right. The album needs more sex appeal. The songs need to be catchier—more commercial, more viral.

Months of rewriting and re-recording, tirelessly trying to satisfy them.

His mouth flattened in a line. He tapped his index fingers together. "This partnership is no longer working."

The morning sky was drained of color, raindrops painting dark splotches on the concrete as petrichor mixed with petrol fumes.

Pedestrians popped open umbrellas, ducked under awnings, and held newspapers over their heads, but Lennon barely felt the drizzle on her skin or the shoulders bumping against her.

A rod of grief shot through her chest. Lennon sucked in a sharp breath, tamping it down. No way in hell she was going to sob in the middle of Fifth Avenue. Her twelve-hour serving shift started in less than an hour and red, swollen eyes and a stuffy nose wouldn't earn her generous tips from the high-end restaurant's clientele.

Besides some occasional gigs at banquets and events, tips were her sole income now.

The rain picked up to a steady downpour. Lennon wrapped her oversized denim jacket around her torso to protect her white button-up shirt tucked into a black skirt for work. Black combat boots sloshed through puddles in a crosswalk and squeaked down the subway steps as Lennon hugged her messenger bag carrying her work shoes to her chest. She rushed to the platform and slipped through the doors of her train seconds before they screeched shut behind her.

The car was gloriously empty thanks to the morning rush having passed. Damp flyaways from her low, dark bun clung to her cheeks and the soaked denim jacket hung heavy on her body as she dropped into one of the faded orange seats. Lennon expelled a sigh, relieved to finally be at rest, at least for a few minutes. Her lack of sleep intensified all points of discomfort—the fluorescent overhead lights, the hard plastic seats, the moisture and underground chill.

But at least she was sitting. *Alone.*

Wait—no, that was worse. As the train jostled forward, grief bubbled up in the silence, stinging her eyes, demanding to be felt.

Not here. Not now.

Lennon pulled her phone from her bag and opened her Favorite Contacts list where her best friend's name sat. She hesitated. Erin was probably already at work. As the assistant physical therapist for a major league baseball team, Erin's day always started early, and Lennon wasn't sure what time zone the Arden Beach Tidebreakers were currently in since they were on the road. Hell, even Erin's days off started before the sun rose because she was a chronic early bird. Meanwhile, Lennon was practically a walking corpse for having to make it to a 9:00 a.m. meeting on the opposite side of the city. All for the executive to end up being thirty minutes late.

The idea of burdening anyone with her problems sent a wave of shame through her. It's what first inspired her to write music as a kid. In doing so, she'd discovered her most reliable outlet for whatever she felt. It was a place to bare her soul without bothering another human. She'd become a pro at bottling up her feelings until it was only her, a piece of paper, and a guitar. Her sanctuary.

Erin never gave her a reason to feel like a burden—that credit belonged to Lennon's mother—and if she knew Lennon was hesitating to reach out to her, she'd give her a verbal lashing. With love.

Her thumb still hovered over Erin's name. The sensation of her chest splintering made her suck in a breath, attempting to hold the cracks together.

Once she told Erin, it would be real.

Tears pooled as she pressed her eyes shut. Exhaling, Lennon glanced down and through the blurry haze she double-tapped Erin's name, then put the phone to her ear.

It rang a few times before the line clicked.

"Lennon?"

Her entire body froze at the familiar *male* voice.

A voice that felt like an old, favorite song. A voice she'd recognize anywhere.

The sound sobered her like a gush of ice water. She stared at the curved metal ceiling, wide-eyed and white-knuckling her phone. The train's steady rumble and the occasional clattering on the tracks filled the silence around her.

"Hello?" he said, speaking louder over a mix of other voices in the background. His voice still had the low, easy rasp that had always given her butterflies. "Are you there?"

"I … I was trying to call Erin," Lennon finally answered, her voice pitched slightly higher than she would've liked. She cleared her tight throat. "Are you, uh, with her?"

"No, you called me." A soft chuckle tickled her ear.

Her brow furrowed as she looked down at her phone. The screen read *Dylan* in bright white, accusatory letters.

Dylan, whose last name was Strickland and sat directly above his fraternal twin sister's name, Erin, in the list.

Her ex-husband, whom she hadn't spoken to since she left Florida six years ago.

"You … are … correct. I sure did," Lennon confirmed, flinching with embarrassment. She never removed him from her damn Favorites. "It was an accident. Sorry to bother you."

"It's OK, you didn't," Dylan assured her, a little breathless. The background voices receded before vanishing like he'd moved to another room. "I'm … are you OK? You sound a little off."

Dylan's intuitive assessment rattled her. It was too familiar, too comforting, too much like things used to be before he'd thrown a grenade at their life together. "How would you know what I sound like when I'm anything anymore?"

Judging by the silence on the other end, she was pretty certain she'd successfully landed a gut punch. The satisfaction was minor and fleeting. Shame swiftly replaced it. She winced as she tucked her chin. "I'm sorry."

"You don't need to apologize," he quickly said. "I deserved it."

Did he, though? Erin told her about Dylan's desire to make amends. While recovering from his accident earlier that year, he'd written Lennon a letter she'd kept tucked in a drawer with an unbroken seal. It wasn't that she didn't *want* to smooth things over between them; she just … hadn't been able to make herself go there. To reopen that wound.

It was easier to ignore it, like she did with everything that wasn't her music career.

This wasn't how she'd imagined their first conversation going since their divorce.

"I'm having a *really* bad day," Lennon said. "My record label dropped me." She'd intended it to come out as an apology—an explanation for snapping at him. Instead, her voice hollowed out.

"What? No way," Dylan said, as if the idea were absurd. A beat passed without her responding. "Are you serious?"

Lennon readied a sarcastic comment, but a fresh wave of tears strangled it. She choked down the sob trying to claw its way up her throat. "As a fuckin' heart attack."

His low, sorrowful sigh hummed against her ear. "Shit. Lynx."

Her heart twinged at the nickname he and Erin had called her since they were kids. In the space of a second, she heard him yelling to her up in the bleachers from the field during his youth league practice. Wishing her a happy birthday in her ear during her sweet sixteen party. Telling her that he loved her for the first time after a game. His voice was a bit deeper than she'd remembered but still painfully familiar.

"I'm ... so sorry."

"Me too. I'm a broke waitress with a failed record deal." Lennon laughed humorlessly at herself as she wiped the corners of her eyes, carefully avoiding her mascara, though it had probably already melted from the rain.

"Well, I'm a suspended baseball player trying to clean up a PR disaster, so you're doing better than me if that's any consolation."

"That does make me feel a little better actually. Thank you." She sniffled. "I'll cry about it later over wine and pizza like Olivia Pope or ..." She racked her overladen brain for another example.

"*The Golden Girls*?"

"That was pie."

"I think they drank wine, too," Dylan said.

Lennon pictured the little crease between his dark-brown eyes as he shuffled through his memory, trying to convince himself he was right. A flutter rose up her sternum. "I don't think so. I mean, maybe sometimes, but not like, as a regular *thing*."

"Wasn't there an episode with them stomping grapes in a barrel?"

"That was *I Love Lucy*, Dylan. Get your TV shows straight. You should binge-watch them since you have more time on your hands now." As soon as the words left her mouth, she cringed. The stress and exhaustion made her loose with her words, slipping into their old way of joking as if they weren't basically strangers now. "Shit, sorry. That was insensitive—"

Dylan laughed like he always had at her sarcasm, and she relaxed at the sound—boyish and uninhibited—as the train pulled into a station. The doors slid open. "No, you're right. That was a gross mistake on my part. But if it was wine, they probably wouldn't be a good influence," he noted. "I could end up in more trouble, and then it'd be your fault."

A smile formed on her face, but memories from those last few months of their marriage pushed their way in and sucked the tiny bit of joy from her like a vacuum. The nights she'd spent crying in an empty bed, telling herself she wasn't a good enough wife because if she were, he wouldn't be out drinking and partying; he'd be at home, with her.

As a twenty-five-year-old, she now knew that was bullshit—that his actions hadn't been *her* fault—but that understanding hadn't erased the scars and emotional imprints they'd left behind. While she'd handled it the best she could at the time, she still regarded their marriage as a personal failure. They'd proved everyone right who told them they were too young to get married. They'd thought their love was different—something special.

But they hadn't made it a year.

Just like her record deal.

Lennon sucked in a breath as the grief swelled again. The doors shut; the car still empty except for her as the train shoved forward.

"Hey, are you OK?" Dylan asked, his gentleness loosening her grip a little on the shield around her heart.

Lennon caught her lower lip between her teeth. "I knew

something was wrong when they asked me to come in for a meeting this morning," she admitted. "I'd hoped it was to talk about my recording session tomorrow … give me more notes on what they wanted. They've had me change things so many times. But something told me this time was different." She exhaled a dark chuckle. "My last session was … my last. And I didn't even know it."

She'd had this nightmare before, losing the record deal she'd finally landed after years of crawling her way through countless auditions and demos and gigs at seedy bars, the rug being pulled out from under her just when she thought she'd finally made it.

Except this time, she wouldn't wake up.

This was her reality.

"I know what that deal meant to you," Dylan said, the words clipped as if restraining anger. "I'm sorry it turned out this way."

She watched the dark concrete whizz past the windows, the smell of stale, damp air thick in her lungs as the train gently rocked her. The cabin's emptiness reminded Lennon of her apartment, which was as sterile and lifeless, serving as a temporary stop on her way to her dreams. She realized it was a sad reflection of her life, devoid of anything meaningful as she rushed toward something, only now she seemed to be going in circles.

She wondered if Dylan felt a similar emptiness. Baseball was his life, and for now, he'd lost it.

"How did we get here?" Lennon mused, like the dreamy little girl inside had suddenly woken up and looked around and couldn't understand how the hell the adult version had so royally messed up everything.

"I don't know," Dylan answered like the little boy she'd met on the baseball field all those years ago who had suddenly woken up and found himself just as lost. He remained quiet for a moment, and in that space everything she'd wanted to say to him rushed in. *Why'd you break your promise? Why'd you abandon me? Why wasn't I enough? We were supposed to face life together. You threw it all away … you threw* me *away …*

"But at least we don't have to stay here," he said resolutely, the man he was now returning and interrupting her thoughts. "That's what my therapist keeps telling me, anyway."

Lennon sensed a smirk in his voice, but she didn't smile herself. Her heart was too battered to let hope in yet.

To let *him* in.

As much as she wanted to believe herself mature enough to have a friendship with him again—as much as, God help her, she just fucking *missed* him—she wasn't convinced she'd ever be ready to move on from *here*. From this place where she felt more pain than joy in his presence.

It was a day of accepting hard truths.

The metal wheels screeched as the train navigated a sharp curve, jabbing her ribs into the rail beside her seat. "I should go. My stop is coming up."

"Oh … going home?"

"I wish. I have to work. Though it's probably for the best. It'll help keep my mind off things rather than throwing myself a pity party."

"Sorry you got me instead of Erin. She would've probably offered better comfort."

At that moment, Lennon realized her heart was a little less heavy, but she felt too … vulnerable to admit that to him. He'd left her holding the broken pieces of it in her hands, forced to rebuild a life she'd never imagined without him. The fact that he could still reach her that way raised more questions than she currently had the capacity to deal with.

"I'll try to reach her on my break," Lennon said. Now, they'd have two events of emotional upheaval to unpack.

"I'll tell her to watch for your call when I see her."

"She's with you? I thought she was still on the road."

"They got in last night. She came with me to this golf tournament I'm doing, but right now she's holed up somewhere with a laptop, attending a lecture for one of her classes."

"You're playing in a *golf* tournament? You *hate* golf."

Dylan released a long-suffering sigh. She imagined him running a hand through his thick, dark-brown hair. "I do. But it's for charity."

Another man's voice rose in the background. "Hey, man. They want us back on the course in five."

"Well, good luck with your game," Lennon said. Her stop wasn't far off, and she needed some alone time before work to get her head straight.

"Thanks. I'll need it." Dylan paused. Then added, "And thanks for not hanging up on me." He tried to pass it off as a lighthearted joke, but she sensed the truth behind it. His own vulnerability.

"Don't get used to it," she joked back, and she had a feeling he sensed the truth behind that, too. "Bye, Dylan."

"Hey, Lennon—"

She dug her teeth into her lower lip, desperate to get off the phone. "Hm?"

"There's no way you won't be a successful musician."

The confidence in his declaration was a warm, soothing touch to her battered heart.

"You just deserve better than those idiot execs who were too blind to appreciate the good thing they had in front of them," Dylan continued. "Trust me, it's their loss. And by the time they realize what they gave up … they're going to regret letting go of someone like you."

CHAPTER 2

Dylan

Metal *snapped* against the golf ball, sending it soaring into the crisp blue sky. Spectators surrounding the course watched in silent anticipation as the ball arced in the general direction of the flag marking the tenth hole yet plopped several yards away in a sand trap.

Dylan, shielding his eyes with a gloved hand, pressed his lips together as shame struck a match up his neck. The silence at his back burned more than the hot morning sun. He hated losing, and golf was not his game—a fact made worse by his head being a thousand miles away on a New York City train instead of a South Florida golf course.

He'd stopped in the middle of the break room at the sight of Lennon's name lighting up his phone, nearly wearing another golfer's beverage as he narrowly avoided a collision with Dylan. He'd muttered an apology as his heart restarted—and then pounded like a jackhammer.

Finally, after six years.

He hadn't expected it, but a part of him hadn't given up hope that she'd give him a chance to make things right. He'd rehearsed what he wanted to say to her a thousand times. Except the call today hadn't been the appropriate time to say it all.

She was hurting.

Dylan's chest clenched all over again as he recalled the sound of Lennon's voice breaking while he'd helplessly listened in a lounge at a fucking country club. It's how she'd sounded the night she left him—holding back tears, trying not to let him see how much he'd broken her.

Something had broken inside him that night, too.

Dylan felt as useless then as he did now, wishing he'd known what the hell to say, what the hell to *do*, to ease her suffering. He sat there on the line like an idiot, offering sympathy and platitudes from probably the last person she wanted to hear them from.

And guiltily enjoying hearing her voice again. Being in her presence.

"Good thing you're not from a golf dynasty," another golfer quipped, yanking him back to the green. To the blazing sun, sweat lining the inner rim of his baseball cap, and hundreds of people watching him fail at yet another thing. He was zero for two today.

"Yeah, better stick to bigger balls," someone else commented.

Low chuckles murmured around them. Flags brandishing the Arden Beach Country Club logos and other sponsors of the charity event danced in the breeze, drawing Dylan's attention to one of the event photographers crouched beneath one. A reminder of why he was there.

To fix something else he'd broken.

Sweat slid under the collar of his tight polo shirt. Dylan smiled with a nod, taking the hits in his stride on the surface while each one scraped his pride like sand on a sunburn. "Maybe I'd do better if the clubs were wood," he remarked.

That got a bigger laugh.

With the tension successfully diffused, the group of golfers began filing into two golf carts to ride to the next hole. He flipped the club around in his hand and gripped it tightly, glancing at the sand trap where his ball sat alone.

Bunker shots were some of the hardest in golf. He probably had no business being hopeful of scoring, but that wouldn't stop him from trying.

After the tournament—he ended up ranking a pitiful seventy-five out of a hundred and forty-two players on the leaderboard—Dylan made small talk with some of the other players and spectators and stopped to talk to some of the press covering the event. When questions about "the incident" and the future of his baseball career came up, he politely cut the conversation short and made a swift escape to one of the VIP lounges.

On his way, he checked his phone notifications. It was a long shot that Lennon's name would show up again, but his chest deflated a little anyway when it didn't.

He found an empty lounge, further away from the main event area, where he could avoid most of the players and guests busy mingling. A buffet and assortment of bottled beverages lined the tables on a raised veranda overlooking the course. His stomach growled at the sight. As he browsed the table with charcuterie boards, a boy's voice and the sound of sneakers pounding the wooden floorboards stole his attention.

"Hey! 'Scuse me! Are you Dylan Strickland?"

Dylan turned to the boy, who was no more than ten or so. The child's eyes widened in awe. He smiled. "Last I checked," he confirmed. "Definitely not one of the pro golfers, that's for sure." He knelt down. "What's your name, buddy?"

"Caden. You're one of my *favorite* baseball players."

"Really? Aw, man. I'm honored." Dylan pressed a hand to his heart, warmth fanning from the spot.

"Can I have your autograph?"

"Of course—"

"Caden!" A frazzled woman in a red polo dress appeared around the corner, letting out a sigh of relief when she spotted the boy, then immediately tensing again when her gaze fell on Dylan. She took quick steps to Caden, snatching his hand. "I've told you not to run off like that."

"Sorry, Mom, but this is important. I found *Dylan Strickland*. The best starting pitcher for the Arden Beach Tidebreakers! He's going to give me an autograph."

"We don't have time for that. Sorry." Her attention locked on Dylan, the condemnation in her eyes slicing him like a blade.

Dylan slightly recoiled, stunned.

"Let's go."

"But Mom!—"

"Now, Caden." She tugged him away, the boy's expression awash with devastation as he watched Dylan over his shoulder.

Dylan raised a hand to wave goodbye, forcing a smile. "Nice to meet you, Caden," he called out.

As the boy disappeared around the corner, Dylan dropped his hand, remaining in a squat as he tried to process what just happened.

Though he'd primarily been a hermit since the accident, he'd noticed fewer fans came up to him than they used to when he did venture out of his cave. It had never dawned on him that parents wouldn't want their kids near him anymore.

Shame carved an icy pit in him.

Dylan rose and returned to the buffet, trying to shake it off. He plucked a roll of sliced ham and cheese from one of the tiers, popping the entire thing in his mouth as he reached for a buttery roll and some sort of granola cluster.

"There you are. I've been looking for you," Erin said, her voice drifting from behind him.

"How'd you find me?" Dylan asked around a mouthful of food.

"Figured you'd be hiding somewhere food was involved and

other people weren't." His sister's blonde ponytail filled his peripheral vision as she strolled up beside him, acquiring a toothpick from a small ceramic holder and piercing a couple of grapes on the fruit tier.

"Good call."

"I'd be hiding, too, after a game like that." Erin slid the grapes off the toothpick with her teeth.

Dylan glared at her. "Thanks."

"You're such a good batter. You'd think you'd be good at this, too." Her expression twinkled with sisterly teasing as she smiled back. "How's your shoulder?"

She was right—he *should* be good at golf. Although he pitched professionally, batting had always been his favorite position, and those skills typically transferred well to golf. He never could get his head into the game. The slowness of it, the eerie quietness of the course. It was like trying to play a game in a boardroom.

"It's OK. A little sore." Dylan absently rolled it as he finished off the food he'd snatched.

"We should do some PT today. My schedule's clear."

"I'll be alright. Take a day off for once." Dylan ignored the ache in his shoulder, instead brushing off his hands and moving to a cooler beside one of the tables. He plucked a bottle of mango juice from the bed of ice, unscrewing the cap.

Erin hopped up on the wide ledge overlooking the course, scooting back a bit to get comfortable as her legs dangled over the edge. "You know, losing a celebrity golf tournament isn't going to turn the tide in your favor."

"It's for charity, Erin," he said before bringing the bottle to his lips.

"That's what I mean. Everyone knows you're on an image rehabilitation tour. No one sees you leave the house unless you do something like this. It looks a little too ..."

He'd nearly downed the entire juice bottle. Coming up for air, he lifted an eyebrow in her direction. "Go on, say it."

Erin scrunched her nose apologetically. "Desperate."

Dylan snorted a laugh, shaking his head. His sister was more ruthless than any shit-talking athlete he'd ever met. "I've always done charity events. How is this any different?"

"You *hate* golf. And everyone knows you need the good press."

That one hurt. He shot her a sharp look. "That's not why I—"

"I know, Dyl," Erin interrupted. Tilting her head, her light hazel eyes looked at him with sincerity. "I know your heart is in the right place, but the *public* doesn't. And neither does the league's board, who's unfortunately deciding your fate." The last part was bitter on her tongue. She'd never been quiet about her distaste for the politics of baseball, but especially now. "It's about perception, fair or not. And right now, people don't know what to believe."

Dylan sighed. He couldn't win for losing.

He drained the rest of his drink and tossed the bottle into the recycling bin before joining Erin at the ledge. He leaned his forearms on smooth white surface, removing his baseball cap to run a hand through his damp hair. As he stared into the interior of his Tidebreakers cap, the sunlight glinting off the United Baseball League holographic authentication sticker inside, he asked, "How am I supposed to convince people I'm not who they think I am? That I'm not just doing damage control."

Erin offered a faint shrug. "You have to find a way to let people see who you really are."

Dylan looked out onto the vibrant green lawn filled with people laughing and taking photos as they enjoyed a carefree Friday in the sun. He'd forgotten what that felt like—having fun, living for the moment—or even how to do it.

Squinting, he watched one of the professional golfers give a group of kids a lesson in putting. "And what if they don't like what they see?"

A gentle hand came to rest on his bicep. He met his sister's compassionate, unyielding gaze. "I think the real problem is that *you* don't like what you see," Erin said. "You're hiding because you think the real you isn't enough." Her delicate brow furrowed. "Have you forgiven yourself, Dylan?"

The question scratched a nerve. How could he forgive himself? He drank too much one night and it may have cost him his career. He may never pitch the same again. All because he wanted an escape from the pressure.

It almost got him killed.

He wouldn't forgive himself until he fixed everything. *If* he fixed everything.

"Have you had any more nightmares or panic attacks lately?" Erin asked.

Dylan clenched his jaw, staring out across the sunbathed green. He felt like a shadow looming over it. "Sometimes."

"You can take more time off," she said. "You don't have to come back next season …"

They'd had this discussion. He'd told her that wasn't an option.

Dylan flipped his hat around his fingers before securing it on his head. Tilting his chin toward the kids, he said, "Maybe I should join their lesson, so I don't embarrass myself on the course anymore."

The corners of Erin's lips tipped down, and he waited for her to call out his not-so-subtle deflection.

She peered over her shoulder at the boy squaring off with the hole a few yards away. The professional golfer said something to him. The boy poised himself with a putter, then gracefully swung. The golf ball rolled across the green straight into the hole. The other kids gasped and cheered in delight as the pro congratulated him.

"I wouldn't," Erin said. "Getting shown up by kids would be even more embarrassing." She patted his right shoulder—the good one. "Best to quit while you're ahead."

A corner of his mouth rose despite himself. He watched the other two kids excitedly fight for the next turn, jumping around the professional golfer and vying for his attention. Dylan's smile turned somber. The shock had finally worn off, and a knot of shame twisted in his gut, recalling the look on the mom's face as she dragged her son away from him as if she'd found him conversing with a criminal.

He wasn't the one who had been driving the damn boat when it crashed, but to the public, he may as well have been.

Shit. Is that what Lennon thought?

Despite the balmy air, an icy ripple ran down his spine. Maybe that's why Lennon never reached out after Erin gave her the letter. Maybe she didn't care about his apology because she didn't believe him. It was too little, too late.

Dylan couldn't even argue with her about that.

"Hey. You OK?" Erin gently rubbed his upper arm.

His jaw tensed. "I talked to Lennon."

Erin paused, her eyes slightly widening. "You did? When?"

"Today. She was trying to call you, but she accidentally called me," Dylan said, wondering what it meant that she hadn't told Erin about it.

She dropped her hand to the ledge with a sigh. "She texted me while I was in class, but we haven't had the chance to talk yet. She told you about the record deal?"

"Yeah." A rock sat on his chest. He tightened his brow as he looked out over the lawn. "She's heartbroken."

The same pain he felt was evident in Erin's sigh. "I told her I'd have my phone on me all day." She pulled it out of the pocket of her denim shorts, presumably checking to see if she'd missed anything from Lennon. The way she frowned at the screen told him she hadn't. "How did it go? The call."

What a loaded question. One he had no idea how the hell to answer.

Dylan shoved one hand in his pocket, the other reaching to scratch the back of his neck. "Well, she didn't tell me to go fuck myself, so not terrible, I guess?"

Erin's brows rose in encouragement. "That's a good start."

"I just wish it had been under different circumstances. I hope I didn't make what she was going through worse."

"You know Lennon. If you had, she would've hung up on you."

Dylan huffed, the corner of his mouth twitching up. "That's true." Maybe there was hope she'd eventually allow him back in her life. The idea released some of the weight on his chest. Without her, life had lost its color, like a song playing in the wrong key.

"You want to talk about it?"

He considered it for a beat, but something about it didn't feel right. Not when Lennon hadn't had a chance to talk to her yet. "Not now." He gave her a faint smile. "But I think I will take you up on the PT. All those bad swings are starting to set in."

As Erin hopped off the ledge, he turned to wrap an arm around her shoulders. He sucked a sharp breath through his nose at the motion, wincing as his shoulder twinged. If his baseball career never recovered, golf was definitely off the table as an alternative.

"Good job, Dodo," she jibed, employing her favorite childhood nickname for him. "At this rate, you'll be able to play baseball again when you're Dad's age."

"Thanks, Emu. Have I told you lately you're a great sister?"

Erin moved to his other side, guiding his right arm over her shoulders and settling her left around his back. "Not nearly enough. But I'm in town for a few more days, so you have time to make up for it."

CHAPTER 3

Lennon

"Hey, Lennon. Nine needs more bread and seven's getting antsy for the check."

Gordon, another server, peeked into the side station where Lennon was cashing out one of her tables. He had a large, full tray balanced on one of his thick arms.

"Already on it," she said, fingers flying across the touchscreen computer. It momentarily froze—as it often did—and she released a string of curse words under her breath.

The Friday night crowd was in fine form. The restaurant was always booked out months in advance, but it was as if every difficult, impatient guest in the city had decided *that* was the night to eat at Opus 21.

At least it kept her conversations with coworkers to a minimum as they were all busy rushing around. The fewer opportunities there were to chat, the fewer opportunities there were for the topic of her squashed record deal to come up. Even when it was time for her break, Lennon decided not to call Erin, opting to scarf down something to eat while she listened to music in the break room instead.

She had to make it through this double. She could have a breakdown later.

"They also just sat a huge party," Gordon continued over the sound of the small printer finally spitting out a receipt. "We're double-teaming, and I'm in the weeds."

A huge party meant a huge bill and, usually, huge tips. "I got it. I'll grab their drink orders," Lennon said, ripping out the receipt. She placed it in the small leather folio to deliver to her table.

"Thanks, superstar. I'll help you fill 'em in a minute." The nickname stung, but she swallowed back a reaction. He was about to race off when he poked his around the corner again and added, "Oh—and heads up, they're a bunch of *influencers*." The last word was delivered in a stage whisper.

Lennon grimaced. Some influencers made her shifts more fun, while others made her wish she'd stayed home. And, so far, luck hadn't been on her side today.

She quickly rang in another table's order, then dropped off the bill at one and the bread at the other before bracing herself for the party of fourteen sitting in the corner by the tall, floor-to-ceiling windows overlooking the sparkling New York City skyline.

They all looked to be in their twenties, dressed to the nines for a night out like they'd all come from, or were on their way to, a glamorous event. Stopping at one end of the long table, she greeted the line of bored faces and launched into her well-practiced spiel over the hum of the busy restaurant. As she mentioned their selection of wines, a female voice interrupted her.

"Oh, my God, Lennon—is that you?!"

Lennon searched the table for the source in the low lighting, and her eyebrows jumped up as she clocked the beautiful, lithe Cuban Dominican woman leaning forward at the far end. The familiar face glowed under the table's tea light candles. "Avery?"

"Yes! I can't believe it. I didn't know you lived in New York," Avery said.

"Did you move here, too?"

"No, I'm in town for Fashion Week. We're all here for Rochefort."

"Oh, wow. That's … amazing," Lennon pushed out with a smile while her heart dropped to her stomach.

Avery had been invited to Fashion Week. By *Rochefort*.

Lennon wasn't plugged into the fashion industry, but she knew enough from working in a high-end restaurant in Manhattan to know it wasn't easy to score an invite, especially from a huge, century-old luxury brand. Half of the guests in the restaurant were wearing their signature logo and old-money aesthetic.

Avery must have been doing well for herself.

Jealousy stabbed Lennon in the gut, followed by embarrassment flushing up her neck as she stood there serving her rather than reuniting under more … equal circumstances.

One of the guests to Avery's right, who sported a buzzcut and yellow-tinted sunglasses—inside, *at night*—cleared his throat, a drawn expression acutely communicating his boredom. "Can we get some like, drinks or something? I desperately need to not be sober."

"Yeah, of course." Lennon swallowed her pride and plastered on her well-practiced customer service smile, pulling a pen and pad from the black apron tied at her waist.

"We'll talk later," Avery promised.

Lennon nodded, her knuckles white around the pen.

The chaos of her shift kept her mind busy and adrenaline flowing, allowing Lennon to ride the waves without paying attention to what was happening beneath the surface. Until Avery Mora came slamming back into her life and dragged her beneath the current.

Lennon struggled to find her flow again, thrown off-kilter by the uncomfortable shit it kicked up in her subconscious. It was hard enough being a spectator to strangers celebrating career milestones and coworkers landing auditions that took them out of rotation. It cut differently to see someone she'd known most of her life, who was from the same neighborhood and grew up under similar circumstances—with a single parent—catapult miles ahead while Lennon remained stalled on the side of the road.

She did her best to pull her focus back to work, but the Rochefort table seemed intent on making that damn near impossible.

Two of them sent back their drinks to be remade, one had a long list of preferences that somehow *nothing* on the five-star Michelin menu could satisfy, while another wasn't happy when the well-done steak she'd ordered was served with no pink in the center. She then complained the second steak was cold—twenty minutes after it had been served to her. She didn't touch it until she'd taken several photos and videos of the food, herself, and the restaurant.

As Lennon turned away from the table to take the cold steak back to the kitchen, the young woman remarked loudly, "No wonder she's just a waitress. What an idiot."

Lennon bit her tongue, fighting back the urge to spin around and lob the steak at her. *I need this job, I need this job …*

The influencers stayed well past closing, racking up a massive bill with alcohol and unfinished dishes they took more photos than bites of, and keeping part of the staff there long after the rest of the restaurant cleared out. Lennon and Gordon stood by the exhibition kitchen where the chefs and sous chefs were cleaning up.

"You think the one with the frosted tips and fake watch is drunk enough to sleep with me?" Gordon asked Lennon as they observed the group get progressively more drunk and the content they filmed progressively more unhinged.

"You deserve better," Lennon remarked, watching the man he was referring to try to balance his phone in his hand as he recorded himself doing something called the "glass flip challenge."

"After working this God-awful shift, I don't even care. A blowjob is a blowjob, and he clearly doesn't have a fear of choking."

Lennon snorted. One of the guests raised an arm and shouted for someone to bring another round of shots.

"Your turn to tell them the bar's closed," Lennon said before

Gordon could slip away. "I put in my time trying to explain to the redhead with the blowout that the steak she wanted was actually medium and not well-done and the science of food getting colder the longer it sits on a table in an air-conditioned room."

Gordon dramatically sighed before plastering a fake smile on his face and setting his shoulders like he was preparing to go into battle. As he sauntered over to the table, Avery returned from the bathroom. Instead of joining the others, she stopped beside Lennon.

"Man, they're *still* going?" Avery released a soft groan, shifting in her four-inch stilettos as she smoothed out her light pink satin mini dress. She looked like an off-duty ballerina. "I thought this would be done by now. My feet are killing me."

"I can't even feel mine anymore."

"I'm sorry they're making you stay so late."

"It's fine," Lennon said, her hand popping up from her crossed arms to wave it off. "I can make a bed out of the uneaten dinner rolls and napkins if it goes on much longer."

Avery sighed. "These events can be *so* boring if you don't click with anyone, and most of the people I'm with tonight are the type that give us a bad name. I'd leave, but I don't want to send the wrong message to the brand."

"You could say you're sick," Lennon suggested.

"Don't tempt me." A beat passed. She glanced at Lennon. "I'm sorry about what Britta said."

"Who?"

"The one who complained about her steak. She was rude. I would've said something to her, but I'm at work, too. If I start any drama, it'll get out that I'm difficult and—" Avery gently shook her head, her long lashes briefly fluttering shut. "It's all a game, but you have to play it, you know?"

Lennon nodded, all too keenly aware of workplace politics.

"I heard about you and Dylan," Avery said, compassion in her voice. "I'm sorry I never reached out. I didn't know what to say."

Lennon's heart squeezed at his name. At all that came with it, its vibrations like a deep note reverberating in the air. "It's OK. It was a long time ago, and I wouldn't have wanted the sympathy anyway."

"I was really surprised. I always wanted what you two had. I think it threw me into a bit of a crisis about the existence of true love for a while."

"Sorry about that," Lennon dryly joked. *At least your crisis ended,* she chose not to add.

"I'm sorry it didn't work out," Avery said, sounding sincere. "Are you dating anyone?"

"Single as a Pringle."

"Really? You must have beat them off with a stick once everyone found out you were available. I remember all the guys in high school drooling over you."

Lennon blew a dismissive sound through her lips. "That must've been the other weirdo musician you knew in high school because it definitely wasn't me."

"You were too obsessed with Dylan to notice. All the boys were jealous that you were taken by the baseball star."

Avery's version of the past jarred with the one in Lennon's head where she'd been ruthlessly made fun of for her ever-changing hair color, battered combat boots, and showing more interest in doodling lyrics in her notebooks and losing herself in her headphones than interacting with the rest of the student body. Since Dylan didn't go to the same school—he and Erin attended a private school—half of her peers didn't believe they were actually dating. Everyone in Arden Beach knew who the Stricklands were; Lennon was a nobody.

Avery was right about one thing: If it wasn't Dylan or music, it wasn't on teenage Lennon's radar.

"I can't believe I haven't seen you since ... gosh, graduation?" Avery asked, a crease forming between her two dark, elegantly curved brows. "What's new with you? What've you been up to?"

Lennon gave her a quick rundown on how she'd moved to New York after transferring from Arden Beach University to New York University to pursue a degree and career in music. When Avery asked if she'd released any music yet, Lennon rushed through a summary of her defunct record deal. "We ended up parting ways over creative differences," she concluded. Technically, they *did* drop her due to creative differences. The fact that it wasn't mutual didn't seem like an important detail to share.

Not wanting to hear the sympathy Avery began to offer, Lennon quickly shifted the spotlight back to her, asking what had landed her at Fashion Week. In high school, Avery was the quiet student who showed more interest in maintaining her 4.0 GPA than keeping up with fashion trends. They'd both had priority shifts since graduation.

Avery shared how she became interested in fashion and started a blog in college while studying for her business degree. It was a way to have something fun to do on the side. Somehow, it turned into a full-blown career. Her goal, however, was to broaden it into a lifestyle empire. "A modern-day Martha Stewart of Arden Beach," Avery said.

A razor blade cut tiny slashes through Lennon's gut. Not only had Avery easily found success, but she'd found it with something she hadn't even originally intended to turn into a career. It had all simply *happened* for her. Everything had fallen into place as if by divine interference. Meanwhile, Lennon had been clawing her way through thousands of hours of vocal practice, writing, recording, auditions, late nights, debt, and back-to-back serving shifts only to lose her first *real* opportunity. What the hell had she been doing wrong?

"And … I'm engaged," Avery beamed, her perfect teeth sparkling as she raised her left hand where a diamond sparkled even brighter.

"Oh, shit," Lennon breathed. A delayed smile spread across her face. "Congratulations—that's amazing." She reached out to hug Avery. "You seem really happy."

"I am," Avery said as they parted. Joy beamed in her eyes. In that moment, Lennon realized she couldn't remember the last time her own eyes had lit up like that. "Oh—and I'm doing a reality show." Avery laughed at the absurdity of forgetting that little detail.

"Sorry, what?"

"Yeah, it all happened kind of fast." Avery shook her head as if still trying to process the whirlwind of it. "I found out about a show being cast in Arden Beach that's following the social scene there. I auditioned, and one thing led to another, and now they're covering my wedding on the first season."

"Holy shit," Lennon repeated. "That's ..."

"Crazy? I know."

The adrenaline wore off, and the volume of Lennon's exhaustion turned up, along with all the aches and pains in her body that came with being on her feet all day. Her head somehow felt both heavy on her shoulders and light enough to float away.

Her brain demanded a complete shutdown and reboot.

"I think it's going to be a good opportunity, though," Avery continued, oblivious to Lennon's inner turmoil. She fidgeted with her engagement ring as her gaze fell somewhere over Lennon's shoulder. "It's a great way to take my brand to the next level. I love fashion, but it's never been the goal. This could be the platform to get my name out there and into different spaces, hopefully bring in some big opportunities. I'd love to have my own show someday."

Through the haze, Lennon sensed Avery's hesitance. She realized it wasn't that she was oblivious to Lennon's reaction but rather misreading it as disapproval and it seemed to have triggered her own doubts. That sobered Lennon for a moment.

"I'm sure you'll make it happen," Lennon told her. "You've already accomplished so much, like in school when you were always at the top of the class. Everyone admired you. I would've hated you if you weren't so damn nice."

A soft laugh trickled from Avery.

"You deserve to have all your dreams come true." Lennon reached for Avery's left hand, holding her fingers beneath the shiny rock.

Avery smiled appreciatively, squeezing Lennon's hand back. "Thanks, Lennon." A second later, something shifted in her eyes, a light bulb going off. "Hold on—I have the most amazing idea."

Lennon raised a curious eyebrow as exhaustion continued its bid to pull her under.

"Last I heard, they were still looking to cast some more people for the show. Why don't you audition?"

Lennon barked a slightly delirious laugh. "What? I don't live in Arden Beach anymore, remember?"

"You could move back for a few months while we're filming. It'd be a great way to get your name out there and build a fan base for your music. So many people now get opportunities based solely on their social media followings. Maybe you'll even meet someone in the industry who wants to work with you. Oh, my gosh! Lennon—that would be perfect."

Lennon wasn't sure if it was the exhaustion, the mental fatigue of dealing with the table of fourteen, or the emotional hangover from *everything*, but she found herself completely unable to process what Avery was saying. "I can't be on a reality show. I'd be so boring. I can't even get people to follow me on social media *now*. When I'm not working, all I do is sit in my apartment and play music."

"Oh, stop it. You were so much fun in high school, always making the best mix tapes for parties and sneaking us into live shows. Your hair always dyed in those crazy colors. And you're a singer! You're *literally* a performer."

"When I'm making music, yes, but not *in general*." Except for when she pretended not to be dying inside during a conversation like this. "My music is what's interesting—" *though, that had been debatable lately*, "—not me."

"Bullshit. *Those* people are boring." Avery appraised the table of influencers, all staring at their phones as they nursed their free alcohol. "And they have millions of followers. We're all more interesting than we think we are."

Lennon shook her head. "I just can't picture myself on a reality show. That's not my thing."

"I had trouble wrapping my head around it at first, too. Honestly, I still do. But I think about all the benefits and realize I'd be standing in my way if I *didn't* do it. Is it what I imagined for myself? No.

But I'm hoping it will help me get to where I want to go. I mean, did you imagine yourself being a waitress?"

"No, but it's a decent job—"

"And that's all being on a reality show is. A job. A means to an end."

Avery was starting to make sense, but when Lennon tried to picture herself on a reality show, her brain short-circuited. It was fucking *absurd*. She was too private, too much of a homebody, too … *not a reality show star*.

And right now, too tired to give a fuck about anything but getting back to the quiet confines of her apartment and passing out in bed.

"I'll think about it," Lennon said to placate her, though she was pretty confident she knew what her answer would be after a good night's sleep.

Absolutely fucking not.

"OK, but don't wait too long. Filming starts soon, so they'll want to have the cast nailed down ASAP. If you're interested, I'll give you the info and pass your name along to the producers."

"Thanks. I appreciate it," Lennon said with sincerity. Because she did appreciate it. Even if it was never going to happen.

"You have to at least come to the wedding. It's in September."

Lennon's breath turned thick in her throat. The last wedding she'd attended was her own, even though it had been a quick elopement. How would she feel watching someone else walk down the aisle in the same city where she'd left behind the love of her life?

At that moment, she didn't have a good reason to say no and was too wrung out to devise an excuse. Avery would probably forget about her by the next morning, anyway.

"Of course. I'd love to."

CHAPTER 4

Dylan

The meeting Dylan had been dreading for weeks finally arrived. He tugged at the collar of his dark grey button-down as he watched the numbers rise above the elevator's mirrored doors, closing in on the top floor. He thanked whatever cosmic force had spared him from it being a morning meeting.

He would've struggled to make it after staying up all night thinking about Lennon's surprise phone call.

About her.

Thoughts of Lennon followed him to the hotel. How did she feel talking to him again? Was her mind on their phone call as much as his, or did she want to forget about it?

No. Get a grip—obviously she wasn't thinking about him. She just lost her record deal. She had more important things on her mind. He should be focusing on his career, too, given the ventilator it was on.

Dylan met his reflection in the doors. He ran a hand over his short beard, which he'd trimmed that morning. *Should I have shaved?* He adjusted the sleeves of his blazer for the millionth time, sucking in a deep breath through his nose and exhaling through his mouth in an attempt to calm his racing heart. The two cups of coffee he had that morning were doing their job a little *too* well, and now, he was distracted on top of it. This was his first meeting with Eddie since his accident. Besides the brief phone calls and check-ins, nothing formal had been arranged. When they'd last spoken, Dylan promised him he'd fully recover and do everything in his power to get his suspension lifted, then make it up to the team with the best season of his life.

Eddie agreed to put his neck on the line and back him. Dylan owed it to him not to fuck up.

The old Dylan probably would have looked for a way out of the meeting. He had, on more than one occasion, taken advantage of the decades-long relationship between his family and the Carmichaels, but Eddie Carmichael was a notoriously hard man to pin down. When he requested a meeting with you, you made yourself available if you knew what was good for you.

And Dylan knew meeting with the Arden Beach Tidebreakers' owner wasn't just good for him right now. It was a damn necessity. He'd run out of "get out of jail free" cards. In fact, he was pretty sure, at this point, he was operating on borrowed time.

A soft *ding* announced his arrival. The doors slid open to a large, framed black and white photograph of his grandfather on the field celebrating the Tidebreakers' first National Series victory. He set his shoulders before striding down the hall past more photographs, memorabilia, and a timeline of his grandfather's career with the Tidebreakers, starting from the team's establishment in 1969 to his retirement as manager in the two-thousands. They led to an upscale restaurant bearing his late grandfather's name— Merritt's Steakhouse.

His heart skipped a beat as his attention landed on the female figure with long, dark hair standing behind the desk, her back to him. It put a hitch in his step.

Lennon?

The name teetered on the edge of his tongue as her voice echoed in his head again. *"How do you know what I sound like when I'm anything anymore?"*

The shame those words spurred sliced through him.

The hostess turned around, her face a stranger's. Nothing like his ex-wife. His heart settled back in his chest. She smiled, eyes traveling his length, sparkling as they met his again. "Good afternoon, Mr. Strickland. Please, follow me."

She led Dylan to a curved booth tucked away in a quiet corner, where private business meetings could comfortably take place without the threat of eavesdroppers. The restaurant was part of Eddie's business portfolio, though Dylan's father held a stake in it. He'd once told Dylan an office was too formal; you learned a lot more about a person when you broke bread with them.

An unassuming, middle-aged man with thick, black-rimmed glasses rose from the booth to greet him. "Dylan," said Eddie affectionately.

"Hey, Mr. Carmichael." Dylan smiled as they exchanged an embrace.

"I told you, you can call me Eddie now. You're not in grade school anymore, and we're practically family." Eddie squeezed the back of his neck as they parted.

They settled into the booth opposite each other. Mounted on the dark wood paneling behind Eddie was a photograph of Dylan's grandfather mid-pitch during a game. "Hard habit to break," Dylan replied as the hostess handed him a menu. He thanked her before she slunk off.

"Not as hard as some." Eddie sent him a knowing look, one laced with empathy. "It's good to see you, kid," he said, the statement deeper than a pleasantry as he studied Dylan in a fatherly way.

The hostess returned to fill Dylan's water glass, and Eddie waited until she left before continuing. "How are you doing?"

While Eddie was a close family friend he had known since birth, there would always be a thin, invisible barrier present due to the business side of their relationship. Eddie inherited the Tidebreakers when his father passed away nine years ago. Their families had been intertwined ever since Dylan's grandfather, Merritt "Mitt" Dylan Strickland, had become a star player for the Tidebreakers under the Carmichaels' ownership, followed by his son, Merritt "Rhett" Dylan Strickland II, a few decades later. Their shared love for the game and the Tidebreakers' legacy was special. It was a deep-rooted bond, but you could only be so close to someone when your success directly affected theirs.

Sitting before him now, after all his mistakes, Dylan's guilt hit him from two sides: disappointing a family friend and disappointing an employer who counted on him.

"Doing better," Dylan said, the thick leather menu perched between his fingers despite always ordering the same thing. He was just glad to have something to do with his restless hands. "A lot better, actually. The doctor says my shoulder's healing well. Working on getting back to my normal pitching speed."

"That's great. But I meant how you're doing here—" Eddie tapped two fingers to his temple "—and here." He tapped his heart over his crisp blazer.

What a loaded question. "Bruised but still beating," Dylan answered.

The waiter arrived and took their orders. Eddie selected an assortment of appetizers for the table and the grilled salmon for his entree, while Dylan went for his favorite, the braised short ribs. They drifted into small talk after Dylan asked about Eddie's family. His daughter, Savannah, was graduating with an MBA from an Ivy League school the following spring and would be moving back to Arden Beach to work for the family empire. That's how it worked in families like theirs. He wondered how Savannah felt about it and if she was excited or dreading it. He still remembered when he found out he'd been officially drafted to the Tidebreakers. His father threw a party to celebrate.

Dylan had his first panic attack that night. And it was the night he discovered which liquor best took off the edge.

"Bet you're excited to have her back in town soon," Dylan said, forcing a smile as he caught the last piece of yellowtail *sashimi* between his chopsticks.

"Yeah. I just hope our company is still standing so I have an actual job to offer her." Eddie said it wryly as he dipped his tuna *nigiri* in soy sauce, but when he looked up and saw Dylan regarding him with concern, his smile faltered.

"Is it that bad?"

Eddie rested his forearms on the table, the *nigiri* suspended above his plate. His lips pressed into a thin line as he leveled with Dylan. "We had some very ill-timed investments before the pandemic and haven't fully recovered. I'm confident we'll get through this rough patch, but until then, we're hemorrhaging money. We can't keep going like this without something giving." He paused, his jaw tightening. "I'm not sure we can hold on to both the company *and* the team."

The weight of that statement settled over Dylan. He'd heard about the closures and layoffs, but he'd never considered that the team could be in jeopardy. In his mind, the Carmichaels owning the Tidebreakers would always be an immutable fact. He'd never considered that someday, that could change.

"Now, that's my absolute *last* resort," Eddie reassured him, his free hand slicing the air. "I'm going to fight like hell to keep it. It's part of my family's legacy—my daughter's. But if things keep going the way they are with the team … . To put it plainly, I'm getting fucked from all sides." He sighed before tossing the fish into his mouth.

Dylan sat back, running a hand through his hair as he processed all the potential implications of the team going to new ownership. His own father's job security was the most obvious thing at risk. Since they'd been playing a less-than-stellar season, the manager was always the first one people looked at to blame. Pundits questioned Rhett's efficacy as the team's manager, and suggestions of retirement were spreading, especially with his contract up for renewal next season.

The only way his father would retire right now would be in a casket. Rhett had vowed he wasn't going to stop until he got the team a championship win as a manager—with Dylan. Like Dylan's grandfather, Mitt, had done with Rhett.

And ultimately, see Dylan—Merritt Dylan Strickland III— join them in the Hall of Fame.

Dylan's chest tightened. He put down the chopsticks. A bead of condensation slid down the glass of water beside his plate, tracing the curve of the glass. Something stronger would take the edge off, but he couldn't use that as a coping mechanism anymore.

Instead, he cupped the glass, pressing his fingers into the cold, wet surface. Grounding himself.

"Your dad's probably too prideful to say this, but the team isn't the same without you," Eddie continued. "Have you caught any of the games this season?"

Dylan gave a small nod. The accident wiping out three of their strongest players, not to mention all the negative media attention, had taken its toll on them. They were the third-lowest-ranking team in the league at the moment—a shock for a team that had made it to the postseason the last ten years in a row. If anyone could pull off a mid-season comeback, it was his father, but that was increasingly unlikely with every lackluster game.

"Rob and Emmanuel have … strong opinions on how we should turn things around, and they're not in line with your father's," Eddie confided, referring to the team's general manager and director, respectively. "I've been overriding their decisions to stand with Rhett. He really believes in the farm we've cultivated, and the numbers reflect that. Our minor league team is consistently in the top ten. But they're not ready for the majors yet. He wants to keep thinking long-term, and I get it, but …"

"You're worried you won't be able to hold on to it long enough to see it through."

"And I can't guarantee the new owner will see eye to eye with your dad."

The distant murmur of laughter in another booth trickled through a blanket of silence that settled between them. Dylan's injured rotator cuff began to ache, tension corded deep in his shoulders. The neoclassical music drifting through the restaurant did little to ease the pressure steadily building within him. His grip on the glass tightened.

"What about Diego?" Dylan asked.

"What about him?"

"Why not give him another chance?"

"Diego's a rookie," Eddie said. "He's not worth the bad press when we can replace him with someone else."

"A rookie who's easily one of the most promising we've seen in years. He's young, he made a mistake that night," Dylan reasoned, shame coating his throat. The fish churned among the acid in his stomach. "We all did."

"And you see what it's taking for us to rehab your image when you have an entire legacy and proven track record behind you."

Dylan dropped his gaze. He wished he could go back in time and stop himself from getting on that damn boat—from getting so wasted he blacked out. He'd never let it go that far before. Three bad games in a row had sent him into a spiral and he'd just wanted to relieve the pressure. He'd chosen the wrong night to lose control.

He was still paying for it.

Eddie placed his chopsticks down, wiping his mouth with the thick cloth napkin from his lap. "The team's morale is waning, and you know once that starts to go, it's the beginning of the end," he said.

Dylan did know. All too well.

"They need you. *Rhett* needs you."

"I'm doing everything I can to get back out there, but now that the league's in control, it's up to them if or when—"

"They've said they'll consider lifting your suspension before spring training if you keep your head down and get your numbers back up. You've got time. Not a lot, but enough." Eddie leaned in, slightly lowering his voice. "The commissioner is an old buddy of mine from college. We golf together. As long as you make a good enough show to placate the board, we're golden."

Dylan rolled the chopsticks between his fingers, doing the math in his head. That gave him until February—about seven months. It should, in theory, be enough for him to completely heal and get his throwing speed back up to par.

The scar on his shoulder twinged again as if on cue, planting a seed of doubt.

"We need you out there. I'm afraid we won't make it another season without you," Eddie said, sensing his doubt. "I don't want to add extra pressure on you, but you're one of our star players for a reason. You've been the league's MVP. You were the youngest pitcher ever to win the Merritt Strickland Award. You were famous before you were even drafted. People come to games to see you."

Dylan smiled absently, looking out toward the restaurant. "They used to, anyway."

"They will again. Everyone loves a comeback story. And I know you'll be like your father when he shattered his knee. He didn't just break records when he came back. He won the championship. It lit a fire under him. You'll be the same."

"No pressure, right?" Dylan ribbed with a slight lift of his brow, to which he saw Eddie drop his head to the side with a guilty smile. "I appreciate your confidence. I do. I guess I'm just surprised you have as much in me as you do after everything."

"We all make mistakes, Dylan. You took responsibility for

yours. That's why I'm fighting for you," Eddie said firmly. "Not because you're a Strickland, but because you're a good man. The kind who deserves a second chance. The kind I want on my team."

Initially, Eddie's validation warmed him. But a second later, that familiar pressure rose under it, pressing through and steadily expanding outward. Dylan's hands began to tingle. His chest tightened.

Not now. Not here.

He refused to have a panic attack in front of Eddie. He tugged at his shirt collar, loosening it to give himself more air. He thought of the breathing exercise Erin taught him. Inhale for four seconds. Hold. Exhale.

Get a grip, Strickland.

The waiter stopped by to deliver their entrees and top off their water glasses, giving Dylan an excuse not to respond. The brunette hostess led a couple to a nearby booth. As she turned her back on Dylan, waiting as the couple settled in, his thoughts drifted to Lennon again.

"I'm sorry I wasn't enough for you."

The last words she'd said to him before she walked out on him haunted him, wedging a fresh knife in his spine.

If only he'd been man enough to tell her the truth.

"Don't get any ideas," Eddie warned.

Dylan pulled his focus back to him. "Sorry?"

Eddie glanced purposefully at the hostess, who sent a small smile over her shoulder at Dylan before slowly walking back to the front desk, then back to his star player, his implication becoming clear. "There are many different vices to distract a man. Right now, you need to keep your head clear. Stay focused. If you need to … blow off some steam, do so casually. And smartly. That's all I ask."

Dylan let out a small laugh, rubbing the back of his neck. Casual relationships were all he'd had since his marriage. Mostly one-offs, occasionally interspersed with a short fling he'd cut off once he sensed the woman wanted more, despite always making it clear from the start that he didn't. The only one who could get under his skin was more than a thousand miles away.

"Trust me, you don't have anything to worry about there," he assured Eddie. Dylan reached for the sauce to pour over his ribs.

"Dylan," Eddie said, the seriousness of his tone calling Dylan to look up again. "Can I count on you to be ready by February?"

The vice-like pressure around his lungs pulled tighter. His grandfather's fierce, determined expression on the mound loomed in his periphery.

Dylan nodded, projecting confidence he didn't feel. "Yeah. I won't let you down."

CHAPTER 5

Lennon

The mattress springs creaked as Lennon rolled over in bed, her consciousness reluctantly drifting awake. She tried to coax it back to sleep, uninterested in joining the world of the living yet, but it didn't relent. A pounding headache surfaced. Her eyelids were crusted shut and sinuses stuffed like the breadsticks she'd devoured after last night's shift, now digesting in her stomach like a brick.

One shred of bittersweet reprieve had shone upon her in the form of a day off from the restaurant. Bittersweet because she'd been booked for a full day at the recording studio. *Ha, ha.* The universe had jokes.

Lennon reached over her head, fumbling for the phone on the dresser behind her to check the time. Half past one in the afternoon. A few text message notifications sat below it—one from Erin, one from her boss, and a spam message telling her she'd won a free cruise to the Mediterranean.

Rubbing sleep from the corners of her eyes, she opened the text from Erin, received at 5:11 a.m.

Erin: Call me whenever you want, honey. I'll be free
all day. Love you.

Lennon smiled, her bruised heart curling up in the warmth of her best friend's message. By the time she got home from work last night, she'd been too exhausted to talk to anyone. She grabbed a bag of breadsticks and a pizza slice on the way home, inhaling it before even making it to her third-floor walk-up. She showered and passed out.

She needed to pee first before she launched into that phone call and exhumed all the emotions she'd spent the last twenty-four hours repressing. Sitting up, she tapped on her boss's message.

Ray: Hey. I need you to come in this afternoon for
a meeting.

Was he fucking serious? A downside of her being the go-to for covering last-minute shifts: He assumed she didn't have a life outside of work.

The realization that she *didn't* have a life outside of work hit her with depressing irony.

Lennon: Is it mandatory?

Impromptu meetings with the serving staff were rare, unless something critical happened, such as a failed health inspection, a food recall, or an unexpected visit from corporate.

Whatever it was, why did it have to happen *today*? She'd been looking forward to sulking all day in her apartment and not changing out of her pajamas. Her bladder reminded her of all the soda she'd guzzled before bed, so she dropped her phone on the bed and stood, stretching out the kinks in her neck and back.

A new message dinged from the blankets as she slipped on a pair of shorts under her faded, oversized Queen tee and pushed her feet into some sliders, readying herself for the trek down the hall to the shared bathroom. She grabbed her phone.

> Ray: It's important. Won't take long. Can you be
> here at three?

A funny feeling stirred in Lennon's stomach. Her thumbs were poised to tell him to fuck off in a polite, professional way—that she had other commitments she couldn't break—but she couldn't risk making waves. Opus 21 was her only gainful employment.

> Lennon: Sure.

So much for a slow day. She'd have to quickly pull herself together and grab food on the way to the train. She swiped over to Erin's text thread.

> Lennon: Love you, too. I have to go in for a work
> meeting at 3. I'll call you after. Have the popcorn
> ready.

Walking into work on a day off always felt like being at school after hours. Lennon hoped that whatever this meeting was about, it would be quick. She passed Gordon in the hallway, who gave her a look like a teacher seeing a student in the faculty break room.

"Tits. Do you ever take a day off?" he asked.

"What are those?" Lennon quipped dryly. "I'm here for the meeting."

"What meeting?"

An unsettling ripple thrummed through her. The realization hit him at the same time, his eyebrows rising grimly.

"Hey, Lennon," Ray said, calling their attention to where he straddled the threshold of his office, drumming his stubby fingers on the doorframe. He gave her a thin-lipped smile as he tilted his head toward his office. "Let's chat in here."

As he stepped back inside, Lennon glanced at Gordon. He

sent her a "good luck, comrade" expression before she followed their manager.

Lennon's skin turned clammy. She blinked away the flashbacks to walking into the record executive's office yesterday morning, but in their place, she began rapidly analyzing everything she did during her last shift. Had she made a mistake on something? Charged someone wrong? Accidentally accepted counterfeit cash?

"What's up?" Lennon asked as she met him at the door, where he stood waiting.

"Take a seat." Ray gestured to the two chairs in front of his desk. He closed the door behind her, then settled into his faux-leather office chair. A puff of air squeaked out of the mechanism as he sank into it. He clasped his hands in front of him as she lowered herself into one of the smaller stationary chairs across from him, tucking a stray piece of hair behind her ear. "So … I'm just going to rip the bandage off. We received a complaint from a guest."

A little jolt to the heart rocked her system, surprise warring with confusion. "About me?"

"Correct."

"From who? I don't remember anyone complaining about anything recently."

"She was part of the large party you served last night. The one you shared with Gordon."

Understanding chimed. Lennon briefly closed her eyes. Avery's group.

"One of them said you got her order wrong and then argued with her about it," Ray explained. "She said you tried to make her look 'stupid' and embarrassed her in front of everyone, and that her dish still didn't come out right the second time."

"Is this the one who asked for a well-done steak and then complained when it was well-done?"

His exasperated expression suggested he found this situation as ridiculous as she did. With a curt nod, Ray answered her question.

Lennon scoffed. "All I did was tell her that what she was asking for was a *medium*-cooked steak. Then, she was upset because it got cold while she didn't touch it for several minutes."

Ray emitted a long sigh as he circled his thumbs around each other. "I know, I know. I get it. But you know our approach to things like this. The customer is always right."

"Well, in this case, she isn't. I didn't try to make her look stupid. She did that all on her own."

Ray pressed his thin lips into a line. "Be that as it may, she's put me in a tough position. She wouldn't accept any of my offers to fix the situation. There was only one thing she wanted." He squeezed his hands together, the skin around his eyes pinching under his glasses as he looked at Lennon. "I'm afraid we have to temporarily suspend you."

The words bounced off her ear drums, striking but not fully permeating. "What?"

"I'm sorry, Lennon. She threatened to post a scathing review on her social media if we didn't do something about it. She has, like, a fucking million followers," Ray said, a touch defensively as if *he* was the one going through a life-altering situation. He leaned back, the office chair squeaking with the motion. "Hey, she wanted you fired. I'm only suspending you."

Lennon's ears pulsed, the sound of his voice muffled through the rush of blood. Everything else inside her went still. "Without pay?" she clarified.

He stared at her for a moment, then faced his palms out and smiled ruefully in a "that's how it works" gesture.

Lennon pressed her tongue into her cheek, trying to process what was happening. "When can I come back?"

"A month or two should be enough for her to forget about it."

She released a sound between a scoff and a laugh. "A month? I don't have another job, Ray. This is my job."

"Then, I suggest you start looking for one. I'll give you a glowing reference. And hey—you've got that record deal, right? You're not gonna need us soon, anyway."

Lennon blinked back tears, wishing the earth would open and swallow her.

"Look, you're one of our best servers. I'm sure you'll have no trouble finding another job. I hear that diner a few blocks off Broadway is hiring. The one with the singers. That'd be perfect for you."

It took everything in her not to break right then and there.

Lennon looked away from him, sucking in her lower lip and biting down. Her gaze landed on the framed photograph of a mountain with the words "BELIEVE AND SUCCEED" written beneath it, hanging on the pale beige wall.

This can't be happening.

"I'll draw it up and email it to you by Monday," Ray said. "Remember, this is temporary."

This couldn't be happening, but it was.

CHAPTER 6

Lennon

"Who was this girl? I'm going to go report all of her social media accounts."

"For what? Being a dick?" Lennon asked Erin around a mouthful of cereal, standing at the short counter that bumped out from a bank of kitchen cabinets, long enough to fit one small stool, which she'd never bothered to buy. She swiped a drop of milk from her mouth with her thumb. As soon as she got back to her apartment, she caught Erin up on a video chat on her exciting forty-eight hours of losing two jobs back-to-back.

"I'll bet if you told the internet what happened, they'd go on a crusade for you." Erin took out her aggression on the cucumber she'd been dicing as she meal-prepped in her kitchen. "They hate it when people treat service workers like shit."

"With my luck, she'd end up twisting it and making me look like the bad guy. She has millions of followers to send after me. My career would be even deader than it is already."

Ironically, one of the biggest recurring complaints from the re-cord label had been that Lennon wasn't hitting their "target metrics" with her social media following. She'd struggled to keep up with creating content on top of writing and recording music, which she wasn't allowed to share yet, and working full-time. She'd never been able to figure out a balance.

"I feel so stupid." Lennon pushed around the last few pieces of soggy rainbow cereal in the milk. "I can't even get people to follow me on these godforsaken apps. How am I supposed to sell records?"

"You're not stupid," Erin firmly stated. "*They're* stupid for not knowing how to market their artists anymore and putting the burden on you to have a following before you even release anything when all you should be worried about is making good music. Which, clearly, they don't know anything about."

"Their artists have a million awards, and two are in the Rock n' Roll Hall of Fame."

"Even a broken clock is right twice a day."

Lennon snorted. "You sound like your brother." It flowed from her mouth before she could catch it.

The energy shift rippled across the Wi-Fi before Erin uttered a word, her food chopping momentarily ceasing. Tension corded through Lennon's muscles, the sugar in her bloodstream becoming a liability.

"So … how did *that* go?" Erin casually asked, impressively smooth. She was a pro at broaching difficult conversations with care and ease, while Lennon was the type to call her ex-husband for the first time in six years while trying *not* to have an emotional breakdown on a moving train.

Lennon glanced at the screen. Erin was back to chopping—working on a sweet potato now—the camera angling up from its spot propped against a canister at her soft hazel eyes. Her dirty blonde hair was gathered in a light pink claw clip, matching her dusty rose-colored sports bra and high-waisted bike shorts. She looked like a bombshell from a Sofia Coppola movie—naturally, effortlessly beautiful in a girl-next-door sort of way. In the little thumbnail in the corner, Lennon's dark hair stuck out at various angles from where it had come loose from the bun she'd thrown it in when she got home, her faded, oversized Queen tee dwarfing her body again. She'd shed the professional attire she'd worn to the meeting, recommitting to the whole pajamas-for-the-rest-of-the-day thing.

Their aesthetic and lifestyle differences had always amused her—and everyone else. Lennon always said Erin was a Marilyn, while she was a Freddie Mercury. Erin was control, Lennon was chaos. But that was the beauty of their friendship; they balanced each other.

Lennon continued swirling her spoon through the pale pink milk. "I was already in the midst of one emotional breakdown, so I guess it was efficient to kill two birds with one stone. You know what they say, an object in motion likes to stay in motion." Her gaze lifted and settled on one of the chipped spots on the speckled laminate counter, her focus pulling inward as she allowed the memory of the prior night to resurface.

Erin steadily kept chopping in the background, leaving Lennon space to continue when she was ready.

"It was … OK?" was the answer Lennon finally landed on as she dug her thumbnail into the chipped groove. "I mean, as OK as the first time talking to your ex-husband years after your divorce can be. I'm surprised he answered."

"Really? You're surprised?"

Lennon's brows scrunched together, struggling to compute why Erin would be surprised that Lennon was surprised. "Well, yeah. I mean, I've pretty much been avoiding him for years, and then I call him out of the blue? Wouldn't blame him if he didn't want to open that can of worms without warning first thing in the morning."

"He was probably just happy to hear from you."

A strange fluttering sensation spread through Lennon's chest. *Was he probably happy to hear from me, or did he tell Erin he was happy to hear from me?* Something about the way Erin said it had her wondering …

No, she couldn't go there.

Not now.

Lennon set her spoon down in the bowl. "At least the bandage has been ripped off. But I don't think either of us is in the mental space to rehash what happened between us."

"Did you ever read his letter I gave you?" Erin asked with gentle curiosity.

Lennon scrunched her nose, guilt prickling. Her gaze instinctively drifted toward the small chest of drawers at the end of the daybed where she kept a box of mementos nestled among her bras and panties. "No. I was going to. But then, every time I thought about it, I just … couldn't bring myself to do it. I'm pretty sure I already know what it says. He's sorry, he didn't mean to hurt me. It was too much, too fast. We were too young; he made mistakes." And none of that would be what she *wanted* to hear. It was easier to move on than to face the blow of yet another disappointment.

Erin gave her a melancholy smile. "Maybe read it sometime when you're ready. Even if you think you know what's in it, it may help give you more closure to see it in his handwriting. To read it in his words."

Lennon picked at a fingernail. "Yeah, maybe. I'll think about it."

Erin scooped the diced sweet potato into a colorful container, then grabbed an onion and started peeling it. Lennon's eyes almost started watering like a Pavlovian response. "So, what are you getting up to today?"

Lennon blew air through her lips, making them vibrate. She carried the bowl to the sink half a step away as she answered, "Well, I'm debating between going back to bed, crying, or watching sitcom reruns all day. Or I may live on the wild side and do *all three*."

"Whatever you need, babe," Erin encouraged. "Give yourself a day to wallow and process everything. Just don't let yourself spiral too much."

"Spiral? Me? *Pfft*." Lennon rolled her eyes as she rinsed out the bowl. "That's totally *not* something I would do."

Erin raised an eyebrow, shooting her a look that screamed *bullshit.*

"I'm an artist. We have a lot of *feelings,* OK?"

"Why don't you pour some of those feelings into your music?"

Lennon's chest turned to ice. Suddenly, she wanted to crawl out of her skin. "I don't want to do anything with music right now," she said, forcefully scrubbing the bowl with a soapy sponge.

"Why not? That's what you usually do when you're upset about something."

Shame bit at her as she shrugged. "I just don't want to." Lennon moved on to scrubbing the spoon, then rinsed it while Erin remained quiet. Lennon knew she was giving her space to work out her shit while Erin likely debated whether it was beneficial to continue this line of conversation.

As Lennon dried the bowl with a dish towel, she admitted, "Right now, it's a reminder that what I create isn't good enough. At least, not for a career."

Erin abruptly ceased chopping. "Lennon," she said, head cocked to the side with an admonishing look. "Be real."

"I am! I'm trying to be," she replied, frustrated. "I may have to accept that I'm not cut out for being a recording artist. At least, not one in the way I'd imagined, with a big record label, going on tour. The life I'd dreamed of may not be possible for me because I … don't have what it takes."

Pressure built behind her eyes. Which pissed her off even more.

"I get that you're frustrated—you have every damn right to be—but I'm not going to let you talk shit about yourself," Erin said.

Lennon gripped the edge of the counter, leaning onto it. The pressure that began behind her eyes now spread to every inch of her body, desperate to push its way out. "I just … I can't believe they preferred to cut their losses rather than waste more time on me. I wasn't even worth the effort."

The last statement sliced a deep wound open. Its roots snaked through the darkest parts of her. Bullying in grade school. Her father leaving. Her mother refusing to support her dreams. Dylan putting everything else ahead of her during their embarrassingly short marriage.

And now, the one thing she thought she did well—the one thing she thought no one could take away from her, on which she had banked everything—had proved to be yet another way in which she was *not* enough.

Lennon turned her head as a few tears slipped down her flushed cheeks. The hum of the window AC unit filled the silence. After nearly a minute, she found the courage to look back at the phone. Erin had picked hers up, holding it closer to her bare, sun-kissed face. Her eyes shone glassy as she wiped a tear from her cheek. The sight disarmed Lennon.

"I know you've been punched in the gut," Erin said, "and life keeps throwing you curveballs. But Lennon, you're more than enough. Your music inspired them to sign you out of the thousands of other artists vying for a record deal. You *know* better than anyone how fucking hard that is. Who knows what changed? It's a business. I've seen it enough in baseball to know so many variables go into those decisions, most of which have nothing to do with the players themselves. To let one small group of men sitting in a board room determine your worthiness as an artist—at the thing you *love* doing more than anything else—would be an enormous loss to this world.

"You make music because you were made to, not just to help a bunch of people in suits make more money. Don't ever tie up your value in other people's opinions, *especially* ones who look at you and the magic you're creating from your heart as a disposable product. OK?"

Lennon smiled with an overwhelming sense of gratitude for her best friend. They had bonded over being the only two little girls at the Tidebreakers' stadium during spring training when Lennon's mom worked in the office. After Lennon's divorce, she'd moved in with Erin for a few months until she couldn't take all the reminders of Dylan everywhere and needed a change. She moved to New York

City to study music, while Erin stayed in Arden Beach to study to become a sports physical therapist.

Being so far away from Erin had been one of the hardest parts of living in New York. She was the only family Lennon had left after going no contact with her mother.

"OK," Lennon mumbled through a stuffy nose, nodding. She wiped her tears with the heels of her palms.

"Why don't you try producing your own record?"

Lennon sighed. "I've thought about it. But it's so damn expensive. Renting the studio space, hiring engineers to make sure it sounds professional. And then, I have the marketing issue. I don't have the capital to sink into something I'm not guaranteed will make back the investment. I'm still paying off student loans. And now, I'm out of a job for at least a month." A humorless laugh slipped out of her, gargled by her congested nose.

"If you need help, you know I'm here," Erin told her. As Lennon opened her mouth to respond, she added, "And don't you *dare* say you don't want to be a burden. You aren't. You're my best friend. You'd do the same for me."

Lennon snapped her mouth shut into a strained smile, her shame warring with how touched she was by Erin's generosity. "Thanks, Erin. Hopefully, it won't come to that, but I appreciate it … a lot." She rubbed between her eyes where a screw was twisting deep within. "To answer your earlier question—I guess I'll spend the day looking for a new job. Or I could just go on Avery's reality show," she remarked wryly.

"What?" Erin scrunched her brow as she reached for something off-camera, hand returning with some sort of green beverage in a tall, skinny glass. She took a sip from the metal straw.

Lennon grimaced at whatever was in the glass, then filled her in. "It was nice of her to offer, but can you imagine *me* on a reality show?" She picked up the phone and carried Erin over to the twin-sized bed parallel to the wall. She plopped down with a squeak of the mattress, pulling her knees up to prop up the phone.

Erin shrugged, popping her lips off the straw. "Why not?"

"Because it's … not me. I don't know, I wouldn't …" Lennon paused, picturing the glamorous lifestyle and fashion guru Avery, as well as the other guests at dinner. "Fit in."

"Won't that work in your favor? The whole point is to stand out, so you don't get lost in the noise."

Lennon stared at Erin, who casually set down her drink and began cleaning up her meal prep supplies. She put lids on the colorful containers and dropped used utensils in the sink as if she hadn't just said something that flipped Lennon's world on its head. Nerves bundled in Lennon's stomach, her deepest fears laid bare.

"Does it make you uncomfortable because you won't be able to hide behind your music?" Erin asked.

Lennon made a disgusted expression, raising her free hand in a *stop* gesture. "OK, Erin. Stop attacking me with truths I don't want to hear."

"You need a job, right? It would solve that problem and maybe even pay enough for you to produce your album," Erin said, ignoring Lennon's internal crisis. She held up a finger as she leaned into the other hand on the marble counter. "The show's in the entertainment industry, which is a step closer to where you want to be." Another finger joined the first. "It would solve your social media following issue by giving you exposure to a large audience. And—" Digits three and four went up. "You'd be back in Arden Beach with me for a while." A pleased smile twinkled on her face.

"You're not even *in* Arden Beach half the time," Lennon pointed out, though Erin's reasoning had begun tipping things in her brain.

"With the way the Tidebreakers are playing this season, I probably will be soon."

Lennon had avoided the baseball world since her divorce, but it was surprising to hear the team was struggling this early in the season. They usually dominated the season and only struggled in the postseason. Had the accident thrown the whole team off? Erin had told her that, besides Dylan being suspended, two other strong players were also cut from the team.

Dylan must be riddled with guilt.

"Sometimes, we look in the wrong places for the things we want," Erin said, pulling Lennon back to their conversation. "We can get so caught up in thinking it has to happen one specific way that we miss opportunities that could lead us where we're meant to be. Especially when those paths are outside our comfort zone." She washed her hands at the sink, her wispy bangs hiding her eyes as the camera caught her profile, but Lennon sensed the wistfulness in her tone.

"Are we talking about me still?" Lennon asked.

Erin slanted a stern look at the camera. "Don't deflect." As Erin shut off the water and dried her hands, Lennon made a mental note to circle back to *that* at some point. "Are you afraid of coming back here, too? Of seeing … certain people."

Lennon pulled in a long inhale, dropping her head back against the wall as she stared up at the popcorn ceiling. She eyed the old water stains she'd memorized. "My mom's living in Sarasota, so I don't think I'd run into her." She chewed on her lip as Erin waited, both of them knowing Katherine Young wasn't the only person included in that question. "But yes," Lennon finally answered quietly after a long beat, releasing a deep exhale. "That whole city is him. Us."

"Maybe it's time to make new memories. It's your city, too." Erin softly smiled. "Just give it some thought. Go with your heart."

"My heart doesn't have a great track record for making decisions."

"Letting your heart lead is who you are. It's one of the things I admire most about you."

The sincerity in Erin's voice touched Lennon.

"What if they have been the right plays and it's too early in the game to tell how it's all going to shake out?"

"God, you're such a baseball nerd," Lennon lovingly chided.

"What can I say … the metaphors work." Erin shrugged. "And

don't talk shit about my best friend ever again. I'll have to come kick your ass."

"I'll keep it to myself next time, then," Lennon said. Erin picked up her phone and smacked the camera with her hand, making Lennon laugh. "OK, OK. *Sorry.*"

"Apology accepted." Erin kept hold of the phone, leaning back against the counter. "Here's another cheesy baseball metaphor for you—you're only a few innings in, babe. Don't count your losses yet. You may end up with a home run you didn't even see coming."

"From your lips to the music gods' ears."

After a long day of video chatting with Erin, which included a movie musical double feature of their favorites, *Grease* (Lennon's) and *Mamma Mia!* (Erin's), they finally signed off when her best friend's eyelids began to droop around 9:30 in the evening. Lennon slipped out to use the bathroom down the hall. When she returned to her apartment, the emptiness of it hit her like a punch to the chest. She hadn't had a chance to fully sit uninterrupted with her emotions since the meeting with the record label. Now, in the stillness of her dark, quiet apartment, her heartache stretched its limbs.

She pressed back against the door, sliding to the floor. As the blue glow of the television she'd left on a rerun of *Friends* flickered across her slumped figure, she let the tears flow and slip down her cheeks. Let her lungs burn and throat turn raw.

Lennon let herself grieve.

Her twenty-sixth birthday was six months away, and she was on track to be in the same place she was last year. And the four years before that. Same circumstances, same job, same apartment. No further ahead in life.

What if the reality show didn't work out either?

What if it did?

Her mother's presence loomed, casting scrupulous eyes on

her. Lennon was confident—because she'd told her as much—that if Katherine Young could change one thing about her daughter, it would be for her to make safe, measured, low-risk life decisions every step of the way. "Life doesn't favor the bold. It makes a joke of them," Katherine warned Lennon when she asked permission to audition for the eighth-grade talent show. "Do you want to be a joke, Lennon?"

What if her mother wasn't the only one who would think of her as a joke after exposing herself on a reality show?

Lennon was typically a dive-in-first, ask-questions-later type, fueled by the thrill of adventure. This was one of the few times fear made her pause rather than punch the gas. Her string of failures had her questioning herself. And going back home would be even more complicated than leaving had been.

But what other choice did she have?

The bills would keep coming. Time would keep ticking on. If she'd learned one thing while living on her own the past six years, it was that if she wanted to survive, she had to keep moving. The least she could do was explore her options.

Before Lennon talked herself out of it, she slipped her phone from the pocket of her sweats and wiped her tears with her shirt as she found Avery's name in her contacts.

> Lennon: Hey Avery, it's Lennon. It was great seeing you last night. Can you send me the info for that reality show?

CHAPTER 7

Lennon

L ennon pulled her old beat-up suitcase from the baggage carousel. She adjusted the duffel bag slung across her body before rolling her luggage through Arden Beach International.

After Avery forwarded the casting director's information to her, Lennon emailed them an audition tape she recorded the next morning, following their guidelines. She hadn't expected to get a call back at all, let alone one an hour later asking if she was available for an online meeting that same afternoon. Being temporarily unemployed with nowhere else to be, she threw herself together and jumped on the call.

Two weeks later, Lennon signed the contract, gave her landlord notice that she wouldn't be renewing her apartment lease, and packed everything she owned in boxes.

Lennon walked past people in shorts and flip-flops arriving for summer vacation, taking photos next to a large fountain in the central atrium surrounded by tall palm trees. One of the passengers from her flight—a young woman around her age—ran past her into the arms of a group of people excitedly waiting for her with a home-made sign that read "WELCOME HOME, DARCY."

A pang of loneliness reverberated through her.

Erin was back on the road with the Tidebreakers. Without her, there was no one to welcome Lennon home. She hadn't told her mother she was moving back to Arden Beach, and she wasn't even sure where *she* was living those days, either. Last time they spoke, Katherine was in Sarasota with her new husband, but she mentioned they were considering moving to North Carolina. Knowing Katherine, Lennon would probably receive a random text from her one day with photos of their new place and a list of some stable, practical job listings in town for Lennon to check out if she was "finally ready to get serious about her life."

Lennon's father left when she was a toddler, and she had no connections to extended family. Essentially, she was as alone in Arden Beach as she had been in New York.

She rolled her luggage to the pickup area where a stoic, stocky man in a suit waited, holding a sign that brandished her surname with the reality show's production company, High Wave Productions, beneath it. He looked like an off-duty wrestler.

"Ms. Young?" he questioned with a Puerto Rican accent.

"That's me," she confirmed with a halfhearted wave.

"I'm Bruno. Nice to meet you." As they shook hands, his intimidating appearance melted away and was replaced with kind eyes and a gap-toothed smile. He offered to take her luggage. "First time in Arden Beach?"

Lennon lifted the duffel bag from her shoulder, thanking him as she handed it off. "Grew up here actually."

"Welcome home, then." Bruno carefully hooked the bag over his shoulder before reaching for the beat-up, rolling suitcase she'd had for years.

Bruno loaded her bags into a black Escalade parked at the curb. Beneath the jet fuel and exhaust fumes, Lennon picked up the subtle scent of the ocean salting the humid air. Hundreds of palm trees lined the roads they took to exit the airport, the rich green fanning across an equally rich blue sky. She squinted through her aviator sunglasses to see them as the blinding sun reflected off the white pavement surrounding them.

They made small talk over the soft hum of classic Latin pop on the radio as he battled the traffic leaving the airport, like how his twelve-year-old daughter, Rosie, loved the piano and how he'd picked up the job to help pay for lessons. "It runs in the family," Bruno told her. "You'll meet my husband, Darius, soon. He's the lead sound coordinator for the show."

A melancholy smile touched her lips, wondering what her life would have been like if her dad had stayed. He'd loved music, too. "Lucky girl. Do you play music, too?"

"I'm what I call a passionate enthusiast. I love to listen and dance to it, but I can't sing or play an instrument to save my life. I used to make Rosie cry when she was a baby when I'd try to sing her lullabies."

"You just need some good lessons," Lennon said. "Everyone can be taught."

"Your confidence is sweet but horribly misplaced, Ms. Young."

"Careful, Bruno. I love a challenge."

Skyscrapers rose in the distance, their glass facades reflecting turquoise along the beautiful Downtown Arden Beach skyline. She took in the sights as they flew past—endless palm trees, turquoise water, massive cruise ships docked in the Port of Arden Beach. They were soon replaced by rows of yachts in the marina as they crossed from the causeway into the city.

The low rooflines and whimsical, retro charm of Art Deco and mid-century buildings mingled with the sharp angles of steel and glass structures, with the occasional Spanish-style edifice thrown into the mix. This unique patchwork created a medley of quaint beach town, modern luxury, and old-world mystique unique to the city.

As her gaze fell on one of the many billboards, time suspended.

A fourteen-foot photograph of Dylan, mid-throw and clad in his baseball uniform, towered over the street in an advertisement for the Tidebreakers' stadium.

Her heart skipped. Lennon hadn't seen his face much since their divorce, outside the occasional dream. She wasn't aware of how hard she'd been staring until the car turned and she unwittingly craned her neck to follow the billboard until she no longer could.

"Apologies, we're going to be a bit late," Bruno said.

It took a second for his words to penetrate her consciousness. Lifting from her daze, she glanced at the gridlocked traffic ahead, then at the clock. Her meeting with the producers was in two minutes.

Great way to make a first impression.

Fourteen minutes later, the Escalade pulled up to The Blue Iris, a small restaurant a block from the beach known for its Mediterranean fare. Vivid blue umbrellas shaded tables on the sidewalk from the bright Florida sun, which gleamed off the white building. As Bruno opened her car door, he told her he'd be waiting to take her to her hotel.

Lennon ran inside, her black platform sandals making it hard to move as quickly as she'd like, only to impatiently wait behind a couple at the hostess stand. "Hi, I'm here to see Mr. Donaldson and Ms. Greenberg," Lennon said breathlessly when it was finally her turn. She swiped away a few strands of hair sticking to her face.

The hostess ushered her to a table in the back where two people were engrossed in conversation. As soon as they saw her, the man with salt-and-pepper hair rose to greet her. They exchanged introductions while Lennon apologized for being late.

Executive producer/showrunner Huey Donaldson and his co-producer, Maeve Greenberg—both industry veterans—waved it off, making a joke about Arden Beach's horrible traffic. Her anxiety eased a little.

"We've been using it as an excuse to get drunk on Bellinis before noon," Maeve joked as Lennon settled in across from them and accepted a menu from the hostess. She reminded her of a nineties news anchor—glamorous and perfectly coiffed in a crisp, professional way.

"We're not quite there yet though. You got here too fast," Huey added. In contrast, he seemed like the kind of man who would spill coffee on his shirt and hide it with his expensive tie.

"Well, don't let me stop you." Lennon looked up at the server who approached as the hostess left. "I'll have what they're having."

Huey leaned into Maeve. "I like her already."

At first, Lennon felt like she couldn't quite catch her breath, a fine layer of sweat prickling up along her neck, but the morning's chaos gradually settled as they fell into easy conversation. She put her vocal training to work to regain control of her diaphragm while looking over the menu. Once they'd placed their orders, the producers didn't waste a second before jumping into their plans for the show. By the time her spaghetti arrived, Lennon's head was spinning.

"Wow, you guys move fast. You'll really have the whole season filmed and released in—" She did the math for the premiere date they'd mentioned. "Five months?"

"Content moves swiftly these days. You snooze; you lose. Gotta churn it out before people get bored and move on to something else," Huey said between chomps of his omelet. He'd smothered it in hot sauce, salt, and pepper. Mauve had commented on his blood sugar as he generously poured, and he shrugged it off, assuring her that he was "fitter at sixty" than he was at Lennon's age.

"How often will I be filming?" Lennon asked, slowly twirling some spaghetti around her fork.

"Well, we've got the season mapped out, but we leave some room for spontaneity. Never quite know what surprises may be waiting for us that we'll want to jump on. But right now, you're a supporting player within Avery's storyline," Huey answered. "Maybe a couple days a week."

"Not necessarily every week," Maeve chimed in. She picked at her tomato salad, her bold red lipstick somehow perfectly intact, matching her long, acrylic nails.

"Right," he said. "Keep your schedule open. We'll let you know when we need you."

"I was thinking of getting another job while I'm here," Lennon said. "Is that going to complicate things? I don't know how all this works. Filming a TV show is new territory for me."

"If you're not available when we're shooting, you'll miss out on that production time, unfortunately," Huey answered simply, wiping a drop of tabasco sauce from the corner of his mouth with a white cloth napkin.

Basically, less exposure and less pay. She had to fit into their schedule. If she didn't, it was her loss, not theirs. "Will I have a chance to film anything by myself, or will I only be in Avery's scenes?"

"Oh, we *definitely* want to get some footage of you working on your own thing," Huey assured her.

"We *love* the whole struggling musician thing," Maeve agreed, fanning out her hands. "When you told us about losing your record deal, my heart was absolutely *breaking* for you."

"Audiences love an underdog," Huey remarked, glancing at his colleague.

Maeve met his gaze. "*Love* an underdog."

"We wanted someone on the music scene to round out the cast. When Avery told us about you, it was like fate dropped you in our laps in the nick of time. Really saved our asses. I thought we'd have to go with that coked-up DJ for a minute," he said, laughing through a mouthful of omelet.

Maeve's eyes widened with dread as she sipped her second Bellini. "That was an HR nightmare waiting to happen."

"Wouldn't be the first," he remarked sardonically, and the two of them snickered like they were reliving a wild story from the battlefield.

Lennon smiled tightly, trying not to make a face and

encouraging herself not to read too deeply into whatever just transpired between them. She'd gone too far to start having second thoughts or giving herself reasons to run the other way. It *was* the entertainment industry; she'd dipped her toes in it enough to know things weren't exactly a dream behind the scenes.

"So, anyway," Huey continued. "We'll probably want to get you beating the pavement, talking to music producers, schmoozing—you know, working the Arden Beach music scene. Really want to show that struggle."

A piece of feta cheese caught in Lennon's throat. She gently coughed. "Wouldn't it be more interesting to show me making music or putting a performance together? Or maybe collaborating with others? Focus more on the art."

Huey wobbled his head back and forth with an *ehhhh* sound. "I mean, sure, maybe a little bit of that, but people will get all the happy stuff with Avery's wedding. We need drama to balance it out. Provide some contrast. Give 'em someone to … relate to."

The spaghetti and alcohol churned uneasily in her stomach. "I'm the sad story against Avery's fairytale?"

They seemed to realize she'd taken offense to it and glanced at each other.

"You're the one people get to see themselves in and root for," Maeve clarified, leaning forward slightly with an encouraging lift to her voice.

The idea still sat uncomfortably in Lennon's bones, but she knew she wasn't in any position to argue about it. And it's not like it wasn't true; she *was* struggling while Avery was living out her fairytale. The idea of putting herself in that light in the public eye made her insides feel like the ball of pasta on her plate, but if that's what it took to get her to the next level, so be it.

She was used to being vulnerable in her music on stage. She'd have to get used to being vulnerable as herself, too.

"Will I get to perform my music at all on the show?" Lennon asked.

Huey's bushy brows furrowed a bit, and he inclined his head in a sort of half-committal nod/shake. "I'm sure we'll get it in there somewhere."

"Yeah, at least a little taste of it," Maeve assured her, bobbing her dark curls.

That wasn't the answer Lennon wanted to hear. She was about to open her mouth to argue a case for showcasing her music on the show but then thought better of it. She didn't want to appear difficult on the first day. The record label execs had complained about how vocal she was from the beginning. If she was going to take any lesson from that, this was probably a good place to start.

Besides, Lennon had time to figure out how to finagle her music into the show. She'd have to get creative to make it worth their while.

They discussed some other things and informed her that the production assistant who had helped arrange her flights and accommodation would be in touch about all the other boring details, like her schedule and finding housing. Lennon shook both producers' hands as they stood up from the table. "Thank you so much again for this opportunity."

"We're looking forward to having you on the cast," Maeve said with a smile, bright white teeth popping against red lipstick.

"Let's make some good TV," Huey winked.

Lennon laughed nervously, wondering what the hell she'd gotten herself into. Whatever it was, it was too late to turn back now.

Huey swept his arm out, inviting Lennon to take the lead while Maeve checked her lipstick in a compact mirror. The two followed her toward the door a few steps behind. In a split second, Lennon's brain went from whirring about the show to coming to a complete stop, like a car slamming into a tree.

Through the glass doors, a young man with a tall, lean build grabbed one of the handles and swung it open. He stopped to let an elderly couple exit, stepping to the side with a kind smile as he dipped his head. Tufts of brown hair stuck out from the edges of his baseball cap. They thanked him, beaming up at him as he held the door open for them to pass. He said something that made them laugh, and they made him laugh in return. His low, relaxed chuckle carried through the open door, messing with her insides.

As they walked off, he turned back toward the restaurant. He caught Lennon's stare as he stepped across the threshold. He, too, stopped dead in his tracks, dark eyes melting into pools of surprise.

Her heart thumped in her chest, reminding her it was still there, beating—*hard*.

"Lennon," Dylan said, the way someone utters a prayer. "Hey." One side of his parted lips pulled into a smile.

"Hi," she said on an exhale.

Dylan took her in. She suddenly became aware of herself. Once again, she hadn't been prepared—not for the conversation on the train or for the first time seeing him. She pushed a loose strand of dark hair from her claw clip behind her ear, exposing the little music note tattooed by her left lobe, and ran her hands down the front of her black floral sundress, likely wrinkled from the plane ride. The tight schedule hadn't allowed her time to change after landing, so she had to wear something nice for the meeting but comfortable enough for the plane.

But then, Lennon got distracted by the way *he* looked.

The vintage graphic tee hugging his broad shoulders. The distressed jeans hanging off his hips. The scruff on his face and the smooth, golden tan flowing over the muscles in his forearms.

The lanky baseball player she'd left behind had gained muscle—and a short beard—in the years since she'd last seen him. The billboard hadn't done him justice.

He was stupidly handsome. Her heart caught in her throat the same way it would when they were teenagers.

"I didn't know you were in town," Dylan said, drawing her gaze back to his.

"Oh—yeah. I got in this morning," Lennon said. "It was a last-minute thing."

"How long will you be here?"

"A few months at least."

His brows rose slightly. "Really?"

"Yeah." Lennon nodded casually, feeling the exact opposite of casual. He smelled good, exactly as she remembered, like clean laundry and an earthy cologne he'd always loved. Silence stretched between them for a few moments, leaving them staring at each other. In that space, time collapsed.

She was the teenager again who thought she'd found her soulmate. He was her best friend. Her safe space. *Home.* A place she had been aching for and now was in front of her in vibrant, raw, living color.

"Who's this?"

It took a moment for Huey's intrusive voice to register. He and Maeve peeked around Lennon's shoulders, eyes hopping back and forth between her and Dylan with a buzz of curiosity.

Time spread back out, the present sucking her back into place.

They were divorced. He'd broken her heart. She'd lost her record deal, and she was about to go on a freakin' reality show to pay her bills and jumpstart her stalled music career.

"That's Dylan Strickland," Maeve said as though it should be obvious. "Pitcher for the Arden Beach Tidebreakers—one of *the* Stricklands."

A shadow passed beneath his charming smile. No one else likely noticed it, but Lennon did. Her heart twinged.

"You two know each other?" Huey asked. Both producers came to stand on either side of them, creating a circle between the four of them.

"He's my ex-husband." It still felt weird to say. Lennon cleared her throat as a loaded glance passed between her and Dylan.

"You were married to a professional baseball player? Why didn't you tell us?" Huey looked past Lennon to Maeve. "How did we miss this?"

Maeve shook her head, the wheels turning behind her eyes.

"It was a long time ago." Lennon noticed some of the other

patrons were beginning to stare. The space closed in on her. She gripped the strap on her shoulder, pressing the small handbag into her ribs with her bicep to stabilize herself.

She wanted out of that restaurant.

"Hey, uh, I've gotta run," Dylan said, jabbing a thumb toward the door. "I'm just picking up a to-go order and have a training session to get to." When Lennon looked back up at him, he was already focused on her, his eyebrows pulled slightly together.

Grateful for the lifeline he was throwing her, the tension in her body eased slightly. "OK. Good to see you."

Dylan smiled softly. "You too." He held her gaze for a beat longer before shifting his attention to the producers. "Nice to meet you both," he said. He glanced at Lennon once more, then strode past them.

Lennon made a beeline for the door, anxious for the freedom of an open space. Outside, she stopped on the sidewalk—nearly colliding with a woman in a matching athletic set walking a French bulldog—and took in a deep gulp of air. She was barely on the exhale when the two producers flanked her again.

"What was *that*?" Maeve questioned.

"What do you mean?" Lennon searched the street for a black Escalade.

Huey and Maeve shared a look like two conspiratorial teenagers giddy over a secret. "*That*," Maeve reiterated. "The chemistry between you and Dylan-effing-Strickland, one of the biggest major league baseball stars in the country."

"There was no—he's just an ex." The proclamation tasted wrong on Lennon's tongue, but she tightened her jaw to give it solidity. "There's nothing to talk about." The producers looked at each other again, this time like two adults who were aware of something the child between them wasn't. Her patience frayed. "I have a lot to do before filming starts next week, like find a place to live," Lennon said, straining to keep her tone polite. "Are we all set here?"

"Why does that name Strickland sound familiar?" Huey asked, ignoring her. "You said 'one of *the* Stricklands'—"

"He's from a line of baseball legacies," Maeve explained, "and he's been in the tabloids a lot recently. Earlier this year, he was suspended from the team on the heels of that big scandal."

His face lit up. "What scandal?"

"Dylan and some other players from the team got wasted at a party and crashed a boat," Maeve said. "A bunch of people got hurt. They found drugs, too."

"Dylan wasn't doing drugs. And he didn't crash the boat. He was passed out before they pulled away from the dock," Lennon interjected. His stupidity for getting himself in that situation boiled her blood all over again, as it had when Erin first relayed it to her, but they at least needed to get facts straight.

"Oh, *that* scandal! I remember." Huey's eyes bulged. "That was *him*?" The producers were back to having a silent conversation as Maeve nodded slowly. "Shit, I should get into baseball."

"I wouldn't recommend it. The stress takes at least ten years off your life," Maeve remarked.

"You think he'd be interested in being on the show?" Huey asked Lennon.

"What? No, absolutely not—»

"It'd be a great chance for him to tell his side of the story," Maeve remarked. "Clear the air. Build his reputation back up. Get America back on his side."

Was America *not* on his side? Lennon had avoided reading anything about the accident. All she knew was what Erin told her, which included ranting about how the media had twisted and sensationalized the story. The public turning on him was news to her. Lennon assumed the backlash had been limited to behind-the-scenes drama within the baseball league.

The idea made her feel funny. Strangely … protective.

"People love an underdog and a comeback story," Huey sang. "They'd fall in love with him."

"How could they not? He's so handsome, too," Maeve said with an eyebrow wiggle. Lennon tried to ignore the warm knot low in her torso at the memory of him walking through the door. Maeve studied Lennon. "Your dynamic together would also be interesting."

"I don't think he'd be interested," Lennon said. "And I'm barely going to be on the show, anyway—"

"We'll bump you to a starring role," Huey cut in with surprising directness. "That means a bump in pay and exposure, too."

The flush of desire for what he offered was quickly squashed by Lennon's disgust at the idea of selling Dylan out for her benefit. Maeve cut in before she vocalized it as if smelling the reluctance on her. "Think about it. Talk it over with Dylan," Maeve said, preemptively holding off Lennon's repudiation. "You can let us know by the end of the day tomorrow."

"It's a once-in-a-lifetime opportunity," Huey told her. "It could save your career. And his."

CHAPTER 8

Dylan

"You running from something, bro?"

The question posed by his trainer pulled Dylan back to the Tidebreakers' gym—to the whir of the treadmill, his feet pounding the belt, and the empty stadium beyond the glass wall. His heart pumped vigorously in his chest, but running was only partially to blame.

He'd been distracted all afternoon.

"Sorry, what?" Dylan asked, breathless.

"I told you to stop at twenty minutes and meet me outside," Marcos answered, his long, black hair tied in a bun at the nape of his neck. "You're flirting with half an hour like something's chasing you." He leaned an arm on the machine beside Dylan's, crossing one ankle over the other. "I was waiting to see how long you'd keep going, but I got bored."

Dylan lowered the speed to a jog, then a walk, and finally hopped off the machine. Grabbing the towel he'd set off to the side, Dylan plopped down on a weight bench and wiped the sweat from his brow. He sat there for a moment, catching his breath, his thoughts running on a different treadmill over the same topic they'd been stuck on for hours.

Her.

"You wanna talk about what's got you in your head today?"

"What do you mean?" Dylan hedged as he hung his head, elbows braced on his slick knees while the towel hung from his hands.

"You know what I mean. You were late to our session. You forgot parts of the warm-up you do every day. You've barely said two words when I usually can't get you to shut the hell up and focus on your reps."

"I was only a few minutes late, and that's because I was picking up lunch for us, asshole."

And unexpectedly ran into the love of my life in the process, Dylan didn't add.

"The lunch they forgot your stupid sauces for, and you didn't even notice?"

Dylan stilled, the realization soaking in like the sweat through his muscle tank. They had left out the sauce—and he *hadn't* noticed. He'd never eaten his gyros without it before. Not by choice. Once, he'd driven back to the restaurant across town to get them when they were left out of his takeout order. He made a point to check the bag now before he left.

Usually.

On the days when his ex-wife didn't consume his thoughts.

Dylan glanced over his shoulder at Marcos, who was still leaning against the other machine, patiently watching him. After years of training together, they'd developed a friendship, particularly since Marcos and Erin had been helping him rehabilitate after the accident. His teammates had been busy on the road—some had flat-out distanced themselves from him amid the controversy—and he hadn't been in a very social mood, regardless. Some weeks, Marcos was one of the only human beings he saw besides his father and sister, thanks to their rigorous training schedule to get him back in shape for the next baseball season. And because he'd become somewhat of a hermit.

"You planning to add 'therapist' to your job description?" Dylan shot back dryly, dragging the towel around his neck as he faced forward.

"Depends. Do I get a raise?"

The corner of Dylan's mouth nudged into a smile, but his thoughts flowed back to his distraction like water in a trough. "I ran into my ex this morning."

"Shit. Which one?"

The only one that mattered. "My wi—ex-wife."

It had started as any normal Tuesday, and just like that, after simply walking through the door of a restaurant he'd happened to get a craving for, his world shifted on its axis. Or maybe it was put *back* on its axis. The fact that Dylan felt more normal in those few minutes talking to her on the phone and standing in that restaurant with her brought up a landslide of questions he wasn't prepared to answer.

"I thought she lived in New York?"

"She did. She just moved back to Arden Beach."

"*Ay, Dios mío,*" Marcos mumbled. "How'd she look?"

Dylan dropped his head, unable to fight the smile at the memory of her that afternoon. The loose hair framing her face. The small tattoos scattered across her body. Those mesmerizing green eyes and the way her little black dress with flowers on it had swished around her long, smooth legs. His heart pounded like he was still in a sprint. "Beautiful," Dylan said quietly.

He could practically hear Marcos's eye roll. "I meant, did she seem happy to see you or like she wanted to kill you?"

At that, his chest compressed.

Lennon looked like she'd wanted the floor to swallow her up when those people she was with started asking about their relationship. Being connected with him put an immediate target on anyone's back. She hadn't signed up for that. He wanted to do absolutely anything but walk away from her, but he could tell she wanted an out, so he gave her one.

It was hard enough not to think about her when she was a thousand miles away. Knowing she was right there, in the same city, would make it damn near impossible.

Dylan shook his head, drawing a sharp breath as he swiped his hand across his nose. "She was busy. We didn't talk long. But I don't think my life was in danger, so that's a plus, I guess." He dropped the towel beside him and rose from the bench. He crossed the gym to the mini fridge tucked into a wet bar and removed a water bottle. "We talked on the phone about a week ago." Dylan held up the cold bottle and offered it to Marcos.

"Oh yeah?" Marcos asked as he nodded. He caught the bottle that came sailing toward him with smooth, athletic ease.

Dylan grabbed another bottle for himself and cracked it open, leaning back against the bar. "She meant to call my sister but accidentally called me instead."

A thick, dark eyebrow quirked up as Marcos raised his hands, making quotation marks with his fingers around the bottle. "*Accidentally?*"

"Definitely accidentally. She sounded like a ghost had answered the phone." The pressure in his ribs doubled as he recalled how reluctant she'd been both times to talk to him, at her eagerness to get away from him. He drowned the thought with a long, burning gulp of ice-cold water. He'd almost completely drained the bottle when he came up for air.

Marcos leveled a non-judgmental gaze on him. "You need to talk to your therapist?"

Dylan considered it for a moment as he spun the cap back on the bottle. He felt the pull to counterbalance the growing knot in his chest with a distraction intense enough to numb it, but his grip remained strong enough not to give in. For now, at least. "I'm good. Appreciate the check-in, though."

"Let's head to the bullpen, then. Or would you rather sit here pining after your ex for the rest of the day?"

Dylan sent the near-empty water bottle soaring across the room with deadly precision, the lightweight plastic narrowly missing the center of his trainer's chest thanks to a quick sidestep. Marcos laughed as Dylan rolled his shoulder above his pitching arm, his fading surgical scar twisting with the movement. It was still a little stiff and gave a light twinge, but nothing like the searing pain that had plagued him directly after the accident.

"At least your aim's pretty good, even if your game isn't," Marcos chided with a wink as he turned toward the exit.

"We can't all be as smooth as you, Marc."

As Dylan followed him, his gaze fell to the simple gold band around his friend's ring finger as it glinted under the lights. Dylan unconsciously flexed his left hand.

After their bullpen session, Marcos left Dylan to do the rest of his workout alone in the gym so he could meet up with his wife at a Lamaze class. The physical exertion had helped Dylan burn off some of his restless energy. With the team on the road, the stadium was uncomfortably quiet. He could go home and finish his workout there, but it would be just as silent. He'd spent enough of the last four months holed up there.

At least at the stadium, he felt somewhat connected to the team. Not like the outsider he'd become.

To fill the silence, Dylan flicked on the flat-screen television near the weight-lifting machines. He grabbed plates and loaded up the barbell.

"—unfortunate consequence of a string of bad deals and decisions. If Carmichael's making those kinds of mistakes with his companies, that doesn't bode well for the Tidebreakers."

Dylan paused, the man's familiar drawl raking over his nerves. He turned to the television where Nolan Pierce spoke to the anchor of the popular sports newscast *Hour on Sports with Yousef Hajjar.* Nolan wore his typical smug expression, his misplaced arrogance as overbearing as his three-piece suit. Desperate as ever to prove himself.

"And while he's focused on trying to save his sinking ship of a conglomerate," Nolan continued, "who's looking out for the team?"

"With all due respect, you're—what, twenty-five years old?" Yousef asked.

"Twenty-six," Nolan corrected, the corner of his mouth vaguely curving in a smirk.

"What makes you think you know better than Eddie Carmichael, who's been in the business for decades?"

Nolan leaned into his elbow on the chair's chrome arm, his hands clasped together in a relaxed position. His smirk deepened. "A sign of a good leader is knowing when to step down and let new blood take over. The Tidebreakers have been slipping backward, not moving forward. Even the fans have expressed frustration with how the team's been managed recently. While other owners are investing in their teams, Eddie's been stingy to protect his bottom line—and it's costing them." His dark gaze briefly lowered to the glass table between him and Yousef, his smile fading. "I was raised as a Tidebreakers fan, but I didn't have the privilege of growing up as an elite in that world who felt entitled to possess the team. I advocate for the fans who are there for the love of the game, not for what it can do for them."

Dylan's blood steamed. As if Nolan cared about anything but himself.

He shut off the television as his phone buzzed in his pocket. He dug it out—a call from his manager. One of the last people he wanted to talk to. He let it go to voicemail and dropped it on the bench before stretching his arms and back. A few seconds later, his phone pinged with a voicemail. As Dylan sat on the bench, he scrolled through his notifications. Five missed calls from Jeff and a text demanding he call him back "ASAP."

Dylan grabbed the towel to wipe the sweat coating his skin, still warm from the summer sun. Resting his elbows on his knees, he tapped his manager's name to get it over with. Jeff picked up almost instantly.

"Dude, where the fuck you been?"

"Please tell me there's not another fire to put out," Dylan muttered, kneading his thumb and forefinger into his brow. He'd had enough of those in the last several months. Really, since the beginning of his professional career. The media talked more about his life off the field than on it.

"Nope. Luck is finally turning in our favor. A whole damn fire truck showed up today, baby." As Jeff took a dramatic pause, Dylan's sweat-filled brow furrowed, wondering where he was going with this. "Why didn't you tell me you ran into Maeve and Huey from High Wave?"

"Who?"

"At Blue Iris. They said they met you there, with your ex-wife."

Dylan's brain struggled to catch up. What did it have to do with him if she met with music producers? The implication gave him some hope, though—was she already working on another record deal? Was that why she was in Arden Beach?

"They're producing a reality show. *Arden Elite.* One of those shows that follows hot rich people around while they party and shit. She's going to be on it," Jeff continued.

"Wait—what?" That didn't sound like Lennon. "Are you sure?"

"Sure as shit. I talked to them an hour ago. I've been trying to reach you since I got off the phone. They want you on the cast, man."

Dylan didn't know if the intense workout had left him dehydrated or if he was so distracted by Lennon's return that his synapses weren't firing, because none of this made sense. Lennon liked binge-watching reality shows but had always been fiercely private. The idea of fame was the one thing that had unnerved her about her music aspirations, but she'd pursued them anyway because her passion for it had been stronger than her fear. One thing he admired most about her was her bravery in living life on her terms.

Dylan wished he were more like her.

How did they go from Lennon clamming up when that woman in the restaurant—one of the producers, he now understood—recognized him and asked about their relationship to her wanting him on a show with her?

Unless she didn't know.

Lennon would've called him if this were her doing. It must have been happening behind her back. He knew all too well how that kind of shit went down.

"I don't think that's a good idea," Dylan said, hanging his head as he peered between his knees at the black rubber floor.

"Fuck off, bro. You know it's a fantastic idea. This is the perfect opportunity to repair your image, which, as you know, sucks right now. If you want to have a future in baseball and get your sponsorships back before your opportunities dry up, you need to win back the public's support. This could do that for you."

Dylan's jaw clenched, as it often did during conversations with Jeff. He wanted to tell him to fuck off. Selling himself, managing a public image—by far the worst part of his job. But as he'd seen in the last four months, failing at it could end his career overnight.

Part of him wanted it to end. To be free from the pressure, the weight of his family's legacy, the monetization and sensationalism that stripped the fun from a game he used to love. The mere thought shed some tension in his shoulders, unfurling something deep within.

But Dylan had too much to lose. Baseball was his life. It was his identity. His birthright. The reason he had anything in this world. And it wasn't only about him. Too many people were counting on him to return to the game.

He was done disappointing people, so he had to figure this out. Getting in Lennon's way to do it, however, was not an option.

Dylan breathed steadily through his nose, readying himself for diplomacy. "I've stopped drinking and going out. I've been serious about getting my shit together—"

"But the public doesn't know that. The old you is stuck in their minds," Jeff interrupted, reminding Dylan of his conversation with Erin at the tournament. "The way to change it is to *show* them—to let them see what your life is like now. What *you're* like. A reality show is the perfect platform for that. People fucking love a comeback story. They'll eat that shit up. Sponsors will be *begging* you to hock their crap. Teams will be taking turns sucking your dick trying to sign you."

Dylan ran his fingers through his damp hair. As much as he loathed to agree with him, he knew what Jeff was saying made sense, but he doubted Lennon was on board with it. If she was going on a reality show, there was no way he was going to step on her toes and screw that up for her. He'd done enough damage in her life already.

"I can't," Dylan said with finality, lifting his head.

"Dude, listen—"

"The answer's no, Jeff. I gotta go."

"Damn it, Dylan. Just think about—"

Dylan ended the call. He blew a gust of air from his lungs. Looking at his phone, he debated calling Lennon to let her know he'd turned them down.

He slipped the phone back in his pocket. He'd promised not to impose himself on her. If she wanted to talk about it, she'd call him.

His ears rang in the silence of the gym. In the stillness.

Dylan unloaded the barbell. He needed a different outlet to burn off the tension in his body.

CHAPTER 9

Lennon

Lennon tapped her room card on the digital keypad, unlocking a door on the hotel's eighteenth floor. During check-in, the front desk clerk had informed her they were preparing a new room after receiving a last-minute upgrade request. The studio put her up in a mid-range hotel chain, recently renovated with sleek, modern finishes. Opening the door, she stopped short and gawked at the suite, complete with a kitchen, living room, and separate bedroom. At the far end, the city peeked through a gap in the sheer, white curtains. She passed her luggage, which the staff had already deposited beside the low-profile sofa, and pushed the curtains aside.

A blue strip of ocean, a few blocks in the distance, hugged the horizon. Tiny sailboats floated between the white skyscrapers that sliced her view of the Atlantic. The city's chorus—traffic, seagulls, sea breeze—was dulled by the glass, but it was enough to feel its heartbeat.

Home.

The word was sung in a whisper through her bones. Lennon

had never imagined herself leaving. Not until it hurt too much to stay.

Lennon let go of the curtain and the memories, continuing to the bedroom. A large gift basket sat on the king-size bed. In it were various self-care items like a silk sleep mask and an organic body scrub, a generous gift card to the hotel's spa, an expensive bottle of wine, and a few boxes of chocolate. Lennon flipped open the attached card on thick card stock. "A little taste of what's to come for our stars," the card read, which was signed by Huey and Maeve of High Wave Productions.

All the bribery in the world wouldn't get her to say yes to their offer to drag Dylan into this, but she would enjoy the fruits of their effort.

The melody belonging to him thrummed somewhere deep in her ribs and rose along her sternum. As she closed her eyes, his look of surprise when he saw her in the restaurant stole her breath all over again. One side of her heart beat for him, while the other ached over how things ended. She didn't know how to lean into one without the other.

Ignoring them both had been the only answer.

But in the space of two weeks, Lennon had already tripped into two accidental encounters with him. Now that they were living in the same city again, avoidance would be tricky, if not impossible.

It was time to deal with it.

Lennon kicked off her black platform sandals and sank her feet into the plush carpet before climbing onto the bed. Her lunch knotted itself in a lead ball as she reached for her phone lying next to the gift basket. Maeve's words about getting America back on his side echoed in her mind.

Before she talked to him, she needed the complete picture of what was going on.

After their divorce, Lennon avoided the baseball world as if any acknowledgment of it would sentence her to a horrible death, like watching that video in *The Ring*. It was pretty easy in New York, given the city had its own major league teams to focus on. If you aren't actively engaging in the baseball world, you're mostly oblivious to what's happening within it.

Lennon ripped open one of the boxes of chocolate, shoving a tiny piece in her mouth for moral support before lying on her stomach and kicking up her feet. She opened an internet tab and typed Dylan's name into the blinking search box.

With a deep breath, she tapped *Go.*

Dylan's boyish, soulful eyes stared into hers from his baseball headshot. The chocolate slowly melted on her tongue as she took him in through the series of photos. Standing on the pitcher's mound as he eyed his mark with intense focus. Celebrating on the field with his teammates after pitching a no-hitter game. Smiling in a fitted suit with an arm around his father at some event.

Lennon tore her gaze away. Scrolling, she shuffled through the various articles about the "downfall of a baseball legacy."

An hour later, from the depths of the rancid rabbit hole she'd tumbled down, anger and disgust flowed hot in her veins over the wild speculation, conspiracy theories, and outright lies people spread about him.

And about *them.*

The so-called journalists speculated that Lennon and Dylan's "failed teen marriage" was either the cause or the first sign of his "reckless behavior." Some postulated affairs. Others theorized that there was a secret pregnancy she terminated or that Lennon had gotten jealous of his success and left him. Several media outlets had reached out to her for a comment after the accident, but she'd declined to speak to any of them. Now, she wondered if that had served to fan the flames of conjecture.

The aggressive public scrutiny was brutal. Dealing with one's demons in private was bad enough. Lennon was nervous about having a small part on a reality show, meanwhile Dylan was dragged through the mud in tabloid fodder and media discourse he hadn't asked for. If her music career ever did take off, she could potentially find herself in the same position someday.

He'd made a mistake, but he didn't deserve *this*. No one did.

Swiping out of the browser, she pulled up her contacts and stared at his name under her Favorites. Pressure mounted in every molecule of her body.

Before she could talk herself out of it, Lennon smashed her thumb on his name.

As it rang, she reached into the box of chocolates from the gift basket for another piece, shoving it in her mouth.

"Hello?" Dylan answered, sounding a little out of breath.

"Hey, it's me—Lennon." She pushed herself up and crossed her legs. "Did I catch you at a bad time?"

"I know who it is." He chuckled, the raspiness of it making her skin tingle. "No, you're good. I'm on a run."

"Oh, we can talk later if you're—"

"I'm free."

Lennon's heart drummed in her chest. "Actually, can we switch to video?" They needed to have this conversation face-to-face. Maybe she should have asked to meet in person, but she didn't have the patience to wait any longer.

"Yeah. Sure," Dylan said with a tinge of either excitement or apprehension—she couldn't tell which.

Lennon tapped the button to request the video call. Her muscles pulled taut around her organs in the few seconds it took for him to accept it and the video to connect. A blurry, pixelated outline of him appeared before stabilizing. The blue sky framed him as the phone bounced with his jog. He wore his deep blue Tidebreakers hat backward, tufts of dark hair peeking out of the sides that connected to his short beard. But that was the only article of clothing in the frame. Sweat glistened across his bare shoulders and broad chest, rising and falling with heavy breaths.

She experienced instant regret for suggesting a video call.

Glancing down at his phone, he smiled. "Hey."

Lennon realized her lips had parted. She clamped them shut, swallowing around the chocolate melting on her tongue. "Hey. You sure this is a good time?"

"Yeah, I was just blowing off some steam." The undulating hum of the ocean underpinned his voice. He lifted the camera higher and angled it toward the sea, giving her a glimpse of the vast stretch of aquamarine that sparkled in the sunlight. And more of his lean, well-defined torso. "Not a bad view, huh?"

"If you like that sort of thing," Lennon joked. His laugh came as a low rumble that made her limbs warm. Before he lowered the camera, she noticed a faint shimmer on his left shoulder as the muscles shifted with the swing of his arm. A pale slash with slightly jagged edges traced a line from his collarbone to the tip of his bicep.

The heat simmered to sadness. What happened to him suddenly became strikingly real. Erin had called from the emergency room and kept Lennon in the loop throughout his recovery, but *seeing* the scar made her stomach flip. The nightmare burst alive with a new kind of intensity.

Dylan slowed to a walk. Looking at her, his smile faded. He glanced at the scar. "It looks worse than it is."

"Yeah, it only needed half a year of recovery," Lennon remarked wryly, not surprised he still brushed off his injuries.

"Gave me a chance to catch up on TV," Dylan retorted casually.

Lennon glared at him. As he sat down on the sand, a dune at his back, she said, "I'm sorry for the awkward run-in, for how they ambushed you and drew all that attention to us."

"It's OK, I'm used to it." Dylan swiped his forearm across his brow. "Are you OK?"

"Yeah, I'm fine." Despite her answer, something worried his brown eyes. "Why?"

His forehead scrunched, squinting toward the sky. "I'd understand if you wouldn't want to be seen with me right now."

"You think I was *embarrassed*?" Lennon raised an eyebrow. He shrugged. She had been, but not for the reasons he assumed. "I'm not embarrassed to be seen with you."

One side of Dylan's mouth twitched as he watched the horizon. "You may want to reconsider that."

"I'm not afraid of what the media's saying. They can go fuck themselves."

Dylan's eyes snapped to her. His expression sat somewhere at the crossroads between surprised and amused. "I agree."

Lennon rolled the hem of her dress between her fingers, resting her hand on her knee. "Obviously, I imagined it going a lot differently when we finally saw each other again."

He waited a beat. "Does that mean you *wanted* to see me again?"

Her teeth bothered her bottom lip. How did she even put an answer to that into words? *Yes, I've been dying to see you, but also no, I wasn't sure my heart could take it.* "Well, it was inevitable our paths would cross eventually now that I'm back in Arden Beach," Lennon reasoned. "We needed to clear the air at some point. Which is why I called."

Dylan nodded, his throat bobbing. "I'm glad. I know I already said everything in the letter Erin gave you, but I've been hoping for a chance to say it to you in person. Or at least, over the phone. I didn't want to force it on you when you were already going through a lot."

Guilt needled her heart. The letter—still sealed—was in a box waiting to be shipped from New York to wherever she ended up living in Florida. "To be honest, I haven't read it yet. I haven't … been in the headspace for it." Her heart clenched at the disappointment in his expression. "But you don't need to say anything."

"I want to—"

"I'd rather you didn't," Lennon said. He stared at her. "I don't want to get caught up in the past. We've both been through a lot. We've grown a lot." *At least I have,* she didn't say out loud. *I don't know about you yet.* "Let's just agree to start with a clean slate."

His expression was unreadable. The Dylan she divorced would have been relieved. Not even serving him divorce papers—her last desperate attempt to reach him—had cracked him open. Instead, he'd signed them.

That signature had finished splitting her heart in half.

Lennon recognized the irony of their roles flipping, but it had taken years for the hard scab to form over that wound. Like hell she was going to rip it open now while the rest of her life was on fire. Nothing he could say would heal it, anyway. The vows he made to her before had meant nothing, so why would she believe them now?

Muscles flexed along his jawline before he dipped his head. The gentle waves in the background filled his long pause. "OK," Dylan said, eyes softening on her. "Can I say one thing? And then we don't have to talk about it again. Unless you want to."

The wounded, carefully guarded side of her heart stiffened, afraid. The other nudged her, aching for closure. "Just one thing."

"I'm sorry, Lennon," Dylan said, those three words punching the air from her lungs. "I'm sorry for letting you down. For breaking so many promises to you. For putting you through hell—for bringing you into *my* hell. You deserved better. You deserved everything and I … I couldn't give it to you. I should've never promised you I could."

Lennon bit down on her tongue, tears blurring the edges of her vision. Otherwise, she remained completely still, unable to move.

"You were my best friend. I shouldn't have shut you out. I'm so sorry, Lennon. I'm so, so sorry," Dylan said quietly, his voice breaking slightly. Heavy with what sounded like regret. He swiped a hand over his jaw. It may have been a trick of the light, but before he turned his head, his eyes seemed glassy.

For a while, they sat in silence. Lennon tamped down the wave of emotion beating against the dam in her chest. Even though it wasn't enough to heal everything, she hadn't realized how much she needed to hear that from him. The side of her heart carrying the wound breathed a little easier, beat a little less painfully.

"Thank you," Lennon said. Was all she could say.

Dylan waited a moment before lifting his head, his expression now stoic. Awkwardness swelled between them. "So, um … are you really going on a reality show?"

Lennon cringed and groaned at his effective—but unfortunate—way of breaking the tension. It snapped her out of it, even if it did come at the cost of her embarrassment. "Yeahhh," she admitted. After a moment, she snort-laughed, which prompted him to release a laugh he'd been holding onto, which prompted her to release a full-bodied laugh. "Shut up." She reached back for one of the fluffy pillows and buried her face in its sweet floral scent.

"No, no, it's just … not something I would've expected, is all." Dylan's laughter tapered off. "You used to watch them all the time, but you always said you'd sooner strangle yourself with a guitar string than ever go on one."

"Well, having your dreams go up in flames and not wanting to relocate to a cold slab of concrete under a bridge will change your perspective on things."

"You could've chosen one of the ones with grass or a nice little pond."

"Wow. You can't hit a home run or tell a funny joke anymore."

"Kinda hard to hit home runs as a pitcher," Dylan pointed out. It'd be nothing but a sarcastic remark to anyone else, but a tightness crept into his voice, betraying the bitterness buried beneath it.

He'd shown promise as a two-way player growing up, possessing strong skills in both batting and pitching. Batting had been his preferred position, but his father had strongly encouraged him to become a pitcher when he went pro. Dylan had fought him on it but ultimately relented.

"Sounds like an excuse," Lennon joked back, keeping things light.

An amused smile pulled at the corners of his mouth as he shook his head. "In all seriousness, I get it. It's a great opportunity for you to get yourself out there. Once people get to know you, they won't be able to help falling in love with you."

Warmth spread through her. It noodled her brain for a moment as she rested her chin on the pillow, until something occurred to her. "How'd you even know about the show?"

Dylan made an uncomfortable, restrained sound as he scratched the back of his neck. "My manager told me. He uh, got a call from the two producers you were with."

Lennon didn't even have to wait to find out where this was going. She already knew. Rolling her eyes, she momentarily dropped her forehead into the soft cotton. "Of course they went over my head. I told them you wouldn't be interested, but they're very … *persistent.*" She had a few other words in mind for what they were.

"They'll get along great with my manager," Dylan remarked bitterly. "He's been bugging me all afternoon. He thinks it would be good for my image." The shift in his voice was subtle, but she felt it. The quiet ache of remorse.

"What exactly happened that night?" Lennon knew the basics, but she wanted to hear it from him.

Dylan adjusted his hat. A nervous tick. "We'd lost the last three games in a row, including the one that afternoon. It was my fault. My head wasn't in it. I made mistakes. I knew it, but everyone made it a point to let me know." He swiped his tongue through his lips, tightening them. "Drinking always took the edge off bad days, but I went overboard that night. I'd never passed out like that before." Fear laced the admission. He avoided her gaze.

Lennon wanted to reach out to him, brush her fingers down his cheek. She had wanted him to wake up, but not like this. Not by almost dying. And not with it sensationalized in the media like juicy, entertaining gossip.

"I get that you made a mistake, but you weren't the one driving the boat, and you weren't conscious when he crashed," Lennon pointed out. "I don't understand why the media—or the league, for that matter—is giving you such a hard time."

"Some people who were there that night sold fake stories. Said I encouraged Craig to take the boat out and pretended to pass out—oh, and that I was doing drugs, too, even though my tests were negative. All my sponsorships dropped me because brands don't want to be associated with controversy, and the league is cracking down on players' code of conduct. They're not convinced I'm worth keeping around. Especially if I'm not pitching as well as I used to after the injury."

"I thought it was the team's management that had the final call on suspensions?"

"They used to. Last year, several of the UBL's board members were lobbying to have control over players transferred to them, and they won. They also got rid of our union." The long grass sprouting from the dune swayed behind him. Dylan's gaze went inward. "That's not even what bothers me the most about all this, though."

Lennon waited, sensing there was something deeper weighing on him—something he needed to release. His brow sunk low.

"Kids used to come up to me with my jersey on, wanting to take pictures. Have me sign things for them. They told me they wanted to be like me when they grew up. It was one of my favorite parts of the job." A smile ghosted Dylan's lips.

A pang shot through her heart.

"One of the bright spots, even when I was miserable. But now … their parents guide them away from me when they realize who they're talking to."

Lennon winced at the sorrow beneath his casual tone, something squeezing deep in her chest.

"I know I'm not a good role model but … I'd like to be someday. Not just for baseball, but for actually being someone worth looking up to. The way I looked up to my heroes when I was a kid."

Lennon ached to touch him. She remembered how much it meant to Dylan when kids came up to him or sent him letters. He always took the most time out of any of the players to talk to them between innings and after games, to toss them balls and wave to them from the field. She didn't need to hear the sadness in his voice or see it in his eyes to know how much that hurt him.

And she didn't have to use her imagination to understand the shame behind his words—the deep desire to be someone worth admiring. That was a hole in her own heart she was desperate to fill.

"Does your manager really think the show would help?" Lennon asked.

"The twenty-three text messages he's sent me about it would indicate yes." Dylan removed his baseball cap, releasing a mess of thick, dark hair. He drove a hand through it.

Lennon's thumb troubled the edge of the pillow. "Would *you* want to do it?"

Dylan's fingers paused in his hair, eyes meeting hers. He mirrored her hesitant tone. "Would *you* want me to do it?"

She ran her teeth along her lower lip, unsure of her answer to that. "They were very interested in our relationship. They'd probably be looking for drama or a reunion. It'd invite more scrutiny from the public, too."

"It would," Dylan said, dropping his hand.

"But it could also give us a chance to control the narrative. Show everyone the truth," Lennon reasoned. "Tell our side of the story."

"We don't owe anyone an explanation."

"No, but it would be satisfying to have the last word."

Dylan smirked. With a hint of mischief in his eyes and his hair a mess like he'd just rolled out of bed, she saw a glimpse of the boy she had fallen in love with at the ballpark all those years ago. In another lifetime.

He'd made mistakes, but he didn't deserve to lose everything over them.

When Lennon remained serious, his expression tumbled through confusion to realization. "Are you seriously asking if I'd want to do the show?" Dylan asked.

Lennon asked herself the same question.

With the media breathing down Dylan's neck, it was a matter of time before they started hounding her, too, now that she was in the same city. Filming a reality show, no less. Whether she liked it or not, their fates were intertwined. They both had problems the show could solve.

If they could get ahead of it and take control . . . .

"Maybe," Lennon answered.

They were both quiet for a moment, thinking to themselves, having a silent discussion with each other as they weighed the decision. He narrowed his eyes, darting back and forth between hers. She pressed her tongue into her molars, brows knitted together.

Dylan finally said, "Do you want to—"

"Should we just—"

"Go for it?"

"Maybe? It'll either be the smartest thing we've ever done or the dumbest," Lennon said.

"I've worked with worse odds."

"Me too."

A beat passed. Dylan hesitated. "Are you sure?"

"No." Excitement and trepidation swirled into a familiar adrenaline rush, sparking her impulsiveness. That exhilarating feeling of standing on a cliff's edge. "But let's fucking do it, anyway."

The corner of his mouth arched. Something seemed to spark alive in him, too. That same sense of danger—thrill.

"OK," Dylan said. "Let's fucking do it."

CHAPTER 10

Lennon

NINE YEARS AGO

A blanket of baby-blue unbroken by a single cloud.
Crisp January air that smelled of possibility.
Distant laughter and the crack of wood on leather—
her comfort soundtrack.

Lennon sat in the empty bleachers, bundled in an oversized sweatshirt and shorts for a Florida winter. Her high-tops were propped up on the faded blue seat ahead as she scribbled lyrics in a monogrammed notebook on her lap. She'd had the notebook a month—a sweet sixteen birthday gift—and had already filled nearly half its pages. She should slow down, preserve it longer. But she didn't want to. She loved it too much.

A sharp, clean whistle called her attention. Dylan stood along the railing separating the field from the bleachers, away from the other players practicing behind him. Even from her spot at the top, Lennon could make out the little tilt of his smile as he bit one side of his lower lip. His cap shaded his eyes, but she felt their singular focus on her like a cool breeze shooting through a warm sunbeam.

Dylan raised his arm, holding the baseball up momentarily to communicate what he was about to do. Lennon dropped the pen in the crease of the journal before he pitched. The ball arced through the air straight toward her, and she caught it.

Black ink caught her eye between the red stitching. "WILL U BE MY GF?"

Her heart soared to her throat.

Lennon bit the inside of her cheeks to keep from grinning too hard. Opening her journal, she wrote her answer on a clean sheet of paper in big, bold letters and held it high.

"YES."

Dylan beamed. The guys yelled at him, calling him back to the field. He rubbed a hand over the left side of his chest as he took a couple of slow steps backward, then turned to jog back to them. The other boys teased him with kissing sounds.

When Dylan took his place on the pitcher's mound, he looked up at her again.

She should slow down, Lennon thought to herself, but she didn't want to.

CHAPTER 11

Lennon

The show's high-strung supervising producer, Carol Anne, who became Lennon's primary point of contact for the show after her meeting with Huey and Maeve, found Lennon a beautiful, fully furnished one-bedroom apartment two blocks from the beach. Her new contract as a "main player" on the show included fully paid-for accommodation throughout filming, so long as Lennon allowed them to film inside the apartment if needed. While she enjoyed her pampered life at the hotel for a week, she looked forward to no longer living out of a suitcase.

The white Art Deco-style apartment building built sometime in the eighties instantly charmed her. While the architecture was vintage, the interiors had been recently renovated with upscale, contemporary finishes—a far cry from the sterile, outdated studio apartment she'd called home for the last few years. She nearly cried when she saw the spacious open floor plan, bright natural light, balcony, and not one but *two* bathrooms inside the unit.

For the next three months, it was all hers.

The thought of having to leave once filming ended nearly smothered her joy, but a fire burst the lid back off.

A fire to finally *make* something of herself.

Lennon saw enough during her brief apartment search to know there was no way she could keep a place like this from waiting tables alone unless she landed a unicorn job, so she needed this reality show gig to pay off.

She *had* to get her music career off the ground.

The dozen or so boxes shipped from New York were delivered that afternoon. After a few hours, Lennon was almost entirely unpacked and settled in, marveling at the extra space she'd have even after unloading everything she owned. The apartment wasn't that big compared to the average home's square footage in Arden Beach, but to her, it might as well have been a mansion. She especially enjoyed arranging her record player and vinyl collection on the living room shelves. They'd been relegated to a box under her bed for the past six years.

While unboxing her sweaters into a dresser drawer in her bedroom, she came upon a shoebox from an old pair of combat boots she'd worn into the ground. Sitting back on her heels as she knelt on the carpet, Lennon lifted the lid. Right on top, above her NYU and ABU acceptance letters and various ticket stubs and sheet music—including an autographed program from her favorite Broadway show *Grease*—was Dylan's letter, staring up at her expectantly.

As her fingers brushed the smooth paper, she froze, unable to break the seal. She tried to work up the nerve, jolting when a knock came at the front door.

Knowing who waited on the other side, her entire body thrummed like a plucked guitar string.

Lennon had invited Dylan over to discuss what they would and wouldn't talk about on camera regarding their relationship. They both agreed it was a good idea to make sure they were on the same page to avoid any awkward moments or slip-ups, especially when the producers had a vested interest in their divorce and reunion.

She also didn't want their first *actual* in-person reunion to be on the show.

"Be right there," Lennon called out. She dropped the letter back into the shoebox and shoved it into the drawer.

Lennon stopped to check her reflection in the full-length mirror hanging by the front door. She had gone back and forth on what to wear before settling on a pair of distressed denim shorts and a crocheted black crop top tickling her navel. Barefoot, her black pedicure popped against the glow of a fresh tan from afternoons lying by the hotel pool. Lennon spotted traces of the girl she once was in the fresh freckles across her nose and the natural flush on her cheeks. The one who loved to spend long, lazy days at the beach with her guitar, writing music with the sun and the sea as her accompaniment.

Or at the ball field, watching her ex-lover practice.

The ex-lover waiting on the other side of the door.

Lennon pushed her onyx hair behind her ears—her hands oddly shaky, like her blood was rushing too fast—and took a deep breath before opening it.

Dylan looked up from his crisp, white sneakers. His pupils dilated as they quickly swept her from head to toe. "Hey," he said, one side of his mouth lifting in his signature crooked smile. His thick, dark hair was tousled but in an intentional fashion, like he'd put some effort into styling it. A blue Henley hugged his lean torso over dark blue jeans.

If she hadn't known better, she would've guessed he was going on a date. Warmth curled low in her abdomen. "Hey." She stepped aside, holding the door open. "Welcome to my new, humble abode."

As Dylan stepped past her, she inhaled a breath of his cologne, and the warmth curled tighter. She watched the way his jeans hung perfectly around his hips, a place she used to stare at often, especially in his baseball uniform. He hadn't missed many workouts in his time off.

"Wow. This is nice," Dylan said, glancing at her over his shoulder. She quickly looked up and shut the door, a surge of panic shooting through her at almost getting caught checking out his ass.

"Yeah, thanks. Carol Anne really came through. Since they're covering the cost while filming, I expected a cardboard box an hour outside the city. At this rate, I'm ready to sell them my soul if they ask for it."

"Don't let them know that. They'll probably take it." He shoved his hands in his pockets as he surveyed the apartment.

"I'm not sure I haven't already."

Dylan released a small, dark laugh. "You and me both." His gaze returned to her, and for a moment, they simply stared at each other. *Every Breath You Take* by the Police drifted from her wireless speaker sitting on the kitchen counter.

Her blood rushed a little faster.

Lennon tore her attention away, maybe a little too quickly to be natural. "You, uh, want something to drink before we start working on how we'll protect what's left of our souls?"

"Definitely need hydration for that sort of thing."

Lennon padded over to the refrigerator, which she'd stocked with as much as her arms could carry on a walk from the grocery store around the corner. She pulled out two dark-brown glass bottles and offered him one. He eyed it, then gave her an uncertain look. "It's root beer," she quickly clarified.

Dylan's face split into an "of course" smile, flushing a little red as he accepted the non-alcoholic beverage from her. "Thanks." They popped the caps and took swigs. On a refreshed sigh, he said, "Man, I haven't had one of these in years."

"Remember when we used to drink them as kids at the ballpark because we thought it made us look cool, like all the grownups with their real beer?"

Dylan laughed—a boyish, throaty rumble—turning the bottle over to look at the label. "I do." A shadow dampened the joy in his eyes. "You think such stupid things are cool when you're a kid." His energy shifted downward, as if shame were tugging him below the surface.

"You know what—I forgot to eat dinner," Lennon said, drawing him back. "I've been running around all day trying to get settled in. You hungry?"

He brightened a little. "I'm always hungry."

They agreed on takeout from the Chinese restaurant down the block. While they waited for the delivery, she hoisted herself up on the kitchen counter, letting her legs dangle while he leaned back against the island a few feet from her. Lines of muscle pressed through the fitted sleeves of his shirt as he braced a hand on the edge of the marble countertop, the other lifting the bottle to his lips. His tall, broad frame dwarfed the kitchen. Even with the high ceilings, he could have reached up and brushed the smooth surface with his fingertips.

Lennon clenched her thighs together to stop the pressure mounting there as she imagined him slotting between them perfectly at this height. Inwardly, she slapped herself out of the fantasy.

That was the *last* distraction she needed.

The fact that Lennon hadn't been with someone intimately in months didn't help. The last was a guest from the restaurant she used to sleep with whenever he was in town for business. Nice and easy, no strings attached. Out of her hair most of the time. Usually, she was too busy and exhausted to give a shit.

But her hormones were awake now.

As if things between them weren't already complicated enough.

"We should talk about the show," Lennon said, shifting on the counter. She saw his dark eyes flick to her legs with the motion, then away, a muscle feathering in his jaw. "I think the less we say, the better. It's no one's business what happened."

Dylan swirled the root beer around the bottle absently, watching it. "You know it's OK if you do ever want to talk about it, though, right?"

"I'm sure your manager would *love* that." If he thought his reputation was bad now, imagine every jaded woman rising against him after she shared her story.

"The truth is the truth." Dylan looked up at her. "You don't need to hold back for me. I can deal with the consequences."

Surprise struck her. Lennon searched him and found raw sincerity. He seemed to mean it. Even if it meant his reputation would take another hit.

Coming from the man who had acted more married to baseball than her, she had a hard time swallowing it.

Maybe he *had* changed. But it hadn't been that long since the accident. What was keeping him from eventually slipping back into his old habits, especially when the pressure on him was higher than ever?

"I'm not looking for revenge, Dylan," Lennon said. "I don't want to relive the past, especially not for someone else's entertainment. Like I said, clean slate." He nodded, but the look in his eyes suggested he knew their slate was far from clean. "Friends?" she suggested. "No drama."

A soft smile touched his lips. "Friends."

They clinked glasses. Their gazes remained locked as the moment lingered. The twinge in her heart and ache between her legs whispered *liar*.

A loud knock at the door startled them both.

"Damn, that was fast," Lennon said, grateful for the delivery person's well-timed interruption. She hopped off the counter and reached for the wallet in her bag.

"I've got it," Dylan said, already slipping his wallet from his back pocket as he strode toward the door.

They ended up on the floor of her living room, dining on their takeout and reminiscing about the drawer in their first apartment together that was filled with sauce packets from various takeout places because 1) he was obsessed with his sauces, and 2) neither of them could cook.

Dylan's gaze landed on the record player and albums on the shelf behind her. "Remember how we used to listen to music for hours on my bedroom floor?" He reclined against the edge of the white leather sofa, his long legs stretched out in front of him with his feet crossed at the ankles and a small amount of beef and broccoli left in the box on his lap. "What was that game we used to play? Where we'd play the first notes of a song, and the other had to guess what it was …"

A grin spread across her face. "Name That Tune."

"That's right. You'd always cheat and play like, half a note of some obscure song no one had ever heard of beside you and the musician's parents."

"That's not cheating, that's superior skill," Lennon corrected.

"The game was rigged against me."

"I was encouraging you to broaden your musical horizons."

"By cheating."

"You discovered a lot of new music through me, didn't you?"

"That is true," Dylan reluctantly admitted. "I just had to suffer the shame of losing in order to get it. Not really a fair trade."

Lennon blew a dismissive raspberry. "That's a *totally* fair trade. Nothing compares to the gift of discovering great music." She popped a small piece of sweet and sour chicken into her mouth.

"You used to make me paint your nails and watch *Grease* for the five-hundredth time."

She smiled wickedly around her mouthful of chicken, glancing upward in sweet remembrance. "I loved that game."

"I'm sure you did."

Lennon arched an eyebrow at him. "Want to play it now?"

Dylan assessed her with trepidation. "Why, so you can beat me again and destroy the self-esteem I've painstakingly rebuilt over the years?"

She rolled her eyes. "Stop being so dramatic. I knew you were competitive, but I didn't know you were *that* afraid of being a loser."

His eyebrows jumped up as he released a sharp laugh. "I didn't know you managed to become an even bigger savage than you already were."

"Like wine, I get better with age," Lennon remarked proudly.

"And more bitter," Dylan added.

She stuck her tongue out at him. "Come on." Lennon nudged his foot with hers. "You used to be fun."

"I also got more bitter with age."

"A bitter loser."

Dylan rolled his head back, groaning. "Fine."

Lennon excitedly sat up, pulling her legs in to sit cross-legged. She grabbed her phone to open a music streaming app.

"But *no* weird, obscure songs from Europe or a small 1920s jazz band or anything like that."

They played a few rounds of the game, giving each other three chances per round and keeping score based on how long it took them to figure it out, if they managed to do so at all. Dylan surprisingly held his own better than he had in the past. She was impressed—and a little turned on. He still, however, did not win any of the rounds, though he came close on the last one.

Lennon laughed so hard, her side hurt at the fit he threw when he narrowly lost. He was so proud of himself for coming close and so disappointed with his ultimate defeat over Queen's *These Are the Days of Our Lives* clinching her win. She hadn't admitted it to him, but she was sweating a little up to the very end.

Dylan was correct—it *was* rigged against him—but his hyper-competitive aggravation was part of the fun. And, like when they were kids, she enjoyed the excuse to share music with him that he hadn't heard before. She appreciated the way he intently listened when she described why each song was special, word-vomited background on the artists, and pointed out the techniques used in their production.

For the last song, she broke out her noise-canceling headphones—a birthday gift from Erin—so Dylan could properly hear all the details she described to him and *feel* the music. "And so, we can fix the embarrassment of you not knowing this song," Lennon added.

"I know the song," Dylan asserted, running a hand through his hair. One of his habits when he was frustrated or nervous. Or both. "I just couldn't peg it from the first few notes."

"It's OK to admit you'd never heard it. It's not one of the more well-known Queen songs. I won't judge you. Much." She flicked an eyebrow up as she calibrated the sound to be perfect for the song.

"I've heard every Queen song at least once," Dylan said as she handed him the headphones. Their fingers brushed. Her stomach tightened.

"They're my favorite."

"I know."

Something about the way he said it, paired with the soft, serious look in his eyes, held more gravity than she expected. A flutter rippled through her.

Dylan slipped the headphones over his ears and closed his eyes, resting his head back against the sofa cushion as she pressed play.

Lennon watched him experience the music. The small muscle contractions in his face. The gentle tap of his long fingers on his thighs. The rise and fall of his chest as it gradually fell in time with the music. Her gaze followed the sinews in his forearms beneath the pulled up sleeves of his Henley, the deep blue stretching over his sculpted biceps. She studied him again, getting lost in the dip of his cupid's bow and the little scar above the left side of his lip from a stray ball splitting it open when he was six. The wisp of hair that curled over his forehead. The little line between his eyebrows illustrating his concentration.

Brooding. Achingly beautiful.

Her heart stretched and reached out, yearning to touch him. She curled her fingers into the fluffy rug to avoid indulging herself.

The way her soul breathed a sigh and glowed with warmth in areas that had long been cold, dark, and dormant brought sadness with it in her realization that, like this apartment, it wasn't hers to keep. It was temporary, wrapped in conditions. They may be sitting on the floor, laughing and listening to music together like they had when they were younger, but it didn't erase all that had transpired between them.

All the times he chose his career and teammates over her. All the times he shut her out. All the times she needed him, and he wasn't there.

All the reminders that, while he may have loved her, she had obviously loved him more.

If she had been so easy for him to put aside then, why wouldn't she be now?

As the song drew close to the end, Lennon began to scroll through her phone, so it looked like she'd kept busy while he listened to the music. When it finished, Dylan opened his eyes like he was coming out of a daze. He pushed the headphones down to hang around his neck. "Wow," Dylan said. "That song is …"

"I know, right?" The lyrics captured the feelings of nostalgia that had been creeping in and haunting her lately. Maybe subconsciously, that's why she chose it in the last round. Music had a funny way of finding you when you needed it. "Makes me feel sad in a good way."

The corner of his lip twitched up, his expression a bit spellbound. "Yeah. That's it."

"Truly great music does that for you. It's a sort of catharsis."

Dylan looked at her. "Someone is going to feel like that about your music someday."

Lennon's heart swelled and contracted in quick succession. Grief and doubt smothered the part of her touched by his comment. She closed the music app. "I hope so."

"Have you worked on anything lately?"

"Not since the label dropped me." Lennon reached out for the headphones. He slipped them away from his neck, handing them back. They were warm.

"Why not?"

Lennon shrugged. "Haven't felt inspired."

"You sure you're not avoiding it?"

She glared at him for calling her out like that.

"Look, I know you," Dylan said. "When you're hurting, you hide from whatever it is that's causing the pain. You put up a wall around it."

"Anything else I should know about myself, Dr. Freud?"

"That you're a gifted artist, and it's not your music that let you down, it's the people you trusted with it who did."

His words struck her like a cord being snapped deep in her belly, vibrating outward all the way to her fingertips. He didn't seem to be only referring to her music.

Lennon hated herself for doing precisely what he said and erecting her walls, but she couldn't help it. It had been a long day. A long couple of weeks.

A long six years.

She was tapped out.

His sitting there across from her like this—on the floor, at night, in such a strangely intimate way—had her head and emotions all muddled.

"Well, I should probably finish unpacking," Lennon said, placing the headphones back in their case, zipping it. "I have a brunch thing tomorrow morning with Avery. I'm meeting the other girls on the show and filming my first official scene."

"Hope it goes well," Dylan said encouragingly.

"Thanks." Lennon smiled weakly.

"I'm starting later this week. They want to film a day in my life. I told them it would be boring, but, hey, it's their show. What do I know?" Dylan extended his arms above his head, the hem of his shirt lifting to reveal the soft hair trailing from his navel into his jeans.

Lennon averted her attention before he caught her. "That's what I said when this whole thing first came up. They're probably going to regret it when they find out all I do is write music, play music, listen to music, and talk about music. If I'm not doing any of those things, I'm eating or asleep."

"Same, except replace it with baseball."

They both laughed. An awkward moment followed, the eye contact and easy rapport suddenly too intimate in her quiet, cozy apartment. Lennon stood, and he followed her lead.

As Lennon led him to the door, she said, "So, to recap, we reconnected again recently when I moved back. We've both been busy living our own lives. We're friends now, no bad blood or grudges. Nice and boring."

Dylan smiled, but it didn't quite make it to his eyes. "Right. Friends."

Lennon studied him, her instincts tingling that he was holding something back. A troubling thought occurred to her. Was he worried she still harbored romantic feelings for him? That she may try to reignite that part of their relationship and he'd have to pull away from her again? Had he caught her staring at him—seen something that made him nervous that she expected something from him?

"I'll make it very clear to everyone there's nothing else going on," Lennon assured him. "And I'll let you know if the producers try to do anything to force a different narrative."

Dylan nodded. "Sure. I'll do the same."

As she opened the door, he stopped beside her. Silence hung

between them for a moment. She wondered if he was about to throw up that barrier.

"To be honest, I haven't been feeling a lot of hope for the future lately," Dylan admitted hoarsely, a window to the pain he harbored briefly cracking open in his eyes as they avoided hers. "But … I'm starting to feel different. Like, maybe there is a light at the end of this long, dark tunnel." He finally met her gaze. The vulnerability in it made her breath hitch. "Thank you for giving me a chance to be in your life again. And for letting me go on this crazy adventure with you. I hope it'll end up being something good for both of us."

Lennon put on a smile even as her heart squeezed. "Me too," she said, swallowing the lump in her throat. She gripped the edge of the door. "Have a good night, Dylan."

"You, too, Lynx."

CHAPTER 12

Lennon

The sun had barely risen when a "glam team" of three descended on Lennon's apartment. Led by a British, six-inch-stiletto-wearing, green-haired stylist named Freema, their crew consisted of Greg, a hair stylist whose mane nearly reached the waistband of his distressed jeans like a member of a nineties grunge band, and Deb, a petite, round, makeup artist who looked like someone's sweet grandmother until you got a closer look at her silver heart-shaped earrings engraved with the words "fuck off" in a pretty script.

They were Lennon's kind of people.

Carol Anne told her the other cast members had personal glam teams, so the show sent their resident stylists to "help her out"—another perk of her new main player status. While Greg and Deb went to work setting up a temporary glam station in Lennon's living room out of the large black trunks they'd hauled in, Freema rolled in a rack of designer clothes with matching shoes and handbags brandishing luxury labels. Bright, neon colors and skintight silhouettes hung before her. Lennon's own closet was a mix of Sandra Bullock in *Practical Magic* and Joan Jett. She stared at the selection in her oversized flannel shirt and distressed denim shorts, nary a loose floral dress or hint of black leather to be found among the two-piece sets and mini dresses.

"This is all gorgeous, but none of it looks like me," Lennon pointed out.

"You're playing a part, darling," Freema purred. "Think of television as a stage. *Embrace* it."

They had a point. Treating it like a performance and stepping into a character made this reality show thing sound a *little* less daunting. Maybe that small delineation between "Show Lennon" and "Real Lennon" was what she needed to get through it.

A month's rent for the apartment they stood in cost less than the handbag Freema ultimately opted to pair with the selected outfit and shoes. While Greg pinned Lennon's hair in wide curlers and Deb painted her face, Carol Anne dropped by to sign off on the final look. In contrast, Carol Anne's plain tee was coffee-stained and ill-fitted, and her hair was haphazardly tied in a low ponytail. Although she appeared to be in her mid-thirties, she looked like she'd lived nine lives and hadn't slept during any of them. Her frenzied energy made Lennon's blood pressure rise and feel like she needed to hurry, though for what, she didn't know.

After the supervising producer snapped a photo of her on her phone, Lennon asked, "How's the audience going to believe I can afford all of this as an aspiring musician?"

"That's the point. It's a splurge. A reward. If they see it on someone like you, they'll believe they can have it, too." Carol Anne didn't look up from her phone as her fingers flew across the screen.

Something about that didn't sit right with Lennon, a faint tightness curling in her gut. "Can we at least incorporate some things that are a little more my style?"

"The sponsors send us what they want us to feature," Carol Anne answered before addressing Freema. "Can we get more boob?"

"There's not much there to work with," Freema replied, eying

Lennon's modest chest with an arched brow. "But I'll see what I can do."

"Work your magic."

Lennon gave them a withering look. "Are we selling them breasts, too?"

"We're selling the dream." Carol Anne went to the door. "I'll be back in five for last look."

Freema pulled two rubber things that looked like chicken cutlets out of their Mary Poppins bag and held them up. Not wanting to be difficult on her very first day, Lennon bit her tongue.

Choose your battles, she reminded herself.

Twenty minutes into her first day of filming and Lennon was already sweating.

The brunch took place at a travel blogger's dream luxury boutique hotel on the beach—a pink facade, black and white striped awnings, and gold fixtures. Bruno escorted her in his Escalade, but they filmed her arrival as if she'd walked there, capturing various angles of her strolling down the sidewalk past designer stores. Who knew how hard it would be to walk naturally, especially in stilettos in the blazing summer heat, while being filmed? It was as if Lennon had forgotten how to walk at all, like a mannequin who had recently come to life. They had her do it five times before Carol Anne finally waved a hand and said, "They'll fix it in post."

By the time Lennon made it to the restaurant overlooking the ocean, her feet were screaming. She smiled through the pain of fresh blisters forming as she approached Avery's table.

The other four women waited around a circular table on the sprawling patio, shaded by a black and white umbrella. Water and bread sat untouched in the middle. Vibrant colors adorned each of them except for Avery, who wore a white mini dress. At least Lennon didn't look out of place in her neon green crop top and matching high-waisted mini skirt.

Avery spotted her first. Her face lit up as she stood to meet her around the side of the table. "Lennon! Hi."

"Hey, sorry I'm late. It took a while to film the, uh—" Lennon covered her faux pas with an awkward cough. "I mean, it was a long walk. From my place." She inwardly cringed. *Off to a great start.*

"You look amazing," Avery said, guiding her into a delicate hug. "So do you."

Avery addressed the table. "Everyone, this is Lennon Young, the musician I've been telling you about. We went to school together. She just moved back from New York."

The other three women offered friendly greetings as Avery introduced her bridesmaids, Tana and Candace, and her maid of honor, Kelsey. The surreality of the situation hit Lennon. It was as if she had climbed into her television while watching one of these exact scenes play out on countless other shows. The flawless, celebrity-like beauty of the cast. The glamorous, picturesque setting. If it weren't for her throbbing feet and the mic pack digging into her spine, she would have to pinch herself to confirm it was real.

As Lennon squeezed around the corner to get to the empty chair, her foot caught on the leg of Avery's and dragged it a couple of inches, the metal loudly scraping along the polished stone floor. "Shit!" She stumbled, barely avoiding a full face-plant. She grimaced at the cameraman positioned nearby. "Sorry—am I allowed to say 'shit'?"

Avery's friends exchanged awkward glances while a soft, gracious chuckle drifted from the bride. "You're good," she assured her quietly.

Lennon cleared her throat, cheeks warm as she smoothed her hands down the sides of her skirt. *Off to a great fucking start, Lennon.* She took a seat between Avery and Candace.

"Linen—like the fabric?" Kelsey asked, amusement twinkling

in her blue eyes with small winged tips. Her bleach-blonde hair shimmered in the sunlight.

The silent, tickled look that passed between Kelsey and the bridesmaids brought Lennon back to her childhood. "Wow. Haven't heard that one since grade school," she remarked coolly. Lennon refrained from adding *you're as original as an eight-year-old, Kelsey. Congrats.*

Kelsey's eyes narrowed slightly.

A waiter filled Lennon's empty glass with ice water, and she thanked him before he disappeared as quietly as he'd arrived. The coolness of the glass in her hand helped her relax a bit, slowly bringing her racing heart down. "It's actually like John Lennon," she explained. "My father was a huge fan of the Beatles." Speaking of him made a hollow, tinny vibration ring from the pit his absence had carved in her heart after he ran off to follow his own dreams, leaving her and her mother behind. Where those dreams had led him, she had no idea.

"Cute," Kelsey said as the waiter returned.

As he took their orders, Lennon noted a few cameramen stationed around them, catching a glimpse of at least one unmanned camera hidden behind a large banana leaf tree planted in a stone pot. Avery ordered a round of mimosas for the table and one virgin mimosa for Candace, who sported a small baby bump. Kelsey called for a toast when they arrived.

"To Avery," Kelsey began, raising her glass. Everyone followed suit. "For being such a beautiful, inspiring, boss bitch. May your wedding be everything you've dreamed of and more."

"Cheers," they sang in unison before clinking their glasses together.

The fresh orange juice bit at that satisfying place at the back of Lennon's cheeks. She savored it, hoping the tiny bit of champagne would help her loosen up a bit. Her whole body seemed to be stretched taut from the inside out like a drumhead.

Her attention gravitated to the cameras again. How was everyone else but her acting so natural, ordering their salads and drinking their mimosas like millions of people wouldn't watch this later like an afternoon soap opera? She couldn't shake the hyper-awareness of everything she did. Every move she made, no matter how small or ordinary, operated on manual rather than automatic.

"Not to get sappy so early in the day, but you all inspire *me*," Avery said, pulling Lennon's focus back to the group. "I mean, look at this table. I'm so lucky to be surrounded by such incredible, successful women. We're all going after our dreams. Tana, your beauty and skincare line is amazing. I'm so proud every time I see the well-deserved love it's getting," she said to the tall, Amazonian beauty who could have walked here straight from a runway. Tana's striking bone structure was emphasized by the long, onyx braid flowing down her back. "And Candace, I'm so excited to meet your new little one. I'm in awe of how you make being a wife, a mother of three, and running your own boutiques look so effortless. I hope I can be half as good at juggling it all one day."

"I can give you some tips. I'm sure that day's not too far off," Candace said warmly with a wink.

Lennon realized why her big, wide-set eyes and pixie cut looked familiar. Her boutique hosted a pop-up shop recently near Opus 21 that had attracted a line around the block. That day, everyone in Manhattan seemed to carry around shopping bags with her doll-like face on them.

"Chad is going to put a little quarterback or fashionista in there *fast*," Tana remarked, snapping her fingers.

Avery laughed, shaking her head. "And Kelsey," she said, turning toward her maid of honor. "Your huge heart and all the philanthropic work you've already done at such a young age have inspired me so, so much. I can't wait to see your movie when it comes out next year. I'm going to miss you when you're a huge actress and too busy hanging out with A-listers to spend time with me anymore."

"Are you going to have time for *me* when you're busy running your huge lifestyle brand?" Kelsey arched an eyebrow as her champagne flute dangled from French-tipped fingers.

Avery's lips curved into a smile. "That's the dream," she said with a sigh.

"Well, I'd say you're already on your way." Candace rested her chin on delicate hands. "You've got the career, the husband, the TV show. Next stop, babies and an empire."

"Get that bun in the oven and cash in the bank, baby!" Tana wiggled her shoulders, large gold hoops swaying from her ears. Applause and sounds of agreement rang across the table.

As Lennon listened to Avery list everyone's accomplishments, the air thickened around her, pressing until she felt impossibly small. She wished she had achievements to celebrate. Instead, shame and disappointment nipped at her. She reached for the glass of water.

"Oh, and of course, Lennon—" Avery turned to her. Lennon wondered if it was a gracious way of covering that momentarily she'd forgotten about her. "I'm so inspired by your creativity. I remember you singing in the school talent shows and now you're following your dreams. You're totally going to be selling out venues someday."

Lennon smiled, tight-lipped. "Thanks, Avery."

"Also, now that you're officially back in town, I wanted to ask …" Avery glanced at the others before she reached out, placing a hand on Lennon's. "Will you be one of my bridesmaids?"

Lennon's head whipped to Avery, her glass clinking loudly against the ceramic bread plate as she narrowly missed the table while lowering it. Everyone jumped a little.

That was a question she hadn't expected.

"What? Seriously?"

"Yes!" Avery laughed.

"Wow. That's … wow," Lennon repeated, a laugh stumbling from her throat. "Sorry, I'm a little surprised. Aren't you knee-deep in planning already at this point? The wedding's in September, isn't it?"

"Yeah, but that's a few months away. There are a lot of things you can be a part of. We can make up for lost time."

Something twinged low in Lennon's belly at the suddenness of it all, but closer to the surface, her chest ached for sisterhood and connection. "Yeah. Of course. I'd love to."

Avery's dimples deepened with her smile. "Also ... will you sing something for us at the reception?"

Lennon's lips parted. Still reeling from the last question, she'd barely found her bearings before that second shockwave. "I'd be honored."

Avery pulled Lennon into an embrace. "It's going to be great."

"So, Lennon," Tana said as Lennon settled back in her chair, "what kind of music do you do?"

"Alt-pop and rock, mostly," Lennon answered. The sea breeze had finally cooled her clammy skin, her hair no longer sticking to her neck and shoulders.

"How many albums have you made?" Candace asked.

A prick of grief stung her heart. "Um, none yet. I had a record deal, but it didn't pan out."

"Uh-oh," Tana said around her straw. "What happened?"

As she opened her mouth to answer, fate stepped in and did her a solid. The waiter and his assistant returned to the table with trays of food. The question got lost in the shuffle as they marveled at how good everything looked and smelled.

Lennon's appetite had abated a little, but the incredible smell of her eggs Benedict aroused it again. She drizzled some syrup over it and took a bite. It melted on her tongue. At least the food was delicious. And free.

"So, why'd they dump you?" Kelsey asked, piercing a small piece of salmon with her fork before delicately placing it in her mouth.

The unceremonious way in which she'd asked the question caught Lennon off guard. Her throat constricted around the untimely piece of egg she'd just swallowed. "Excuse me?" she pushed out with a tiny cough.

"The record label," Kelsey clarified, the sun glinting off her diamond necklace. "Why didn't they want to work with you anymore?"

"We parted over creative differences," Lennon said evenly, taking a sip of water.

"What does that mean? They didn't like the music you were making?"

Lennon studied Kelsey, something grating against her instincts. "They didn't get the music I wanted to make, and I didn't like the music *they* wanted me to make. We just weren't a good fit. It's disappointing, but it happens."

"Mm. I've heard how unpredictable the music industry can be," Avery said with a frown and a sympathetic nod.

"Then, why did they sign you in the first place? Didn't they have you audition or listen to your demos or whatever before you signed a contract?" Kelsey pulled a confused face, glancing around the table. "Seems kind of weird you'd both not know what you were getting into so no one wasted their time."

The others chewed small bites of their food as their eyes bounced between Lennon and Kelsey.

"Things changed once we started recording," Lennon explained. "We were no longer on the same page. It's really not that complicated."

"That had to be so disappointing when they let you go," Kelsey said, sounding sympathetic, but it felt hollow. "You must've waited a long time to get one, too. Aren't you almost thirty?"

Lennon smiled tightly. "I'm twenty-five."

Kelsey's eyes expanded momentarily. "Oh, wow. I applaud your commitment." She speared a Brussels sprout.

"How old are you?" Lennon asked.

"Twenty-two. So, what are you doing for work, then? Or do you not have to work?"

Lennon cut into her eggs, slicing off another piece despite the rock forming in her stomach. "I'm between jobs now, but I was working in New York as a waitress while recording."

"I've heard it's hard for aging female artists. It's *so* sexist." Kelsey rolled her eyes. The other women all nodded, mumbling sounds of agreement. "It must be stressful, especially when it's probably putting you in the position of choosing between your career and starting a family soon."

Lennon couldn't help the humorless laugh that slipped out of her. Everyone turned to her with expressions of confusion.

Kelsey canted her head. "What's so funny?"

"It's just … you're making it sound like I already have one foot in the grave and assuming I can only be a mother or a musician, not both, if starting a family is even something I want. I mean, how is it any different from Candace running a boutique with three kids?"

"She's not living on a tour bus and going to sleep in a different city every night," Kelsey pointed out, her brows scrunching together as though it should be obvious. "You were married young, right? I figured having a family must be important to you."

Lennon blinked, stunned by Kelsey's audacity. "That's a lot to assume about someone you don't know. How did you even know I was married?"

"Is settling down and starting a family *not* important to you?" Kelsey asked, ignoring the follow-up question.

"Kelsey doesn't mean any harm. She's just a really straightforward person," Avery cut in. "It can be a little jarring at first, but she means well." She tossed Kelsey a "tone it down" look.

"I'm trying to get to know you. I don't like wasting time on bullshit. It's so pointless," Kelsey remarked casually, waving her fork.

Lennon bit her tongue, holding back the part of her that wanted to throw down her napkin and fight. She was technically at work, and she'd be spending a lot of time with these women. On television, no less. She needed to keep her cool. "My career is my main focus right now," she asserted calmly.

"Then, why come back to Arden Beach instead of trying get another record deal in New York or in LA?" Kelsey tossed out the question as if she already knew the answer, not even looking up from her plate. "Aren't there more opportunities in those cities?"

A gust of salty air washed across the patio, blowing up the scalloped edges of the umbrellas to flap against the canvas. The silence at the table was loud. They all waited for her to answer. Even the cameras seemed to lean in a little closer.

Lennon considered throwing back a sassy remark. *Why are you so curious, Kelsey?*

But that probably wouldn't earn her any favors—with Avery's friends or with anyone watching later. She heard Erin's voice in her head. This was a chance for people to get to know her. To let her walls down a little.

To stop hiding.

"I never really gave Arden Beach a chance after high school." *Because I was running away from my heartache,* Lennon held back. "When the opportunity came up, I realized it'd be nice to return to my roots. And it's nice seeing old friends. New York got lonely after a while."

The corner of Kelsey's pout gently ticked upward. Her blue eyes narrowed slightly as if analyzing Lennon. "Your ex-husband lives in Arden Beach, too, doesn't he? Dylan Strickland."

Lennon's stomach twisted. Hearing his name on Kelsey's tongue rubbed her the wrong way. "How'd you know about Dylan?"

"Avery told me."

Lennon passed a questioning look to Avery, whose doe-like eyes expanded slightly under the possible accusation she'd been gossiping. "I mentioned it in passing when I told her I'd run into you in New York," Avery explained. "He knows Chad, my fiancé. I was saying what a small world it is."

Tana stopped a forkful of kale an inch from her mouth as her attention shot to Lennon. "Wait, hold up. Dylan Strickland is your ex? As in, pitcher for the Arden Beach Tidebreakers?"

Here we go.

"We were married for a little while when we were teenagers," Lennon explained.

The bridesmaids exchanged looks as if some *very* juicy gossip had been shared, their expressions alight with interest. Lennon shifted uncomfortably in her chair, picking up her knife to slice off another piece of her food.

"Didn't he almost die in some big accident?" Tana questioned.

"Oh, my God," Candace exclaimed, nearly choking on her food. She touched the small, gold cross resting on her collarbone. "What?"

"He was on a boat that crashed. Everyone on it was wasted." Tana nodded slowly as she spoke, eyebrows lifted. "One guy got arrested and kicked off the Tidebreakers. Dylan was suspended. *Huge* scandal."

"Was anyone hurt?"

"I heard he was in the hospital for a while and may never play again," Tana answered Candace.

"He will," Lennon said, driving her knife through the English muffin. "He's doing a lot better now."

"So, you two are in touch, then?" Candace asked, the question sounding innocent enough. Her round eyes betrayed a deeper intrigue.

"We reconnected recently when I moved back."

Tana leaned forward. "Do you think you'll ever get back together?"

Even though she'd been waiting for that question, Lennon's stomach squeezed. "We're friends. His sister's my best friend, so we'll always be in each other's lives."

Kelsey's lips curved into an empty smile. "Wow, how nice that you happen to be in town to support him during this difficult time."

Lennon locked eyes with the blonde as her knife finally hit the ceramic, severing the piece of eggs Benedict. The way Kelsey watched her felt like a challenge. Any hope she'd had that these women would become her friends vanished with it.

It became clear that they may have been Avery's, but they certainly weren't Lennon's.

"What lucky, lucky timing," Kelsey mused over her champagne flute.

CHAPTER 13

Dylan

At the crack of dawn, Dylan pulled into the parking lot of one of the national beach parks. The barely risen sun cast a soft, diffused glow over the dense trees and wooden administrative cabins. While the camera crew unloaded their gear from the vans, the production team rushed around in the throes of prep.

Despite Dylan's packed schedule, the week had dragged on with more of the same. Baseball practice, physical therapy, talk therapy, workouts, repeat. Even his first day of filming for the show consisted of cameras following him for an afternoon of workouts and batting practice. When he got the invitation to participate in a beach clean-up that weekend, he jumped at it. Not only was it for a good cause that didn't require him to play golf, but it was also a chance to do something different.

And Lennon would be there.

He hadn't seen her since the night at her apartment almost a week ago.

"Morning," Dylan said when Lennon ambled over to him. Her oversized denim jacket dwarfed her sleepy frame, eyes barely cracked open. He couldn't get over how cute she was, even half-asleep and cranky. "Coffee?"

They'd been directed to wait near the craft services table until the sound team was ready to hook up their mic packs. Hot coffee and various packaged pastries—muffins, doughnuts, bagels—were arranged on platters.

"Can you send it straight to my veins?" Lennon asked, voice adorably hoarse and groggy. She released a wide, bear-like yawn. Mornings had never been her thing. Dylan remembered her always staying up late to write music. Seeing her like that—in the same jacket she'd owned for years with her collection of patches all over it—brought him a pang of joy and heartache at the same time.

She deserved so much better than he'd given her.

"I don't think they've set up the IV machines yet." Dylan approached the table, smiling at the grey-haired woman in a burgundy apron. "Morning. Two cups, please." He rattled off Lennon's order, then his, and as she went to work preparing the coffees, he surveyed the pastry situation.

"How the hell did you remember my coffee order?" Lennon asked. "Especially this early in the morning. I can barely remember my own name right now."

Dylan shrugged. "It's not that hard to remember. *Lennon.*"

"Thanks, Darren," she retorted before another yawn.

Dylan studied her face. Her makeup looked different from how she usually did it. And there was a lot more of it. "Why do you look like you're going to a photoshoot? Aren't we cleaning up trash on the beach?"

Lennon closed her eyes as if taking a mini nap. "That's what I told them, but they insisted on full glam, anyway."

"Who's 'they'?"

"My glam team."

"You have a *glam team*?"

"I'm moving up in the world, Daryl."

A smile tugged at his lips, and an ache at his chest. Damn, he'd missed her. "So, first time we're officially filming together." Dylan glanced around to ensure no one else was listening, then dropped his voice. "After we're mic'd up, should we have a code word, or some kind of special hand signal to let each other know when we need to be bailed out of anything awkward? Like if they're trying to get us to say or do something we don't want to do."

Lennon scrunched her brows together, opening her eyes. "That's actually a really good idea."

"I have those sometimes."

The server passed her the first coffee. Lennon wrapped her hands around it, seemingly siphoning its warmth in the crisp morning air as she considered his suggestion. "What about the ones we used to do with Erin when we were kids? You know, when we'd find dirt on the team you were playing against and feed you tips from the bleachers."

A grin split across his face. "That was great. Until Dad found out. What were they again?"

They shuffled through their memories for the various hand signals and meanings they had created as kids. His father discouraged them from doing it once he found out, but Dylan always thought he was a little impressed with them and sorry he had to be a fair grown-up about the whole thing.

To send each other an SOS, they settled on the gesture she and Erin used to get his attention when they had some pressing intel to share. They applied new meanings to a few others, as well, like flicking their noses to say "all good."

"Well, this is a nice way to start the day," another woman's voice interrupted. He turned to a blonde with French braids standing by the table, smiling up at him. "Hi." She offered her hand. "Kelsey McCroy."

"Hey. Dylan." He accepted his coffee from the barista, thanked her, and then shook Kelsey's hand.

"I know who you are." Kelsey popped an eyebrow. "You're one of the greatest baseball players of our generation."

A mangled sound somewhere between a grunt and a laugh shot out of him. "Oh, I know a lot of people who would disagree."

"The stats don't lie." Kelsey gave a small shrug. "They're just bitter."

"Hey, Kelsey," Lennon said, peering around Dylan with a stiff wave.

"Oh, hey, Lennon." Kelsey grabbed a protein bar from one of the baskets. "Well, see you on the beach," she said, holding eye contact with him over her shoulder as she turned to walk away.

Dylan lifted his chin in acknowledgement, then took his first sip of his coffee. The burn felt good. One of the production assistants called Lennon over to the sound area where a few people were getting their mic packs hooked up. He tried not to take it personally when her eyes lit up at some piece of equipment and she hurried toward it like a little kid.

Leave it to something music-related to wake her up.

Dylan watched with a small smile as she excitedly asked the crew member working on it some questions. The guy was young. Tall. Had a strong, muscular build. Not exactly the stereotypical tech nerd.

His smile faded. A twinge of jealousy tugged at him.

"Little Prince," came a deep, booming voice behind him.

Dylan winced at the nickname his teammates had given him when he'd entered the professional league. An affectionate—and sometimes, not-so-affectionate—jab at him being the son and grandson of two baseball legacies and his thin frame in adolescence. Hadn't taken long for the fans and media to catch on and adopt it, too. Unfortunately.

Dylan turned to the tall, broad-shouldered man demonstrating his impressive wingspan as he held his arms out.

"Bricks," Dylan responded warmly, a grin spreading across his face. As they said in the south, Chad "Bricks" Mormont was built like a "brick shithouse." A much better nickname. They slapped their hands together, pulling each other in for a hug. "Good to see you, man. What're you doing here?"

"I'm here with the wife-to-be," Chad said, jutting his chin toward Avery as one of the production assistants finished attaching her mic pack.

Avery approached them with a smile as she readjusted her white tank top. "Hey. It's good to see you, Dylan."

"You too," Dylan said, leaning down to hug her. "Congratulations, by the way. I didn't realize you were Chad's Avery."

Her smile deepened. Chad pulled Avery close, his tree-sized arm nearly engulfing her petite frame. Their size difference was comical. "You're coming to the wedding, right?"

"No way I'd miss it," Dylan said.

"I wanted to elope, but she wanted a big wedding," Chad remarked. "We compromised and settled on a big wedding broadcast on a reality show."

Avery elbowed him in his ribs. He barely flinched, laughing instead. He squeezed her into his side. "You know I'm just playin', baby."

Dylan smiled at them, but a deep ache rippled through him. He glanced at Lennon. She'd removed her jacket, holding it in front of her, as the sound guy in a quarter-zip carefully fed the wire under the neckline of her top from the back. He remembered the day they ran off to get married. They'd eloped on a whim. The memory was as vivid as if it were yesterday.

One of the best days of his life.

"So, you're the famous baseball player we've been hearing so much about." A tall woman wearing a black bodysuit and a tight, slick bun approached Dylan. His grip tightened around his coffee, assuming she meant the media. "You were a big topic at brunch the other day. I'm Tana." He relaxed as she held out a hand with long, pointy fingernails. "This is my husband, Trey."

Dylan shook their hands; pretty sure he'd seen Trey in cologne ads or something. Tana looked familiar, too.

"Hey, where's Candace?" Tana asked Avery.

"She's having a bad case of morning sickness," Avery explained with a frown.

"*Ew*. Bummer." Tana smacked her chewing gum.

"OK, people," Carol Anne called out, storming into the center of the crew's makeshift headquarters. She made the ex-drill-sergeant-turned-trainer Dylan had in high school seem mellow by comparison. "Let's go over the day's schedule. You two—why aren't you mic'd up yet?" She waved her pen at Dylan and Chad. "Do it while I'm talking."

"Yes, ma'am," Chad said before sneaking an amused "get a load of this lady" glance at Dylan.

Lennon smirked at Dylan as he approached the sound area. "You got in trouble," she sang quietly. She'd slipped her denim jacket back on and dropped her aviators in place.

Dylan leaned down to whisper in her ear teasingly, "I thought you liked that."

He couldn't see her eyes, but the way Lennon's head turned and cheeks slightly blushed told him enough. Satisfied, he continued to the production assistant, who was waiting with his mic pack, as Carol Anne quickly relayed the schedule.

"Ezra and Steph are from the Seas the Mission Foundation. If you have any questions, they'll be your liaisons for the clean-up," Carol Anne announced.

Dylan noticed Chad's face drop in surprise. He followed his line of sight to the Seas the Mission crew members. Across the parking lot, a man with dreadlocks tied in a bun and a redheaded woman in a blue polo shirt unloaded equipment from a truck.

Steph. Chad's *ex*-fiancée.

Avery snapped a questioning—and worried—look at Chad, who appeared to be second-guessing every life choice he'd ever made that led him to this exact moment.

"OK, let's head to the beach," Carol Anne said, tapping her pen on her clipboard. "We'll start with Ezra and Steph introducing the organization and explaining what you'll all be doing, then you'll grab your gear and begin the clean-up. Let's go." She marched toward the path that led to the beach.

Steph picked up a bin and turned to carry it in the same direction, glancing their way. Her eyes widened when she clocked Chad. Ezra said something to her, and after a beat, she faced forward, answering as she followed him.

"I swear—I had *no* idea she worked with Seas the Mission when I set this up," Kelsey insisted to Avery.

Tension pulled the cool morning air taut. Avery and her two friends followed Carol Anne. Trey gave Chad a look of condolences before going with them.

"Fuck me," Chad groaned right as the crew member switched on his mic pack.

Falling to the back of the group, Dylan and Lennon walked beside each other as they headed toward whatever awaited them on the beach.

"Who is she?" Lennon quietly asked him.

"Chad's girlfriend in college," Dylan answered. "They were engaged, but he broke it off."

"Oh, shit." Lennon observed Avery and her friends huddled together as they walked ahead, engrossed in conversation. Chad trailed a few paces behind them. "Well, at least the drama won't be focused on us."

As sorry as he felt for Chad, he was grateful for a reprieve from the spotlight. Dylan relaxed slightly, one corner of his mouth lifting as he glanced down at Lennon. Knowing she'd be there with him also brought him some comfort.

This might even turn out to be fun.

Dylan flicked his nose at her.

CHAPTER 14

Lennon

The clean-up began smoothly. Once the coffee kicked in and the producers had all the establishing shots they wanted with the group, Lennon and Dylan walked along the beach as they collected debris from the shore. It allowed her space to get lost in her thoughts, with the ocean at her side and the crisp morning air filling her lungs before the humidity ramped up. The seagulls cawed, searching the sand for food, and the pastel seashells carried in by the surf looked particularly majestic in the soft morning light.

Lennon hadn't seen the beach that early in the morning in a long time. It was beautiful.

As the air warmed, she shed her jacket. Beneath it, buttery yellow, high-waisted bike shorts and a matching sports bra clung to her body. Freema had even provided her with padding to make her chest look more endowed. Dylan did a double take as she tied the jacket around her waist, clearing his throat and fixing his eyes on the sand again when she looked up at him. She fought the urge to smile.

Though they mostly remained silent, wandering in their own little worlds, she and Dylan fell into each other's orbit, occasionally exchanging comments. The majority of the cameramen focused on other conversations happening down the beach.

Lennon wondered what the others were talking about—what was interesting enough to be filmed. She hadn't given much thought to what Avery and the others were choosing to share on camera besides the obvious. How personal were they getting?

One cameraman followed Lennon and Dylan, maintaining a safe distance but keeping a close eye on them in case anything interesting happened. Being watched like that was a strange sensation. Lennon would think of something she wanted to say to Dylan, only to catch herself, not wanting to share it with an audience. Like at brunch, she became hyper-aware again of every facial expression she made, every word she said, and every move she made, as if she were on stage but without anything specific to perform.

More worrying was how close she came to forgetting about them. How easily she realized she could become content and let the wrong thing slip. It was like her own version of *The Truman Show*.

They were just following her around, waiting for her to be … interesting? Say something scandalous? Admit something personal and shocking? Make out with Dylan on the beach?

That last thought stirred something low in Lennon's abdomen and magnetized her attention to him. To his biceps flexing as he squeezed the trash picker to grab a crinkled water bottle and toss it in his bag. His sculpted arms and part of his shoulders were exposed in his fitted black tank, which stretched under every movement, revealing more ridges and valleys of muscle. He was so lean yet *solid*.

Lennon noticed the cameraman looming in the distance along the brush, and she quickly began searching the sand in an overt, almost comical fashion.

Shit.

If it hadn't been obvious enough she was checking Dylan out, her overzealous attempt to hide it probably sealed the fucking deal. Thank God her sunglasses at least hid her eyes.

Lennon slowed her pace to no longer match Dylan's, and

gradually veered closer to the surf to put more space between them and—hopefully—calm the rising pressure in her pelvis. She was at work. *And* volunteering. *And* already breaking the rules they'd set for themselves, for God's sake.

Calm down, Lennon.

Dylan glanced to his side, then past his shoulder, brows dipping as he found her several paces behind him. She sent him a tight-lipped smile, which he returned, but something in his eyes made her heart sink a little. She sensed sadness in them, making her wonder what had been plaguing *his* thoughts that morning. Her lips parted to ask, but the cameraman and his black cargo pants lurked in her peripheral vision.

Not the time nor the place to ask something personal.

"Hey, Strickland," Tana called from the other end of the beach. Lennon and Dylan both looked behind them, finding Tana standing with Chad and Trey. "Can we get some more muscles over here?"

"You think that's code for 'come help me with something seemingly innocuous so I can interrogate you on camera'?" Dylan asked.

"Most definitely." Lennon gave him a pitying smile. Hopefully, he'd have an easier experience than she did at brunch. "Send me a signal if you need me to cause a distraction and bail you out."

"If you don't come fast enough, I'll just feign an injury. I already have one I can work with."

"Ask not what you can do for your injury, but what your injury can do for you."

Dylan sprinted toward Tana. She directed the guys to some large items further down the beach, presumably to be hauled to the area where all the collected trash and debris were being organized. Lennon went back to picking up trash on her quiet stretch of seashore.

A couple of minutes later, the crunch of sand announced Kelsey's arrival. Lennon silently thanked her sunglasses again for hiding her knee-jerk eyeroll.

"Hey, girl. Can we talk?" Kelsey's tone was honeyed, like they were friends who'd had a minor quarrel. Designer sunglasses rested atop her head, and two hot pink triangles held in place by a string barely covered her breasts. It was a miracle she could perform the tasks at the clean-up without having a wardrobe malfunction. "I feel like we got off on the wrong foot at brunch the other day."

"What makes you think that?" Lennon asked with a touch of sarcasm. She continued scanning the beach for manmade debris. Some seagulls rushed away from the rising surf, then followed it back toward the sea as it retreated.

"Well, you seemed upset. I don't know if I said something that triggered you, but obviously, that wasn't my intention." Kelsey used her picker to swat away the seagulls as they approached them, sending them scattering and cawing. It then went back to its place at her side with her near-empty bucket hanging from her elbow like a handbag. "I was just trying to get to know you. Now that you'll be in the bridal party, we'll be spending a lot of time together. This is one of the most important events in Avery's life. I don't want anything to mess it up."

Lennon glanced at the cameraman following them along the beach. "Well, since we're being honest, it didn't feel like you were trying to get to know me. It was more like an interrogation."

Kelsey pulled a confused expression. "Avery's my best friend. Wouldn't you do the same for yours?"

"If she'd already decided the person was worthy of her friendship, I wouldn't need to. I trust her judgment."

Blue eyes analyzed her. "Why did my questions make you uncomfortable?"

Lennon used the picker to dig a crushed water bottle from the sand. "Well, they felt a little invasive." She dropped it in her bucket. "And you were basically telling me I was too over the hill for a music career and needed to switch my focus to popping out babies before I'm too old for that, too."

Kelsey's eyebrows jumped up. "OK, that's *not* what I said."

"Except it is. It's literally on tape."

The blonde popped her glossy lips. "Look, I came to smooth out any drama and misunderstanding between us, but now you're putting words in my mouth. I don't appreciate it."

"They were *your words.*" Lennon almost laughed at the absurdity of this conversation.

"I was showing compassion for you getting dumped by your record label. I felt *bad* for you. I don't know how you got all of that other stuff from what I said."

"You don't need to feel bad for me. I'm fine," Lennon stated sharply, her patience wearing thin.

Kelsey huffed a little chuckle. "I'm sure you are now that you're back in touch with your famous ex-husband," she remarked, looking down the beach.

Lennon stopped short, facing her. "What are you implying?"

Kelsey eased to a halt. "I'm not implying anything. All I'm saying is, things are looking up for you. You're on a TV show and part of a big, glamorous wedding thanks to Avery, and you seem to be getting pretty cozy with Dylan. That solves a lot of your problems, doesn't it?"

Waves rolled and crashed along the shoreline as Lennon's frustration crested. "I didn't come back to Arden Beach for Dylan's money, if that's what you're saying."

"There you go putting words in my mouth again," Kelsey said flatly. "But, I mean, if you did, you could just admit it. People respect honesty. No one likes people who pretend to be something they're not."

A low, dark laugh escaped Lennon's throat. "Wow. That's rich coming from you."

Kelsey crossed her arms. "I don't appreciate your tone."

"Well, I don't appreciate yours."

"I'm trying to be friends with you, *Lennon.* For Avery's sake."

Lennon smiled at the mocking emphasis of her name. "You have a funny way of doing it, *Kelsey.*"

Kelsey shook her head again, chuckling humorlessly. "Wow. I

don't know what your problem is, but I can tell this conversation is going *nowhere*, so I'm going to get back to work."

Yeah, I'll bet you've been real *busy.*

Kelsey turned back toward the rest of the group at the other end of the beach, mumbling "I tried" with a dramatic sigh.

For a moment, Lennon stood there, the surf rising to engulf and slide away from her feet as her blood buzzed uncomfortably under her skin. The cameraman who had followed them kept his lens trained on her, while another, who Lennon hadn't noticed before, followed Kelsey.

A pit formed in her stomach.

As the sun blazed brighter near its apex and the air warmed to a sticky heat, the clean-up came to a close. The organization's team instructed everyone on the final steps of the process while the production team packed the film equipment, though some camera operators continued capturing footage. The cast helped dump the sacks full of debris onto a large blue plastic sheet to be sifted through and reorganized by material.

Dylan remained busy with the guys, hauling heavier debris and supplies.

After Lennon finished up, Darius—the sound coordinator who turned out to be as lovely as his husband, Bruno—removed her mic pack so she could clean off the sand and grime at the beach's outdoor shower station on the upper level of the boardwalk. She bothered him with some more questions about capturing clean audio outdoors without all the ambient interference, and he graciously indulged each one until duty called him away.

At the showers, Lennon kept her shorts on, only removing her jacket and shoes to wash her legs and torso. As she rinsed off her sneakers, voices drifted from a lower level of the boardwalk.

She peered through the wild foliage surrounding the shower area, catching Chad and Trey splitting off to reunite with their partners while Kelsey and Dylan remained together on their own, talking. They stopped to get their mic packs removed.

Kelsey placed a hand on Dylan's bicep as she threw her head back, laughing. Lennon's blood pressure spiked.

They finished with Darius and started up the winding boardwalk a level below Lennon, their voices traveling. Lennon caught some of their conversation as they moved closer.

"Thanks for coming out today," Kelsey told him.

"No problem. It was fun."

"It's *so* hard to get people to do these things. A lot of them need priority checks."

"I can't judge," Dylan admitted. "Mine were pretty messed up for a while. The accident made me reevaluate a lot." His voice lowered. "Pretty much everything."

"Crazy how life will do that to you, huh? Give you a major wake-up call and have you rethinking your whole life."

"Yeah. Just wish it happened sooner."

"Everyone makes mistakes," Kelsey said. "I don't judge people for things that happened in the past. I care about who you are now. But it must be hard being around people who can only see your mistakes when they look at you."

Lennon's heart skimmed her stomach. She stilled as the water continued running over the sole of her shoe, washing off the sand.

Dylan didn't say anything. Lennon couldn't see his expression, the backs of their heads shrinking until they rounded the corner. Lennon looked away as though she hadn't been eavesdropping on them, turning off the water and hooking her sneakers on her fingers. She grabbed a towel from the pile Seas the Mission had set out for them.

A cameraman followed Kelsey and Dylan up the boardwalk. Even though their mic packs were gone, they weren't off the clock yet. Lennon imagined there were probably others around, hiding in the trees. Listening. When Dylan made eye contact with Lennon, he smiled, and she smiled back with a casual tug at her earlobe: *We're being watched.*

He gave a small nod of understanding.

"Thanks for your help, Strickland," Kelsey said as she approached one of the vacant shower heads.

"No problem, McCroy."

Lennon inwardly gagged at the use of the last names. Like they were already *buddies.*

While Lennon toweled off her arms and legs, Kelsey peeled off her shorts, leaving her in a hot pink string bikini, and began to rinse off her body. Dylan left one of the shower heads open between him and Kelsey, slipping off his shoes and then stripping off his dirt and sweat-stained shirt. Lennon did a double take at his tanned, well-defined torso, his back muscles flexing as he spun the valve on and rubbed the stream of water over his arms, then turned to get his back, giving her a glimpse of the ridges cutting across his chest and abs.

"Hey, can you check my back and tell me if I missed any spots?" Kelsey asked Dylan.

Her question was like a dump of cold water. Lennon glared at Kelsey, who had angled her nearly naked backside toward Dylan, gathering her blonde hair away from her neck.

You've got to be fucking kidding me. Lennon suppressed another gag but didn't bother suppressing an eyeroll. She could only do so much.

Dylan passed a quick look at Kelsey, then returned his attention to rinsing the sand from his swim shorts. "You're good."

"You sure?"

"Yep."

"Thanks. This stuff gets *everywhere.* I'll probably find it in all sorts of places later."

As Lennon swallowed the sharp comments burning in her

throat, Tana and Trey approached the shower area. "Wow—you two are *hot*," Tana remarked. "Should we give you some privacy?"

"You're such a horndog, Tan," Kelsey remarked with a smirk, arching her back as she focused the stream of water on her chest.

"Hey, I'll see you up front," Lennon told Dylan.

Dylan glanced over his shoulder. "OK. Be right there."

Better to walk away before she said—or did—something she'd regret.

CHAPTER 15

Lennon

A low moan squeezed out of Lennon as large, strong hands kneaded into her bare back.

For a moment, she forgot the cameras were around, nearly losing herself in the masseuse's blissful ministrations as he loosened knot upon knot. After the beach clean-up, Avery reached out to Lennon about spending some one-on-one time together. The bride invited her for a spa day later that week at a five-star hotel, with one catch: It would be filmed for the show.

"They're following me everywhere until the wedding," Avery lamented via text.

Lennon wasn't in any position to decline because she, too, was under contract for a certain number of hours. And they were paying her rent. Besides, who was she to complain when "work" those days meant going to the spa with a friend?

The skilled masseuse—if any gods existed, they'd surely blessed this man's hands—continued working at her shoulders where the bulk of her tension coiled.

"This feels so good after all that work on the beach," Avery remarked, her voice languid and slightly distorted from her cheek pressing into the soft massage table.

Lennon tensed at the reminder of that day. Kelsey's accusations had annoyed her, but the conversation she overheard between Kelsey and Dylan gnawed at her more. It planted a seed of fear she couldn't shake.

Is that how Dylan felt every time he looked at Lennon—shame over what happened in the past? Was she a tether to all his mistakes? A reminder of his failures? Would that baggage always be there, weighing him down so long as she was in his life?

The fear that she'd never be able to let go of what happened between them wasn't new, but the thought of her representing something negative to *him* cut differently.

The masseuse must have noticed she'd stiffened because his hands paused momentarily before repositioning and increasing the pressure.

Blessed by gods or not, nothing could unfurl the tightness wound deep within.

After their massages, Lennon and Avery slipped into swimsuits and submerged themselves in a jacuzzi nestled in a private room covered in polished marble with gold veining and shimmering glass mosaic tiles. Avery had slicked her hair back in a perfect low bun, showing off delicate pearl earrings. A server brought them champagne as they settled into the hot, bubbling water.

It would have been a dream if it weren't for the two cameramen with rigs strapped to their bodies spoiling the vibe.

"It was nice to see Dylan again," Avery said, her posture gracefully straight and her skin flawless despite having been pressed into a hole for an hour. Lennon's limbs felt like goo after the massage. "He seems to be doing well."

Lennon smiled softly, watching the water bubbling around her as she thought of walking along the beach with him. It used to be one of their favorite things to do when they were together.

"The way you two were with each other, I almost forgot—"

Avery stopped short with a tight smile. Her cheeks reddened slightly. "I'm happy you're friends again."

Lennon's heart gave a hollow throb. "Me too."

Avery's smile softened. "Just between the two of us, is the door for more completely closed?"

The camera loomed over Avery's shoulder. "Just the two of us?" Lennon remarked with a quirked brow.

Avery's dimples appeared again as she rolled her eyes up, stifling a laugh at herself. But the question still hung between them.

"You're the one getting married soon. Why are we talking about me?" Lennon parried back coyly, opting for an obvious evasion tactic instead of giving—or thinking about—an honest answer. She prayed Avery didn't press it.

For a moment, it seemed like she might, but Avery conceded, the look in her eyes suggesting she understood. Lennon silently thanked her with her own.

"So, I wanted to talk to you about something," Avery said hesitantly, as though wading into uncertain waters. "Kelsey told me you talked at the beach, and things didn't exactly ... go well."

Oh, boy.

Lennon placed her flute down on the flat, wide edge of the jacuzzi. It was better that she didn't have alcohol in her system for this conversation. Even a little bit. "That's a fair assessment. What did she tell you?"

"That she tried to smooth things out, but you weren't exactly receptive. And ... that you accused her of saying things she hadn't."

A low scoff slipped out as Lennon rolled her eyes. "Here's the thing: She *did* say those things."

Surprise flashed across Avery's face. "That you're trying to get back with Dylan for his money? She said that?"

"It was strongly suggested," Lennon said. "And you heard the comments at the brunch about my age and having to choose between my career and a family, which she tried to deny on the beach."

Avery's lips pressed together, her expression caught somewhere between guilt and incredulity. "Kelsey can come off strong sometimes, and her intentions are often misunderstood. She doesn't always have the best bedside manner, but she has a good heart."

That was debatable.

"Look, I know she's your best friend, and I don't want any drama," Lennon said carefully. "But I think Kelsey knew exactly what she was saying."

Avery lowered her gaze, her long, dark lashes falling like a curtain. "I'm sorry you feel that way. I can see both sides." When she looked up, Avery wore a placating smile. "Can you give her another chance? I told her you were probably getting used to everything. Moving back to Arden Beach, getting to know everyone, and healing from what happened with your record deal. It's a lot."

Lennon furrowed her brow. "I don't think *I'm* the problem here," she remarked in partial disbelief, pressing a hand to her chest. Her pulse pounded beneath her fingers, her stomach going uneasy.

"I mean, relationships are a two-way street," Avery said, softly lifting her shoulder. "It requires effort from both sides to make it work. I'd love for you and Kelsey to get along, especially since you're both in my wedding. It'll be a lot more fun if we're all friends." She smiled, hope alight in her eyes.

Lennon's blood pumped harder at the implication she'd had anything to do with her and Kelsey not hitting it off, and that it was now *her* responsibility to fix that. She wanted to say her instincts told her Kelsey couldn't be trusted, but this was Avery's best friend and maid of honor they were talking about. She was never going to side with Lennon.

And it was clear that Avery wanted to avoid conflict.

Without Avery, Lennon wouldn't have been cast on the show, and she invited her to be a bridesmaid when she had no obligation to do so. Lennon would seem ungrateful—and like she was trying to stir up drama—if she denied her this one request.

Avery watched her expectantly. Lennon gritted her teeth and

called upon the skill she had mastered in her years working in customer service.

"I'll do my best," she said, forcing a convincing though painful smile.

"She's trying to make me look like a fucking gold digger."

Lennon fisted a jar of peanut butter and dumped it in the shopping cart, where her phone sat perched against her bag in the front basket. On the screen, Erin jogged on a hotel treadmill. The distant whir of the machine and pounding of Erin's sneakers hitting the belt in Lennon's earbuds overlayed the soft pop/rock music and ambient noise of the grocery store.

Lennon had spent the better part of half an hour venting. Bruno dropped her off at her apartment after filming, and she immediately dialed Erin as she walked off some of her frustration on the way to the market.

Ironically, an afternoon at the spa had had the opposite of its intended effect. Lennon's blood roiled. She had *new* knots on top of the old ones.

"She even made it sound like I used my friendship with Avery to get on the show," Lennon continued, her voice pitched low but sharp. "Which, I guess, technically is true, but that's not the full picture. It was *Avery's* idea."

She wandered a couple of aisles over to the baking section. A disturbing thought slammed into her as she reached for a bag of flour. "She said something at the brunch when we talked about Dylan," Lennon recalled. "How it was 'convenient' that I returned while he was rehabilitating."

"That's a weird thing to say," Erin remarked, a little breathless as she bobbed with every step in her jog, her blonde ponytail swinging behind her.

"I think she was suggesting I'm trying to take advantage of what he's going through to get close to him again. *Fucking A.* This woman is a psycho." Lennon dropped the flour in the cart with a thud. "Kelsey is twisting everything to make it seem like I'm some opportunistic manipulator. She's been baiting me, and I've fallen right into it."

"Mean girls really don't leave it behind in high school, do they? They just find bigger stages."

"I can't believe she's Avery's best friend." Lennon collected a few more items—sugar, cinnamon, cream of tartar. "Avery is so sweet. It's like Snow White and the Evil Queen being besties."

"Avery probably doesn't see it. Or she doesn't want to," Erin reasoned. "But it sounds like Kelsey may be threatened by you, and she's doing everything she can to push you out."

"Threatened by me? For what? She's the one who *filmed a movie,* after all," Lennon said mockingly. She turned down another aisle, cans and bottles of soda lining the shelves to her right. The same glass bottles of root beer she and Dylan shared at her apartment brought her to a stop.

Another sickening realization clicked. "She wants Dylan."

Erin glanced at the camera, her sweat-beaded brow furrowing. "How do you know?"

"She was flirting with him at the beach. She all but rubbed her scent on him. And I overheard them talking. They sounded like they were …" A dull, twisting heat pooled in her stomach. "*Bonding.*"

Lennon had never been the jealous type. She had plenty of experience watching women hit on Dylan when they were together. After all, he was a professional athlete. It came with the territory. But she'd been secure in their relationship. Even when he started partying with his teammates, Lennon only questioned his loyalty once, and he assured her he hadn't stepped out on her. Plenty of people had openly expressed how stupid she was for believing that.

To this day, she didn't believe he'd cheated on her. Whether he had *wanted* to, though, was another matter.

Seeing Kelsey with Dylan had triggered feelings she hadn't before contended with. She wrestled with a strange sense of possessiveness, even though he wasn't hers. She had no claim on him. No right to be jealous.

What she *did* have was the right to feel protective of him. Even Kelsey supposedly believed in protecting friends. She blamed Lennon for trying to exploit this vulnerable time in his life for her own benefit, but what if Kelsey was the one doing that?

"He won't fall for it," Erin said, interrupting Lennon's dark spiral. She slowed to a walk on the treadmill to begin her cooldown. "He doesn't go for girls like her."

"What, beautiful blondes who stroke his ego? That's every man's type." Lennon turned to the other side of the aisle and tossed a bag of potato chips into the cart, then grabbed a box of microwave popcorn further down.

"Trust me, he's not interested in dating anyone new right now." Erin glanced at her phone. "Do you eat *anything* that isn't processed?"

Erin's confidence in Dylan's dating life brought a wave of relief and disappointment. Lennon didn't want to think too deeply about why she felt the latter.

"People's souls," Lennon answered Erin's question absentmindedly. She grabbed a box of Cracker Jacks—the classic ballpark snack—and shook it in front of the camera with a sly grin. "Remember these?"

Erin smiled, nostalgia dancing in her eyes. "Of course." As Lennon tossed them in her cart and then reached for a container of peanuts, Erin tapped some buttons on the treadmill to slow to a stop. "Did you tell him what happened?" she asked as she dismounted. "At the beach."

"No, not yet." Lennon thought it better to give him space. While they'd agreed to be friends and do this show together, she didn't want to overstep and interrupt his entire life with her return.

And Lennon's own feelings were getting confusing. She needed to maintain some boundaries for the sake of her sanity.

"You should tell him, so he knows what's going on," Erin suggested, patting the sweat from her face with a small pink towel.

"I can talk to him tomorrow before we meet up with you for dinner."

"I can't wait to see you guys. Especially you. I mean, I miss Dylan, too, but I miss you more." She lowered her voice as she crossed the empty gym. "Don't tell him I said that."

"I think he already knows, but I won't confirm it." Lennon smiled at the phone. "And I'm looking forward to it, too. Arden Beach isn't the same without you." The promise of seeing Erin got her through the week, even if it meant going to dinner at Rhett's house with her and Dylan. They hadn't all been in the same room together since before the divorce. Something that had once been a normal, weekly affair now had Lennon's stomach in a knot every time she thought about it.

Navigating the new dynamic with Dylan was complicated enough. How would it feel to have dinner with his family when she was no longer part of it?

"I wish I could stay more than a couple of days," Erin said. "I'm so tired of being on the road."

"I mean, you've been traveling with the team your entire life. I'd be surprised if you weren't starting to get a little burned out on it." Lennon grabbed butter and eggs, completing her shopping.

"At least I don't have to do it in the off-season." Erin popped the straw on her stainless steel water bottle, drawing a few sips from it.

"That's what I keep telling myself about the show. I just have to make it until September."

"Try to spend as little time as possible with Kelsey for the rest of it."

"That's going to be a bit difficult, given the whole show is pretty much centered around Avery's wedding and Kelsey's, you know, the maid of honor."

"You have to remember that she's baiting you, like you said. She *wants* you to react," Erin said as Lennon made her way to the front of the store. "She knows the cameras are there, and she's playing to them. So, don't walk into her traps. Try not to engage at all."

Lennon snorted. "You make it sound so easy. Have you met me? It's the downside to my passionate, highly expressive natu—" She drew up short at the entrance to a closed checkout lane. "What the fuck," Lennon loosed under her breath.

"What? What is it?"

Lennon pulled into the lane and snatched *Star Pulse*, a popular tabloid, from the shelf above the conveyor belt. She stared at it for a few seconds, her gut churning, before flipping her phone's camera around to show Erin.

Splashed across the glossy cover was a grainy photo of Dylan and Kelsey at the beach clean-up. The bold, bright yellow headline read: DYLAN STRICKLAND'S NEW LOVE?

"Oh, God," Erin groaned. "You've got to be kidding me."

Lennon set the magazine on her bag, then flipped through it with one hand while she kept the camera trained on it for Erin. She found the page with more photos of them and a short article accompanying it.

"They're just standing near each other talking," Erin pointed out.

And laughing. And smiling. Apparently, that's all that was needed to sell a supposed romance.

"What does the article say?" Erin leaned closer to the phone, scrunching her eyebrows. "It's too small and blurry on the camera."

Lennon read it aloud:

Fallen baseball star Dylan Strickland looks to be falling for someone new. The Arden Beach Tidebreakers star was spotted with a mystery blonde while volunteering on the beach. Though they were joined by a group, including recently retired football star Chadwick Mormont and his wife-to-be Avery Mora, Dylan and the blonde bombshell kept close to each other and were even spotted leaving the beach together. Dylan was suspended from the Tidebreakers back in February following an injury from a boating accident while under the influence. Could a new romance be helping his road to recovery?

Lennon stared at the page, her head spinning. Dread crawled through her body.

"Articles like that are a dime a dozen. He's been linked with so many random women over the years that he barely even spoke to," Erin assured her. "They're just trying to sell magazines."

"They didn't even mention I was there," Lennon observed. "He walked off the beach with her but left the park with me."

"Who knows why they choose to print what they do? Maybe they didn't get good enough photos of you two together, or they didn't fit the narrative they wanted to push."

Maybe the article would fly under the radar and be old news by next week's issue. But her alarm bells were ringing. It felt like the first sign of an oncoming storm.

Forces were at work that she was not privy to—that much was clear. It was the same thing she sensed around Kelsey. Lennon didn't like the feeling of being a pinball kicked around in a machine by other players.

If this was the story the press were going for, what did that mean for the show? Could she end up being squeezed out of that, too if she didn't give them what they wanted?

"I need to start playing the game," Lennon said, the realization solidifying.

Erin raised a curious—and somewhat concerned—eyebrow. "What do you mean?"

Lennon flipped the camera back around so Erin could see her face. "I've been treating this show like a regular job, but it's not. It's a game. All of this is." She looked at the article open in front of her. "I've been playing defense while Kelsey's playing offense. I need to turn the tables."

Erin's gaze sharpened, the wheels turning. "What's your plan?"

"I don't know yet." Lennon shut the magazine. "But I'm sure as hell done being the pawn in theirs."

CHAPTER 16

Lennon

As the sun set the following evening, Dylan picked up Lennon from her apartment and they rode together to his father's house. She anxiously tapped her fingers on the plastic container holding peanut butter snickerdoodles—a favorite of Rhett's—she'd baked that afternoon.

It was just dinner. She needed to get a grip.

At least Marcos, Dylan's trainer, would also be there to make it slightly less awkward. He was hired shortly after their divorce, so Lennon had never met him, but she'd heard plenty about him as he became a family friend over the years.

Dylan drove his SUV through the gate of a sprawling traditional-style manor, its cedar shingle cladding, black shutters, and carriage house garage doors reminiscent of homes in the Hamptons. After parking, he jogged around to open Lennon's door. She barely made it up the walkway before Erin swung open one of the tall front doors, barefoot in loose jeans and a white tie-front cropped top.

Lennon jogged to meet her halfway and collided with her in a bear hug. After Erin finished squeezing Lennon, she lunged at her brother. Dylan expelled an exaggerated groan, feigning pain until she smacked him. He laughed as he returned her embrace, rocking her back and forth.

Lennon's heart leapt at the sight of them, struck by a mix of joy and heartache at the same time.

"*Qué pasó, hermano*? You're late," a deep, softly accented voice called from the doorway. A muscular man—Marcos, Lennon presumed—emerged from the house. His jet-black hair flowed freely over thick, broad shoulders, and though his tone was reprimanding, his dark eyes crinkled in a teasing smile.

Erin released Dylan from her grasp. Dylan and Marcos clasped each other's forearms in greeting.

"Seems to be becoming a habit," Marcos remarked. They exchanged a loaded look. Dylan appeared halfway between laughing and killing Marcos, who peered past him. "You must be Lennon."

"You must be Marcos."

"Tell me—" Still holding Dylan's forearm, he jerked his head toward him. "You got any good dirt on this guy?"

"You kidding?" Lennon arched a brow. "I know things you wouldn't believe."

Marcos grinned. "Good thing we have all night, then." He patted Dylan on the shoulder before releasing his arm.

"Getting you two together was a terrible idea," Dylan remarked regretfully as Marcos led Lennon to the door.

"This is going to be *great*," Erin crooned with delight.

Inside, they met Rhett as he walked in from the patio, several floor-to-ceiling sliding glass doors pushed open to the backyard, creating one sprawling indoor-outdoor space. The mouth-watering scent of a wood-fired grill wafted through the house as he carried in a platter of grilled meat. Erin took the platter from him and put it on the table with the others, filled with grilled vegetables and baked potatoes.

"Hey, Dad," Dylan said, embracing him.

"Hey, son." Rhett lovingly slapped him on the back. "Hey, Lennie," he said over Dylan's shoulder. He opened his arms to her next.

"Hey, Rhett." Lennon's heart trembled a little in her chest at the fatherly presence welcoming her as though she'd never left. A surge of emotion surprised her. As they embraced, part of her didn't want to let go. Pressure built in her sternum. She inhaled his woody scent, keeping it at bay as they parted.

"You look great, kiddo," Rhett said as he gave her a proud once-over.

"So do you. Opted out of the whole aging thing, huh?"

"Tell that to my knees and back." Rhett chuckled a deep, gravelly sound. Lennon always thought Erin favored Rhett more with the light eyes and blonde hair, while Dylan favored their mother's darker features. It wasn't until either man smiled that the charming crookedness of it gave them away as father and son. "That what I think it is?" He eyed the plastic container in her hands.

"With extra cinnamon," Lennon confirmed.

"Don't tell my doctor—or Erin," Rhett conspired quietly, and Lennon winked in response.

"I heard that." Erin sent them both an admonishing look. "Where's Michelle?" she asked Marcos.

"She's at a spa retreat with her sister 'til tomorrow," Marcos answered as he helped her set out the food. "She sends her love and asks me to bring home a doggy bag of Rhett's famous steak. She's been hungry nonstop since getting pregnant."

"I'll put two plates together. One for her and one for the baby she's eating for." Rhett smacked Marcos on his back with affection.

They all gathered around the massive, solid wood dining table. Rhett sat at the head with Lennon and Erin beside each other on one side and Dylan and Marcos across from them. They all gave brief updates on their lives. Erin shared how her first semester in her master's program was going while balancing her job with the team. Marcos talked about his excitement—and nerves—over the impending arrival of his first child. They asked about the reality show with no shortage of curiosity, and Lennon and Dylan shared some of the funnier stories that had happened so far.

"They asked me and the other guys to haul these old car parts from the beach. Turns out, the show brought them in to make the clean-up look more dramatic than it was," Dylan said. "Really got on the nerves of the people hosting it. Carol Anne didn't make any friends that day."

"I'm not sure Carol Anne makes friends any day," Lennon remarked.

They fell into an easy rhythm as if no time had passed since they last shared a meal. Evenings like this had been a regular occurrence when they were kids. Lennon hadn't realized—or maybe hadn't let herself realize—how much she'd missed it until now, reliving it again.

A bittersweet ache rolled through her.

Eventually, they slipped into reminiscing about the days when Lennon's mother worked part-time at the Tidebreakers stadium, where she'd first met the Stricklands.

"I remember when they started calling you the third Strickland kid," Rhett mused with the faint, crooked smile that reminded her of Dylan.

"We even gave you your own nickname to make it official." Erin popped a piece of broccoli in her mouth as she glanced at Lennon.

"What is this about nicknames?" Marcos asked, lifting an intrigued brow.

"Oh, no," Dylan groaned with a drop of his head.

Erin grinned around her broccoli. "Dylan and I made up nicknames for each other when we were little. Lennon wanted one, too."

"Is that so?" Marcos looked at Dylan. "And what are these nicknames?"

"I'm never going to hear the end of it," Dylan warned Erin.

"I'm his Emu," Erin said, ignoring her brother. "And Dylan is my pain in the ass little Dodo."

Marcos's lips slowly curled into a smirk. "That is very fitting for you, *hermano*."

"I figured you might think so," Dylan said.

Erin turned back to Lennon. "And she's our Lynx."

Lennon smiled at Erin before her eyes flicked to Dylan. He watched her with a soft, easy joy that shot a blast of warmth through her.

"You were always hangin' around, hidin' when it was time for your mom to go home. Drove her nuts," Rhett shared, lifting his glass of iced tea and shaking the ice around in it. "I finally told her I'd drive you home at the end of the day if she wanted to leave you there when we practiced late." He brought the glass to his lips.

"That was your idea?" Lennon asked.

Releasing a sigh after a few gulps, Rhett lowered the glass. "You kept Erin company. Though you were a little distracting for Dylan, who was supposed to be watching the team." He passed his son a sideward glance, who pressed his tongue into his cheek to hide a smile. Dylan drove his spoon through his sweet potatoes and took a bite. "I was worried it would be a problem at first when you started coming to his youth league games, but he actually played better when you were there."

Lennon's amusement shifted into butterflies. She and Dylan looked at each other simultaneously again. Her heart did a little flip.

"Guess he wanted to impress you," Rhett continued, cutting into his ribeye. "It worked. For a while, anyway."

Lennon watched Dylan's effervescence deflate as though someone had suddenly flipped a switch and snuffed out the light inside him. It startled her.

Everyone went quiet, sensing the energy shift. The only noise was the clatter of metal on ceramic.

"So, what do they have you up to on the show? Been in any catfights yet?" Marcos joked, successfully releasing the tension and lifting the room's energy back up as Dylan cracked a smile.

"Saving that for the finale," Dylan retorted.

"Now that I *have* to see," Erin said, pointing her fork at him.

"Please sneak me onto set that day. Dylan's the most non-confrontational person I know."

"It'll be a very respectful catfight," Dylan clarified wryly.

"How much time does that take?" Rhett asked. Off Dylan's questioning look, he specified, "Filming. How many hours a week are you spending on that?"

"Uh, so far about …" Dylan glanced at Lennon as he did the math in his head, inviting her to step in. "Fifteen? Maybe twenty hours a week? Like a part-time job, I guess," he said.

Lennon nodded in agreement. "Yeah, that's been the average for me so far. There's all the prep beforehand—hair, makeup, getting different shots—and the interviews in between."

Rhett sliced off another piece of meat. "You don't think it would be better spent working on your game? If that suspension is lifted, you don't want to get back out there only to embarrass yourself."

The muscles in Dylan's jaw flexed with a tight, bitter curve of his lips, the light snuffed out again. This time, the tension in the air became outright uncomfortable. Lennon, Erin, and Marcos exchanged glances. Dylan fixed his gaze on a random spot on the table, zoning out.

A chill passed through Lennon. She knew that look.

She *hated* that look.

"The show's going to help with his image," Erin interjected. "That's the whole point. To help him get back on the team."

Rhett kept his attention on Dylan. "You don't think there are less time-consuming ways to do that?"

"My manager thought it was a good idea," Dylan stated, voice flat with an edge of annoyance.

"Maybe you need a better manager. One who understands your priorities," Rhett returned. "Maybe you could use a refresher on them, as well." He cut another piece of steak. "How's your velocity looking?"

Dylan ground his teeth, his grip on his fork tightening as he pushed his food around on his plate. "Been averaging around eighty-nine."

"You were at a hundred and six before the accident."

"I'm working on it."

"He's getting stronger every week," Marcos said. "Can't rush these things. Recovery takes time."

The shake of Rhett's head was almost imperceptible, but Lennon saw the ripple effect it had on Dylan. Shame took root. His expression went hard, numb, but she saw the pain locked behind it.

Lennon fought the urge to reach across the table and take his hand. She had experienced similar treatment from her mother regarding her music career. Nothing was ever good enough.

Lennon bit her tongue, unsure if she should get in the middle of it. She wasn't a part of their family anymore. It wasn't her place to get involved.

"You might as well retire with numbers like that," Rhett commented before tossing another piece of steak into his mouth. Dylan pressed his eyes shut.

"Dad—" Erin reproved, her fork clanking against her plate as she dropped her hand.

"What? It's the truth. He's below the league average now. The accident set him way back. He should be doing everything he can to get back to where he was. When I tore my ACL, I worked fifteen hours a day, seven days a week to get back on my game. That's the year we won the championship. Best season I ever played. He should be much farther ahead by now. He's just not putting the time into it. Do you actually care about getting back on the team?"

Dylan released a dark laugh, shaking his head.

"Dad, why the hell would you even ask him that?" Erin hissed.

"Because right now, it doesn't seem to me like he does, Erin."

"I do care," Dylan said firmly, voice rasping. "Every free moment I have is spent training. It's hard to put as much time in as I used to between therapy, meetings, and filming, but I'm devoting every second I can to it. My trainers have all said I've made more progress than they expected at this stage."

"It's true, he has," Marcos confirmed.

"The producers know Dylan will be a huge draw for viewers," Lennon interjected. "They practically bent over backward to get him on the cast because of the value he brings."

Dylan looked up at her. His dark eyes slightly softened, gratitude piercing through the tension.

"She's right," Erin agreed. "This show's going to remind people why they love him. And maybe even inspire some people who aren't into baseball to take an interest in it just to support him. That'll help the Tidebreakers, too."

"They won't love him so much if he costs the team wins his first season back," Rhett stated blankly.

The table was stunned to silence again. Erin gaped at her father, incensed, while Dylan's nostrils flared, muscles flexing in his jaw.

"You could drop the therapy and spend that time training," Rhett suggested.

"I can't do that—" Dylan began tightly.

"You're just paying someone to listen to you talk. You get better by *doing*, by getting back out there—not talking about it."

Dylan abruptly stood from the table, the legs of his chair scraping along the hardwood floor. "Excuse me," he said, dropping his napkin beside his plate. "I need some air." He strode out of the dining room, sneakers pounding against the hardwood until he reached the patio.

"I'll go talk to him," Marcos said as Erin rose. A look of understanding passed between them before he excused himself and followed Dylan outside.

"What the hell was that?" Erin spat at her father as soon as Marcos left. "Why do you have to be so hard on him? Can't you see he's trying? And don't even *get* me started on what you said about therapy."

The awkwardness of sitting between them during an argument had Lennon feeling as though her skin turned inside out. She wanted to bolt up from her chair. Wondered if she should excuse herself, too.

"He's the one who got himself into this mess. Trying doesn't mean shit if he's doing the bare minimum." Rhett wiped his mouth with his napkin. "This is the major league. He can't phone it in. It has to be his entire life."

"When it was his entire life, it was *killing* him." Erin let that one sit in the air for a few seconds. "You should show him more compassion. The pressure he's under has stressed him out to the point where he can't even enjoy the game anymore. Or his life, for that matter."

Lennon looked at Erin, the gravity of that statement rooting her to her chair. Even though he'd never admitted it to her, she'd always known the pressure weighed on him. She just hadn't realized how deep it ran.

"My grandfather grew up in a tiny house with no running water and worked from the time he was ten years old. He fought like hell to make a better life for himself. To dig himself out of poverty," Rhett said calmly, though his voice—and the look in his light hazel eyes—held an edge. She'd struck a nerve. "Dylan was born with every opportunity handed to him thanks to the legacy my father started for us. He's made millions of dollars and he's not even thirty. What the hell does he have to be stressed about?"

Lennon bit her tongue. She understood where Rhett was coming from. As someone who grew up with a single mother who barely made enough to scrape by for a while, it wasn't lost on her the impact money—or a lack thereof—had on a person's life. However, the suggestion that having it should preclude any other type of stress was flat-out wrong.

"Everyone's situation comes with different stresses, Dad," Erin said. "And Dylan's wired differently than you."

"He needs to toughen up, then. Stricklands are strong. It's in his blood." Rhett swept a piece of steak through the juice on his plate and the last of his potatoes, enjoying his meal as though he hadn't had a massive confrontation with his children.

Lennon gazed across the patio at the silhouettes of Dylan and Marcos framed by pines and oaks. She wished she could help him.

She wished he would let her.

CHAPTER 17

Dylan

The amber glow of streetlights threw the interior of the vehicle in and out of shadow. Dylan rested his elbow on the windowsill, fingertips bothering his upper lip as his mind wandered. The ride back to Lennon's apartment was mostly quiet beside the hum of the motor and rush of the wind between the open windows.

Rhett's words had taken root, making Dylan question everything.

Was he not doing enough? Training hard enough? Was he not pushing himself as much as he could?

He couldn't use his injury as an excuse, and this wasn't the time to be holding back.

The headlights lit up the street sign leading to Lennon's place. Guilt pulled at him for ruining her night. She was probably desperate for it to end.

"Want to take a walk on the beach?" Lennon asked.

Dylan surfaced from his daze, meeting her eyes with gentle surprise at the question. And relief.

They found a quiet place to park and headed down the moonlit boardwalk. They kicked off their shoes, letting their bare feet sink into the sand, and then strolled along the edge where the cool foam grazed their ankles.

After a long walk down the mostly deserted beach, where lights from private homes and the moon provided a soft glow for their journey, they returned to the boardwalk. They stood along the railing, enjoying the comforting sound of the ocean and the simplicity of the dark, endless expanse stretching before them. The ocean had a way of creating space for complicated emotions and thoughts to roll in and out like waves, applying a balm to the soul in a way only nature could.

Lennon gave Dylan that same space with her silent but steady presence. Leaning on her forearms, she hung her hands over the railing with her sandals dangling from her fingers. Dylan stood beside her, his hands stuffed in his pockets, his shoes on the wood slats next to him. Pensive again, lost in thought.

"I'm sorry about dinner," he finally said after a while.

A little crease formed between her eyebrows. "What do you have to be sorry about?"

"It was pretty awkward." Wry humor poorly masked his embarrassment, a heavy weight sitting in his chest. "And the way I reacted …"

Lennon studied him. He felt naked under her stare, like she could see everything. Every weakness. Every fear. "You were fine. Your dad is the one who should be embarrassed."

"He's under a lot of stress. It can't be easy from his position, having the enormous responsibility of the team weighing on him. And dealing with a son like me."

A pained expression struck her, and for a moment, the idea of her pitying him knocked a wave of aggravation through him. The only thing he hated more than being shamed was being pitied.

He regretted saying anything. He tore his gaze from her, rubbing the back of his head.

"My mom never made an effort to hide her disappointment

in having someone like me as a daughter, and I swallowed the pain of it—accepted it—because I understood what a burden it must be for us to be so fundamentally different." Lennon was facing the ocean when he looked at her, his frustration ebbing.

Sorrow and a pang of guilt mellowed him as he realized her sorrowful expression hadn't been from pity.

It was empathy.

A storm turned in her eyes. "I'm sure it hasn't been easy watching you go through what you've been going through, and I know his job is stressful," Lennon said, as if it burned on the way out, "but a lot of peoples' jobs are. That's no excuse to talk to you like that. To berate you. He should be supportive, now more than ever."

A muscle in his jaw ticked, Dylan's gaze sharpening on the black horizon. "There are some problems that my situation has made worse." He braced his palms on the rough, weathered railing. "The team has been steadily losing money for the past few years. Between losing key players to other teams that offered them more money and others sustaining injuries, it's been a string of bad luck. We keep making it to the postseason but can't cinch a championship. I was supposed to help turn the tide when they drafted me, but we've had a lot working against us. And now … Eddie's worried he won't be able to keep the team. There are already buyers circling. One in particular." His name was bitter on his tongue. "Nolan Pierce."

Lennon's brows pinched together as it appeared to trip something in her brain. "Why does that sound familiar?"

"Nolan's named after his father, who goes by Lan. They're both entrepreneurs. Nolan's a tech billionaire who doesn't know shit about actually playing baseball but thinks he knows what's best for the team just because he owns the world's largest sports streaming network."

It took a second, but her eyes expanded slightly as recognition clicked. "He recently bought Rhythmi," Lennon said, referring to the most prominent music streaming platform in the world. "They pay artists peanuts to stream their music."

"Lan was my dad's stepbrother until their parents got divorced.

They remained close for a while." Tension corded through Dylan's body, his blood heating. "Lan wanted to be a baseball player, but he wasn't good enough to go pro, and he blamed my dad for not helping him.

"Lan turned on him after that. Spread a bunch of lies. He ended up getting kicked out of college for running a gambling ring on school grounds and lost all the grant money for a project he had been working on, but he found investors to start his first company the same year my dad almost made it to the Champion Series. Where he got injured in the playoffs.

"After the game, rumors spread that it wasn't an accident. The player who hurt him had a connection with Lan."

The energy shifted, as if all the particles in the air had collectively stilled. Lennon's eyebrows slowly lifted. "You think Lan paid someone to hurt him on purpose?"

Dylan met her horrified expression, his silence affirming her question. "My dad was humiliated on the field. Their rivals won that game, and then the championship." His stomach churned at the thought, as though he'd lived it and not only heard about it second-hand his whole life. "I think it's why Nolan wants to buy the team. To finish what his father started. Dad has never been quiet about his dream to take the team to the championship as a manager and win it alongside me."

"Damn. Jealousy really is a disease," Lennon mused with contempt. "That's fucked up."

"Yeah. And I paved the way for him to do it." Dylan pushed off the railing, disgusted with himself. He paced in a circle in the middle of the boardwalk.

"Hey, this isn't all on you. You're not responsible for Nolan's stupid revenge fantasy or an entire baseball team's success."

"Well, I'm certainly not helping, am I?"

Lennon twisted to face him. "You're allowed to make mistakes, Dylan. The important thing is whether you learn from them or not."

Dylan stared at a distant point on the boardwalk where it trailed into the dark. "And what if it's too late?" A hollow pressure built behind his ribs. "There's so much on the line. I made a commitment to the team—to my dad—and I let everyone down. I don't think he'll be able to even *look* at me if he not only loses another chance at the championship but also the entire team because I couldn't get my shit together."

"If your dad's love for you is conditional on how much time and effort you've put into baseball, then it's not you with the messed-up priorities. It's him."

Something glinted between two of the wood slats. Dylan knelt to retrieve the quarter-sized pearlescent seashell. "Baseball's his life. Our family's legacy." He rolled the smooth shell between two fingers. "It's the most important thing in the world to him."

"It's not more important than you."

Dylan glanced up at her, his heart stumbling over a beat.

That's what he should have told her before she left. What he should have made sure she *knew*.

Dylan swallowed thickly and stood. Peering out across the sand, he pulled his arm back and heaved the seashell into the shadows. His shoulder lightly twinged. Like it did every damn time.

"Does it hurt?" Lennon asked.

"Sometimes it aches, especially after a long training session." Dylan rolled it. "Mostly, it feels a little ... off when I use it."

"Does your dad know?"

The corners of his mouth quirked ruefully. "He'd tell me to suck it up like he did when he busted his knee." Dylan leaned against the railing with a long sigh, the ocean breeze gently blowing through his hair. "Ever since the suspension, I can *feel* the shame and disappointment. I see it when he looks at me. Which he can barely do these days."

Lennon pushed a frustrated sigh through her nose. "The pressure he's put on you isn't fair," she said. "You didn't ask to be born into this and have all those expectations on you. That would be a lot for anyone to live with."

"I've hurt people because I didn't handle it well, though." Dylan pinned her with his gaze, the weight of a stadium on his chest. "That part's on me."

Pain briefly flashed in Lennon's eyes, quick but sharp enough to cut. Her expression turned unreadable after that as she looked away from him.

He didn't know what that meant. If she was tired of his apologies, or if he was only hurting her again every time he forced her to relive their past. Dylan watched a thin cloud pass in front of the silver moon, the light piercing through it.

Gentle pressure settled over his hand.

He looked down at the little black heart tattooed beside her thumb, her fingers resting on his. A slow, quiet ache spread through him.

It was the first time they'd touched since she'd left. *Really* touched.

"He loves you," Lennon said with certainty. "That's not conditional on baseball. Maybe he just doesn't know any other way to express it." While she focused on their hands, Dylan focused on her. "When you were in the hospital unconscious that night, you should've seen him. He was a wreck. Wouldn't leave the place, kept harassing all the doctors for updates. He barely slept. I don't think he would've done that for any of the other players on the team."

Dylan's hand tensed under hers. He knew she was right, and that made the shame he carried over the night of the accident punch through him with such force, he wanted to hurl himself off that boardwalk and let the sea engulf him.

Until something clicked.

"Wait." Dylan studied her. "How do *you* know what he looked like that night?"

Lennon tensed. "Erin told me." As Dylan watched her closely, she turned away, as if looking at him made her uncomfortable. "And we did a video call that night. She was with your dad. She was really scared." Lennon paused a beat. "So was I." Dylan's face softened at the rawness in her admission. Guilt surfaced in her eyes. "I'm sorry I didn't come to see you when you were in the hospital."

"You don't have to be—"

"I wanted to," she said, bowing her head. "I almost bought a plane ticket, but then Erin called and said you'd woken up and were doing surprisingly well. That you'd gotten lucky. Then, after the relief washed over me …" Lennon met his gaze, and he could feel her remorse. "I was angry at you for getting yourself in that situation at all. I didn't know how to process everything I was feeling, so I figured it'd be better if I stayed away. I didn't want to make things worse for everyone."

"You wouldn't have," Dylan said.

"It wasn't my place."

Dylan read between the lines. *I was no longer your wife;* he imagined her thinking. As though that also meant she was no longer part of his family.

He hadn't realized he'd technically taken that from her, too. It drove a knife through his chest. "You'll always be part of our family. So long as you want to be." Dylan lifted his thumb to gingerly—tentatively—wrap it around the side of her hand.

Lennon stiffened under his touch, her eyes glistening. He brushed her pinky with his thumb. After a moment, her eyelids shuddered, and she gently pulled her hand back, then rubbed them both up her arms as though she'd suddenly felt a chill.

Pain lanced through him. Dylan cleared his throat, shoving his hands in his pockets.

"I should get to bed. I have an early call time for filming tomorrow," Lennon said, slipping her shoes on.

Dylan did the same, and they started walking back to his car.

"So, what are you filming?" he asked, cutting through the silence.

"Apartment hunting. Finally getting my first solo segment."

"You're moving already?"

"No. They're setting up some fake showings for me to look at, and then I have to view mine as if I've never seen it before so I can decide *that's the one!*" Lennon raised her hands in mock excitement. "They told me I can talk about my music, though. Test the acoustics of each place with my singing. Not exactly a behind-the-scenes feature, but it's something."

"It's just the beginning. You're a great musician. Now that you have a platform to show it, it's a matter of time before something clicks."

"Let's hope. Though, if Kelsey gets her way, I'll be begging people to let me sing at their kids' birthday parties again." Lennon waited for a car to pass before crossing the street to his vehicle.

"Who's Kelsey? That girl from the beach clean-up?" Dylan opened the passenger door.

"Yeah, the one you're supposedly dating," she said tartly, shooting him a look before slipping inside.

"Dating? I barely know her."

"The tabloids and the internet would like to believe otherwise."

Dylan shook his head, hanging his wrist over the top of the door. "I ignore that garbage. You should, too." She looked up at him before he shut the door, her brow furrowing slightly.

Dylan settled into the driver's seat and turned on the engine. "So, what does Kelsey have to do with your music career?"

Lennon rested an elbow on the windowsill, tangling her fingers in her hair. She released an agitated breath, which he was glad not to be the cause of for once. As he backed out onto the street, she relayed a conversation she'd had with Kelsey on the beach.

Dylan laughed. Not because it was funny, but because it was flat-out ridiculous.

"We've known each other for years," he said. "*You* divorced *me* and wouldn't even let me pay spousal support. How could you possibly be a gold digger?"

"It doesn't have to be true. It just has to be believable."

"No one's going to believe that."

"You sure about that?"

Dylan clenched his jaw. No, he wasn't. It was exactly the kind of narrative the media and the public would devour and then pick their teeth with the carnage.

"Let's get ahead of it, then. What do we need to do?" Dylan focused on the near-empty road, waiting for her response. A few seconds of silence passed. He glanced and found Lennon staring at him. "What?"

Her expression suggested surprise but otherwise didn't give away what she was thinking. Had he said something wrong?

Lennon finally turned her attention to the window, pulling her legs up. She'd slipped out of her sandals again, resting her bare feet on the edge of the leather seat as she wrapped her arms around her legs, seeming to sink into thought.

She used to sit like that when they drove around as teenagers, the same black nail polish on her toes. Her feet would dance to music on the radio while she sang along.

A small smile snuck to the corner of his mouth. Dylan faced forward, scrubbing a hand across his upper lip to hide it.

"I think we should ignore it," Lennon finally said. It took him a second to remember what they were talking about. "At least in the sense of not arguing with her about it. Either of us trying to defend me will just make me look guilty and give her more ammunition to use against me. I need to *show* people the truth. Let them see it with their own eyes."

"Well, that's easy," Dylan said. She sent him a questioning look. "They just have to see us together. It's obvious how we feel about each other." He turned down the street to her apartment complex. Putting the vehicle in park, he kept his hand resting on the shifter between them. Lennon was giving him that look again. The one he couldn't read, that made him wonder if he'd missed something. "We're friends, right?" he asked. "Or has that changed since we last talked about it?"

Lennon narrowed her eyes, humming with uncertainty and nearly giving him a heart attack. A teasing smile tugged at her lips. "No, it hasn't."

"Then, let's show them."

Lennon seemed to think about it, fixating on the streetlamp illuminating the hood of the vehicle. She rested her head back against the headrest. "We have to figure out *how* to do that. We need an excuse to film something together."

Dylan tapped his fingers on the shifter. "Actually, I have an idea. Eddie's receiving an award from *Playmakers Quarterly* tomorrow. Erin and Dad will be there. It's this whole stuffy black-tie thing, but the show's filming some of it. Eddie's idea. He said it'd be a good opportunity to show we're a united front and help get people reinvested in the team." He paused, an unexpected rush of nerves tightening his breath. "You want to be my plus one?"

"You sure? I don't want to intrude on something important to your family and career—"

"I told you, Lennon. If tonight wasn't proof enough, we'll always think of you as family. For better or worse," Dylan said with a wry curve of his lips. "I would've invited you sooner, but I didn't think you'd want to go. These things are always boring, and I was worried you would be … uncomfortable if I asked."

Lennon's eyes softened. She faced the windshield again, the amber light casting a warm, dreamlike glow across the planes of her face and through the loose strands of hair framing it.

Fuck. She was the most beautiful woman he'd ever seen.

"Well, I guess I need to hunt down a dress for a black-tie event in less than twenty-four hours." Lennon sent him a sidelong glance with a conspiratorial smile.

Dylan returned it, his dread for tomorrow turning to excitement. He gripped the shifter, fighting the impulse to reach for her hand. "Thank you for tonight. For everything you said and for just … being there."

Lennon dropped a shoulder. "I never turn down free food."

Dylan laughed—a real, genuine laugh—and her smile widened. She didn't move to unbuckle her seatbelt, instead sitting there for a moment, seemingly contemplating something. He waited patiently, happy to sit there with her for as long as she'd let him.

"I can see how much you've grown. How hard you're trying," Lennon said, catching him off guard. His chest drew tight. "I hope you don't let your father's unreasonable standards, and a douchebag billionaire take that from you."

Dylan stared at her, struck by what she'd said. He swallowed and sent her a small smile. "Thanks," he said, his throat tight. "I hope you don't let your mom take anything from you, either."

Lennon's eyes turned sad, as they always did at the mention of Katherine. Even through a smile, he saw the grief behind it. The doubt rooted there. He wished he could take it from her and carry it himself, so she didn't have to.

"You deserve everything you want," Dylan told her. "You're going to make it. I know it."

Her lips parted, seemingly as struck by this as he had been by her comment. His gaze fell to her mouth. Of all the times he'd wanted to kiss her recently, the urge now was particularly overwhelming. Lennon's eyes raked across his face, settling on his lips, and his heart rate quickened. Dylan leaned closer.

"I should go," Lennon said.

He stopped, regret hitting him fast and hard.

Dylan nodded and sat back. As Lennon unbuckled her seatbelt, he asked, "Want me to walk you up? Since it's late."

"I'll be OK." She smiled. "Appreciate it, though."

"I'll wait until you're inside, at least."

They said goodnight to each other, and he remained parked outside until the light in her apartment clicked on. A moment later, she appeared at the living room window. She flicked her nose. He chuckled and waved back, then reluctantly rolled away.

As the distance between them grew, so did the ache deep inside him.

CHAPTER 18

Lennon

NINE YEARS AGO

A sunset bathing the trees pink and orange. The first blossoms of spring sweetening the air. Distant music and laughter celebrating a victory.

Lennon sat on the metal bridge across the back of a billboard-sized electronic scoreboard, right behind the outfield of the Arden Beach Ballpark. Beyond it, conservation stretched a couple of miles until it tapered off to a quiet beach. No one had any reason to go back there unless they were servicing the sign, and the huge concrete wall below it made the area completely unobservable from anywhere but the immediate vicinity.

Her high-top sneakers dangled as she enjoyed the peaceful seclusion of it, waiting. Soon, the sound of someone climbing the ladder brought a smile to her face. "Congratulations, Mr. MVP."

Dylan humbly dipped his head as he stepped onto the grated metal, freshly showered and changed from his baseball uniform into a t-shirt and jeans. His hair was tousled and damp, pieces curling around his ears and forehead. As he lowered to sit beside her, he winced, sucking air through his teeth.

"What is it?" Lennon scanned his body as he much too carefully hung his long legs over the side. "Dylan—are you hurt?"

"It's nothing," he reassured her, sounding as if he were holding his breath. "Just bruised my ribs a little when that guy slammed into me on second base."

Anger flared hot again. Lennon had yelled obscenities from the stands, wanting to race down to the field and knee that other idiot player in the groin. "Let me see—"

"I'm fine, baby. I promise." Dylan laughed and immediately winced again, earning a reproachful look from her. "I'm fine," he repeated unconvincingly through a grimace he tried to twist into a smile.

Lennon grabbed the hem of his faded comic book tee and yanked it up, revealing a splotch of purple the size of a handprint blooming along the side of his abdomen. He sighed, conceding. Her heart rose to her throat. "Shit, Dylan .... That looks awful. You sure nothing's broken?"

"Yeah. Dad got it checked after the game. It looks worse than it is."

He always said that about his injuries. New cuts and scrapes and bruises appeared on his body regularly because the boy had no fear on the field. He'd thrown himself into walls, slid into bases, been hit countless times. But this one .... She felt light-headed, like she might slip off the edge of the railing. Heat formed behind her eyes.

"Hey, you OK?" His deep brown eyes searched hers under a low, concerned brow. "You're gripping me pretty hard." The corner of his mouth raised a bit.

Lennon hadn't noticed her fingers had tightly curled into his shirt, turning her knuckles white. She didn't want to let go. She didn't want to let *him* go. "I just realized how much I don't want anything to happen to you," she said, a little dazed.

Dylan's expression softened with surprise. "You weren't sure you cared that much before?" he joked, though he watched her intently. His throat bobbed.

"Obviously." She half-rolled her eyes but couldn't stop looking at the bruise. It felt like her heart was outside her chest, beating in front of her. "I guess … I didn't realize I—"

"I love you, too."

Lennon's stomach flipped over, and warmth fanned through her. The words seemed to spill out of him like there had been no thought leading up to them, only a rush of truth pushing its way out. He stared at her wide-eyed, lips parted, looking as struck by it as she was.

After several seconds without her saying anything, his eyebrows twitched upward. "S-sorry, I shouldn't've assumed—"

"No, you're right," she said, a smile growing that she tamed by biting her bottom lip. The truth settled over her like a blanket. It was one she'd known for a while, she realized. She'd just been too scared to admit it. "I do."

Dylan's eyes brightened. The corner of his mouth slanted upward. "You do … what?"

Lennon's face warmed, and he apparently noticed, his lip lifting a little higher. She glanced at the faded scar on it, then back to his eyes. "Love you," she said softly. "I love you."

How he looked at her melted her heart, making it pool in her ribcage. Like he couldn't believe she was real.

She could hardly believe he was, either.

Dylan leaned forward, brushing the tip of his nose against hers. Goosebumps skated across her skin. Lennon closed her eyes, gently tugging on his shirt again, and he pressed his lips to hers in response. Soft, chaste, like their first. The hard metal beneath them and the celebration on the other side of the wall drifted away. For a moment, the only things existing in her world were this slow, sweet kiss and this boy who loved her … for her.

If she slipped off the railing right then, she would probably float over the trees.

No wonder so many people wrote songs about this.

CHAPTER 19

Lennon

As soon as filming for her "apartment hunting" scenes wrapped, Bruno dropped Lennon off at Erin's luxury high-rise on the Arden Beach River. With only a couple of hours to prepare, Lennon raced to the elevator.

Erin answered the door of her twenty-first-floor condo wearing a baby-blue silk robe and curlers pinned in her blonde hair. "I have fuel, dresses, and moral support ready for action," her best friend told her, holding up a pink smoothie in a tall glass. She invited Lennon inside with a tilt of her head.

"You're a lifesaver." Lennon accepted the frozen beverage. "All my evening gowns are in storage with my Grammys and multiplatinum record plaques."

The sunset cast a cotton candy glow over the picturesque view beyond the balcony, turning the canal and other buildings shades of pink and orange. A pink punching bag hung from the ceiling in the corner, next to a little meditation altar with a floor pillow, candles, and crystals.

Erin, in a nutshell.

Having not had a break to eat that day, Lennon took advantage of the tiny sandwiches and snacks Erin had arranged to fuel them through the beauty process while Erin showed her the dress options she'd scrounged together in half a day. All but one were from Erin's collection from years of attending events like these with her family.

"This one is special," Erin said as she hugged a black wardrobe bag and then lovingly unzipped it. "It was my mom's. She wore it to my dad's Hall of Fame induction. I'd planned to wear it someday, but it's never felt like me." She carefully lifted the dress from the bag. "But I thought it'd be perfect for you."

A gasp caught in Lennon's throat at the beauty of it. "Er, are you sure?" she asked, eyes wide as they devoured the gown.

Erin smiled. "There's no one I'd be happier to see wear it."

Purple lights illuminated the white facade and striking modern architecture of the Arden Beach Museum of Science, reflecting off the calm waters of the bay. Royal palm trees lined the walkway as patrons poured inside. Banners with *Playmakers Quarterly's* logo on them—the famous sports magazine—welcomed them to their thirty-sixth annual awards ceremony.

Lennon and Erin walked arm in arm up the steps and into the aquarium wing, where guests mingled in tuxedos and gowns among white-clothed tables and glass cases showcasing colorful corals. Massive, circular windows surrounded them, peering into a blue world of marine life that was engaged in its own slow-motion mingling. A string quartet played an ethereal soundtrack fitting the otherworldly blue and green glow cast over the low-lit space.

Photographers and cameramen from various media outlets moved inconspicuously among the guests, wearing lanyards around their necks, including some Lennon recognized from the show's production crew. She was relieved the event's organizers had only agreed to let the show cover the event as bystanders, like other press in attendance, and not as active participants. As a result, she didn't have to worry about wearing a mic pack or doing any additional prep for it.

She'd had enough of filming entrance scenes and cutaways. Besides, she had plenty of other things on her mind to worry about that night.

Starting with feeling like a tiny fish foundering in a sea of strangers.

"Dad and Dylan should be around here somewhere," Erin said, declining a flute of champagne from a server in a crisp white jacket. "They had to be here early to get in as much elbow-rubbing as possible."

Lennon also politely shook her head, and the server moved on. "Dylan must be *loving* that," she remarked, sarcasm thick on her tongue.

"Shit. That's one of my professors," Erin lamented in a whisper.

"One of your favorites, I'm guessing?" Lennon followed her gaze to a woman with stick-straight posture and a pinched expression who looked like she was judging everyone in the room, including the fish.

"Apparently, her kink is to include stuff on tests she hasn't covered in class and penalize you for getting them wrong. Because of her, I'm having an *amazing* time fighting to maintain my 4.0 GPA." For Erin, that professor might as well have declared an act of war.

"Wow, everyone's dream professor. Should we try to push her into one of these tanks? I can cause a distraction."

"The sharks will probably mistake her for one of their own." Erin sighed. "I guess I should go do some of my own elbow-rubbing. Maybe we can come to an understanding. Please bail me out if I'm still fighting for my life in ten minutes."

"Sure. However, if you end up needing bail *money*, I'll have to go find your brother."

"Let's hope it doesn't come to that."

"Says the girl who kicked her fifth-grade P.E. teacher in the shin because he said girls couldn't play baseball."

"I said let's *hope*."

Erin untangled her arm from Lennon's and approached the couple standing beside one of the floor-to-ceiling, circular windows showcasing the main tank. As Erin flashed the rigid woman a megawatt smile, Lennon, now left to her own devices, fought the urge to run after her. She drifted aimlessly through the crowd, attention latching on to one of the coral exhibits in the middle of the room to help her feel less awkward. She read the accompanying information, then peered into the cylindrical fish tank, the size of a small car, and studied the beautiful, vibrant structure around which tiny fish floated.

A figure in a fitted black tux appeared on the opposite side of the vertical tank as the small blue tang she'd been watching swam around the coral toward him.

Dylan smiled as their eyes met through the glass, the water's cerulean glow refracting on its subtle ripples, encapsulating him in a dreamlike bubble. Her breath caught in her throat. His thick, brown hair was styled in graceful waves, his short beard neatly trimmed above a black bow tie.

Damn, he looked handsome.

For a moment, they were the only two people drifting among the coral, the tension in her head and heart floating away.

If only they could stay in that bubble forever.

Dylan moved to his right and she to her left, meeting each other at the end of the glass. He reared back slightly as they came into full view of each other. His lips parted, eyes taking in the strapless, black sheath gown that clung to her figure, a slit cutting a line from her left thigh to where the fabric pooled around a simple pair of stiletto sandals. Fitted detached sleeves hugged her arms from her biceps to her wrists, an elegant updo leaving her shoulders bare.

"Wow," he released on a breath.

"You recognize it?"

Dylan's gaze rose back to hers, somewhat dazed. "What?" He studied the dress again. Recognition sparked a second later. "My mom had a dress like that," he recalled quietly.

"It is hers. Your mom's. I didn't have anything to wear, so Erin let me borrow it."

"She wore it the night my dad was inducted into the Hall of Fame. I have a photo of them."

Lennon scrutinized his dark eyes, trying to read the emotion in them. "Are you OK?"

The corners of his mouth gently lifted. Dylan nodded. "Yeah." The muscles in his neck strained, like he was holding back.

Lennon began to lift her arm to touch him, but another server—this time a woman—appeared at her left with a small tray of champagne flutes. "Good evening," she said with a pleasant smile. "Champagne?"

Dylan cleared his throat. "Uh, no. Thank you."

Observing the tension in his shoulders he was trying to hide, the realization swiftly hit her. "Do you have any sparkling water?" Lennon asked.

"Yes, ma'am. How many would you like?"

"Three, please." Lennon looked at Dylan. "One for Erin when she gets back."

Once the server had excused herself and glided away, Lennon took a step closer to Dylan. Quietly, she asked, "Is this your first event like this since …"

Since the accident.

His wistful expression was all the confirmation she needed.

"Eddie wants the board members to see my progress," Dylan explained, tugging down the cuffs of his jacket. "Which is the nice way of saying, try to get the board to hate me a little less so there's a shot in hell they'll let me back on the team next season."

"That's a lot of pressure for one evening."

His lips curved in a wan smile, watching the little blue fish swim back around to the other side of the tank. "Could be worse. You could've said 'no' to coming with me."

Lennon's chest swelled, and her heart floated in the vacant space, turning all the vibrant colors of the sea life surrounding them.

The server returned, handing them the flutes of sparkling water before gracefully departing again.

Lennon raised her glass. "To fresh starts."

Dylan smiled. "And old friends."

They clinked their glasses together.

The string quartet played a cover of Billie Eilish's *Ocean Eyes* as they wandered the exhibits. Erin soon caught up with them, hopeful she'd successfully charmed her professor.

As they viewed a stingray and a shark gliding across one of the large picture windows, a crisp male voice commented, "It looks so peaceful in there. You'd never know one was the other's predator."

They all turned to Edward Carmichael as he stepped in next to Dylan. Rhett put his arm around Erin. Eddie stood a few inches shorter than the other two men, but what he lacked in height, he made up for in quiet, palpable confidence. Growing up with a silver spoon in his mouth had imbued him with the composure of a man who knew the power a simple flick of his pen could wield.

"Interesting way to describe baseball," Dylan quipped. "Good to see you, Mr. Car—Eddie." He corrected himself off a look from the older man.

"I'm glad you're here. You look great." Eddie settled his hand on Dylan's shoulder. "Though, of course, not as good as these beautiful ladies." He smiled warmly at Erin and Lennon as they each hugged Rhett in greeting.

"Is the award they're giving you tonight one for flattery?" Erin questioned.

"I can't take credit for speaking the truth." Eddie gave her a gentle peck on the cheek. His attention then slid to Lennon through his thick, black-framed glasses. "Well, this is a nice surprise. Dylan didn't tell me he was bringing a date." He sent Dylan an inquisitive look, a glint in his eyes.

To save Dylan from having to navigate the implication, Lennon joked, "He said these events were boring, so being the great friend that I am, I agreed to keep him company."

"Ah. That is mighty gregarious of you." Eddie glanced between them, seemingly unconvinced but cordially playing along. "They could put a toddler on a sugar high to sleep, couldn't they? They lured me here with the promise of an award, and I never refuse an opportunity to have my ego publicly stroked."

"I hear you're receiving a Lifetime Achievement Award," Lennon said. "I'd suffer through boredom for that, too."

"Yeah. Feels a little like a back-handed compliment, though. Are they trying to tell me in a nice way that it's time to retire?" Eddie laughed good-naturedly. "It's good to see you again, Lennon." He studied her and Dylan for a beat, then passed a glance around the room. "My daughter's here somewhere. She'll be excited to see you all."

"She should be graduating pretty soon," Rhett commented.

"Yep, her master's program ends in the spring. I'm proud of her, but eight years away from home has been … a long time. We're not all spoiled with our daughters studying in Arden Beach and working on the road with us," Eddie said, looking at Erin and Rhett.

Rhett smiled warmly. "Savannah'll be running Carmichael Enterprises with you soon enough."

Eddie's smile seemed to falter slightly, something passing over his eyes. Lennon wondered if it had something to do with him potentially selling the team, though she wasn't sure why that would affect his other businesses.

Someone stole Eddie's attention across the room. "Oh, hey—there's the commissioner. And he's talking to a couple of the board members. Perfect." He fixed his attention on Dylan. "Time to work your magic, kid."

The reaction was infinitesimal—a minute flinch at the corners of Dylan's eyes—but Lennon noticed it. Both older men regarded him with expectancy. Lennon discreetly brushed her fingers against his. When he met her gaze, she sent him an encouraging look. "You've got this."

One corner of his mouth gently rose.

As Dylan walked off with Eddie toward the commissioner, Erin said, "I'll refresh these," taking Lennon's empty flute. She'd been drinking as if something in the water could calm her nerves. "Dad, you want anything?"

Rhett shook his head. "I'm good. Thanks, honey."

Erin disappeared into the crowd. Lennon's heart beat a hard rhythm in her chest as Dylan approached the group of men and one woman across the room.

"Erin gave you that dress?"

Lennon turned to Rhett, who faced the aquarium with his hands in his pockets, glancing sidelong at her gown as the water cast him in a cerulean glow. He'd never been one to reveal much, but she sensed the ghosts behind his eyes. Her heart softened.

"Just for tonight," Lennon answered.

Their eyes met momentarily, his expression a cryptic mixture of wistful and stony, before he followed a school of fish beyond the glass again. Together, they watched the group of dozens of silver fish wind through the water as one.

"Amazing how they instinctively move together. It turns them into this formidable force against predators hundreds of times their size. But if one loses focus and falls out of line, it becomes a target. Its chances of survival plummet."

The school of fish cut across the glass, then looped around a rock formation and back, their shape morphing but never losing harmony.

"Dylan lost focus, and look where it got him," Rhett remarked, voice dropping low to keep the statement between them. "It's imperative he doesn't lose it again."

Lennon's abdomen tightened. "He's more focused than I've ever seen him. And you know I've seen him at his worst."

"He needs to stay that way, or he'll lose everything we've worked so hard to build."

"He seems committed."

"That's because he got a taste of losing it all," Rhett said. "The game, the team—it has to be everything to him. He can't afford to get distracted again. None of us can." He rolled his tongue around his mouth in thought, the weight of that statement thickening the air. "I get the idea behind doing the show, even if I disagree with it. But that needs to be where the distractions end."

It took her a moment to understand what he was getting at—until he settled his gaze on her. For once, his expression spoke volumes.

"You're worried I'm a distraction?" Lennon asked, caught off guard. His unwavering stare wasn't simply an affirmation. It was a declaration. "We aren't dating. We're just friends."

A small chuckle rumbled out of him as he briefly broke eye contact. After a beat, Rhett said, "The game and his team should be his only friends right now."

"With all due respect, I disagr—"

"It's barely been six months, Lennon. Do you honestly think he can handle more than what's currently on his plate?"

The question stunned her to silence. Or more so, its implied subtext did. *He couldn't juggle you and his career before. What makes you think he can now, when the pressure is at its highest?*

"I know firsthand how much this game takes from you," Rhett continued, solemnness weighing down the words. "What has to be sacrificed. Either by you or the people you love."

The implications slowly sank in.

"Man, it took me forever to track down someone without

booze," Erin said as she returned, two freshly topped flutes of sparkling water in hand. "Ironically, I had to go to the actual bar."

"Thanks," Lennon said, accepting one of them. She took a sip as she tried to regain her equilibrium.

"I wonder how Dylan's doing," Erin mused, eying him across the room.

Rhett gave Lennon a meaningful look. "We'll know soon enough."

"Excuse me. I'm going to find the restroom," Lennon said, her stomach uneasy. Erin took her glass back and directed her toward the bathrooms, to which she made a hasty exit.

Lennon took a few minutes for herself in the quiet restroom to get her racing mind under control. Her hands shook a little as she ran them under the faucet. She touched up her lipstick, made sure her hair was in place and no toilet paper was stuck to her shoes, and then took a deep breath, readying herself for the rest of the evening.

As Lennon exited the restroom in a quiet corridor of the museum, someone called out her name. She turned to a man with a small gut poking through a cheap and slightly wrinkled tuxedo. A press badge hung around his neck.

Her instincts thrummed.

"I'm not going to talk about him," Lennon stated firmly.

A pair of wiry brows jumped up his forehead. Following a breath, a low chuckle scratched his throat. "You're a quick one. Is that why it didn't work out? Couldn't get anything past you."

"You're obviously not here to do a story on me."

"Something tells me it would be a good one." A tiny smirk touched his lips. "You're right, though. I am interested in Dylan's story. The real one. I'm Harold Cranston, freelance journalist."

"You can watch the show when it streams, Harold." Lennon turned on her heel.

"If you think a reality show is the best way to get your side of the story out, I hate to be the one to break it to you, but … you're being naive," Harold said bluntly. She reluctantly stopped. "The genre's name is an oxymoron. They're entertainment, not documentaries. They're going to exploit and twist what you give them to their benefit, and their benefit only. Especially if you're working with the likes of Huey Donaldson." Contempt dripped from the name.

Lennon cocked a dubious brow. "As if you won't?"

Harold's expression hardened, like he'd taken offense. "I told you—I care about the truth. I'm not the only person interested in his story, but I am the only one willing to listen to the actual source rather than draw my own narrative to make a quick buck."

"Thanks for the concern, but we've got it under control," Lennon said with a glib smile. She continued down the corridor.

Harold followed her. "Has anyone questioned the convenient timing of you showing up in Arden Beach and spending time with your rich, famous ex-husband a month after your record deal fell through?" Her smile faltered as her stomach pinched. "Pretty good way to create more sympathy for the recovering baseball star. Can't trust anyone around him, even his ex-wife. No wonder he spiraled …"

Lennon dug her nails into her clutch, swallowing the pressure tightening in her throat.

"What does your family think about all of this?" Harold asked.

She stopped again and sent him a withering look as he came up beside her. "You mean you *don't* already know everything about me?"

Harold chuckled. "I'd rather hear it from you. Something tells me people aren't too interested in what you have to say, but more in what they *want* you to say."

That hit deep in her core.

Lennon kept her expression neutral, but inside, the thread

Rhett had pulled unraveled further. She hated how perceptive this guy was. How much he was getting under her skin.

Harold narrowed his eyes. He tapped the flaps of his jacket, seemingly thinking to himself. "I'm going to give you some advice, Lennon," he said, his voice softening a little. "As long as you tie yourself to Dylan, you're going to be in his shadow. His mistakes are a reflection on your judgment, so long as you're connected to him. Right now, to the world, you're a player in *his* story. And if he falls again—by his own doing or by the hand of others who have a vested interest in seeing him fail, of which there are many—you need to be careful he doesn't take you down with him."

CHAPTER 20

Dylan

Dylan's attention waned as the commissioner droned on about the yacht he'd rented for his recent two-month vacation in the Mediterranean. He'd politely listened to Bud Walden go on about it for the last ten minutes, and while Dylan was relieved the conversation wasn't focused on him, the anticipation of its inevitable shift in that direction had his blood hopping.

He wished he had something to take the edge off. Something—anything—to ease the pressure cooker in his chest. He avoided looking at the glass of scotch in Bud's hand and the champagne flutes held by the other board members.

Dylan's gaze wandered past the commissioner's shoulder, only to land on another guest holding a glass of whiskey. Dylan followed it as the man raised it to his mouth to take a sip. His own hand twitched at his side, clenching and flexing.

"You own one, don't you, Ed?" Bud asked.

"I did," Eddie replied. "I recently sold it."

"Ah. Wish I'd known. I'm in the market for one." Bud cocked

his head, pausing a moment. "Word on the grapevine is you're considering selling something else."

Dylan's attention snapped to Bud, while the commissioner and the other two board members focused on Eddie.

"I presume you mean the rumors about selling the team," Eddie said, unflustered.

"There have been rumblings," remarked Barbara Callaghan-Spencer, a grocery chain heiress who took her father's spot on the league's board when he recently retired. Diamonds hung from her ears, matching the ones circling her neck.

"I assure you, I'd tell you something if there was something to tell. I'm too excited for what the team has in store, especially when Dylan returns next season." Eddie put his hand on Dylan's shoulder, smiling. The ease with which Eddie conveyed unwavering confidence when Dylan knew what was really going on was one of his most impressive talents. He needed to work on own bullshitting skills.

"Your injury was pretty bad. Are you sure you'll be ready by then?" asked Clifford Boucher, a technology mogul after whom the observatory in that very museum was named.

"I do, sir," Dylan said, projecting Eddie's confidence.

"Whether he's ready physically isn't the most important issue," Barbara stated. She pinned her icy gaze on him. "You've had questionable behavior since you were signed to the minors. That was, what, almost seven years ago? Why should we believe anything has actually changed since spring training, and this miraculous turnaround isn't just … temporary?" The little smile on her face was devoid of warmth.

Everyone's attention deferred to Dylan.

"Because I hadn't accepted that I had a problem until the accident," Dylan answered earnestly. He didn't need to bullshit his way through this one. "I was in denial, but that was a rude awakening. I couldn't ignore the truth anymore. I was putting the work into the game but not myself. Now I am. That's what's different." He held her gaze even as she regarded him with incredulity. "And I respect your skepticism. Trust is earned. I'm doing everything I can to deserve the league's, the team's, and the public's trust again. If I get a second chance—" Dylan's focus swept over each board member in turn "— I promise, I won't take it for granted."

Barbara's lips gently curled, a condescending gleam in her eye. "They've trained you well."

The suggestion he was insincere was a slap in the face. Dylan dropped his eyes to his sparkling water, biting his derisive smile through the inside of his cheek.

"Baseball is a family sport," Barbara said, addressing the others. "It's supposed to uplift people and represent the backbone of what this country stands for. I think we've strayed too far from that, and it's high time we returned to our core values." She fixed her attention on Dylan again. "Our players should be role models, not cautionary tales."

She may as well have shoved his face into the ground and stepped over him. Frustration burned up his neck. He didn't know what to say without making it worse.

"Heroes who have fallen and had the strength to get back up are more inspiring than those who pretend to be perfect," a different female voice interjected. Everyone's attention turned to Savannah Carmichael, the tall, gazelle-like brunette who appeared at Dylan's side. "We've all made mistakes. Most of us are just lucky we don't have to live them out in the public eye." Savannah smiled at Barbara. "I mean, imagine if your affair with your husband when he was still married to his pregnant first wife had been splashed all over the news, Mrs. Spencer. I doubt the public would've been very forgiving."

Bud nearly choked on a sip of scotch, giving a gentle pound to his chest as he coughed while Clifford and Eddie stifled smiles. Meanwhile, Barbara bristled, her eyes shooting daggers at the young Carmichael.

"Dylan is exactly the modern role model we need," Savannah

said, addressing the men with calm authority. "Someone who takes responsibility for their mistakes and doesn't let them define them." The earnestness in her eyes as she looked at Dylan touched him. The list of those willing to champion him was short these days. He didn't take those who did for granted. "That's what the game teaches us, right? When you strike out, you try again. And you keep trying until you win. That's how legends are made."

Eddie smiled proudly at his daughter while Bud and Clifford appeared to ponder her statement. Barbara, meanwhile, remained a statue.

"She's right," Eddie agreed.

"If you'll excuse me, I'm going to steal Dylan," Savannah said, linking her arm through his. "We haven't seen each other since last Christmas, and knowing us, I probably won't see him again until the next one."

"I'll catch up with you in a bit," her father said, eying both of them.

As they strolled away from the group, Dylan whispered in her ear, "Thanks for saving my ass, Sav."

"No need to thank me. Having an excuse to insult Barbara Spencer made my night. She needs to find a new husband to steal. Maybe then she'd be a fraction less miserable."

They slowly wound through the crowd, keeping their voices low. "You ever considered going into politics?"

"I am in politics. It's called business."

Dylan released a dark chuckle. "Yeah, I'm realizing that's another name for pro sports, too. At least you like it."

"*Like* is a strong word. I'm … *accustomed* to it," Savannah said breezily. "And, like you pointed out, very good at it."

"The apple didn't fall far from the empire."

"Ditto."

Dylan cast her a sideways glance. In her heels, they were the same height. "Have you ever considered doing something else?"

"You mean, walk away from CE?" she asked, referring to

Carmichael Enterprises. Off his affirmative look, she canted her head, scrutinizing him. "Please tell me you haven't had anything to drink."

"Just five glasses of whiskey and a few shots." He threw her a look as she dismissively turned away. "I'm serious. Are you happy about moving back? Joining the company."

Savannah's arm seemed to tense slightly against his, though her expression remained unbothered, exactly like her father's. "I've been preparing for this my whole life. Of course, I'm ready."

"That's not what I asked."

Savannah appraised him now. They were roughly the same age, but she'd always possessed a poise and gravity that felt worlds ahead. "We're two of the luckiest people in this room. We've had to work hard, but the opportunities were always there waiting for us. We didn't have to fight just to get a foot in the door. I won't ever take that for granted."

Dylan couldn't argue with that. He felt that gratitude in his bones.

"And it's an honor to be part of something so special," she added. "To carry on something bigger than me."

He smirked. "Spoken like a true politician."

Savannah slid a glare his way, though the corner of her mouth quirked up. Up ahead, his father and sister were engaged in conversation by a different window into the aquarium than the one he'd left them. He searched the space around them, but Lennon wasn't there.

"Sometimes, I daydream about it, though," Savannah admitted, pulling his attention back to her. "I wonder what it would be like to be able to choose a different future, something entirely my own. Who I might have been in a different life." Her eyes went distant, somewhere only she could see. After a moment, she met his gaze. "But everyone does that. We always think the grass is greener on some other imaginary side, but it's a fantasy. I'm choosing to water what's real."

A handful of paces away from Rhett and Erin, Dylan came to a stop. He guided Savannah into a hug. "You're a good one, Sav."

"*Ew*, don't tell anyone else that. You'll ruin my reputation." Savannah hugged him back. Quietly, she added, "So are you."

Dylan smiled before they parted. As they approached his father and sister, he said, "Look who I found."

Savannah lifted an eyebrow. "Look who *you* found? How quickly my valiant gesture has been forgotten."

"I don't know what you're talking about."

"Must be all those balls you've taken to the head affecting your short-term memory."

"More like *selective* memory," Erin remarked. "Seems to be a defect in the male DNA."

Rhett and Dylan exchanged a look. "Don't say anything, son."

"Trust me, I wasn't planning to."

"At least you can train them," Erin said with a wink.

Savannah hugged them both. "Now, there's a face I haven't seen in a while," she said over Rhett's shoulder, her attention latching onto Lennon. Relief settled over Dylan.

As Lennon joined them, something seemed off. She looked shaken, even as she smiled. "Hey, Savannah."

"You look fucking amazing." Savannah's dark eyes traveled the length of Lennon's gown.

"So do you, as always."

"I heard you've been living in New York. Are you back for good?"

"Yeah. Well, while the show is filming, anyway."

"What show?"

Lennon glanced at Dylan, who jumped in with the question, "Eddie hasn't told you?"

"Are you kidding? My father's the worst with gossip," Savannah remarked. "They're not trainable in everything."

Dylan cleared his throat. "Lennon and I are doing a reality show together." His attention bounced to his father for a second, who looked away, disapproval sharp in his eyes. It sliced across Dylan's ribs.

Savannah observed him like she was waiting for the punchline. "Are you messing with me?"

"They're not," Erin confirmed with a bounce of her eyebrows.

Savannah's eyes widened slightly. The corner of her red lips lifted in a small smile. "Oh—you have to tell me everything."

"Good evening," an elegant female voice said over the speakers. "At this time, we ask you to please take your seats in the Brenner Hall. The ceremony will begin in five minutes."

"Immediately after the ceremony, you're catching me up to speed," Savannah amended.

"Should I mention they're here filming?" Dylan asked.

"I'm going to kill my father."

"At least wait until after he receives his lifetime achievement award," Dylan suggested.

CHAPTER 21

Lennon

Everyone filed into the Brenner Hall, a two-story, dome-shaped room with a large window at the ceiling's center offering a view into the aquarium. Marine life floated above them. A stage stood at the far end while several round tables, each with seating for eight, filled the rest of the space.

The Stricklands and Carmichaels had a table reserved at the front. Eddie and his wife, Janine, joined them. Lennon's gaze wandered the room, almost missing that Dylan had pulled out a chair for her and waited for her to take a seat. "Oh—thanks." She smiled at the gesture.

As they settled in, Lennon continued to search for Harold, assuming the press were allowed into the ceremony. Her spine pressed rigidly against the chair's gold spindles.

Dylan rested his hand on the back of her chair, leaning toward her. "You OK?" he asked quietly.

"Yeah. Fine."

"You're lying," he whispered. "Did something happen while I was gone?"

Just your father and an uncomfortably perceptive stranger telling me I made a mistake coming back.

"We'll talk later," Lennon insisted.

Dylan assessed her a moment longer, concern etched in his expression, but he ultimately relented.

Once all the guests had arrived, the media followed, lining up at the back of the room. Two High Wave Productions cameramen flanked the space to cover both angles while her buddy Harold stood beside the one directly facing Lennon and Dylan. He sent her a smile and a little nod.

Lennon subtly scratched her nose with her middle finger, then planted her attention at the front of the room as the lights dimmed. A statuesque, voluptuous brunette took the stage, introducing herself as one of the magazine's frequent swimsuit cover models and the ceremony's host for the evening.

Dylan was right—the ceremony *was* boring. The magazine handed out several awards for people in the sports industry, some of whom were athletes, but most operated behind the scenes. After a very long hour and a half, it was finally time for the Lifetime Achievement Award.

"To present one of the most prestigious awards of the evening is a special guest—one of *Playmakers Quarterly*'s esteemed board members," announced the host, a little glint in her eye. "Please welcome to the stage, Nolan Pierce."

As the room erupted in applause, the Strickland/Carmichael table went notably still. It took a few seconds for the name to click in before Lennon remembered he was the billionaire trying to buy the Tidebreakers.

The son of the man Dylan was convinced had arranged his father's injury at Rhett's first shot at the National Series.

The color drained from Dylan's face. Lennon followed his attention to Rhett, whose stoic expression had turned particularly cold. They exchanged glances around the table. Eddie silently communicated his displeasure to their circle but raised his hands to join the applause, encouraging them to do the same.

A man in a slim-cut tuxedo jogged up the stage steps as he buttoned his jacket. Though not classically handsome in the way some of the athletes that had graced the stage that night were, he was roguishly good-looking—a slightly crooked nose, a full bottom lip, and dark eyes framed by a strong brow that had the beautiful host preening when he fixed them on her. He carried himself with a smooth, easy stride and a hint of trouble in his smile, which deepened as he took her hand. He whispered something that made her blush before he settled in at the podium.

"Good evening," Nolan said as the applause abated. "I'd apologize for being late, but judging by the glazed look in everyone's eyes, for once, I may be the smartest person in the room." Laughter trickled through the audience. "The board and I will have a chat about making things more exciting next year. I almost didn't make it tonight, but as luck would have it, I was able to get here in time to hand out the most prestigious award of the night." His gaze found Eddie, sharpening around the edges. He inclined his head slightly. "Though, I'll admit, when they asked me to present the Lifetime Achievement award to Edward Carmichael, no one was more surprised than me." Nolan paused to watch the audience, the room suspended in quiet uncertainty. "I mean, the man doesn't even have grey hair yet. At least, not that we can see."

Everyone relaxed into another wave of laughter. Eddie smiled tightly.

"Actually, I admire Edward," Nolan said, his rich, warm timbre sinking lower. "It's no secret we have our differences. But what we do have in common is our dedication and love of baseball, and I respect commitment when I see it. Over the last few decades, he and his family have contributed more than $100 million in funding and resources to youth and outreach programs, particularly in underprivileged communities. If he did decide to walk away from it all tomorrow, he'd have a hell of a run under his belt."

Nolan regarded Eddie again, this time with a smile loaded with subtext. A muscle pulsed along Dylan's jawline. Lennon reached out under the table, curling her fingers around his hand resting on his leg. He exhaled slowly and squeezed her hand back, his glare fixed on the stage.

"Everyone, give a round of applause for Edward Carmichael," Nolan declared, leading the charge.

Thankfully, the Lifetime Achievement Award was the last of the evening, with only a few closing statements to follow. While the Carmichaels hung back to accept congratulations from fellow attendees, Dylan clearly couldn't get out of that room fast enough. He bolted for the doors.

Lennon and Erin followed him out to the exhibits, where small clusters of guests were passing through to head to the bar, restroom, or exit entirely, while the majority stayed behind, giving him space to let off steam in a quiet corner. The press hadn't even dispersed yet.

"Well, that surprise was about as fun as your period starting during sex," Erin remarked as she leaned against the smooth wall, crossing her arms over her chest.

"I didn't even know he was involved with PQ." Lennon gently arched her back in a stretch, thankful to be standing and for the blood to be flowing back to her legs. "That guy seems to have his hands in everything."

Dylan paced between them, hands shoved in his pockets. "Yeah, well, I'll be damned if he gets them on the Tidebreakers."

The man didn't know stillness when something bothered him. It was like all the energy from it went straight to his muscles and the only way he could expel it was by moving. Lennon imagined that was part of why he liked to drink—it was the easy way to shut it off. Easier than it had been to talk to his wife about it. An all too familiar sense of dread pressed against her ribs as she watched a storm build behind his eyes.

"That sounds dangerously close to a threat," Nolan remarked as he strolled up to them, one hand relaxed in his pants pocket. He sounded almost bored as he checked his watch. "Should I be concerned?"

Dylan came to a stop but didn't bother turning all the way to face him, glowering at him sidelong. "We don't all resort to hurting people to get what we want. That's more your family's style, Nolan."

"You sure about that?" Nolan shifted his gaze to Lennon. She scowled at him for using their marriage as a way to hit back at Dylan. His eyes ventured lower with a devilish glint, hooking on her dress.

Dylan stepped between them, partially blocking Nolan's view of Lennon. "Don't you have a company to poach or a streaming channel to go talk shit on about things you know nothing about?"

Nolan simply canted his head, momentarily regarding Dylan with amusement before returning his attention to Lennon. "Tell me. What is it about the allure of baseball players that makes smart, beautiful women abandon their better judgment?"

"Just say you can't get a date without paying for it, Nolan," Erin remarked, still reclining against the wall. It was past the early bird's bedtime.

Nolan chuckled a deep, throaty sound. "We're all paying for it in some form, aren't we?" He winked at her. Erin's apathetic expression didn't budge.

"I don't see anyone here supporting you," Dylan pointed out. "All that money can't buy you respect."

The corner of Nolan's mouth ticked up. His smirk held, but his eyes turned cold as they landed on Dylan. "No. But apparently, a name can."

Dylan matched his smug demeanor with a slant of his lips. "You're really hung up on that, aren't you?" He shrugged a shoulder. "I guess it makes sense. Your father couldn't make it as a baseball player on his own merit, and now, you're trying to buy your way in.

But that's not working so far, either, so all you can do is throw a fit about how unfair life is because you're named after a twice-bankrupt businessman who made his name from exploiting people rather than athletes respected for their talent and hard work."

A long, soft whistle blew through Nolan's lips. "Big words from a guy who tanked his marriage and career because he can't keep his shit together, and now he's waiting for Daddy Strickland and Uncle Carmichael to bail him out. I'm curious, how long do you think you'll last if they aren't there to clean up your messes?"

Beneath their calm façades, something volatile was brewing. A chorus of familiar voices spilled through the doors as Rhett and the Carmichaels emerged from Brenner Hall. Their laughter died unceremoniously as attention fell to the heated confrontation between Dylan and Nolan.

Lennon noticed one of the High Wave Productions cameramen looming in the corner. He'd caught it all.

Shit.

"Everything OK out here?" Rhett asked gruffly, the question posed to Dylan while holding Nolan in his crosshairs. Next to him, Eddie cast a shrewd glare while Savannah studied the scene with quiet intrigue.

Nolan emitted a soft, derisive laugh under his breath. "Impeccable timing."

Erin linked her arm through Dylan's and Lennon followed suit on the other side. "Come on, Dylan. Let's go home," Erin said. "If I wanted to watch a child throw a tantrum, I'd go hang out at a playground."

As the three of them passed Nolan, Lennon glowered at him. His eyes followed her with something like pity.

They swept through the museum, following signs for the event, which led them to a different exit where the valet was set up. They stepped out into the warm, fresh air under a porte-cochère that faced a street perpendicular to the bay. The sounds of engines and horns from Saturday night traffic contrasted with the quiet, elegant museum. Dylan and Erin handed their tickets to the valet, and two attendants promptly broke into a jog toward the parking lot to retrieve their vehicles.

Dylan blew out a gust of air as he drove his fingers through his hair. "That son of a—"

"Hey, Dylan! Is it true you're considering offers from other teams?"

Bright camera flashes burst in rapid succession as a mob surrounded them. It all happened so fast, Lennon didn't even see them coming. Suddenly, several people walled them in. They shouted invasive questions at Dylan and shoved photographs, jerseys, and baseball cards at him to sign.

"Is your suspension going to be permanent?"

"Do you think your father should retire?"

As they all fought for his attention, a man barreled into Lennon, slamming her against the tall valet desk. Sharp pain exploded in her arm and shoulder. She folded her arms against her torso as the stranger's heavy, sweaty body pressed against her, caging her in as he thrust a jersey at Dylan while he recorded him on his phone.

"HEY! Don't touch her." Dylan fisted the large man's shirt and shoved against his chest with his forearm. The crowd gasped as the stranger, a man around his father's age, almost lost his balance, his phone flying out of his hand and crunching against the pavement.

Dylan turned his back on everyone, creating a barrier between them and Lennon with his body. His attention was locked on her, tense and protective.

"I'm OK," Lennon assured him, nodding. Her heart jackhammered beneath her ribs. They both searched for Erin, who waved at them from the doors where she'd retreated from the crowd. Two security guards emerged beside her. They tried to tame the crowd, but the orders they shouted got lost in the chaos.

"Is Nolan Pierce going to buy the Tidebreakers?" someone yelled. Cellphones and printed photographs jostled around Dylan's shoulders.

Dylan's nostrils flared, a firestorm in his eyes. He glanced over Lennon's head and his gaze sharpened. "Come on. Stay close to me." His fingers threaded through hers. "Move out of the way," Dylan yelled, shouldering his way through the crowd toward the street. Lennon gripped him tightly as she followed him to a luxury sports car as the valet attendant rolled to a stop in front of them. Dylan yanked open the passenger door and guided her inside.

"Wait, Erin—" Lennon said.

"I'm right here," Erin shouted back as she came around Dylan's side. Her convertible was pulling in behind his.

Lennon climbed inside and Dylan shut the door, muffling the noise. Through the rearview mirror, she watched Dylan and the valet attendant help Erin settle safely into hers. She kept him in her sightline until he'd jumped in beside her, the shouting momentarily swelling again before he slammed the door, shutting it out.

As he pulled the car forward, Lennon locked eyes with Harold, who stood off to the side. The rock in Lennon's stomach sank lower. The journalist quirked an eyebrow at her as if to say, "I told you so."

CHAPTER 22

Dylan

The sharp hiss of a steam wand welcomed Dylan into Bembe's Café, followed closely by the rich aroma of Cuban coffee and freshly baked bread. Music with the café's namesake, a Cuban drumbeat, blended with the chatter of patrons and the bustle of baristas within the cracked plaster walls. He removed his sunglasses, his eyes adjusting from the high sun as he scanned the tables, bar, and seating area.

He found Lennon sipping a *cafecito* in one of the thick leather armchairs.

"Hey." Dylan smiled. The sight of her was better than a shot of espresso.

Lennon looked up from a magazine in her lap, legs tucked under her to the side and the hem of her black mini skirt riding up her thigh. He thought of the tattoo that marked her a bit higher, a line about the wings of butterflies from Queen's song *The Show Must Go On* written in a small script. He used to love tracing it, with his fingers and his—

"Hey." She smiled back. "That one's yours."

It took a half-second longer for him to make sense of her words than it should have, his gaze darting to the steaming espresso cup on the mosaic-tiled coffee table. "Oh—thanks." He lowered himself into the armchair perpendicular to hers and reached for the cup. Taking a sip, he relished the sweet, frothy *la crema* on top.

"So, how've you been?" Lennon asked, the question a loaded one.

"Why, did something happen?" Dylan hedged with a dry, heavy dose of sarcasm. He reclined back in the chair, his legs spreading and arms resting leisurely as if his insides hadn't been in knots the past few days.

The media had been having a field day with what happened after the *Playmakers Quarterly* gala. They were eating up Dylan's "feud" with Nolan and his "outburst" against a fan. Videos of the latter had gone viral, and the public was divided on it. Half said he'd overreacted while others praised him for protecting Lennon.

He'd gotten a particularly contentious call from Eddie, who reminded him of his conversation with the board members and how he was supposed to be *avoiding* drama, not inviting it.

"I should be asking you that," Dylan said. He'd never forget the sight of her being shoved into that valet desk. He licked the froth from his lips as steam threatened to rise inside him again.

"For the millionth time, I'm fine." Though spoken with an edge of annoyance, a small smile tugged at Lennon's lips. It faded as her eyelashes lowered. "I appreciate you protecting me, but I'm sorry you had to. That they rushed you like that. It's not fair that you're getting shit for how you reacted."

"They can say whatever they want. I'd do it again."

Lennon's gaze lifted to his with surprise—and something else. Something that seared straight through his chest. The sounds of the café shrank behind the weight of her stare.

Ceramic crashing against the polished concrete floor broke the connection.

Dylan glanced back toward the noise where a woman was

profusely apologizing for her child knocking over an empty coffee cup. The young barista calmly waved it off as she fetched a broom.

"You never told me what was bothering you that night," Dylan said, recalling the shaken look in Lennon's eyes before the ceremony.

Lennon's shoulders curled in slightly as she shook her head. "Oh. It wasn't a big deal." She folded the magazine and dropped it on the coffee table. "Just some reporter that's been sniffing around. He cornered me when I came out of the bathroom, and it gave me the creeps."

Dylan leaned forward. "Some guy did *what*?"

"He's legit. I looked him up. He's trying to do a story on you."

"I don't give a shit if he's legit. That doesn't give him permission to stalk you. What's his name?"

"Harold Cranston. He's not the first one, but they usually stick to annoying phone calls." Lennon took a sip of her *cafecito* as if she were sharing an offhanded anecdote, but Dylan's stomach turned to lead.

"How many have there been?"

"I don't know. At least a dozen? Most of them were right after your accident, but I guess I should've expected things to pick up again now that we're doing the show together."

It felt like someone had punched him in the gut. After the accident, Dylan worried reporters would bother her. They were contacting everyone from old colleagues to his elementary school teachers. Erin confirmed some had, but a man approaching Lennon in person while she was alone crossed the line.

Anger burned in his chest. At the asshole who cornered her, and at himself for putting her in this position.

"Did he scare you?" Dylan asked.

"No. It was just …" Lennon chewed on her bottom lip. "Some things he said got under my skin. I shouldn't have let it." Her forehead crinkled, as though something had suddenly occurred to her. "Harold said he was at the gala because he contributes to *Playmakers*

Quarterly. He and Nolan had some similar takes on your situation. Do you think Nolan hired him to do the story?"

"I wouldn't put it past him." Dylan's expression hardened, the desire to protect her overwhelming him. "Tell me if that Harold guy or anyone else tries to bother you again. I'll take care of it."

Lennon released a soft sigh. "So, are you ever going to tell me the purpose of this impromptu rendezvous?" she questioned with a cocked brow.

Dylan checked his wristwatch. He'd been told to stop by for the meeting any time after two. In a few minutes now.

He stood, extending his hand with a smirk. "Come with me and find out."

The way Lennon's eyes danced with delight made his heart accelerate. She loved surprises, and he knew she'd especially love this one. She put her hand in his, his thumb brushing across her knuckles as she rose from the chair. As he quickly finished off his *cafecito*, she started toward the main door.

"This way," Dylan said, motioning toward the back of the café. Her eyebrows arched again.

Lennon followed him through a door that said, "EMPLOYEES ONLY." The barista and Dylan exchanged a nod as they passed through the hallway leading to the back door, which opened onto an alley. He punched a code into the lock on a wrought iron gate with "PRIVATE" etched into the elaborate design, leading them into a private courtyard tucked between the Spanish colonial buildings. Lennon shot him a look loaded with questions. All he gave her was a knavish smile.

They passed a large stone water fountain with bright blue mosaic tile burbling in the center of the courtyard, surrounded by lush tropical foliage, to a staircase concealed in the corner of the building. At the top, they were met with a pair of tall wooden doors embellished with more elaborate wrought iron and stained glass. Dylan pressed a button to the side with a small black camera above it, then casually shoved his hands in his denim pockets to wait.

"Where are we?" Lennon whispered. "Is this someone's house?"

Dylan dramatically lifted his shoulders and eyebrows in an "I don't know" gesture, earning an eye roll from her.

He was enjoying this too much.

After a few moments, a distorted shadow appeared through the glass, growing larger as someone approached. A beautiful, grey-haired woman opened the door, adjusting a flowy, short-sleeved cardigan in a bright floral pattern over her shoulders. Under it, a black leotard with leggings clung to her petite form. She smiled, eyes twinkling at the sight of him. "Hola, Dylan," she crooned flirtatiously.

"Hola, Agueda," Dylan said, smiling back. A slight blush rose to his cheeks under her stare. He canted his head. "This is Lennon."

"Nice to meet you, Lennon." Agueda stepped aside, opening the door wider for them.

"Nice to meet you, too."

Dylan gestured for Lennon to walk in first, then followed her into the circular foyer encompassed by a two-story rotunda. Arched windows surrounded the top, casting light on a breathtaking mural that depicted a heavenly, Michelangelo-like scene on the ceiling. The polished marble floor sparkled against textured walls.

"Perfect timing. I just finished Pilates," Agueda said. She fixed her short hair in a mirror hanging by the door. "Can I get you both something to drink?"

"I'm good, thank you," Dylan said, gently placing a hand on her arm and eliciting another smile from her.

It took Lennon a beat before she tore her eyes away from the ceiling. "No, thank you."

Agueda waved them to follow as she turned. "He's waiting in his study."

They followed her deeper into the home, which likely took up half the block. As they passed through the living room, a gilded gramophone trophy gleamed inconspicuously from one of the shelves among books and decor. He watched Lennon spot it, then mouth, "Who the fuck lives here?" to him.

"You'll see," Dylan mouthed back.

Down a wide hallway, multiple framed gold and platinum records adorned the wall. He could just imagine how much Lennon was freaking out inside. He smiled at the thought. They stopped at another pair of double doors, one of which was cracked open but angled away from them, obscuring the interior. Agueda knocked, then poked her head in. "Dylan's here."

"Send him in," a deep male voice answered.

Agueda returned, gesturing them in with a wink.

"*Gracias*," Dylan said, then glanced at Lennon, her expression a mix of anxiety and restrained excitement. He let her step in first, following closely behind.

Floor-to-ceiling windows stretched along the entire back of the office for an uninterrupted view of the strikingly blue Atlantic Ocean. It framed a large mahogany desk and two leather club chairs facing it, with an even more massive leather office chair on the opposite side. To the left, a white grand piano filled the corner. An imposing man stood at the window, staring out at the rolling sea.

He turned as they entered, regarding them with a slanted grin. "So, this is the girl you've been telling me about," he remarked in a thick Cuban accent.

As soon as Lennon saw his face, Dylan watched recognition strike.

"Lennon, this is—"

"—Oscar Alonso," she finished for him, reverent. "You're a legend. Wow, it's … such an honor to meet you."

"According to Dylan here, it's an honor for me to meet *you*," Oscar quipped as he came around the desk. Though he was in his seventies with thick salt-and-pepper hair, he looked like he could take someone down with a single punch without breaking a sweat. He shook Lennon's hand. "You should hire him as your publicist."

Dylan shrugged before accepting Oscar's greeting next. "I'm just telling the truth."

"He's easy to please. His walk-up song used to be *Good Vibrations*," Lennon jibed, to which Dylan answered with a glare.

"Well, I'm not," Oscar said squarely. He jabbed a thick thumb over his shoulder toward the grand piano in the corner of the room, positioned with a perfect view of the ocean and clear blue sky. "You play?"

"Yes, sir."

Oscar inclined his head toward the instrument. "Then, show me what you've got."

CHAPTER 23

Lennon

It was like an out-of-body experience. Lennon felt as if she was watching herself from a distance as she sat at a piano that probably cost more money than she had made in her entire life. She adjusted her skort. "What would you like to hear?"

"He says you write your own songs," Oscar remarked. She confirmed with a nod. "One of those, then. Whatever you feel. Let the muse tell you what to play."

Her muse was currently freaking out, but she told it to pull itself together. Chances like this were rare—*not* the time to freeze up. Lennon set her fingers on the keys, feeling their smooth surface, their weight. Her hands shook a little. She squeezed them into fists to steady them.

Lennon hadn't picked up a guitar or played her keyboard or even written anything since the label dropped her. Well over a month. It was the longest she'd ever gone without making music, and before that, she'd been beating it into submission in failed attempts to please the label. It'd been even longer since she played for her enjoyment. It felt like a piece of her had been missing.

Would that piece return on command after being neglected for so long?

What should she even sing?

The first song that came to mind was one the label had scrapped. It used to be one of her favorites to play, but she'd let it go without much of a fight because she assumed they knew better. They were the ones with millions of record sales and awards, after all. What if they'd been right about it? Better not risk it and find out now. Lennon quickly filed through the songs they *had* liked and landed on one she used for her demo, the one that had cinched her the record deal—a simple ballad about young love.

Having the person who inspired it standing behind her almost made her more nervous than playing for Oscar. Almost.

Time slowed, matching the rolling tide beyond the glass. Stretching her fingers over the keys, she took a deep, anchoring breath and began to play.

Lennon had performed that particular song so many times for various auditions that it came easily to her. She knew every inflection, every note like a well-practiced routine. By the end, when she brought it to a close on the last notes, she sighed with relief, satisfied with herself. A clean performance with no words stumbled, no pitch problems, no fumbled keys. Technically perfect.

As the final note drifted off, two sets of applause rang out behind her. Lennon turned to face them, gratitude warming her cheeks and chest, her skin buzzing.

"You wrote that?" Oscar confirmed, sitting on one hip on his desk.

"Yes, sir." Lennon's eyes briefly flicked to Dylan, who held an expression she couldn't quite read.

Oscar seemed to be in thought as he tapped his thumb against the other hand resting on his bent knee. His expression was also agonizingly unreadable.

Did he like it? Did he hate it? Was he about to tell her she needed to put all her eggs in the reality star basket and hope for the best?

Time slowed to a crawl again as she waited for him to speak. She glanced at Dylan again, who stood with his arms crossed, thumb rubbing absentmindedly across his chin as he watched Oscar. He met her gaze, and his eyes softened into a smile. One of pride and encouragement.

Lennon relaxed a little.

"The record label you were signed to," Oscar said, drawing their attention back to him. "Who were they?"

"Goldrush Records," she answered, the name tasting bitter on her tongue.

Oscar's mouth pressed into a disapproving line. "They don't take the time to develop their artists. They're too focused on the market—the market this, the market that." He shook his head. "I don't believe in that. I believe in *creating* the market. You make something great, the market follows. Everyone starts copying you rather than the other way around. Goldrush wants a machine to make easy money, and they do make a lot of it with that method, sure. Money is great; I love money. It makes life comfortable. But art—that's what gives life meaning." The corner of his mouth turned up in a smirk. "I want both. You make great art in this business, the money follows."

Oscar's ethos resonated with Lennon more than anything she ever heard from the label executives during her time at Goldrush. It felt *right*.

But what was he implying about *her*? That she wasn't making great art? She wondered if she'd made a mistake—maybe she should've played a different song.

"Why do you want to be a recording artist?" Oscar asked.

What a complicated question. She wished she had a good answer prepared. The record label had never asked her that; no one had. But it was something she should have thought to have ready.

After a moment, Lennon said the first thing that came to

mind. "Because of exactly what you said—art makes life worth living. Music has gotten me through every bad moment in my life and given me something to live for when everything else was falling apart around me. It's my one constant. It's there when I need to dance, when I need to cry, when I need to figure shit out. It's kept me company when I'm alone. It's helped me put the pieces back together when my heart was broken." Lennon swallowed, avoiding Dylan when she saw his head slightly dip. "If I can create music that does for someone else what so many artists have done for me, then I believe that's one of the best contributions I could make to the world. Like I'm paying it forward."

Oscar stared at her for a few long moments, and she was pretty sure her heart had stopped in the interim. Finally, his lips curved into a small but meaningful smile. "That's because you're a true artist," he stated. The blood suddenly rushed back through her system, her heart pumping fast, with a rush of … joy. "You have a beautiful voice, easy to listen to but distinct. Your writing has a lot of promise, too." He squinted in consideration, nodding. "You're talented."

Lennon's voice lodged in her throat for a second. "Thank you," she finally squeezed out. "I appreciate that."

"Did the label say why they ended things?"

"They said I wasn't fitting their 'creative vision,'" she answered, trying not to sound *too* bitter. And likely failing miserably.

Oscar chuckled, and she wondered if it was because she had, indeed, failed miserably. "It's good they dropped you," he said. "That's code for 'our analysts pinpointed a new trend, and you don't fit the mold.' Means you're not a karaoke chameleon. You have a distinct sound. Like an artist should." He opened a polished wooden box on his desk and removed a cigar, which he proceeded to unwrap. "What are your plans?"

Lennon reeled from the rush of his validation, not to mention the perspective shift he'd offered about her killed contract. She would have to process it all later when she was alone. She blew a gust of air through her lips. "Honestly—I don't know. I was cast on a reality show here in Arden Beach, hoping it would help me get some exposure and make connections. I'll probably start submitting demos again soon."

"Been making new music?" Oscar kept his attention on the cigar, carefully trimming the tip.

Lennon glanced at Dylan, who had been standing quietly to the side. She recalled him gently calling her out for avoiding her music since the label let her go. Instead of giving her an "I told you so" look, she found reassurance in his expression. *See, you're talented; there's no reason to hide.*

"I've been taking a break. I haven't felt very inspired lately," Lennon admitted, shame and guilt creeping in like she was admitting to neglect of a loved one, though it had felt more like being rejected by one.

"Breaks are good, so as long as they don't go on too long," Oscar advised. "It's a muscle. Don't let it atrophy."

A knock came at the door.

"Sorry to interrupt," Agueda said, then looked at Oscar with an expression that said, "get a load of this." She planted a fist on her hip. "Raquel is here for dinner."

Lennon's eyes widened slightly at the name—the one on several of the platinum albums hanging around his office that he'd produced. The same Latin pop albums Lennon herself owned and had practically worn out over the years.

Granted, he could know more than one Raquel ... .

Oscar shook his head languidly. "That woman is always early. Doesn't matter if it's a recording session or a party. She was even born premature," he said to Dylan and Lennon. Lennon's stomach clenched at the words *recording session.* "Tell her I'll be there in a minute."

Agueda disappeared down the hall.

Lennon decided not to express how big a fan she was of Raquel Rosas, and instead played it cool, despite the orchestra erupting inside her. Dylan's lips dimpled at the corners in amusement, undoubtedly aware that she was on the verge of losing her shit.

"Well, thank you for taking the time to meet with me," Lennon said. "It's been an honor and a pleasure." She rose from the piano stool, her legs a little shaky.

"You like Cuban food?" Oscar asked as he opened the box of cigars again.

"Who doesn't like Cuban food?" Lennon answered.

"I think it's a requirement when you live in South Florida," Dylan agreed.

"Stay then if you don't have other plans. My sister made *paella*. It's the best. Makes your tongue come out of your mouth and slap the back of your head."

For a moment, Lennon wondered if this had been part of Dylan's surprise, but when they exchanged a look, she realized he was as caught off guard as she was.

"We'd love to," Dylan said, a smile tugging at his lips as he watched Lennon, who tried not to nod too enthusiastically.

Oscar took out two more cigars from the box. He offered them to Dylan and Lennon, who politely declined. He shut the lid on the cigar box before standing. "Alright. *Vamos*. Let's eat."

Raquel was every bit the goddess Lennon had dreamt one of her childhood idols would be. She had glowing skin, humidity-defying hair, an intoxicating scent like someone had just been feeding her fruit in a tropical paradise, and apparently, the grace of an angel, not showing how unnerved she probably was when Lennon nearly broke into tears at the sight of her.

Lennon's humiliation was overshadowed by her unbridled joy. And shock.

"Good thing I brought tons of food. Let's go eat our feelings, babe," Raquel told Lennon as she wrapped an arm around her shoulders, leading her outside.

They dined on the large rooftop terrace overlooking the ocean while Oscar told the story of how he got his start in the music industry before he and Agueda immigrated from Cuba in the seventies. After they both lost their spouses—Agueda widowed, Oscar to multiple divorces—they moved in together, and Agueda took over managing the household.

Lennon could have spent all night listening to their wild stories from decades in the entertainment industry. Some of them felt illegal to hear. The famous names Agueda and Raquel casually dropped, much to Oscar's dismay, had Lennon's jaw hanging open.

After that night, she'd have enough material to blackmail half the music industry if she wanted to.

A particular club in Arden Beach, called The Starbird Lounge, came up a few times, as it had been one of their favorite haunts for decades. Raquel credited their weekly karaoke nights with helping her overcome her stage fright early in her career.

"I've never had stage fright, thankfully, but I have been feeling creatively … empty lately," Lennon shared as she reached for another piece of *plátanos maduros*. The savory, crisp texture of the fried crust mixed with the sweet, creamy interior was addictive. Her stomach was packed with Cuban bread, salad, and *paella*, but she couldn't stop herself from stuffing it with more. The flavors were an edible equivalent of a song you want to listen to over and over again.

"You can't force the muse. You must seduce her like a beautiful woman," Oscar said affectionately from the head of the table, his sister flanking the opposite end. He glanced at Dylan to his left, who offered a firm nod of agreement.

"He means feed her," Raquel interjected from beside Lennon, and laughter rippled across the table. "You need to fill up your creative well. Give it some nourishment. Have you been under any stress lately? Pressure?" Lennon snorted, and Raquel made a "there you go" motion with her fork. "That shit will suck the creativity right out of you. You're running on empty, babe."

Lennon picked at the remaining pieces on her plate. "I don't know what to do about it. Music usually helps me *de*-stress, and it's not doing its job lately."

"That's because you're treating it like one." Raquel leveled a sobering gaze on her.

The revelation hit Lennon like a ton of bricks. "Shit. You're right."

"You've put too much pressure on it to *do* something for you, to *be* something for you," Raquel continued, her soft Texan drawl coming through. It made a charming, melodic sound with her Mexican lilt. "When's the last time you played with music for the fun of it?"

The answer made Lennon's heart pinch. "Honestly? I don't know. And here I am calling myself an artist." That familiar shrinking feeling of not belonging slipped in. Her attention flicked to Dylan across the table. He seemed to have retreated within himself, too, his thumb gliding over the condensation on the rim of his glass as his thoughts wandered somewhere else.

To his relationship with baseball, she imagined.

"That's the most artist thing you could say," Oscar told her, drawing her attention to him. "Half my job was convincing them that they knew what they were doing."

Raquel's curls bounced with a reluctant nod. "It's true."

Lennon smiled. "You're like a musical godfather."

Oscar snapped his fingers, pointing at Lennon. "Hey, I like that. I need to call my lawyer and have that trademarked."

"You're retired," Agueda reminded him.

"Still in the business of being a legend," Lennon noted, and Oscar's eyes twinkled at her.

Raquel rolled hers. "No wonder he likes you. Words of affirmation are his love language."

"I helped you come out of your shell, didn't I?" Oscar retorted.

One of the staff members brought out a platter of homemade churros Raquel had made, along with a selection of chocolate, caramel, and *dulce de leche* for dipping. As everyone filled their plates, Dylan asked Oscar, "Hey, how's Miles doing?"

"Can't stop talking about winning the championship," Oscar said, pride gleaming in his smile. "Tells everyone with an ear. He's already excited about next season."

Dylan continued asking Oscar questions about this boy named Miles, who Lennon gathered was one of Oscar's grandsons. She dunked a small churro in *dulce de leche* and nearly melted through her chair at the first bite—the perfect crunch of fried dough, sugar, and cinnamon with a warm, soft center.

Raquel smacked the table, startling everyone. "Hold on! I know what you need, Lennon."

After dinner, they gathered in Oscar's living room, where he'd set up a makeshift karaoke situation that would rival most karaoke bars.

"Alright!" Oscar clapped his hands together. "Who's first?"

"Lennon. Time to feed the muse, gorgeous," Raquel said, kicking off her sandals. She wiggled her eyebrows as she sank into the deep, plush sofa. "Let's have some fun."

Dylan guided Agueda to the sofa, her arm linked through his and sat down next to her. "I can't wait to see what you sing, *guapo*," Agueda told him.

"Oh, no," Dylan said with a shake of his head. "I won't be doing any singing."

"Sure you won't." Agueda winked at Lennon.

Lennon stifled a laugh at the dread that passed through Dylan's eyes.

Nerves crawled up her insides, but she also felt something else she hadn't in a while—excitement. Exhilaration.

Lennon flipped through Oscar's catalog and chose the first song that sprang to mind. She used to jam out in her bedroom to it when her mother wasn't home. She needed to channel some of that rebellious, free-spirited energy now.

Air guitar and all, Lennon took to the center of the living room and sang her heart out to Joan Jett's *Bad Reputation.*

After generous fanfare for her performance, and Oscar sharing a story about meeting the band back in the eighties at a club in New York, the others took turns singing classic songs and offering critiques. Raquel told Oscar he needed more "hip action" during his performance of *La Bamba* and Oscar told Raquel she "may have a promising future in music" if she stuck to it. Agueda did a moving, passionate rendition of *La Vida Es Un Carnaval* that proved musical talent ran in the family.

The highlight of Lennon's night would have been when she and Raquel did a duet of one of Raquel's classic hits—an experience Lennon would *never* forget so long as she lived—if it hadn't been followed by them all convincing notoriously stage-shy Dylan to get up there.

He agreed on one condition—that Lennon perform with him.

And she agreed on one condition—that she get to choose the song.

They sang and danced their way through *Summer Nights* from *Grease,* Dylan surprising everyone when he hit John Travolta's famous high note at the end.

As they finished to applause, Lennon and Dylan looked at each other. Cheeks warm with color, breath short. His brown hair was tousled, the skin crinkling around his eyes. Remnants of a boy less burdened by life's heartaches surfaced.

For a moment, they were both teenagers again. Carefree. Optimistic.

Laughter bubbled up from her throat, which triggered his laughter, which made hers plunge even deeper. They clasped hands and bowed.

For the rest of the night, Lennon couldn't stop smiling.

As the sky slipped into purple and pink hues, casting a dreamy, romantic haze over Arden Beach, Dylan drove Lennon home.

The streetlamps and skyscrapers twinkled like the evening's first stars. The crisp night air swept through the open windows of the vehicle, cooling their flushed skin just enough to let her coast on the adrenaline rushing through her system without snuffing it out. Lennon held an arm out the window, surfing her hand on the wind and enjoying the feeling of the fresh air whipping across her face.

"I can't believe that just happened," Lennon said over the roar of the wind, resisting the urge to pinch herself and check to see if she was dreaming. If she was, she didn't want to know. She wanted to enjoy the dream for as long as she could. "How did that even happen?"

"His grandson's a big Tidebreakers fan," Dylan answered, his arm stretched out to rest a hand atop the steering wheel, cords of muscle in his forearm flexing. "I spent an afternoon giving Miles lessons for his birthday last year and have kept up with him. Mr. Alonso told me to let him know if I ever needed a favor in return. He'd been away on vacation, but he got back last week. I called it in, and he offered to make good on it today." He said it as if it were all so simple, so unexceptional.

"I can't believe I was in his house," Lennon mused, slipping into a sort of daze. "I was in Oscar Alonso's *house*. I played his *piano*. I sang and danced with *Raquel Rosas*. We harmonized. I ate the homemade churros she brought. She made those in her *kitchen* with her *hands*."

Dylan laughed, glancing away from the road to watch her like a parent watching a child excitedly open their gifts on Christmas morning.

"And he liked my music," Lennon said, the memory reactivating gravity. She'd been flying and suddenly sunk into beautiful, grounded bliss. "I can't believe it."

"I can."

"And you fucking nailed that Danny Zuko note."

Dylan winced, but a reluctant smile also slipped through. "Yeah, that feels like a fever dream. I'm glad there were no cameras around, so it won't wind up on the internet tomorrow."

"I can't believe you have that entire song memorized. You weren't even looking at the lyrics."

"You kidding? You made me listen to it almost every day."

"You secretly love it."

"I do. It always makes me think of you."

The words fell from his mouth so smoothly that it took a moment for her to process exactly what they meant. Dark eyes slid to her, then back to the road, hand tightening slightly on the wheel. His throat bobbed through a swallow.

Lennon rested her head back as she kept her gaze on him, feeling her heartbeat through every pulse point in her body. "Thank you."

"I didn't do anything," Dylan said with a shrug. "Just arranged a meeting."

"Just accept my gratitude like a normal person."

He huffed a laugh. "Fine. You're welcome." A few moments went by, the occasional whoosh of a passing car drifting in and out before Dylan spoke again. "Thank you."

"For what?"

"This is the first night out I've had in a long time where I didn't want to crawl out of my skin. I didn't want to escape any of it or look for a way to numb myself. I actually felt …" He paused, a gentle lift at the corner of his mouth. "Alive."

Beneath the golden glow of the streetlights and the sunset diffusing into nightfall, her heart melted. She studied his profile, finding traces of something she hadn't seen there in years.

Peace.

The breeze drifted through the open window where his other forearm comfortably hung, softly blowing through the thick waves of his hair and the collar of his shirt, lifting it away from his smooth, tanned chest. Stray pieces of her onyx hair whipped around her face, the scent of the salty sea, city diesel fumes, and restaurant grills mixing in the air.

Lennon was experiencing something for the first time in years, too.

She was falling in love with life again.

Or maybe, she'd never truly fallen out of it.

Back home, Lennon changed into a pair of cotton shorts and a soft, oversized sweatshirt and lit a few vanilla candles around her apartment. She switched off all the lights except the under-cabinet ones in the kitchen, bathing the space in a soft, amber glow.

She dug out her notebook from the bedside drawer and placed it on the coffee table with a pen. Barefoot, she tucked her feet under her to sit cross-legged on the sofa and nestled her guitar in her lap.

Unlike other failed sessions lately, this time, it didn't feel like a chore. She was excited to pour the energy the afternoon had infused her with into *something*. Her endorphins were still pumping, adrenaline a mere memory away from a fresh spike. Being around all that creativity and experiencing something so special had gratitude—and hope—swirling within her that needed to go somewhere.

Taking a deep, centering breath, she didn't force the words or melody to come. She sat with the feelings of the day, letting them wash over her and settle in. Soon, those feelings became sounds. Notes. She hummed, tasting them on her tongue, allowing them to vibrate in her chest. Eventually, her fingers followed.

And finally, the words.

Lennon wrote and played until 3:00 a.m., and fell asleep on the sofa dreaming of music, dancing, and of a boy she couldn't seem to let go.

CHAPTER 24

Lennon

String lights against a twilight sky. Fryer oil, booze, and a salty tang in the humid summer air. Live music and the bustle of festival goers.

The country band finished a cover of *Friends in Low Places* to an enraptured, mostly drunk crowd singing along to the chorus. They cheered loud enough that people blocks over probably heard them.

Tough act to follow for an eighteen-year-old with a guitar and an amp.

It was Lennon's first paid gig—a weekend festival on the beach with local vendors, artists, and live music. White tents and food trucks lined the street beside a small stage erected on the beach. It may as well have been Madison Square Garden, as proud as she'd been when she booked it. What felt like half the city had crowded onto the beach.

Everyone, except her mother.

A hole widened in her chest as Lennon took the stage and

scanned the crowd for someone who wasn't there. But then, she saw *him* instead.

A mess of dark-brown hair stuck out at all angles like he'd just rolled out of bed, his long legs lifting him at least a head above everyone else. Dylan's eyes brightened over a crooked grin. He cupped his hands around his mouth, shouting encouragement while Erin's blonde ponytail swung as she bounced on her heels and cheered as if an actual rockstar was about to perform. Rhett stood behind them, a large pretzel with a bite out of it in hand and his mouth full. As his eyes met Lennon's, he nudged the pretzel in acknowledgment.

The rest of the night, she was on a high.

Lennon played three thirty-minute sets and finished her last as the vendors packed up. Some people approached her between sets to compliment her, and leftover adrenaline buzzed under her skin as she walked along the empty beach with Dylan, eating a slice of pizza he'd saved for her before everyone closed up shop.

"You were amazing, baby," Dylan said, the easy reverence in his voice making her heart flutter.

Her cheeks hurt from smiling so much. "Thanks. It feels surreal." Still, something kept her from fully sinking into it, like a blister forming on her sole, cutting deeper with each step.

The muffled sounds of the city—cars, sirens, music—underscored the ocean's roll at their side. "So, you wanna tell me why your eyes look so sad?" Dylan asked.

Lennon finished the last bite of pizza crust, brushing off her hands. "I can't believe she didn't come," she said after swallowing, watching her black toenails sink into the sand. "She told me she wasn't going to, but I thought she'd change her mind at the last minute."

He released a small, strained sigh beside her.

The fact that Lennon was getting paid to play music, even if it wasn't much, hadn't made the impression on her mother she'd hoped it would. Just like getting accepted to two universities' music programs hadn't. To Katherine, it was all a "waste of time." Music was a foolish way to spend her summer before college and an even more foolish way to spend her life.

But it was *her* life. She was eighteen now. She didn't need anyone's permission.

"It's OK," Lennon said, infusing her voice with strength despite the crumbling feeling inside her. "Once I get a record deal and I'm selling out arenas, she'll come around."

Dylan dipped his head as he glanced down at her, a soft smile tugging at the corner of his mouth. His long fingers found hers, interlacing them together. The warmth of his palm soothed her.

"Are you scared? About this next chapter of our lives," Lennon asked, watching the lights blink on a passing plane slowly cutting across the inky sky. "Everything's about to change this fall. We're starting college. You'll most likely be drafted soon, and I've started sending out demos to labels, so who knows what could happen with that …"

Dylan curled his lower lip between his teeth, following her gaze toward the sky. "Yeah. Kinda terrified, actually." A small laugh trickled out of him. His hand tensed a little in hers, so she pressed her body closer, fitting her arm around his.

"Me too," she admitted quietly. Fear prickled under her skin. "I *want* everything to change, for us to build our own lives and live our dreams, but I don't want *this* to change." She leaned her head on his bicep, too short in her barefoot state to reach his shoulder. As if holding on to him tighter would keep him from slipping away.

"It won't," Dylan said with certainty.

The sea breeze blew strands of her sweat-dried, post-show hair across her face. Lennon wanted to believe him. Everyone had made it a point to tell her that everything would change when they went to college, and even more when he became a pro baseball player. Her mother was first in line, warning her that he would leave her behind once he got bored, like her father had. He would want his own life. His freedom.

"What if you meet someone else—"

"Lennon—"

"I'm the only girl you've ever dated. I'm not naive. I know you're going to have a lot of opportunities, and I'd get it if you wanted to explore other options without feeling tied down. I don't want to be a burden."

Dylan abruptly swung around and stepped in front of her, making her stop short. She had to crane her neck to look up at him when he was that close.

"Hey." His deep brown eyes locked on hers, a tiny crease forming between them. "Do *you* want to see other people?"

Lennon released a sigh. "No, but if you did—"

He bent down and interrupted her with a kiss. His hand came up to support the back of her neck as his mouth gently coaxed hers open, his tongue sinking inside as if to send a message. *You're mine. I'm yours.*

Their fingers still tightly intertwined, she wrapped her other arm around his waist, pressing her torso flush against his.

"Does that tell you what you need to know?" Dylan whispered, his breath warm against her lips and his thumb drawing small circles along her jaw. His long, dark lashes hung over his eyes as he stared into hers.

Lennon licked her lips, the taste of him lingering on them. "I'm just … afraid you'll change your mind," she admitted, embarrassed to be so vulnerable.

Dylan's eyes grew heavy with a look she couldn't quite read before he lowered to one knee.

"Oh, my God. Dylan, you don't have to—" A small gasp caught in her throat as he pulled a ring with a marquise diamond from his pocket. "Oh, shit," she exhaled.

"I've been carrying this around all summer, trying to decide how to ask you." He sounded nervous, a little breathless. "I know we're young. But you're right—life's only gonna get crazier from here. We'll have college, and at some point, I'll go pro and you'll get your record deal, which won't take long because you were born to make music. They're probably gonna fight over you." Dylan smiled at the laugh that poured from her. He went quiet momentarily, his puppy-like eyes turning a little sad. "Losing my mom taught me that we never know how much time we have. Why wait when I know I want you for however long that ends up being?"

Her heart split open. Lennon dropped to her knees, so they could be face-to-face. And because they were weak. And because she needed to be closer to him.

Moonlight caught his unshed tears. His gaze fell to the ring, sparkling like one of the stars above them. "This was hers," Dylan said softly, the pain rasping his voice. "She left it for me and told me to give it to someone who felt like home." He looked back at her with his heart in his eyes. "You're the best thing that's ever happened to me, Lennon. You're everything."

The ocean's roar was nothing compared to the one in her chest. She gripped his knee to hold herself steady. Her voice broke a little as she said, "You're my home, too."

Lennon offered him her trembling left hand, and his eyes widened slightly. His breath hitched. Cradling her fingers, he gently slipped on the ring. She scooted forward on her knees through the sand and grabbed his face, pressing her lips to his several times.

Lennon sat back on her heels, tucked between his legs as they caught their breath and admired each other. They would be OK. They weren't her parents—they were their own people. Whatever life threw at them, she knew in her heart they would find their way through it.

Dylan kissed her knuckles. "Forever."

Lennon smiled as tears wet her cheeks. "Forever."

If this moment were a song, she would've listened to it on repeat.

Forever.

CHAPTER 25

Lennon

The next couple of weeks passed in a blur.

Lennon threw herself into anything that would keep her busy. Writing music, looking at job listings, rehearsing the song for Avery's reception, going to every pre-wedding event she was invited to and smiling through it. She even began attending the free cycling classes her building offered after she discovered, while walking by to grab her mail, that one of the trainers had excellent taste in music. Erin went back on the road with the Tidebreakers, and Dylan remained busy training.

They hung out a few times when their schedules allowed it and had slipped into texting daily in one long, continuous conversation. The couple of days neither of them had time to touch base felt weird. And the fact that it felt weird, felt weird. It was almost like the six years apart had never happened.

Late Saturday morning, they video chatted while Lennon sipped coffee on her balcony and Dylan worked out in his home gym. She spent the majority of the conversation lamenting her weekend plans. The invitation to Avery and Chad's joint bachelorette/

bachelor party had been hanging menacingly on her fridge. Kelsey and Trey were hosting it at a mansion on the beach. Everyone had been invited to stay overnight after the party on Saturday and relax on the beach the next day.

All filmed for the show, of course.

"The idea of basically being stuck in a fishbowl—with Kelsey, no less—for twenty-four hours is going to seriously test my ability to keep my mouth shut," Lennon said. She propped her feet on the railing as a warm breeze swept through, gently rustling the palm trees against the building. At least the show would wrap soon. The wedding marked the end of the first season in another two weeks, so the party was one of the last times Lennon would have to play nice with Kelsey.

"It's going to be fun watching you try." Dylan smirked at the camera as he curled heavy weights, the veins in his biceps bulging. Even though he wasn't a groomsman, he'd been invited to join them.

It would be the first party he'd been to since the accident.

"How are you feeling about tonight?" Lennon asked.

"What do you mean? Bachelor parties are the pinnacle of moral conduct. What could possibly go wrong?"

Lennon pressed her lips into a flat, unimpressed line at his sarcasm. "I know the show's pressuring you to go, but you don't have to, y'know. Chad would understand." She ran her thumb along the rim of her Freddie Mercury mug.

"I know. But then you'd have to go alone," Dylan said, his face straining against the final rep. He dropped the weights with an exhale. "I'm also leaving tomorrow evening for that ten-day boot camp up in the Panhandle, so … it's my last chance to see you for a while." His eyes met hers.

Emotion swelled behind her ribs. She'd been dreading him leaving for almost two weeks and wished they could have spent his last night in town differently. Since she had no choice in the matter of her attendance, she was glad he'd be there with her. It soothed some of her anxiety around it.

A knock at the door dragged a sigh from her. "That's my glam team."

"Already? That seems … early."

"Tell me about it," she said as she dropped her feet from the railing. "Apparently, it takes several hours to make me look presentable enough for television." Inside, she caught her reflection in the glass door as she slid it shut. Her hair balanced like a bird's nest atop her head in the same bun she'd worn to bed, and her chin donned a purple star-shaped pimple patch. "Actually, that's fair."

"Nah. You're perfect."

Lennon stuck her tongue out, but she knew he meant it. Her heart liquefied. "See you later. Hope you recognize me when they're done."

They signed off as she answered the door. Freema, Greg, and Deb marched in with their trunks in tow, along with a spray tan artist and her portable spray tan booth.

"Oh, God," Lennon said as she eyed the rack of small, lingerie-like outfits Freema parked in the living room.

"You mean, oh *gods*," Freema corrected with a flourish. "The party's theme is sexy Mount Olympus, honey, so sexy Mount Olympus they're going to get."

Once Lennon's body had been sufficiently airbrushed, Deb lathered her in shimmery oil that made her look like a delicious, glazed doughnut. Freema completed her transformation into a "modern-day Greek goddess" with a white corset, matching asymmetrical miniskirt, and nude gladiator sandals.

Bruno whistled as she strode out to his black Escalade by the curb. "Goddess Athena, your chariot awaits," he said, sweeping an arm toward the backseat as he opened the door.

"I guess that makes you Charon," Lennon remarked dryly. He chuckled at her reference to the ferryman to the Underworld with a "you're not wrong" look. She passed him the handle to her small rolling luggage but kept hold of a small pink cardboard box. "I went to that bakery on Sixth Street that Darius told me about." She lifted the lid, revealing three large cupcakes. "Got one for each of you. As a thank you. You and Darius have helped me stay sane through all this."

Bruno's eyes turned glassy. "Damnit, *mija*. Don't make me cry. I've got to be on camera soon." He smiled, his cheeks dimpling. "It's been my pleasure. Truly."

With his help, Lennon carefully climbed into the vehicle.

"*Ay Dios.*" Bruno sighed. "That body makeup's going to be hell to get out of the leather."

The sun was setting when they pulled through a pair of massive, imposing gates surrounded by tall hedges. Bruno first dropped her off at the mansion's tennis court and accompanying villa toward the front of the property, where the production crew had set up their base for the weekend. As Darius connected her mic pack, Carol Anne briefed her on the shots they planned for her arrival. Lennon half-listened as she watched one of Darius's assistants tinker with the sound board. Once Carol Anne left, Lennon bothered Darius with a few questions. He'd gotten used to her curiosity and was always generous with his time, which she was normally mindful not to encroach on too much. But tonight, she used it to wilfully procrastinate until an assistant sent by Carol Anne poked her head in and passed on the message to "hurry the fuck up."

"Oh, hey. Before you go, I have something for you." Darius reached into a pocket of his black jeans, which he wore with a fitted V-neck pullover. He always looked like he belonged on the cover of a Ralph Lauren ad.

"What a coincidence," Lennon said. "I left something for you with your husband."

Darius lifted an intrigued eyebrow before handing her a small envelope. "It's a year's subscription to my favorite media library," he said in that deep, rich voice she could listen to wax poetic about sound production all day. It was perfect for the podcast on the topic he'd mentioned wanting to produce—the one she'd been doggedly urging him to pursue if only for her own selfish reasons. "They have all the best samples and stuff on the market. It was in a swag bag at an event I went to, but the studio already comps a subscription for me, so I thought you could use it."

"Wow—absolutely. Thanks, Darius."

Between that and the dinner with Raquel and the Alonsos, the universe seemed to be nudging her back into music. It gave her a little boost to get through the weekend.

A reminder of what she was fighting for.

Lennon carried that motivation with her as Bruno slowly rolled up to the motor court and parked in front of the manor steps. A drone hovered while a cameraman waited outside the door to catch her stepping out. For now, the vehicle's tinted windows concealed her from watchful eyes. Dread sat like a stone in her stomach.

Why did she feel like an animal wandering into a trap?

"Looks like we're both in for a long night. I work as a rideshare driver when I'm not chauffeuring, and I'll be on call tonight." Bruno gave her a meaningful look through the rearview mirror.

Aware of the device pressing into her spine, Lennon silently pulled her phone from her gold clutch. She swiped open the New Contact screen before handing it to him. "Thanks, Bruno," she mouthed with a smile, heart warm with gratitude. He winked at her as he passed it back.

While Bruno unloaded her small suitcase from the trunk, Lennon released a long exhale, steeling herself. Time to flip into "show" mode.

He opened the door to the drone buzzing overhead. They filmed Lennon rolling her suitcase up the paved circular driveway to what looked like an actual palace. Boy, had they *committed* to the Mount Olympus theme. Two statuesque male models, their skin painted gold and clad in matching togas, flanked the palatial front doors. They opened them in tandem as she climbed the marble steps.

Her heart stopped when she approached the threshold.

It was like Lennon had walked into one of the luxury night-clubs on the strip—servers with bronzed bodies wearing nothing but gold tassels and G-strings served guests hors d'oeuvres, dancers with white wings writhed in elevated gold cages, and champagne trickled down a literal fountain in front of a double staircase. All surrounded by a *fuckload* of people. Way beyond the main bridal party and groomsmen. At least a hundred people were packed in the foyer with cameramen lurking among them.

"Lennon!" Avery's voice pierced through the loud music and hum of the crowd. "You look amazing." Delicate wings spread from Avery's back, matching her white mini dress that looked more like lingerie than cocktail attire.

Lennon snapped her jaw shut. "Hey—thanks. So do you." They exchanged a kiss on the cheek. She glanced around again and laughed awkwardly. "Sorry, I'm reeling a bit. This is not what I expected. There are … *so* many people here."

Avery laughed with her. Apprehension flashed in her eyes, suggesting even she was slightly intimidated by it. "I know, right? Kelsey knows how to throw a party." She waved over one of the gilded models, a tall man with blond, wavy hair. "Alexei will show you to your room. Meet back here when you're done. The party's officially starting soon."

Alexei silently led Lennon to one of the many guest bedrooms upstairs. Its opulence reminded her of Versailles. Two queen-sized four-poster beds were arranged between the paneled walls clad in floral wallpaper, and a private balcony overlooked the ocean. He informed her she'd be rooming with Tana, who had already claimed one of the beds.

"She's not rooming with Trey?" Lennon asked.

"He's with the groomsmen on the other side of the manor. Also, phones aren't allowed at the party."

Lennon had nowhere to hide it in that outfit, so she stuffed it inside her luggage.

As she followed him back to the party, nerves skittered under her skin. Most guests already had a drink in hand from the champagne fountain, pre-gaming for the night. Energy crackled in the air, poised for a release. Lennon searched for Dylan. Usually, she could pick him out in a crowd by his height alone, but the room was filled with athletes and models, and everyone but the staff wore white. A voluptuous blonde balanced the stem of her champagne flute between her breasts as she leaned over the fountain, filling the glass as a small audience of men watched in awe. The fact that none of it splashed on her was impressive.

"This is like an X-rated version of *Hercules.*"

Lennon turned to Dylan, who regarded a gilded model serving chocolate-dipped strawberries to guests with bemusement. "Gives a whole new meaning to the term 'golden shower,'" she quipped back.

Dylan snorted, but his amusement melted into something else when he faced Lennon. Deep brown eyes slowly skated over her. Greg had sprinkled gold glitter through her long, crimped waves cascading down her bare shoulders, and Deb had brushed gold over her eyelids. "You look beautiful," Dylan said, his voice dragging low. Flutters raced along her spine.

"Thanks. You don't look so bad yourself." Lennon took in his flowing button-down and matching pants. The crisp white fabric made his tan look particularly golden, especially where the first few buttons of his shirt hung open, revealing the hard planes of his chest.

Heat spread through her.

Lennon diverted her attention. "This is … not what I expected when they said combined bachelorette and stag party," she said, scanning the people packed around them. "I thought it was only going to be the wedding party."

"Guess my invitation wasn't so special after all," Dylan remarked. The muscles in his jaw twitched at a glance at the fountain.

As the realization clicked, her neck flushed with a wave of anger. No wonder the show had pushed for him to come. They wanted to throw him in the deep end and watch what happened.

"You OK?" Lennon asked.

Dylan nodded, his brow firm. "Yeah." He smiled. "I'm good. Promise." Something in his eyes—sincere confidence and resolve— reassured her.

"If at any point it's too much, we can sneak away somewhere quiet," she told him.

"That a promise?"

The corner of her mouth lifted at his playfulness and the flirtation dancing in his eyes.

"Little Prince! You made it." Chad's booming voice easily cut through the noise. A broad hand settled on Dylan's shoulder, playfully rocking him. To Dylan's credit, he barely moved.

"Yeah. Felt bad after beating you at golf," Dylan said as they locked hands.

"You actually managed to beat someone at golf?" Lennon raised an eyebrow, earning her a glare from Dylan. She shoved her tongue in her cheek to stifle a smile.

"I let him win," Chad remarked quietly as he leaned toward Lennon.

"Sure you did," returned Dylan.

"Well, I'll be damned. Look who's come out of retirement." A man with ginger hair and a southern accent came up beside Chad. He fixed his gaze on Dylan. "Now it's a fuckin' party." Another muscular man with a buzzcut and a silver cross hanging from his neck joined him.

The line of Dylan's jaw hardened.

"Been a while since we've seen you around," the one with a buzzcut said. He had a few tattoos on his arms—another cross, some numbers, and the logo of the professional football team Chad used to play for. Probably a player himself. He glanced at the ginger. "Told you he'd be back. No one parties like Dylan fuckin' Strickland."

"Not anymore. This is a one-off." Dylan shoved his hands in his pockets. "Sorry to disappoint."

The newcomers exchanged looks of skepticism openly. "What? You too good for us now?" Buzzcut asked with a small, derisive smirk.

Dylan regarded him with cool indifference, but his eyes held an edge.

"We're both coming out of retirement tonight. One last blow-out before the wedding," Chad interjected. He knocked his elbow against Dylan's. "Appreciate you coming out tonight, man."

The warmth returned as Dylan shifted his focus to Chad. "Of course, brother."

The ginger nudged his chin toward Lennon. "This your girl, Strickland?"

Dylan's gaze settled on Lennon. The question hung in the air. The music stopped.

"Hey—listen up, people! All my goddesses come with me," Kelsey shouted over the hum of the crowd. She stood on a gold chair, cupping her hands around her mouth. Lennon almost did a double take at her outfit, or lack thereof. If Avery's looked like lingerie, Kelsey's was made from whatever tiny strips of fabric had been left over.

"And all the guys follow me," yelled Trey. He lifted his hands above his head to motion toward the back of the house.

The sea of people all mobilized at once. Lennon was swept away with the bridal party, and Dylan with the groomsmen, as the two groups broke off in opposite directions.

"I'll find you later," Dylan shouted over the crowd.

Kelsey led them to a vast living room with a wet bar and private out-door space. It covered about as much square footage as Lennon's entire one-bedroom apartment, if not more. Lennon heard some-one say the house was owned by one of Chad's professional foot-ball player friends. A vacation home that he used a few times a year.

All the gilded male servers lined up with trays loaded with shots. Kelsey led Avery to an ornate gold throne in the center of the room. Everyone cheered her on as the bride carefully lowered into it, staring at Kelsey with a cross between panic and excitement.

That's when the room turned into an ancient Greek mythology version of *Magic Mike*.

The servers discarded their trays and started dancing as dirty hip-hop music played through the speakers. They focused their energy on Avery but occasionally broke off to grind on other guests. The last thing Lennon wanted was *that* kind of footage out in the world, so she sank to the back of the room with her non-alcoholic cocktail, watching the debauchery unfold from afar.

Lennon could only imagine what was happening at the groom's side of the party. She and Dylan would have to trade war stories later.

God, she hoped he was being smart and avoiding anything that could get him in trouble with the UBL's board.

After the performance, the party poured out onto the sprawling patio. A spattering of stars twinkled in the deep blue sky. The bridal party—Avery, Lennon, Candace, Tana, and Kelsey—gathered around a sleek gas fire pit where flames licked a bed of turquoise fire glass. Lennon indulged in one shot but opted out of the following round with Candace, who hadn't been drinking. Lennon needed to keep her wits about her. Impaired judgment in a house full of voyeurs was a recipe for disaster.

She came on this show to help her career, not blow it up in a single evening.

Once they'd thrown back their second round, Tana eyed Lennon. "You sure you don't want another?"

"Nah, I'm good. I'm too much of a lightweight," Lennon said. "I'll end up passed out and drooling on the sofa for the rest of the party." That was a lie, but she knew from spending time with Erin, an actual lightweight, that the excuse worked.

Tana crossed her long legs, leaning her elbow on one knee and cupping her chin in her hand as she studied Lennon. "So, is this bringing up any weird emotions for you?"

"What do you mean?" Lennon adjusted her miniskirt to ensure the cameramen weren't getting a free show.

"Like, about your divorce. Is it hard to go to weddings and be around all this stuff?"

The truth pinched, but Lennon didn't let it show. "I haven't really thought about it."

"*Euck*, I'd hate it," Tana said, grimacing. "Weddings used to make me sad before I found someone because I was afraid I never would."

"Are you completely over Dylan, then?" Kelsey asked, stirring a tiny straw around her margarita.

Lennon relaxed into the white cushion and propped her arm on the back to let her forearm hang casually. She was feeling bold. "Why are you so curious, Kelsey?"

Everyone's attention snapped to Lennon.

Kelsey's brow arched. Her blue eyes sharpened. "I was wondering if you'd be OK with it if he dated someone else."

While other partygoers remained in the throes of celebration, their immediate circle fell into a pocket of stillness, hanging on her answer. Lennon's nerves frayed at the edges, but she maintained a mask of indifference. "He can go out with whoever he wants."

A soft curve tugged at Kelsey's lips. "So, you wouldn't care if we did?"

Lennon bit the inside of her cheek. Guess they were doing this, then. A couple of cameramen skulked around them. Lennon matched Kelsey's steady, unblinking gaze.

"I just want to make sure I won't be stepping on your toes," Kelsey continued, pressing a hand to her chest. "I'm a girl's girl. I don't want any drama."

It took every modicum of her willpower not to laugh in Kelsey's face, but Lennon couldn't help the sardonic smile that stretched across her lips. "That's the worst, right?"

"Totally," Kelsey agreed. Both were playing the game, carefully moving pieces across the board. "I'm glad you're so cool and understanding."

"Of course." Lennon lifted her hand and rested her head on

her fist. "Power to you for wanting to make the first move and put yourself out there."

Kelsey's lashes flickered slightly. "I'm … not planning on asking *him* out," she said with a small laugh. "I have a feeling he'll be asking *me* soon, and I wanted to check with you before things got serious."

"Oh, really? Huh." Lennon's eyebrows scrunched together. "We talk every day. You've never come up."

Kelsey's smile could cut glass. "Maybe he didn't want to hurt your feelings."

Lennon matched it. "I don't think I'm the one who needs to worry about having their feelings hurt."

The way Kelsey's smile faltered gave her a rush of satisfaction.

"Oh-kayyy," Tana drawled. She lifted her empty glass. "How about another round of shots, ladies, before we go find the boys?"

"What the hell, I guess I'll have one more," Lennon said, sitting up. Tana waved down one of the gilded servers carrying a tray of shots.

Once all but Candace had one in hand, who still nursed a virgin mojito, they clinked them together and then tossed them back in unison. Lennon and Kelsey watched each other over the crackling fire as they swallowed the liquor. Lennon welcomed the burn. Her entire soul would need a cleansing after this.

As Avery lowered her glass, her face blanched. "What is *she* doing here?"

Lennon followed Avery's stare behind her to Steph—Chad's ex, the redhead from the beach clean-up—standing by the bar in a sheer white bodysuit. She laughed with another woman who had long braids.

"Because I invited her," Kelsey declared. Avery shot her a look of betrayal, but her maid of honor was undeterred. "She's probably the one who planted those rumors in the tabloids about them getting close again in a desperate attempt for relevance. She needs to know you're not threatened by her. You and Chad are solid. He's yours now." Kelsey locked onto Steph, who caught on to the attention. "Let the bitch see it."

Avery didn't argue, but she didn't look entirely convinced either. The redhead's smile faded. She looked away.

"Are you OK?" Lennon asked. "I thought everything was fine with Steph."

After a beat, Avery nodded with a tight smile. "Yeah. Of course." She glanced at Steph again. Uncertainty swam in her gaze.

"She was getting a little *too* cozy with Chad at the beach," Tana said.

Lennon hadn't noticed anything strange that day, but then again, she wasn't with them the whole time. And she'd been avoiding the tabloids and gossip websites since the photos of Dylan and Kelsey had nearly sent her into a spiral. She hoped the rumors about Chad and Steph were as baseless.

"You can never be too careful with ex-girlfriends," Kelsey said. "One moment, they're claiming they've moved on, all while secretly plotting to steal them back."

As the other women continued discussing Steph, Kelsey's focus was now pinned on Lennon. Challenging her.

Lennon received the message loud and clear: *Prove me wrong.*

CHAPTER 26

Lennon

Some women from Avery's sorority descended upon the fire pit and interrupted the conversation. Lennon jumped at the opportunity to excuse herself.

She needed a breather. And to find Dylan. And to avoid wringing Kelsey's neck before the end of the weekend.

This was going to be a long night.

After downing a cup of ice water from one of the bars, Lennon followed the music pumping through the hidden speakers to the dance floor. Sweaty, writhing bodies packed the dark space from wall to wall. A DJ manned the raised booth, headphones over his ears and a toga draped across a bare, tattooed torso.

She hadn't planned to stay, but the addictive beat crept into her. Her shoulders moved with the rhythm, the rest of her body following. The little bit of alcohol she'd had buzzed in her bloodstream as the music lured her deeper. It'd been so long since she'd gone to a club and just *danced*. The bodies packed tightly around her, shrouded by darkness except for a spinning disco ball, offered her a reprieve, if only for a minute.

Lennon hid herself in the crowd and let the music take her. The vibrations melted the anxieties percolating under her skin. Her muscles unfurled in a wave carried by the rhythm. The other bodies faded into obscurity, becoming no more than a collective energy undulating around her.

If she had a drug of choice, this was it.

The song smoothly transitioned to a slower, more sensual rhythm, and she matched the pace. Her eyes drifted shut as her head rolled back, her chest and back arching forward as her long hair swept the exposed flesh above her corset. She lost any sense of time and place as one song seamlessly flowed into the next.

Lennon dragged open her heavy lids. Through the swell of music and bodies and scattered lights, their eyes met.

Her heart skipped a beat.

Dylan leaned against the door frame. One hand in his pocket, a plastic cup clutched in the other. The lights danced across his face, throwing him in and out of neon color as he watched her. Transfixed.

A thrill coursed through her, leaving a trail of fire in its wake.

Those first few open buttons of his shirt taunted her with a wide slit of smooth, sculpted skin. Heat pooled low in her torso as she held his gaze. Her free hand roamed her body, dragging along her curves, down the swell of her breast, dip of her waist, curve of her hip. He followed reverentially.

Lennon inclined her head, her fingertips slipping through the sweat on her collarbone to her neck. She imagined his hands on her. His breath tickling her skin, teasing it with a brush of his lips. She felt his warmth as though he were right in front of her. His lean, muscular form pressed against hers, moving as one. She drove her fingers through her hair, wishing they were tangled in his.

She wanted to know what he felt like now.

She *needed* to know.

Lennon drifted toward him through the swaying bodies. He slowly pushed off the door frame. The music crested, the erotic beat pulsing with each step. His lips parted. She wet hers. What did he taste like? How would kissing him again feel after waiting so long? Her heartbeat outpaced the music, desperate to find out—to get to him—as she wove through the other dancers.

Light glinted off a lens in her peripheral. A cameraman loomed nearby, concealed by the darkness in the back corner of the room.

Reality hit her with a cold, hard snap.

Lennon went rigid. Dylan's brow lowered and he followed her stare. His jaw tensed under the flash of lights.

Lennon had been careful not to reveal her complicated feelings on camera, and she'd just fucking blown it. Vulnerability and regret clawed at her.

The sweat on her skin turned sticky. The lights became too bright. Like she was naked under them.

She held her stomach, swallowing back a wave of nausea. Dylan's eyes found her again. Concern flashed in them.

Lennon turned. She squeezed through sharp shoulders and elbows until she reached the main hall. The noise pulsed in her head. She tracked down a bathroom in one of the less crowded corridors. As she pulled the door shut behind her, a hand slotted through and stopped it. A gasp slipped from her.

"It's me," Dylan said. He braced his other hand on the door frame.

Lennon looked past him to see if any cameramen had followed. Two couples peppered the hall, too busy making out to notice them. She grabbed a fistful of his shirt, pulling him inside and locking the door.

The noise of the party dampened to near silence. The tightness of the bathroom became immediately apparent. Though the ceiling was high, the space only held a pedestal sink at one end and a fancy toilet at the other. Two long sconces flanked the mirror over the sink, casting a dim glow over the black crocodile walls that nearly receded into a void. Lennon's heartbeat drummed in her ears. It punctuated Dylan's shallow breaths as he gazed down at her, his face cast in shadow.

"What hap—"

Lennon pressed a finger to his lips. His pupils dilated slightly. Twisting, she pointed to the small mic pack hidden beneath her corset's silk lacing. "Turn it off," she mouthed over her shoulder.

Dylan mouthed back, "How?"

Lennon gestured instructions, all those conversations with Darius paying off, and then gathered her long hair to the front. The party was an obscure vibration in the background. Dylan carefully untied the silk ribbons at the bottom to loosen her corset. Calloused fingers brushed her skin, sending a tingle up her spine. The device clicked off. The lacing gently tugged at her waist as he retied the bow.

As Lennon faced him, he directed her to the device under the back of his shirt. She lifted the fabric away from the smooth skin of his lower back where the mic pack was taped. The lighting was too low to be sure, but his muscles seemed to tense slightly. She turned it off.

Above Dylan's head, the air vent lingered. They'd been told the bathrooms were off-limits to cameras, but what if the producers had lied? Lennon glanced back at the mirror, unable to shake the sensation of being watched.

"Hey—what's wrong?" Dylan's warm baritone filled the small, quiet space.

Lennon focused on her reflection. She looked like a skittish dog. "Sorry. I'm such an idiot," she said, shame thick in her blood. She braced a hand on the sink. "I don't know what I was thinking. I lost myself."

"What are you talking about?"

She briefly shut her eyes. "The dance. I forgot about our agreement. The cameras. I should've been more careful."

"I'm glad you weren't."

Lennon met his gaze in the mirror. The same heady look he'd worn on the dance floor stared back at her. Heat momentarily melted her frustration.

But they weren't alone. Not really.

"I don't know if I can do this," she said, keeping her voice low in case anyone had followed them. She didn't even trust the thickness of the door. "Being entertainment. People treating our life like—like nothing more than a storyline. One they can twist to their liking."

"You can't let them get inside your head."

"Yeah, well. It may be too late for that," Lennon said wryly. The long bow he'd tied, a little more haphazardly than Freema had, concealed the bump of the mic pack on her lower back, but the device still pressed into her flesh. There would be a red indent there later. "I don't know if it's worth it."

Dylan's gaze drifted lower. Down her body. His eyes darkened. "Why does it matter if they saw us?"

Lennon turned away from the mirror. "I don't want them to take it and ruin it."

"They can't," he said in a low rasp.

She watched the rise and fall of his chest. "They think I'm a gold digger, Dylan. That I came back for your money. Looking like I'm trying to rekindle things with you here would play right into Kelsey's hands."

His brow stitched together. "Why do you care what they think? I know the truth."

"You better than anyone know it's not that simple. That's not how the game works."

"Well, maybe I'm tired of playing it." Dylan's voice struck like a gavel. "You can't stop people from making shit up, Lennon. Maybe the real mistake here is trying to control something uncontrollable and letting it determine how we live our lives."

Lennon shook her head. "There's too much at stake right now," she said, straining to keep her voice low. "My whole career's on the line. I can't afford to take that risk. Neither can you, especially after what happened at the gala."

Dylan's brow dipped low. He studied her. "Are you saying it's too risky to be with me?"

Rhett's and Harold's warnings echoed painfully. *He can't get distracted again. You need to be careful he doesn't take you down with him.*

Lennon's heart squeezed. "I'm saying it may be too risky for both of us."

Dylan's chest rose with a deep, strained inhale. She could run her hands along the exposed skin there, tangle them in his hair. Act on her fantasies in this dark, locked room. Against the sink. Against the wall.

Say *fuck it* to the game and let the chips fall where they may.

She was tired of it, too.

Someone banging against the door made her jump. "Hey, your mics aren't working," came Carol Anne's muffled voice. "We need to check them."

Lennon clamped her eyes shut, biting back expletives. They really couldn't escape—not even in the bathroom. There were probably cameras mounted in the hallway.

That sickening, grimy feeling slithered under her skin again.

"Let's stick to the plan," Lennon whispered.

Dylan's throat flexed through a swallow. "I can't hide how I really feel about you."

Carol Anne banged on the door again.

"Try," Lennon said.

Before Lennon changed her mind and did something that would complicate things even more, she quickly unlocked the door and swung it open. She caught the supervising producer mid-knock. "Sorry. We turned them off so I could puke in private. Those shots got the better of me." Carol Anne cast a suspicious glance at Dylan. "He was holding my hair back."

"Right." Carol Anne regarded them like a couple of lying teenagers caught behind the bleachers. She looked out of place in the middle of the party, wearing her wrinkled black tee and headset. "You have to keep them on when we're filming. It's in your contract." She moved to the side to let one of the young production assistants step forward.

Lennon rotated so they could reach the mic pack taped to her back. Their eyes briefly met before Dylan shoved his hands in his pockets and looked away, a muscle cutting a sharp line through his jaw.

The cacophony of music and voices swelled around them as they returned to the party. Carol Anne had slithered back into the walls somewhere, but Lennon felt her eyes on them. It only took a second to clock a cameraman who must have followed them when they left the bathroom.

"I should probably find Avery," Lennon said. She could at least try to be a halfway decent bridesmaid.

"Hey, Lennon," Tana shouted over the music, popping up beside her. The smell of tequila spoiled the air. "Can we talk?"

Lennon glanced at Dylan. He'd gone somewhere distant, only half-present. Guilt pulled at her. Her fingers ached to reach out. They needed to talk—*really* talk—but they couldn't here.

"I'm gonna get some air," Dylan told her.

"OK." Lennon hid her disappointment with a weak smile.

Dylan seemed to see through it—he always did—by how his eyes softened slightly. She saw the pain behind them.

She always did.

Dylan descended the few steps to the sunken living room, heading toward the doors that led to another patio.

"Yo—Dylan!"

One of the guys they ran into earlier—the one with ginger hair—raised a cup from a crescent-shaped sofa. Buzzcut and some others sat with them. A blonde lounged on a hip along the back of the couch.

Kelsey.

Dylan hesitated for a moment before joining them. He sat on

the other end of the half-circle. Kelsey tossed her hair over her shoulder and leaned forward as she said something to him with a smile.

Lennon's blood iced.

"It's *so* loud in here. Let's find somewhere else to chat," Tana said.

Marching down those steps and plopping herself beside Dylan was damn tempting, if only to ruin Kelsey's game. But blowing off Tana would make it look like Lennon was threatened by her. Dylan could handle himself.

"Sure," Lennon replied.

She followed Tana to the kitchen. It was a mess of scattered plates of half-eaten food, empty cups, and other party paraphernalia, but thankfully, no other partygoers. The music receded to a distant, thumping bass. Lennon welcomed the quiet and the soft glow of the under-cabinet lighting, though she clocked the cameras this time—a cameraman who had followed them and crouched in the unlit dining area, a surveillance camera under one of the cabinets, and another attached to the ceiling. She pressed her back against the cool surface of the subzero fridge. Her heart thumped in her stomach.

"You looked like you were having fun dancing earlier." Tana's dark red lips curled into a smirk. Lennon stiffened. She hadn't even noticed Tana on the dance floor. Straight, jet-black hair fell over her shoulders as the model leaned over the expansive island. She braced her elbows on it and set her chin in her hands. "I'll bet all the guys were enjoying it, too."

Tana hadn't spotted Dylan. Lennon released an inward sigh of relief.

"So, I wanted to ask you something, woman to woman. You said you and Dylan are friends," Tana began, slurring a little. Lennon's heart rate spiked, but she kept her expression even keeled. "Be real with me. Can he be trusted?"

That wasn't the question she expected. "What do you mean?"

"Like, is he a good guy, or should a woman interested in him run in the opposite direction?"

Lennon wasn't sure what Tana was getting at, but she didn't like the feel of it. "I don't—why are you asking me this?"

Tana sighed, biting the corner of her lip as she appeared to debate what to say. "So, obviously, Kelsey has a thing for Dylan, but I think she like, *really, really* likes him, and I think he feels the same way."

Lennon fought back an eye roll. Not this again.

"I mean, why wouldn't he? She's a fucking catch," Tana continued, oblivious. "But she deserves the best, and I just don't know about him. Like, after what happened between the two of you and the whole thing with the accident—I'm a little worried, y'know? I know he's on this whole redemption thing, but is it genuine? Has he really changed, or is my girl getting set up for a huge heartbreak?"

Lennon sighed, absolutely *sick* of this charade. She dropped her head back against the fridge as she crossed her arms. "Honestly, Tana, you don't need to worry about it because Dylan's not interested."

"How do you know?"

Lennon still felt the heat of Dylan's gaze radiating on her skin. "Trust me, I just know."

Tana narrowed her catlike eyes, drawing slow circles on the marble countertop with a long fingernail. "Well, let's say hypothetically, he was. Do you think Dylan can be trusted?"

"He's a good man," Lennon said firmly. "I think people need to stop putting so much pressure on him."

Tana sighed. "Kelsey does love a project."

"Dylan's not a project. He's a person."

Tana arched an eyebrow, studying Lennon for a beat. "You sure you don't have feelings for him?"

The cameraman crept behind Tana. Lennon tightened her arms around her ribcage. "I'll always care about him. We've known each other since we were kids," she answered carefully. "But we're just friends." The lie chafed against her heart.

Tana smiled lazily. "I guess everyone deserves a second chance, huh?"

If only it were that simple.

Silence stretched between them for a few seconds before Tana abruptly rose. "Alright. Let's get some more shots and dance our asses off. I'll tell the DJ to queue up something good."

"Actually, I'm going to look for Avery. Have you seen her?"

"Not since the fire pit. She got pretty upset over seeing Steph and wandered off somewhere. Bring her with you to the dance floor when you find her."

They split off in opposite directions. Lennon purposely backtracked to the sunken living room as she searched for Avery. Different people now crowded on the crescent sofa—Dylan nowhere in sight. Or Kelsey. She checked the patio he'd initially been headed toward but recognized no one.

Where the hell did he go?

Lennon continued through the palatial manor, poking her head into various rooms. An art gallery, a formal dining room, another living room. How many fucking rooms did this place have?

As Lennon passed the library, she stopped short and did a double take. Avery sat slumped in a leather club chair as she received a lap dance from two half-naked gilded models.

Lennon almost didn't recognize her at first. It was strange to see student president, lifestyle guru, always put-together, sweet-faced Avery getting a lap dance from a topless woman painted gold while a buff man in a thong rubbed her shoulders.

Lennon rested a hand on the doorframe, not wanting to, uh, *intrude.* "Hey, Avery—have you seen Dylan by chance?" She waited a moment. "Avery?"

The bride-to-be rolled her head up. "Who? Oh. No. Sorry," Avery replied with a heavy tongue. Her eyes were half-mast, clearly drunk to oblivion.

Lennon's stomach turned to stone at the cameraman's smirk. His thin, dark hair was tied in a rat tail at the nape of his neck and a sweat stain permeated his black shirt in the middle of his back.

Lennon strode into the room. She reached past the gyrating

model to clasp a gentle but firm hand around Avery's arm hanging over the side of the chair. "I think it's time to get you to bed."

"Noooo," Avery whined, but her eyes fell shut. Her head slumped back against the chair again. "I'm having fun. I never have any fun."

For a moment, Lennon reconsidered. They weren't close, so how did she know if this was what Avery would want? After all, it was *her* bachelorette party and *her* reality show, and Avery was an adult.

"Why don't you join us?" the male model asked, amber curls framing his chiseled face. He let go of Avery and languidly stepped around the chair toward Lennon. She slapped his hand away as he reached for her.

"Don't touch me."

He gaped at her before shifting to disgust. "Bitch," he murmured under his breath.

"Come on, Avery," Lennon said, tugging her arm. Avery could be angry at her later. She wasn't taking any chances that she was in a situation she'd regret once sober. "Let's get you some water. If you still want some fun after you've sobered up a bit, I'm sure some will be waiting for you."

The female model stopped dancing. She sent Lennon a small, apologetic smile as she moved out of her way.

As both models slinked off, Lennon pulled Avery to her feet. She was almost deadweight. Lennon threw Avery's arm over her shoulder and wrapped her own around her waist, and they stumbled out of the room together.

Lennon glared back at the cameraman, who looked every bit like a teenage boy whose fun had been ruined. She shot him a bird. She didn't care that he caught it on camera.

Since Lennon didn't know which of the five thousand bedrooms was Avery's, she brought her to hers and Tana's. Another cameraman tried to follow, but she slammed the door in his face. Lennon lowered Avery on her bed, then went to the wet bar to grab a water bottle from the mini fridge. By the time Lennon turned back around, Avery had slumped onto her side.

"Hey, drink some of this first." Lennon sat beside her and gently guided her up.

Avery groaned but obliged. She accepted the open bottle from Lennon and took long, slow gulps. Once she'd had enough, Lennon put it on the table between the two beds as Avery sank her head into the pillows.

"What if he's making a mistake?" Avery mumbled.

"Who?" Lennon asked. "You mean Chad?"

"They were together for so long. Like you and Dylan. What if she's his Lennon?"

Lennon froze, unsure of what to say to that. A knock rapped on the door. If it were a cameraman or that male model, so help her.

"I'll be right back," Lennon said.

Cracking open the door, Lennon released a sigh of relief at the petite pregnant woman on the other side.

"Hey, is Avery with you?" Candace asked, clear-eyed and sober. "My husband said he saw you bringing her to your room."

"Yeah. Where've you been?" Lennon didn't bother to hide the judgment in her tone. Why had no one been looking out for the bride, especially when she was upset over Steph?

"We've been hiding out in my room. He stepped out to find me some food." Candace cradled her baby bump through her simple, draped dress. "I dipped out shortly after you left the fire pit. Everyone was starting to get too shit-faced."

Lennon opened the door wider. She gestured toward Avery as Candace stepped inside. "She's in a very … vulnerable state. I didn't want to leave her alone."

Lennon shut the door on the cameraman again. Candace's delicate brow sunk inward at Avery curled up on the bed, the expression on her face suggesting guilt. And dread. "I didn't think this party was a good idea," she remarked quietly.

"Why'd you come, then?"

Candace's expression hardened, mouth flattening into a line. "Same reason you did."

While the comment was vague enough, Lennon knew what she meant. *Money.*

Candace's round eyes flitted to the ceiling—to a white, spherical device mounted in the corner opposite the beds. At first glance, it looked like a security system or smoke detector, but the truth hit Lennon with a wave of nausea.

A camera. Probably equipped with night vision.

Carol Anne *had* told her the bathrooms were the only rooms safe from cameras. Silly Lennon for thinking the bedroom would afford her privacy, too. How many partygoers were too drunk to remember the fine print and were unwittingly performing acts on camera that they would later regret?

Lennon's stomach churned. This really was a hellscape.

"Have you seen Dylan?" Lennon asked, every muscle in her body pulled tighter than a violin string. She needed to warn him.

"No. He's probably with the guys."

"I need to let him know I'm leaving." Lennon rested her hand on her abdomen, wrinkling her forehead to really sell it. "I'm not feeling well."

Candace gave her a knowing look but didn't say anything.

Lennon dug her phone out of her luggage and checked her messages in case he'd gone back to his room. Nothing. She sent him a text just in case.

Lennon: Where are you?

Lennon checked on Avery while Candace went to the bathroom to run a washcloth under water. She'd drifted off to sleep.

Lennon couldn't stay here. No amount of money was worth it.

As Candace returned and folded the damp cloth over Avery's forehead, Lennon pounded out a text to Bruno.

Lennon: Hey, it's Lennon. How fast can you get back here? I'm leaving.

As the text flew off, Lennon said, "I'm going to see if I can find Dylan."

"I'll look after Avery," Candace assured her.

Lennon tucked her phone in the waistline of her skirt as she strode toward the door.

"Hey, Lennon—" Candace smiled softly as Lennon turned to her. "Thanks for looking out for Avery."

Lennon returned the smile, not wanting to think about what would've happened if she hadn't found her when she did.

She made her way down the hallway back to the party, the cameraman on her heels.

Lennon wound through a maze of booze, bodies, and bubbles. She wasn't sure where the latter had even come from. Dubstep music pumped omni presently through hidden speakers, and gold G-strings and bras hung from the crystal chandeliers lining one of the main hallways.

Someone clipped Lennon's shoulder as they ran past her. "Hey, watch it—" The sight of bare, bouncing breasts stopped her short as the woman stumbled past her, giggling at the rumble of animalistic noises following her. A drunk man in a toga made a strange combination of monkey/howling noises as he raced after her with a cup in hand, beer sloshing over the top onto the floor. Lennon tucked into the wall as he barreled past her. The splash of booze narrowly missed her.

Across the hall, beyond a dining room, white soap suds filled an entire Olympic-sized pool like a bed of clouds. Arms and heads peeked out from the fluffy substance.

The party had made a swift descent into chaos.

There had been a few memorable times in her life when Lennon hadn't felt safe, like being alone in a handsy record executive's office or walking back to her apartment alone at 2 a.m. after a gig at a dive bar. Tonight carried that same energy.

Filming for the show had been uncomfortable at its worst, awkward at its best, but this felt different. Lennon's instincts buzzed with warning.

She needed to get the hell out of there, but she couldn't leave without telling Dylan first.

Lennon checked her phone again. The text to Dylan was still trying to send, but Bruno replied that he was fifteen minutes out. Why wasn't the one to Dylan going through? Had he switched his phone off? She thanked Bruno and shot off another text to Dylan.

After a several minutes of searching, Lennon spotted Chad exiting the billiards room. He was at least a head taller than everyone else. She sprinted down the hall to catch him. "Chad—hey!"

Chad stopped, turned. It took him a moment to recognize her in his drunken state. "Heyyyyyy. Lennon."

"Have you seen Dylan?"

"Uhhh … yeah, he was heading upstairs by himself. Not surprised he tapped out early."

Neither was Lennon. Her guilt weighed heavier by the minute. He'd come for her. "Do you know which room is his?"

Chad could only point her toward the groom's wing on the opposite side of the manor from the bride's.

Lennon climbed the winding stairs, slipping past the tangle of bodies making out on them. The noise of the party tapered off as she reached the top and a long, vast hall.

Alexei, the model who had shown her to her room earlier, stepped out of one of the rooms. The gold makeup around his mouth was smeared. He stopped when he saw her.

"Hey, do you know which one Dylan Strickland is in?" Lennon asked. Her attention darted briefly to the handprints across his abdomen.

He directed her to the second door on the left, then passed her without a word.

As she approached it, music seeped out from the other side. Something wasn't right. Maybe Alexei had gotten the room wrong.

Lennon swallowed and knocked. "Hey, Dylan? Are you in there? It's me."

An unsettling feeling roiled in her gut as seconds passed with no answer. She was about to knock again when the door opened. The music—a dark, sultry beat—poured into the hallway. A brunette clad in a white bra and a micro skirt leaned on the door.

"You bring us more shots?" she slurred. Rhinestones glued above her breasts spelled out BRANDIE.

Lennon tried to look past the stranger's shoulder as more laughter came from inside, buried under the loud music. With a swift, forceful push, Lennon sent the door swinging open and the stranger staggering backward.

"Ow! What the hell?" Brandie whined.

Kelsey guided Dylan's hands around her waist as she danced against him. Dylan took a step back and stumbled onto the bed— with Kelsey. A yelp launched out of her as she fell on top of him, her legs tangling with his, a hand braced on his chest. One of his arms hung around her waist, flopping to the bed after a moment. She giggled into the crook of his neck.

Lennon's heart sank to her stomach.

"Who are you?" questioned Brandie.

Kelsey lifted her head and caught sight of Lennon. "Oh, shit. Lennon—" A breathy laugh slipped from her lips.

Dylan looked like he was struggling to stay awake. Dazed. He rolled his head to the side, groaning.

It snapped Lennon out of her frozen state.

He wasn't sober.

Fire lit through her veins as she crossed the room. She clasped a hand around Kelsey's arm and wrenched her off Dylan. The blonde gracelessly stumbled off the bed, nearly falling.

"What the fuck are you doing?!" Kelsey ripped her arm away from Lennon.

"What the fuck are YOU doing?" Lennon shot back. "What happened to him? Why is he unconscious?"

Kelsey rolled her eyes. "He's not *unconscious.*" Dylan dragged his head to the center, bringing a hand to his face. "See? He's just relaxed."

The music pounded against Lennon's skull. "What happened to him?"

"What do you think?"

Lennon's gaze fell to the plastic cups and empty liquor bottles littering the end table. It didn't make sense.

Had their conversation in the bathroom sent him over the edge? Had she pushed him too far?

The cameraman settled into the corner of the room. A chill swept through her.

No. Dylan wouldn't. Not here. Not with everything at stake.

Lennon's body vibrated—practically *shook* with rage. She fixed her attention on the bed. "Dylan," she said through gritted teeth. "*Dylan.* Wake. Up." She grabbed his arm lying across the bed and shook it.

Dylan swept his hand down his face. His chin squished against his chest as he lifted his head, squinting. "Lennon?"

"You his girlfriend or somethin'?" Brandie picked up one of the cups from the other end table. She sniffed it, then took a sip.

"Ex," Kelsey interjected. She pushed her fallen strap up her shoulder and rested a hip against the bedside table. "Honestly, Lennon—you're starting to look desperate. It's kind of embarrassing."

"What's embarrassing is forcing yourself on someone," Lennon bit back without turning around.

Kelsey laughed. "Are you serious right now? Are you really this delusional? I'm not the one forcing herself on him, babe …"

"What's going on?" Dylan mumbled, the words clumsy on his tongue. His eyelids seemed to fight against staying open. *What did they do to him?* Fear clamped a fist around her.

"We're getting the fuck out of here," Lennon answered. "Where's your phone?"

Dylan swallowed. "Pocket."

Lennon checked, relieved to find it deep in the left pocket of his pants. Turned off. "Come on. Let's go." She balanced a knee on the bed for leverage and guided him to a seated position.

"*Oh*, my God," Kelsey said as if suffering secondhand embarrassment. "Where the hell are you taking him? This is *his* room."

"Home." Lennon wrapped her arm around his torso as he flopped his arm over her shoulders. "Can you stand?" Dylan mumbled an affirmation. He was a lot heavier than Avery as she guided him up. He reeked of booze and Kelsey's perfume.

Kelsey was lucky Lennon's hands were full.

Lennon led Dylan toward the door. They passed another cameraman in the hall.

She clung to a singular focus: Get downstairs and out of that fucking mansion.

CHAPTER 27

Lennon

Flickering light from the television. Burnt coffee
and lemon ammonia. The steady patter of rain on
the windows.

When the key finally jiggled in the door, it was almost 4 a.m. Dylan had texted that he was getting drinks with the guys after practice, a routine he'd taken to since getting drafted. She listened from the sofa, lying under a blanket, as he shuffled inside behind her. His keys clanked against the glass table by the door, then hit the floor. He groaned sluggishly seconds before the keys scraped against the tile.

Lennon briefly shut her eyes, a thick wave of disgust rolling through her. More shuffling.

"Oh—hey. You're still up," Dylan said, the words dragging on his tongue.

"Yeah," she answered, staring at the television. An empty mug, textbooks, notebooks, highlighters, pens, and her laptop littered the coffee table.

Dylan continued into the kitchen, grabbing a glass from the cabinet and pressing it to the built-in water dispenser on the refrigerator door. Sitting up, Lennon watched him fill the glass, leaning his forehead against the stainless steel. The water overflowed, and he barely reacted, pulling it away from the door and dumping some in the sink before gulping the rest down. His throat contracted with each swallow until he finally came up for air.

Dylan set the glass down, then braced his hands on the counter's edge, staring off into space. His eyes were hazy, red. His face ruddy. Barely there—everything about him dulled and distant and slightly foreign.

Lennon hated it when he was this kind of drunk. It wasn't like when they'd get buzzed at parties, loose and silly. When he came home like this, he was a shell of himself. Like a stranger.

All the warmth left her body.

"Did you burn something?" Dylan lifted his head with the sudden revelation, his brows drawn together.

"Coffee." After half the bag of coffee grounds spilled on the counter, floor, and her. She'd been so busy cleaning everything up, already distracted by him not being home yet or answering any of her texts—three hours ago—that she let it brew for too long.

Dylan hummed in response. He swayed a little as his eyes slid shut.

The anger that had been simmering in her all night boiled over. "Why do you keep coming home like this?"

He let out an exasperated exhale, hanging his head. "Can we talk about this later?"

"No. You never give me a straight answer. I'm sick of you deflecting." Lennon's voice pitched a little higher as her nerves unraveled through her exhaustion. "This isn't like you. Staying out late partying, coming home fucked up all the time. Ever since you were drafted, you've been acting differently. We barely see each other, and when we do, you're usually coming home like this. What the hell is going on?"

"Just blowing off some steam," Dylan answered laggardly, a touch of annoyance sharpening the edges.

"Bullshit."

Dylan blew a sharp stream of air through his nose, his head low. He didn't answer. Just kept his arms braced on the counter, leaning forward, only his mess of hair visible.

"Goddamnit, Dylan." Lennon shoved the blanket away as she stood, padding toward the kitchen to stand on the opposite side of the counter. She gripped the back of one of the barstools. "I *know* you. I know when something's wrong, so stop treating me like I'm an idiot and actually *talk to me*. This has been going on for months." She analyzed his tense shoulders. "Are things not good with the team?"

A muscle flexed in his jaw. "No. Everything's good. We're on a streak."

"Then, what's wrong?"

The low murmur of the television hung between them as she waited.

"Nothing. I'm just … tired. S'all," Dylan answered flatly.

"I'm tired, too. You're not the only one working full-time and going to school."

"Working at a record store and playing on a professional baseball team is a little different."

Lennon's body clenched, almost in a gasp. Shock and a tinge of shame stabbed her in the gut—shock that he'd said it and that she felt some kind of way about it. He didn't seem to realize he'd landed a blow, his head still lowered like he'd fallen asleep right there.

"Well, some of us didn't grow up with a fast track to our dreams," Lennon shot back.

Dylan's only response was a tightening of hands on the counter, the muscles in his arms flexing. He didn't talk much about the team. He'd been playing on the Tidebreakers' minor team for almost nine months, and all she got in response when she asked how things were going were noncommittal answers. It was like he wanted to keep their life together and his baseball life separate. It didn't help that their schedules rarely overlapped. She couldn't leave to go with him on the road because of school and her job, which she needed to pay bills and her student loans. She'd gone to a couple of games in town but couldn't go with him to the celebratory parties afterward because she always needed to go home and study or work on her music.

They'd gotten married to ensure their lives remained intertwined, and somehow, the opposite had happened.

It seemed like Dylan didn't want her to be a part of his new one. Lennon couldn't shake the nagging feeling in her gut that he was hiding something from her. That he was intentionally shutting her out.

It was driving her fucking crazy.

"Are you sleeping with someone else?" she asked boldly.

Dylan's head shot up. "What? No. Lennon—no. You know I'd never do that." Despite the slight slur of his words, he infused them with assurance that left no room for question.

Which left only one other possible answer.

"Are you regretting this?" Lennon's voice trembled slightly. He appeared to think about it, his eyes darkening as they shifted away from her. Her stomach bottomed out. "Oh, God, you are," she released on a breath. Tears stung her eyes. "I told you we didn't have to get married yet."

Dylan's gaze snapped to hers after a delayed second, his brow sinking again. "What? No, that's not—no." He shook his head, scrunching his face as if thinking were physically painful. He pushed off the counter, pressing the heels of his palms to his eyes. "I'm sorry, I really can't do this right now. I have a splitting headache."

It felt like the blood was rushing out of her—like she'd been sliced open, and it was pooling at her feet. Suddenly, everything was wrong. This room, the air, her body. Like she didn't belong there.

Like she wasn't *wanted* there.

"I'm gonna shower. Try to get some sleep. I have a training in the morning," Dylan said, his voice heavy with exhaustion. He walked over to where she stood frozen by the barstools, staring at the wilting potted plant neither of them remembered to water. The smell of hard liquor closed in on her. Beer used to comfort her from all the years of smelling it at the ballpark, but this scent made her sick. A reminder of the stranger he'd become.

"Hey." Dylan's hand gently clasped her elbow, his thumb resting in the crease. Lennon turned her head, glancing up through her lashes. She could see how bloodshot his eyes were this close. And how haunted. "It's not you." His voice cracked with guilt, barely above a whisper. "I promise." Dylan brushed his thumb along her skin, leaning in to press chapped lips to her temple.

She listened to him shuffle into the bedroom, shuck off his shoes, open and close a drawer, and finally shut the bathroom door.

Dragging herself back to the sofa, Lennon dropped to the cushion and opened her laptop. The rejection email from her dream record label stared back at her. It kicked her in the gut again, as it had a hundred times since she'd opened it that afternoon.

Swallowing thickly, Lennon closed the window and shut everything down before lying back on the sofa, pulling the blanket over her.

CHAPTER 28

Dylan

A sputtering noise struck his consciousness. Dylan slowly rose from a void, the strange sound taking form with a quiet melody floating behind it. He peeled his lips apart and unstuck his tongue from the roof of his mouth. Dragged a hand down his face. A fan spun on a ceiling he didn't recognize. White sheets bunched around his legs instead of his dark grey ones. A small, black spiral notebook sat on the end table next to a bottle of black nail polish and a pair of headphones hanging from a charging station. His phone was on the notebook, plugged into the wall. A pile of clothes hung over a chair in the corner of the room.

The warm, sweet scent of amber reminded him where he was. Whose bed he was in.

For one blissful moment, everything in him relaxed.

And then, it all hit him at once.

The party. Lennon. Fragments from a night he'd partially lost.

What had happened to him.

A dark, sickening feeling rolled through him. For a moment,

he couldn't move. His airway compressed in the grip of panic. He broke out in a sweat as anger, shame, and fear rushed him, making him feel as helpless as he'd been last night.

Dylan swung his legs over the side of the bed and sat up, his body immediately protesting the harsh motion. His vision temporarily went dark, and his head swam as he gripped the edge of the mattress. His breath pushed in, out in hard clumps.

The strumming of a guitar pulled his attention toward the gap between the door and the frame.

As the seconds passed, Dylan focused on the music. On *who* was making it.

His heart rate slowed. His lungs stopped fighting each inhale. Dylan lifted the hem of his shirt and wiped the sweat from his face. The fabric smelled of Lennon. He looked down at the Arden Beach University logo on his white tee and his black boxer briefs. He vaguely remembered her slipping the shirt over his head.

Dylan swallowed thickly. What else had he forgotten?

He stood, his muscles stiff, and followed the music through a short hallway to the main living area. The scent of fresh coffee joined the music and murmur of a coffee maker. The early afternoon sun slanted through the windows over Lennon nestled on the sofa with a guitar in her lap, her bare legs folded under her and a small crease between her brows as her fingers gracefully danced along the strings. He leaned against the archway, relieved to find her safe. At peace. Her knitted cardigan hung off one shoulder, her dark hair draped over the other.

He'd always loved watching her play music. He'd missed this. He'd missed her.

He'd missed all of it.

Almond-shaped eyes lifted, and her lips parted. Lennon strummed one final note before resting her hand against the strings. "Hey."

"Hey." Dylan's voice cracked, rough and groggy. He cleared his throat.

"How do you feel?" She scanned his body, the crease deepening between her green eyes. They'd always reminded him of a forest. Wild, deep.

"Like I was hit by a bus and run over. Five times." The wall held all of his weight as anger pierced a hole through him. Dylan pressed his eyes shut. "I wasn't drinking—"

"I know."

It took a second for the words to sink in. He met her gaze, half-expecting her to add a sarcastic remark about him trying to lie his way out of it. After everything he'd done, why would she believe otherwise?

Lennon put the guitar aside and stood, her cardigan slipping further down her arm. Under it, she wore a thin black camisole without a bra and loose shorts. She walked to the kitchen. "Someone drugged you," she said. Calm but serrated. She opened one of the cabinets and removed two mugs.

"Yeah." The truth settled in him like poison. Slow, corrosive. "How did you know?"

"Because I know you." The gurgling stopped, and the coffee maker chimed. Lennon poured the contents of the carafe into one of the mugs. "If you were going to drink, it wouldn't have been there. Not with the cameras. Not with—" Her hand stiffened around the handle. She finished filling both mugs and began preparing his the way he liked it.

Her trust in him, the kindness she was showing—it nearly overwhelmed him. He bit back a wave of emotion pressing against his eyes, lumping his throat.

"What do you remember?" Lennon asked.

Dylan took a moment to steady himself before releasing a low, strained sigh. "Only about half the night. I remember everything until we left the bathroom." His chest twisted at the memory of their conversation, every bit of it painfully clear. "Everything after that is fuzzy. Just flashes of things. You saying my name. Dr. Callow putting an IV in me."

"I wanted to take you to the ER, but you begged me not to. Told me to call him instead. He met us here."

"He's our family physician," Dylan said. "I trust him. If I went to the ER, it would've gotten out to the press."

"You're lucky he answered the phone. I wouldn't have given a fuck about the press." Lennon held the mug out to him.

Dylan stepped into the kitchen to accept it from her as his mouth twitched in a half-smile. He didn't know what he did to deserve her still giving a damn about him, but he was thankful she did. "Thanks." Steam rose from the mug, warming his palm.

Lennon finished preparing her coffee. "You don't remember where you were?" Her voice dragged low. "When I found you."

Dylan pulled his brow tight as he shuffled through the fragments of his memory. The more he tried to home in on the gaps, the tighter the wrench twisted in his skull. He shook his head, frustrated. After the accident, he'd *sworn* he'd never be in a situation like that again.

Except, this was different. He'd always been in control when he got wasted. He'd chosen to push past his limit the night of the accident, stupid as it was. This time, someone forced him past it.

Violated him.

Sickening rage churned in a slow but violent cyclone, eating through him.

"You were in your room," Lennon said flatly as she stirred her coffee. "With Kelsey."

It took a second for what she said to register. "What?" Dylan didn't even remember seeing Kelsey after they all split up. How did they end up in the same room? He looked up at Lennon to ask, but the expression on her face knocked the wind out of him.

Pain filled her eyes. She couldn't even look at him.

"No," he breathed. "We weren't—we didn't—"

Lennon gave a small shake of her head, her lashes briefly pressing into her cheeks. "No. It hadn't gotten that far."

Dylan blew out a sigh of relief, dropping his head back. He

set the coffee on the counter and braced his hands on the edge. "Fuck. *Fuck.*" He swiped a hand down his jaw. "Lennon, I—I'm sorry."

"It's not your fault," she said tightly. "It's the bastard's who spiked your drink." Lennon tapped the spoon against the ceramic. She lifted the mug like she was going to take a sip but then put it aside instead. Her lip curled slightly as if she were nauseated. She pushed her cardigan up her shoulder and wrapped it tightly around her. "Who knows how many victims there were. How much footage they have of people doing things they can't even remember."

Bile churned in his empty stomach. What if it had happened to Lennon? What if they had both been fucked up, and he wouldn't have even been able to protect her? The edge of the stone counter dug into his flesh as his grip tightened.

"I think Avery may have been one of them," Lennon said quietly. Her gaze drifted out of focus. Haunted. "And they kept on filming. Eating it up."

Dylan pushed up, then paced beside the island. His heart pounded against his ribcage. He drove a hand through his hair. "I should've known what would happen once I saw how many people were there. I've been to enough of them to know what kind of shit goes down if you aren't careful."

"I didn't think people would be that stupid with all the cameras around." Lennon scoffed. "Turns out I was the stupid one."

"You weren't stupid," Dylan said firmly. He was. He shouldn't have left her alone. He should have gotten them out of there as soon as they realized it wasn't what they thought it would be.

"I knew just as well as you that it was a bad situation," Lennon said. "But I didn't want to lose out on the money. Or the game." She looked away with a gentle shake of her head, disgust on her face. "Dr. Callow took your blood to test it. Said we'd find out in a few days what it was, but he doesn't think it was a roofie. It was probably something recreational, and you had a bad reaction to it."

Had he been personally targeted, or were they spiking things randomly and he happened to get lucky? How long had it been in his system before it kicked in? All he drank was soda and lime—one during the bachelor party, and one after he left the bathroom. He hadn't paid attention to the mixing process. He'd been stuck in his head, distracted.

It could've been dropped into the wrong drink—never meant for him. Dylan knew several of the guys there used. To them, it had been just another Saturday.

To him, it could cost him his entire career.

"I can go with you as a witness to file the police report before you leave tonight," Lennon offered.

"I think I should wait," Dylan considered, mired in thought.

"What do you mean?"

Dylan continued pacing, his focus turned inward. "There were cameras everywhere. Whoever did this knew that. They probably covered their tracks," he reasoned. "If I go to the police and they don't find any proof, my career's as good as dead. Everyone will think I'm covering up another bender with some bullshit excuse. And if they find out it was drugs, I'm definitely done."

Lennon stared at him in disbelief. "What do you think they'll say when the show comes out, Dylan?"

"Nothing, if I can convince them to bury the footage." Dylan stopped and faced her. "I'm going to call my lawyers. Maybe the studio will work with us to help us find who did it, and then we can take the evidence to the police."

"Anyone who was there could sell the story in the meantime."

"The show makes everyone sign NDAs, remember? No one can legally talk about it until it airs."

Lennon's nostrils flared, clearly wanting to argue further. But the fire in her dwindled. Her eyes became glassy. She pressed them shut, going quiet for a few moments. "I was so scared," she finally said, her voice small in a way he'd rarely heard. His chest splintered. "I can't stop thinking about what could've happened if I hadn't found you."

"Hey—c'mere." Dylan strode around the island to her as she buried her face in her hands. He drew her into his arms, wrapping them tightly around her. "It's OK. I'm OK."

Something deep inside him relaxed at the feeling of her pressed against him. He hadn't held her like this in years. He wished it wasn't because she was hurting. Because of him.

"None of this is OK." The long sleeves of her cardigan hiding her hands muffled her voice. "I hate this."

Dylan's lungs deflated with a sigh, guilt scraping through them. "Me too." She'd been right—being with him was a risk. Especially now. He gently rested his chin on her head as he rubbed her back, memorizing the way she felt. In case he didn't get another chance. "I'm sorry you got wrapped up in this. I shouldn't have dragged you into it."

"I decided to do the show. I got on this ride willingly."

"But you don't have to stay on it."

Lennon's hands slid away from her face. She rested her fists on his chest as she looked up at him. "What are you saying?"

"Most of the chaos you've been caught up in since you came back has been tied to me," he pointed out. "I have a target on my back, and you're getting caught in the crossfire."

"Would you have gone on the show without me?" she parried. "To that party?"

The muscles in his jaw tensed. He searched her eyes. "I know why it's a risk for you to be with me, but what did you mean when you said it was risky for both of us?"

Lennon's eyelashes flickered slightly. She lowered her gaze to her fists curled into her sleeves. They gently rose and fell with his breath. "This is one of the most important times in your career. You're still healing from an injury. You're fighting to get back on the team while Nolan tries to take it out from under you. This party could've ruined everything just because you wanted to be there for me." Her voice lowered. "I've been a distraction."

"You've been the best thing in my life," Dylan said. Her focus shifted back to him. "I'll deal with what happened at the party, but I have no idea what the fallout will be. I don't want this hurting you any more than it already has."

Lennon frowned, going quiet for a few seconds. Dark circles shadowed her eyes. He realized she hadn't even washed her face. Gold still shimmered on her eyelids, black smudged around her long lashes. She must have been up all night. She softly exhaled. "I need some time to think. About everything."

Dylan swallowed with a small nod.

"But I think you should go to the police now," Lennon said. "Whoever did this to you needs to pay."

"I won't wait long. I just want to talk to my lawyers first. Cover all my bases. And Chad. See if he saw or heard anything from anyone else."

Lennon released another long, frustrated sigh through her nose. "They're filming more today. I'll call Avery later. I found her wasted last night. If the same thing happened to her, she'll probably want to file a report, too."

Dylan hoped to God that wasn't the case. He hoped he was one of the few and not many living out this nightmare. Others may not have been as lucky as to have someone save them from it.

"Thank you. For everything," Dylan said. "For believing me. For helping me."

"For letting you sleep in my bed," Lennon added, catching him off guard. He shot her a questioning look. "I could've made you sleep on the sofa."

"*You* slept on the sofa?" Dylan's eyebrows rose in horror.

"No, we shared," she answered as if he were an idiot. "I wanted to be close in case anything happened." Fear flickered in her eyes, and they drifted out of focus like she was receding into a memory.

It gave him a glimpse into what she'd experienced last night—how terrified she'd been. The hell she'd gone through.

What she must have gone through every time he came home late when they were married.

It cleaved open his gut.

Lennon blinked. "I told Erin you'd call her when you woke up," she said, her tone shifting. "She's been waiting to hear from you."

"Did you also tell—"

"Your dad doesn't know yet," she said. His shoulders relaxed. Relieved. "We figured you may want to tell him yourself. Or … not."

Dylan couldn't even think about that right now. "I'll go give her a call. Mind if I use the shower after?"

"Please do," Lennon said as her forehead wrinkled. "It was bad enough sleeping next to you last night."

He wished he could remember it. His mouth slanted into a half-smile. "Doesn't seem to be bothering you now."

"I've been holding my breath this whole time."

Dylan tightened his grip on her, pulling her closer. She dramatically feigned disgust as she pushed back. A laugh rumbled out of him before he released her. For a minor second, he forgot everything. Why he was there. Why he hadn't showered.

From the smile on Lennon's face and the flush of her cheeks, she did, too. Her cardigan slipped down her shoulder again. They stared at each other, only an arm's length apart, as their smiles faded and reality settled back in.

"I washed your clothes. I'll put them on the bed," Lennon told him. "Clean towels and an extra toothbrush are in the linen closet."

Dylan glanced down at the Arden Beach University tee. She'd undressed him. Put him in a clean shirt. But no one had been around to take care of her. And now, he was supposed to leave for ten days.

The idea of being away from her felt like leaving a piece of himself behind.

"I don't have to go to the boot camp."

Lennon picked up her mug, wrapping her hands around it. "Do you feel OK enough to go?"

"Yeah, but if you need me, I can stay—"

"No, go. If it'll help you get back on the team, then it's important. I'll be fine. Promise." She smiled. "Now, go shower so I can breathe and enjoy my coffee."

Dylan lifted his arm and smelled himself to make sure she was joking. Thankfully, she was. She smirked over the rim of her mug as he glared at her. "Thanks for the shirt, by the way."

Lennon took a sip, then ran her tongue between her lips as she lowered the mug. "It was yours. I forgot to give it back."

CHAPTER 29

Lennon

Lennon furiously scrubbed her face with a thick lather until her skin burned. A splash of cold water numbed it. She swiped a hand through the steam on the mirror where red, tired eyes stared back. She'd washed her hair, scrubbed every inch of her body, but couldn't rid herself of the gross feeling that clung to her.

An extra toothbrush sat beside the sink. Dylan was probably halfway to the Panhandle by now. Watching him walk out the door had physically hurt, knowing how far away he'd be and how long he'd be gone. Lennon was still raw. She'd barely slept last night, jerking awake at the slightest sound or movement.

The doctor assured her he'd be fine, but it reminded her too much of the night of the boat accident. Then, she'd been helpless in another state. Now, she felt helpless lying right next to him. And partially responsible.

Regret ate at her. Lennon wished she hadn't gone off with Tana at the party. That their conversation in the bathroom had gone differently. That she hadn't been so wrapped up in the damn cameras—the damn game.

The whole thing made her sick.

She'd almost lost him. Again.

Carol Anne left a few messages, trying to lure them back to the mansion. Lennon hadn't bothered to respond. She would have only made it worse with what she wanted to say.

Wrapped in a towel, she padded out to the bedroom's cool air as she combed through her wet hair. Sunlight cutting through the shutters tinted the room blue as day slipped toward night. Even with such a clear marker, time blurred, as if stuck in an endless dream. A pile of freshly washed linens sat in the middle of the bare mattress. She recalled Dylan lying on it, covered in sweat, an older man with a grey beard and age spots on the crown of his head feeding an IV into one of his veins.

The memory morphed into him lying under Kelsey.

Rage burned through her anew.

A white shirt folded on the dresser caught Lennon's eye. Her heart softened at the Arden Beach University logo, glad he hadn't taken it back. She took a step toward it but stopped when her phone rang from the bedside table. She hoped it was Dylan checking in, but Avery's name lit up the screen instead. She quickly answered. "Avery—hey."

"Hey, Lennon," Avery said, her voice soft and sluggish. "I've been so worried. I texted you back and tried calling earlier. I didn't know you'd left until this morning."

"Sorry, I put my phone on 'do not disturb.'" She'd texted Avery to check in on her since she knew the cameras would be there during the day but then silenced it when Carol Anne kept hounding her. Until Dylan had left, only calls from Erin could get through. "How are you?" Lennon sat on the edge of the mattress.

"Exhausted. Last night was … a lot."

That was the understatement of the fucking year.

"Are you OK?" Lennon asked.

"Yeah. My pride's just a little scraped up."

"You don't have anything to be embarrassed about."

"I let my fiancé's ex get to me at my bachelorette party," Avery remarked tightly. "That's pretty embarrassing."

"Kelsey shouldn't have invited her, knowing how it would make you feel. It was supposed to be your night."

"I get why she did it. She was trying to help," Avery reasoned. Her commitment to diplomacy was getting old. How could no one else see how toxic and manipulative Kelsey was? "I appreciate what you did for me. You saved me from mortifying myself further."

Lennon dragged the pad of her thumb over the comb's plastic teeth, her stomach twisting in a knot. "I wanted to ask you about that. Do you think someone may have spiked your drink?"

"What? No," Avery said, her laugh sounding a little nervous.

"Are you sure? You were pretty out of it …. . I've never seen you like that before."

Avery went quiet for a few seconds, almost long enough to make Lennon wonder if the call had disconnected, until she heard a soft sigh. "I had … way too many shots. I got it in my head—" The forced levity dropped from her voice. "I wanted to make Chad jealous. I don't know what I was thinking. It was stupid."

A mix of surprise and relief settled on Lennon. She was glad Avery hadn't been a victim of anything but her own choices, but it would have been easier to make a case for Dylan with someone else to back up his experience. What if no one came forward for the same reasons as Dylan? What if he was right and whoever did this had been careful to cover their tracks?

"So … how are you?" Avery asked, gently if not a little unsteady. "Kelsey told me what happened between her and Dylan."

Lennon's gut twinged. "What exactly did she tell you?"

"That they hooked up. Or at least, they were about to when you walked in."

Shock and rage hit her with such force that Lennon couldn't speak for a moment. When she finally found her voice, it was cold. "That's *not* what happened."

"Look, why don't you come back to the mansion?" Avery

offered, sounding a little uncomfortable. Her voice changed, almost like someone had walked into the room. Or had already been there. "I think it'd be better to talk about everything in person."

The cold suddenly permeated Lennon's skin, raising the hair on her arms. "You're still there?" Water from her hair slowly crept down her spine. "Are they filming you right now?"

"Yeah," Avery answered weakly—a tinge of guilt in it. Lennon's stomach sank. "We're shooting all day, remember?"

Lennon wedged her lower lip between her teeth, inwardly cursing Avery and herself and this stupid fucking show.

"I'm sorry, Lennon. I assumed you knew—" Avery stammered out, but Lennon ended the call before she finished her sentence.

Silence fell around her. She held the phone in her hand like it was a bomb she'd deactivated at the one-second mark.

Lennon couldn't escape being watched, not even in her apartment. Not even when she thought she was having a private conversation with a friend.

She would have to start questioning everything. The way Dylan did.

How could she live the rest of her life like this?

When someone knocked on the door, Lennon was curled up on the sofa, deep in the clutches of a nap. She peeled her eyes open at her cold, half-empty cup of coffee and empty plate on the table, *RuPaul's Drag Race* playing on the television behind it. Since the party, she hadn't left her apartment. The last few days had blended together in a sort of fever dream. Every time she considered leaving, even to get groceries, the anxiety of being observed by strangers held her hostage.

With the blinds shut, she had no idea how long she'd been

asleep, only that there was still daylight. She lifted her head, squinting at the clock on her phone. 2:18 p.m.

Lennon dragged herself to the door with her blanket around her shoulders, yawning, and peeked through the peephole. Her heart nearly jumped out of her chest. She quickly unlocked and swung the door open. "Holy shit. Am I dreaming?"

Clad in a light, cropped cardigan and high-waisted jeans, Erin grinned at her from under a messy bun. "Nope. Go get dressed. I'm dragging you out of your sad girl cave and taking you on a date."

After some convincing, which sounded more like *threatening* at times, Lennon pulled herself together, throwing on something other than her pajamas for the first time in three days. They hopped into Erin's white, two-seat convertible and took a ride a few blocks over to the coast. Being with her best friend as sunbeams bathed her skin and the scent of saltwater blew through her hair was enough to pierce through some of the dark clouds hanging around her heart.

The Tidebreakers were still on the other side of the country, but Erin told her she'd taken the first flight out that morning. "How'd you manage to get away from the team?" Lennon asked over the roar of the wind, tucking a strand of hair behind her ear that had escaped her ponytail.

"I told them I had a family emergency. I've never even taken a sick day, so they didn't give me any pushback. Cheyenne can handle it," Erin yelled back, referring to the team's lead physical therapist. Cheyenne was expected to retire soon, so the plan was for Erin, the assistant physical therapist, to take her place once she completed all the required classes, hours of on-the-job training, and board exams. When she wasn't working, she was usually busy with her studies.

"What did Rhett say about what happened?"

"Nothing because he doesn't know."

"What does he think is the emergency?"

"I'm here for you, silly." Erin bumped Lennon's elbow where it rested on the console between them, her white sunglasses briefly turning to her as blonde hair whipped around them. Emotionally raw as she was, Lennon nearly teared up. "I told him you were going through a rough patch and needed support. Obviously, I'm worried about Dylan, too. We video chatted when I landed, and I'm going to drive up to see him tomorrow with the excuse of a PT check-in."

"I can't believe no one else has come forward," Lennon said. Dylan's investigation had so far come up empty, and he was still waiting to hear if his lawyers had made any headway with the studio. Every day that went by took another shred of hope with it.

"He got the test results back this morning." Erin's hands tensed around the wheel. "It was Xamberal. The same thing Craig was on when he crashed the boat."

Lennon's stomach bottomed out. "Fuck," she exhaled. She propped her elbow on the door, pinching the bridge of her nose. "He probably did get it by mistake. That's why no one's saying anything. They don't want to get caught." And if they didn't find solid proof his drink was spiked, no one was going to believe he didn't take it on purpose, too.

He was almost certainly screwed.

"I'm worried the studio won't hand over the footage without a warrant, or agree to cut his scenes. If they don't, his only option is to go to the police, but …"

"He'll probably lose everything in the process," Lennon finished for her. She sank further down the seat as the pit in her stomach deepened.

They passed a Stonethread store, a popular sportswear brand. A series of large, black and white photographs of athletes from different sports hung over the tall windows. A baseball player was noticeably absent among them. They were one of the brands that had dropped Dylan shortly after the accident.

Any goodwill he'd managed to earn back since then would be gone. The backlash would be even worse. All over a lie.

"I don't know how I'm going to stomach the wedding," Lennon said. The small car jostled over a pothole, rocking her.

"So, you are going, then?"

"I have to. It's part of my contract because it's the season finale." Lennon sighed. "Annoyed as I am with Avery, I agreed to be her bridesmaid and it'd be pretty shitty of me not to show up for her wedding. She's been texting me, trying to make amends. I think it was just a lapse of judgment after a long night."

"As your best friend, I'm not obligated to forgive her."

A smile pulled at Lennon's lips. "Besides, it wouldn't just be for her. I'm supposed to perform at the reception. I'm even booked to record the song at a studio this week. I did this show for a reason, and I'll be damned if I give up my last chance to at least get my music on the show."

Erin smiled, pride gleaming in it. "That's my girl."

She turned down a familiar side street lined with mom-and-pop shops. The brick-laid street clattered under the tires, echoing off the old buildings. Warmth unfurled in Lennon's chest as she realized where Erin was taking her.

The vehicle slowed down to turn into a small parking lot shaded by palm trees, then into a space facing a turquoise stucco wall. Erin shifted the car into park before placing a hand on Lennon's shoulder. "Let's go feed your soul for a bit, shall we?"

They walked around the small building to the street side where the same big neon sign from the seventies hung above the door, welcoming them to WAXED POETIC VINYL. A bell chimed as they stepped inside. The musty scent of aged wood, paper, and cardboard jackets with a hint of incense transported Lennon back to all the weekends she'd spent thumbing through the crates searching for hidden gems. The same vintage posters and framed records hung on the walls up to the dark turquoise ceiling. The orange sofa beckoned her from the back corner beneath Christmas lights, where she used to curl up to sample records with her headphones. Behind it, another neon sign read "Screw normal, I want magic."

Erin couldn't have chosen a more perfect place to bring her. Lennon sent her a look of gratitude and immense love, and Erin winked.

They lazily combed through the vinyl records for the better part of an hour while listening to the immaculately curated playlist drifting from the speakers and occasionally chatting with the owner. Coco, a woman in black overalls with long grey hair, 20mm gauges in her ears, and tattoos covering most of her body, still remembered them.

"Ever heard of this artist?" Erin held up a record with a baby-faced teenage Raquel Rosas on the cover, her debut album from the late eighties.

"You haven't heard? We're practically best friends now." Lennon accepted the record from her and admired the image of Raquel in a white dress on the beach, her signature long, curly hair blowing around her smiling face. "Man, she started so young."

"I used to babysit her," Coco crooned as she dusted the wood shelves behind the register. She was currently wiping down a statue of a gold hand making the devil horns sign. "Sweet kid. Painfully shy."

"Are we talking about the same Raquel?" Lennon joked, only knowing the self-possessed woman and global superstar who could sell out a stadium.

"She came out of her shell on stage." Coco rose up on the toes of her well-worn leather boots to snag one of the framed photos from another shelf, the step stool she was on creaking with the motion. She hopped off with a childlike bounce and brought it around the desk to Lennon. A young Coco in a leopard mini skirt and fringed black leather jacket hung an arm around teenage Raquel's shoulders, who was clad in a stage outfit of tight white pants and a bedazzled crop top. The Arden Beach Music Festival stage was in the background. Coco tapped a chipped, neon green fingernail on it as she leaned an elbow on the tall metal desk. "That was the summer before her record deal."

Lennon performed on that same stage decades later when she was a few years older than Raquel had been. The same night Dylan proposed. An ache bloomed behind her ribs. Erin must have sensed the shift because she jumped in, taking the photograph from Lennon and complimenting Coco on her outfit in it, who began telling her the story behind the jacket. They continued chatting as Lennon turned to look through the crates toward the back of the store.

Soon, Erin's hand came to rest on her back. *Don't Dream It's Over* by Crowded House drifted from one of the speakers above their heads. Lennon continued to pick through the records, even as her gaze shifted inward.

"I'm falling for him again, Erin."

Erin rubbed her back. "I know, honey."

"I'm scared the timing still isn't right for us," Lennon admitted quietly, the truth carving a deep, painful hole inside her. "Things are only getting more chaotic for him, and I don't even know what my future will look like. We may not be in a position for a relationship any more now, than we were when we got married. I don't want to get hurt again." Her throat tightened. "We didn't know any better then, but we do now."

Erin had begun to gently flip through the records in the carton beside her. "That's all true," she said after a moment. The validation gave Lennon's heart a painful squeeze. "But you've never been the pragmatic one. Why start now?"

CHAPTER 30

Dylan

Dylan stepped into the batter's box, his shoes kicking clay onto the plate as he got into position. He tested his grip on the bat.

"You ready, Little Prince?"

He rolled his jaw at the taunting edge of the pitcher's tone. "Ready."

"You want me to go easy on ya in the first round?" Diego tossed the ball up and down in his hand, chewing gum.

Dylan tapped the bat's tip to the plate thrice, then swung it over his shoulder. "Give me all you got."

The twenty-one-year-old gave a quick tilt of his head as if to say, "alright then." Diego glanced past Dylan at a group of players behind the net and winked at them.

Dylan wondered how high the bets were that he'd strike out.

He'd been a two-way player since he was a kid, but he'd had to commit to one position when he entered the minor league. He'd missed batting. His father wouldn't be pleased that Dylan was doing anything other than pitching at this boot camp, but it was easier to ask for forgiveness than permission.

The players at the boot camp were mainly rookies and free agents in the league, working to improve their game, along with a few others like him who were returning from injuries. But unlike Dylan, they didn't have their reputation on the line. He knew they were all waiting to see how far the mighty had fallen.

Dylan had never felt lower than he had after the accident. This would be a walk in the park in comparison.

"Let's go," one of the guys yelled from the bleachers.

Dylan shifted his stance, loaded up the bat, and took a deep breath, slowly letting it out through his nose to settle into it.

Diego spat in the dirt, then casually observed him, loosely rolling the baseball in his hand. The sun beamed down from a cloudless sky, the air thick with the smell of freshly cut grass and pine trees that enveloped the park. The pitcher waited several seconds before suddenly pulling his arm back and hurling a fastball at him.

Dylan's reaction time was good, but his swing was off. He missed it entirely.

He ate the curse that rose in his throat, not wanting to show his frustration. At least now, he knew Diego's form. And his tell.

"You sure you don't want me to go easy on you? At least for a warm-up," Diego offered.

"Only if you need one," Dylan said.

Diego laughed, briefly looking over his shoulder at the players on the field. "Nah. I've been waiting all week for this."

"Then, put your money where your mouth is, rookie."

That got the reaction Dylan expected. Determination flared in Diego's eyes, his smile settling into a hard line on his face. Dylan flexed his fingers around the bat, stretching before repositioning his grip.

He watched Diego closely, saw the moment he mentally wound up—the feathering of a muscle in his neck.

Diego pitched another fastball, this time with even more aggression than the first, but Dylan was ready. The wood cracked against the ball, sending it soaring centerfield. He dropped the bat and took off running as the opposing team scrambled for the ball.

But it was gone—over the fence.

Dylan ran through the bases as applause rang out from the small group of players on the bleachers and his teammates on the field. Even some of the guys playing on the opposing side slapped his hand as he passed them on the way to home plate.

"Welcome back, Little Prince," one of them said as he sprinted past his base.

At least for a few minutes, Dylan felt like he was floating on air.

Man, he'd missed this.

The hot water on his skin and the steam filling his lungs helped him wind down after the game. Dylan braced his arm on the tiled wall, concentrating the stream from the shower head on his left shoulder. It soothed the aching muscles beneath his scar. He would've stayed there for an hour if he weren't in one of the small, grimy locker room showers.

Dylan spun the valve, cutting off the water and throwing a towel around his waist before stepping out into the locker room. He looked forward to a hot meal and an evening relaxing on a heating pad. Alone.

The other guys lingered in the locker room, shooting the shit and rehashing the game while a small television mounted in the corner played the muted local news. Dylan had always been the quiet, pensive type after a match. He liked to replay it in his head, process every play that had gone right, analyze the ones that hadn't. Some of his teammates taunted him about being a recluse. "*He's a tight ass 'til he gets a drink in him,*" they'd say.

Well, that was their problem now.

Dylan grabbed another towel to dry his hair as he strode to his locker. He punched in the code and swung open the squeaky metal door. Hanging the second towel around his neck, he poured some beard oil on his fingers and scrubbed it through his facial hair.

"Whoa, you see that?" asked one of the guys.

"Oh, shit."

Dylan looked back to see what the commotion was about and followed their attention to the television. The headline on the screen read "CARMICHAEL ENTERPRISES STOCK PLUMMETS."

The blood drained from Dylan's face.

"What's the big deal?" one of the younger players asked, his voice and other noise in the locker room receding to the background as Dylan stared at the screen, trying to read the slow-moving captions as they appeared. The anchors were talking about rumors of upcoming layoffs and budget cuts.

"They own the Tidebreakers, dumbass," another answered. "Guess the rumors about them having to sell are true after all."

"Maybe it's for the best," Diego remarked. That snapped Dylan's attention away from the television. He found Diego already looking at him, putting his arms through the holes of a white t-shirt and pulling it over his head.

"And why's that?" Dylan asked, humoring him. He screwed the cap back on the oil, shoving it back in the locker.

"Because the team needs some fresh blood. Carmichael's a dinosaur. He's more interested in taking care of himself and his rich friends than actually doing what's right by the team."

Dylan exhaled a short, quiet laugh. He'd been cutting Diego slack out of sympathy for what happened, taking the teasing and snide comments in stride the last few days, but shit-talking his former boss wasn't going to earn him any favors. But Dylan understood, Diego was angry and resentful, and he needed to get it off his chest.

"Why don't you say what you really want to say, Diego?" Dylan squared his body to the young player, facing him head-on.

Diego studied him for a moment, his tongue pressing into his cheek. "Alright." He nodded. "I think if you had a different last name, they wouldn't even be entertaining the idea of giving you another chance because there are plenty of players out here who can take your place and do an even better job at it. And if your father weren't up Carmichael's ass, he'd be out, too. The team's suffering, and all they care about is protecting their legacies. Everyone else is just a pawn."

Though it was nothing Dylan hadn't heard before from sports pundits, it burned to listen to it from someone who had once been his teammate, and even a friend. The locker room went quiet, the tension thicker than the dense, humid air as the other guys caught on to the conversation and exchanged glances with each other.

Dylan set his hands on his hips, briefly lowering his gaze to the concrete floor. "Well, thank you for being honest. I don't blame you for being pissed off. What happened to you wasn't fair."

Diego laughed derisively. "Wasn't fair? I got fucking screwed. I didn't even want to get on that boat. I just followed you and Craig because you were my teammates. I thought I could trust you. Then, you black out and the other fucker crashes the damn thing. I was the only one who tried to stop him, and what did I get for it? Punched in the face and cut from the team I quit college for. All because my name isn't Strickland."

The other guys shifted uncomfortably, some rubbing their chins as others raised their eyebrows. None of them were Tidebreakers— not yet anyway—but Diego clearly didn't feel any loyalty to the team that, in his eyes, had abandoned him.

The worst part was that he was right.

But how could Dylan let him know he agreed that Eddie made a mistake without throwing his boss and a man who was practically family under the bus? His hands were tied.

"There are a lot of politics in baseball that aren't fair," Dylan said, clenching his jaw. "Good people get screwed all the time. We all made a mistake that night, and we're all paying for it. I'm sorry you're off the team. But you're an excellent player, Diego. Someone will grab you, and it'll be the Tidebreakers' loss."

Diego's glare was sharp and unyielding. "You're damn right it will be."

There was nothing Dylan could say to fix Diego's situation, but he couldn't avoid addressing the elephant in the room. The thing he carried with him to every field and every locker room, the invisible barrier that would always separate him from his teammates and cast a shadow over every move he made.

"I know my background is unique," Dylan said. "I've had privileges most people don't, and it's made me question my worthiness more than anyone else. But I promise you, no one loves this team more than Eddie or my dad. Or me. Yeah, it's our legacies. That makes us really fucking committed to protecting it, even when things aren't going our way. There's no walking away from it when it gets tough or jumping to another one. This is it for us."

Dylan glanced up at the television. It showed three images of billionaires who had expressed interest in buying the team, including Nolan Pierce. Anger simmered low in his stomach. "And I can tell you," he continued, "if the wrong person gets ahold of the Tidebreakers, it *will* be nothing but a moneymaker to them, and they'll suck the soul out of it. So, you're damn right we're going to fight to keep that from happening."

Dylan slid the towel from his neck, dropping it on the bench parallel to the lockers. He didn't bother checking the other players' reactions or waiting for a response from Diego, who had listened with the same pissed off expression. He went back to getting dressed and thinking about how to ensure what happened at the party was buried.

Because they couldn't afford one more setback.

Dylan secured the brace over his shoulder, tightening it until the compression felt right—a good ache. The knock came at the door with his food delivery as he was tightening the wrap, and a minute later, he finally settled onto the small sofa in front of the television, kicking his feet up on the coffee table with the hot to-go container on his lap.

He tried to find something to watch on television, but his mind wouldn't release the grip on the conversation in the locker room.

As Dylan skimmed through the stations, frustration rose like a pressure wave through him. He finally shut off the television altogether and tossed the remote to the side. His appetite went with it. He rested his head back on the cushion with a drawn-out sigh, staring up at the flat, white ceiling.

He'd grown up receiving daily criticism, but what Diego had said was personal. It was easier to tune it out when it was from random pundits or disgruntled fans—hearing it from someone who had become a friend before the accident grated like salt in a wound.

Made him feel like dirt under their cleats.

Dylan checked his phone. Still no call from his lawyers. He'd been waiting for the one confirming the footage of him at the party was officially buried. Everyone who was there, including the production team, had signed NDAs. As long as the studio agreed to their terms in exchange for not pursuing a criminal investigation, he should be in the clear.

But the fact that it'd been almost a week and it hadn't been resolved yet worried him.

It felt like the walls were pressing in on him again. Dylan's mind was a ball launched into the air, soaring through the outfield as he fumbled to catch it before it went over the fence. The tightness in his chest made it hard to breathe. A tingle rose in his hands.

The wet bar loomed in the corner. He'd requested they remove the bottle of wine the hotel had gifted him and the other players in their rooms, but they'd left the glasses. He could call room service and have another one at the door in minutes. It would ease the pressure, calm his racing mind so he could breathe and feel the ground beneath his feet again. One glass would take the edge off.

Dylan kneaded his palms into his eyes, then slid a hand down his jaw. Sitting forward, he moved his food to the coffee table before reaching for his phone. He opened his text thread with Lennon. They hadn't talked much since he left. He'd been busy. And giving her space.

The guilt nearly ate him alive that he'd pull her into his mess. If she changed her mind and wanted out, it'd gut him, but he'd understand.

Dylan typed out a message—erased it. He wanted to hear her voice. His thumb hovered over the button to call her when his phone rang. His father's photo stared back at him with a video call request.

One of the last people he wanted to speak to at that moment.

"*Shit.*" Dylan hung his head, tempted by the red button to decline it. But if he didn't answer now, he'd have to answer later. He may as well get it over with so he could have the rest of the night to—hopefully, finally—decompress.

Dylan punched the green button. "Hey, Dad," he said, forcing a lift in his tone when his father's moving, pixelated image appeared on the screen. "How's … where are you again … L.A.?"

"Yep. Game's tomorrow. Just got back from drills." The phone was angled up at his chin, his weathered face swaying in and out of frame as he walked down a nondescript hall somewhere, presumably at his hotel. "How's summer camp?"

"Got my fire-starting badge today," Dylan joked back. He decided to strike a match—his father would likely find out, anyway. "Actually, I did hit a home run."

Rhett slanted a look at the screen. "Did the accident affect your head more than we thought and you forgot what a pitcher does?"

"This pitcher does both," Dylan reminded him, lighthearted enough. Beneath the surface, resentment chafed. Everything had been decided for him. Everything controlled. "Don't worry, it was one game."

His father was silent for a beat. Dylan waited for the lecture.

"Showed the rookies how it's done, huh?" Rhett said, surprising him. He stopped, and a second later, the lock on his hotel room door beeped twice before he let himself inside. "How'd it feel?"

The adrenaline rush echoed in his body as he replayed the memory of running through the bases—the cheering, the wind across his face, the feeling of invincibility. "Amazing." He realized his eyes had gone out of focus and pulled his attention back to his dad, who had sat down at a table, watching Dylan with a subtle smile.

Rhett seemed to be lost in thought for a moment, too, his chin perched on his thumb and his forefinger resting over his upper lip. "You heard the news?"

"About Carmichael Enterprises? Yeah."

Rhett's smile faded. "I just got off the phone with Eddie a little while ago. Needless to say, he's not exactly having a home run kind of day." He sighed, heavy and tired, as he leaned back in his chair. "The commissioner's under pressure to force a sale of the Tidebreakers if Eddie doesn't do it himself."

Dylan hung his head. He knew, logically, that's where things were headed, but the reality of it sank cold in his bones. He couldn't believe it was happening. "What's his plan?"

"Well, we have an idea, but I told him I needed to run it by you first," Rhett said. Dylan didn't like the way that sounded or the pause that followed. "Eddie's calling an emergency meeting with the board to make his case for more time. And to get your suspension lifted."

"You think them knowing I'll be officially returning next season is enough to help?"

"I think you returning *this* season is."

His father's words took a moment to permeate fully. "You mean … coming back *right now*?"

Rhett waited a beat. "Are you ready?"

What a complicated question. One Dylan never thought he'd have to consider so soon. Medically, his doctor had cleared him for it, and he was almost back to where he'd been before the accident by all measurable metrics. But *almost* wasn't good enough. What if his father was right—if he went out there now, did Dylan only stand to embarrass himself?

They were banking on his return to help them turn things

around and win games, as well as to draw people in and support the team. What if it did the opposite? What if it was too soon for the public to have his back?

"Cooney hurt his ankle yesterday on the field. It's not looking good. I think we're going to lose him, too." Rhett gently shook his head to himself as his gaze fell somewhere distant. Cooney was one of their best pitchers. He'd stepped up after losing Dylan and Diego from the roster.

They couldn't catch a break.

"If you need me, I will be," Dylan said.

Rhett's attention drew back to him. He remained quiet for a few moments, studying him. "Are you sure?" His tone left no room for uncertainty. He needed to know that Dylan was committed before they went all in on him.

Cement poured into his ribcage, filling all the empty spaces until it rose to his throat. Dylan swallowed it down, resolute.

"I'm sure," Dylan said. "Tell me what to do and I'll be there."

CHAPTER 31

Lennon

Flowers. *So* many flowers.

On the tables, along the double staircase, hanging from the massive chandelier, in the arms of staff crossing through the foyer. Standing in the middle where the champagne fountain had been, Lennon gaped at how the mansion—the scene of the crime—had been completely transformed from a salacious nightclub into an elegant wedding venue akin to something out of *Bridgerton*. Staff hurried back and forth, carting around decor to finish setting the stage for a fairytale.

Her stomach churned, the memories of that night still haunting her. The reality of it still threatening to destroy Dylan's career. But she was expected to act like nothing happened. Dress up, smile, play a part in the fairytale.

Lennon grabbed a small bottle of water from a nearby craft services table. She dug out a box of pink chewables from her bag to help with the nausea and popped one into her mouth, chasing it with a few gulps of cold water.

As she went to screw the lid back on, Lennon paused. Popped two more. She needed all the help she could get.

An assistant from the production team led Lennon to the bridal suite. Cameras recorded her entrance to one of the palatial master bedrooms, where several beauty stations had been set up for hair and makeup. The other bridesmaids were in various stages of glam as stylists worked on them, the smell of hairspray and acetone pungent in the air.

"Lennon!" Avery jumped up from her chair, eliciting a string of curses from her hairstylist through bobby pins sticking out of their mouth. She shuffled over to Lennon in her white silk robe and slippers. "I'm so glad you're here," she said, relief in her voice.

They hadn't seen each other since the party or spoken since *that* phone call outside of texts. Two cameramen focused on them.

"Of course." Lennon mustered a smile, shoving her hands into the back pockets of her distressed jeans. "What kind of bridesmaid would I be if I bailed on your wedding?"

Avery's smile softened. For a moment, her gaze cast downward. "I am really sorry, Lennon. About everything."

Lennon sensed Avery's sincerity. It softened her a little. They'd both made choices they regretted for the sake of the show.

At least it would all be over soon.

"Water under the bridge," Lennon said. Avery's smile deepened, gratitude in her eyes. "It's your wedding. Nothing else matters today but celebrating you and Chad."

Avery directed her to an empty beauty station beside Tana and Candace, who said hello around the technicians working on them. Lennon caught Kelsey's icy gaze a few chairs over as she lowered into hers. Fury boiled up, but she tamped it down. There was so much Lennon wanted to say to her, but this wasn't the time, nor the place. She only hoped everyone else was on the same page.

A makeup artist stepped between them and began to prep Lennon's face.

Watching Avery prepare for the day turned out to be harder

than Lennon had expected. She knew it would likely be triggering, but she hadn't anticipated the bottomless, hollow pit in her gut that seemed to grow wider every minute. The emptiness, the grief. It snuck up on her in the small moments. Avery's mother gifting her something blue from her wedding to her father. Avery seeing herself in her gown for the first time. Avery reading parts of a letter from the groom to read on their wedding day.

Dylan began writing Lennon letters shortly after they met. Like the one he gave her when they were fifteen telling her he couldn't wait to marry her someday. The one he gave her the night he did. And the one she never read—the one he'd sent her mere months ago, after his accident, still buried in a drawer.

They hadn't seen each other since Dylan left for boot camp. Lennon got a text when he got back in town a couple of days ago, but he said something unexpected had come up and he'd be tied up until the wedding. She had a feeling it had to do with the news about Carmichael Enterprises or the legal battle with the show—or possibly both—but she hadn't pressed it. He'd told her he wanted to talk about it in person.

Yet another thing for her to try and avoid thinking about all day.

Lennon put on a smile in all the photos with the bridal party, then lined up for the ceremony, which took place in the sprawling backyard overlooking a private beach. The setting sun reflected the thousands of flowers filling the space, mostly soft pink roses that matched their bridesmaids' dresses. They wore a flowing gown with a slit at the thigh, heart-shaped bodice, and delicate straps. Candles lined the long aisle, casting a romantic, ethereal glow. When the violin music began, Lennon felt as though her center of gravity shifted. She just had to put one foot in front of the other. Make it down the aisle. Stand there. Smile. And walk back.

Lennon slipped her arm through the waiting groomsman's, glad to have something to help steady herself. Every step Lennon took down the aisle was a step through memories. She pushed them away, focusing on the back of Candace's head before shifting to her gold stilettos as she stepped over scattered rose petals. Lennon watched a few of them crunch beneath her toes. When she lifted her gaze, the next petal she crushed felt like her heart.

The music faded, along with the faces around him. The world diffused to slow motion. Dylan stood at the end of a row in a midnight blue tuxedo, his beard freshly trimmed and his thick hair elegantly styled.

Though his expression was stoic, his heart sat in his eyes. Fixed on her.

Lennon forced her attention straight ahead. As she passed within inches of him, the hair rose on her arms and the back of her neck. She stiffened but continued planting one foot in front of the other until she was at the altar, taking her place with the other bridesmaids.

For the rest of the ceremony, the majority of her energy was spent trying to avoid her attention accidentally landing on him in the audience as the cameras watched closely.

Lennon failed once, during the vows. Instinctively, her gaze found Dylan, and she was thankful he was looking down when she did. She allowed herself to stare at him for a few seconds, for the memory of standing across from him at their wedding to layer over it. She wondered if he was thinking about it, too. Almost as if he heard her, he raised his head and their eyes locked.

This time, Lennon didn't look away.

After the post-ceremony group portraits, Lennon went searching for Dylan in the ballroom where everyone was waiting for the bride and groom to arrive. Massive chandeliers sparkled as hundreds of people filed in. The space was grand enough to hold an entire stage, dance floor, multiple buffets, and tables with seating for the whole guest list.

Lennon was about to text him when her stomach growled, and that's when she knew where to find him.

"Erin would have something to say about us both always gravitating toward the food," Lennon remarked as she found him eying a wide assortment of cheeses on a tall, tiered display. She didn't even know that many types existed.

They made eye contact through the silver serving stands from opposite sides of the buffet, and her heart flipped over in her chest. Man, he looked good. Everything about that day had been disorienting, but as soon as their eyes met, it was like grabbing hold of an anchor. The storm kept blowing around them, but he made her feel solid. Secure.

One side of his mouth tilted up. "Should we send her a selfie, so she doesn't miss the opportunity?"

"It's the least we could do while she's in exam hell."

Lennon waited as he walked to the end of the long buffet, coming around to join her on the other side. Her stomach fluttered, but this time, it was from a different type of hunger.

The man could wear a fucking tux.

"You want to take it?" Dylan asked.

"Huh? Oh, yeah. Sure." Lennon removed her phone from her clutch and swiped open the camera app. He leaned in, the earthy scent of his cologne and aftershave sending a rush of warmth through her as she extended her arm to position them both in the frame with the impressive tier of cheese between them. They each pulled a face as she snapped the picture.

While she sent it off to Erin, Dylan remained close. Lennon felt a little light-headed, and she hadn't even had any champagne yet.

The urge to wrap her arms around him was nearly unbearable.

"So … how have you been?" Dylan asked carefully as he offered her an empty plate.

Lennon wished she could answer him honestly without the mic pack pressing into her back and the cameras lurking among guests, who were stuffing their faces with *hors d'oeuvres* and cocktails. "Good," she said with her customer service smile.

Dylan matched it with his PR-trained one. Even under the veil of the soft candlelight, the dark circles beneath his eyes were barely concealed, the heaviness in them even less so. The designer tuxedo and perfectly coiffed hair couldn't hide the brokenness. Lennon had a feeling the same could be said of her if anyone looked hard enough. "Good," he returned.

From the concerned look Dylan gave her, it seemed he was looking hard enough. The elephant in the room squeezed between them.

"Are you excited about your performance?" Dylan asked, trying to lift the mood as he placed some gruyere on his plate.

"Yeah. I hope they like it." Lennon followed his lead, looking over their options. She'd never heard of half of them. What the hell was *Pule cheese*?

"There's no way they won't."

"I don't know why, but I'm nervous. No, that's a lie. I do know why. I've performed at a hundred weddings, but this one's different." When he regarded her with a questioning dip of his brows, Lennon explained, "Because I know the bride, and it's going to be on TV." *And you're here.*

Dylan had no idea yet that the song was about him.

They always were.

"Come on, you sang in front of Raquel and Oscar. This should be a cakewalk. Or … a *cheese* walk." Dylan sent her a little smirk as he popped a piece of gruyere in his mouth.

Lennon stared at him, then snort-laughed. "Wow. That joke was a cheese walk."

"But it made you laugh."

She rolled her eyes, but inside, warmth curled around her heart.

A feeling she'd carry into her performance.

The bride and groom's arrival kicked off the celebration. Thankfully, the party was significantly tamer than their last. Lennon gritted her teeth through Kelsey's toast and the dinner that followed, grateful the topics at the wedding party's table never strayed into dangerous territory. She glanced at Dylan across the ballroom a few times, catching him laughing with a table of athletes he knew. She recognized some from the party.

Lennon couldn't help but wonder if any of them had been the reason his drink was spiked. Had it been one of the bartenders, or had one of the guests dropped it in their own drinks and accidentally included Dylan's?

Or not so accidentally.

After the couple's first dance, serenaded by a famous R&B singer with *three* platinum records who was another one of Chad's friends, Lennon slipped out to the hallway to warm up her vocals. She had about fifteen minutes to prepare before she was due on stage.

During the lip buzzing portion of her vocal warm-up, Avery came around the corner, searching the hall. The short train of her lace column dress dragged behind her. When her eyes landed on Lennon, she stopped.

"Hey, Mrs. Mormont," Lennon said with a playful smile before keying into Avery's tense body language. "Everything OK?"

"Hey, Lennon …" Avery fidgeted with her new wedding band as she approached her. "I need to talk to you about something."

The filet and champagne Lennon had at dinner churned in her gut. "If it's about the party, we can talk after the wedding—"

"No, it's not that."

Lennon took a breath, steeling herself. "OK. What is it, then?"

"I'm so sorry, I just found out. I wish they'd told me sooner. Maybe I could've done something about it—"

"Avery." Lennon stepped closer, placing a hand on Avery's arm. "What happened?"

Avery's brows dipped over dark, sorrowful eyes. "I was told there were some scheduling mix-ups and miscommunication between the event coordinators and the film crew, and they've had to shift a bunch of things around," she explained, frustration underpinning it. She frowned as her voice softened. "They told me there's no time for your performance. I'm *so* sorry, Lennon."

It took a moment for what she'd said to sink in. "Are you serious?" Avery gave a slight, solemn nod. "Oh," Lennon managed to get out as her brain struggled to process it. The shock, then disappointment, came in swift and hard like a pin pulled on a grenade behind her ribs. "Are—are you sure? I mean, I don't mind squeezing in later—"

"I asked. They said it isn't possible without throwing everything else out of whack. I don't know—I'm not in charge of anything. They've planned it all. I tried to argue with them, but they won't budge." Avery shook her head like she was at the end of her rope. Like perhaps this wasn't the first thing that had gone wrong with the show. "Maybe you can sing it for us another time? Maybe when we get back from our honeymoon." Her brows curved upward, her tone hopeful.

Some other guests joined them in the hall, but their presence barely registered. Lennon nodded, forcing a smile through the shell shock. "Yeah. Yeah, of course. The important thing is that you have a great night."

Avery returned her smile, but it was a mixture of gratitude and sadness.

"Avery!" Carol Anne grabbed Avery's attention over Lennon's shoulder. Avery flinched. "I've been looking for you everywhere. We need some shots of you with the sponsors before they leave."

Avery sighed as she shut her eyes, the glow that should be

radiating from a bride on her wedding day cast in shadow. Lennon wasn't the only pawn whose desires seemed to have been sidelined for the show's priorities. She and Avery exchanged a look of solidarity before the latter reluctantly left to answer Carol Anne's summons.

Lennon buried her face in her hands to keep herself from screaming. *This can't be real.*

"Talk about dodging a bullet. Avery doesn't need Lennon's bad luck tainting her wedding," a haughty voice remarked. Some people snickered.

Lennon slowly lifted her head toward Kelsey. "What did you say?"

The other women—Tana and two others Lennon didn't know—abruptly stopped laughing as their attention snapped to Lennon. Candace also stood off to the side, but she was quiet. They all glanced between her and Kelsey.

"Nothing," Kelsey said, not even bothering to look at Lennon.

Lennon approached her. "If you want to say something about me, say it to my face."

Kelsey raised her eyebrows, acting stricken. "I don't have anything to say to you," she retorted with a small laugh, looking back at her friends as though Lennon were unhinged.

"You always have something to say, Kelsey."

Now, Kelsey looked downright annoyed. "Do you get off crashing parties and attacking people for no reason? For God's sake, you couldn't even let a bride enjoy her own bachelorette party. I heard you dragged her away while she was trying to have some fun."

"She was being taken advantage of," Lennon corrected. "The cameraman was practically salivating."

"That's not what I heard," Kelsey retorted. "She told you she didn't want to leave."

"She wasn't fully coherent." Lennon looked to the pregnant

bridesmaid hanging on the outskirts of the small group. "Candace saw how out of it she was after I brought her upstairs."

Everyone turned to Candace, who started like a deer in the headlights under the sudden attention. Cradling her belly through the dusty rose dress, she glanced at Kelsey before her expression flattened. "She was just a little tired. She rested for a bit and then went back to the party."

Shock jolted through Lennon. Remorse briefly flashed across Candace's face, but she recovered quickly, averting her gaze.

"Sounds to me like you were jealous of the attention she was getting," Kelsey suggested. "Is this little attack on me now because of Dylan? Are you still jealous we got together at the party?"

Lennon pinned her attention on Kelsey, fire surging through her. "Forcing yourself on someone isn't the same as hooking up, Kelsey."

"*Excuse me?*"

"Whoa, whoa, now that's out of line," Tana said, stepping between them. Stern eyes narrowed on Lennon. "You're taking it too far."

"I didn't *force myself* on him." Kelsey put on a show of being affronted. "Dylan took *me* to his room. He couldn't get me upstairs fast enough."

Lennon shoved her tongue in her cheek as she huffed a sardonic laugh. *This bitch.* She opened her mouth to retort, but something Kelsey said stuck in her brain, piercing through the cloud of fury. "You're lying," she said. "Chad told me he saw Dylan go upstairs by himself."

"Well, obviously, he was wrong. Or he didn't want to upset you." Kelsey crossed her arms and canted her head, eyes narrowing. "If you were so concerned about what he was doing, where were you? What were *you* doing? Or maybe I should ask, who? Someone else who could get you your next career opportunity or be your meal ticket since the famous baseball player husband didn't work out?"

"You're really going hard on the whole gold digger thing," Lennon noted. "Makes me wonder if you're projecting."

"I don't need anyone's help," Kelsey said—a touch defensively. "But I guess you're saying those rumors about you sleeping your way into a record deal aren't true, then, either?"

Lennon scrunched her brows together. "What rumors? What the hell are you talking about?"

"I'm just saying, where there's smoke, there's usually fire."

Lennon dropped her voice low. "You don't know anything about me."

"Oh, I've known *plenty* of girls like you, *Lennon*," Kelsey said, standing tall with the others at her back. "You're two-faced. You go around playing the innocent victim, trying to make everyone feel bad for you when you're the one who's lying and desperate for attention. You took advantage of Avery to get on this show, then your ex-husband to get more screen time. No one's even seen you trying to do anything with your music since you got here. You're riding everyone else's coattails because you can't get any opportunities to stick on your own." She took a step toward Lennon. "I see right through you."

Lennon stepped toward Kelsey, locking eyes with her. Her nails dug into her palms. "I see right through *you*, Kelsey. You're a liar trying to stir up drama in a desperate attempt for relevance because you have nothing else to offer. You're full of *shit*."

Kelsey scoffed. "No wonder that record label fired you. Why would anyone want to work with someone so hostile and obsessed with playing the victim? Honestly, it's sad. It's becoming more and more clear why Dylan left you."

"I didn't leave her. She left me."

Everyone's attention shot to Dylan. Kelsey's face fell, her whole body stiffening.

Dylan forced his way through the crowd that had gathered, including a few cameramen, to stand beside Lennon. His arm brushed hers as he gave her a look of reassurance.

The feeling of gratitude that ballooned in her chest nearly stole Lennon's breath.

"Lennon never did anything wrong," Dylan stated before eying Kelsey, his expression turning cold. "Our marriage fell apart because of me. She was always there for me, but I … I wasn't there for her. I didn't know how to deal with my demons, and she paid the price for it." He glanced at Lennon again, his regret palpable. "She's one of the strongest, most honest people I know. She gave me more chances than I deserved. She finally couldn't take it anymore. That's on me, not her."

Glances passed among the crowd, guests mumbling to each other. Kelsey kept her arms crossed, her expression unreadable, but Lennon noticed the slight tension in her jaw and the way her nails dug into her bicep.

"You can apologize to her now," Dylan told Kelsey.

Kelsey's eyes widened infinitesimally. They flicked back to Lennon, and Lennon knew that if looks could kill, they'd both have dropped in that hallway.

Lowering her chin, Kelsey ran her tongue through her lips, then wore a remorseful expression when she lifted her head. "I had no idea about your marriage. I'm sorry for assuming anything," she told Lennon. "I know there are always two sides to everything. I guess I felt protective over Dylan after everything that's happened." She smiled softly at Dylan. "It's hard to imagine you *not* being a great husband. I think you're probably being too hard on yourself. It says a lot that you're owning up to your mistakes and trying to be a better man. That's really … amazing."

Lennon stared at Kelsey, baffled by her switch-up. Talk about being two-faced. She rolled her eyes, exhaling a sharp laugh. "You've got to be fucking kidding me," she said under her breath.

"Look, this is my best friend's wedding." Kelsey dropped her arms, flipping up her palms in a show of surrender. "Can we put aside our differences and focus on celebrating her? I'm not in the mood for drama tonight. No one here is."

The weight of the crowd suddenly pressed in on Lennon. She met the stares of those gathered around them.

A chill spread through her as Lennon realized they were all looking at her as though *she* were the villain.

Tears stung the backs of her eyes, but she held them in. She'd be *damned* if she was going to let them see her cry. "Fuck this. I'm done." Lennon ripped off the lavalier microphone hidden under the front of her dress as she grabbed her clutch from a nearby chair in the hall. She pushed through the crowd, nearly knocking into one of the camera operators.

Behind her, she heard Kelsey remark, "There she goes, running away again."

Lennon kept moving, knowing the fight she wanted to have would make her look worse. The best thing she could do was remove herself, even if it made her sick. As she crossed the ballroom for the quickest route to the front door, she reached into the back of her dress, trying to claw off the rest of her mic pack. She scanned the crowd for Avery but didn't see her. She'd explain and apologize later.

"Hey—where do you think you're going?" Carol Anne jumped in front of her, clipboard clutched in her hand.

"I'm leaving."

"No. Let's talk about this—"

"I said, *I'm leaving.* Unless you want to talk about Dylan being drugged by someone at a party *you* were managing."

For the first time, Lennon saw something akin to trepidation flash in the supervising producer's eyes.

"That's what I thought," Lennon said. She shoved past Carol Anne, making her way out of the ballroom.

In the foyer, she handed the ball of wires and machinery to a confused assistant who happened to be passing by, then continued out the front door and down the steps. Stopping under the porte-cochère, she fumbled with the lock on her clutch to get to her phone.

"Lennon—"

She glanced back at Dylan jogging down the steps, then returned to fighting the clasp so she could order a car.

"You OK?" he asked as he stopped beside her.

Pressure built behind Lennon's eyes again, heat flushing up her neck and ears. When the clasp refused to open after a few more tugs, she let out an exasperated grunt. She nearly chucked the entire clutch across the motor court but stopped herself as she looked around, afraid cameras were still watching.

"They didn't follow us. I made sure of it," Dylan said. She noticed his mic pack was gone, too. "Come on—I've got my car. Let's get out of here."

CHAPTER 32

Lennon

The downtown Arden Beach skyline shimmered against the dark, velvety sky. As the distance between Lennon and the mansion grew, the pressure in her body gradually eased. She still felt on the verge of throwing up.

"What do you need right now?" Dylan asked, his tone calm, though she sensed the anger simmering beneath it. The muscles in his neck and hands flexed as he gripped the steering wheel.

"I'd like to hit Kelsey in the face with a baseball bat," Lennon answered. With sarcasm. Mostly.

"Anything else that won't get us put in jail?"

She considered it. "No."

He chuckled, but then abruptly stopped, a thought cutting it off. A conspiratorial smile tugged at his mouth. "Actually, I have an idea."

Fifteen minutes later, they drove through another mansion-lined neighborhood in a quiet suburb and stopped at a massive iron gate leading to a long driveway. He pressed a button on the roof of his vehicle, opening the gate that led to a palatial Spanish Mission-style home at the end of the winding driveway.

Dylan asked her to wait in the living room, which shared a large space with a dining room. It was the kind of house Lennon had always dreamed of calling home—warm, lived in, full of character. Dark-stained wood beams stretched across the two-story ceiling, while three ornate wrought iron railings framed by arches offered a peek at the second floor. A massive fireplace molded from the Venetian plaster walls had her imagining curling up there with her guitar as a fire crackled in the hearth.

Framed black and white photographs lined the wood mantle. As she waited, Lennon started at one end, admiring each one. His parents when they were young and happy on their wedding day. He and Erin sitting on his mother's lap in the stands at the Tidebreakers' stadium. The four of them on the beach about a year before his mother passed. His parents posing together after Rhett was inducted into the Hall of Fame, his mother smiling in the black dress Lennon wore to the gala.

Another made her heart hitch—a photo of Lennon, Dylan, and Erin in middle school on the ballfield cheesing it up for the camera. She reached out to touch it but then dropped her hand as she heard one of the sliding doors to the backyard open behind her.

Dylan returned with his jacket removed and the sleeves of his white shirt rolled up to his elbows. "Come on," he said, inclining his head.

He led her outside to his batting cage. The air was thick with the scent of sea salt, the ocean only a few yards away. Rhett's house had a batting cage and a large backyard with plenty of room to practice baseball, but Dylan had always dreamed of having one of his own. Pride warmed her heart as she approached the cage, knowing how much it must have meant to him the day he contracted someone to build it. He opened the metal door and picked up the bat leaning next to it before gesturing for her to enter.

As Lennon stepped inside, she followed his nod to a bullseye at the far end of the cage. She realized a photograph was taped to it.

A photograph of Kelsey.

Lennon expelled a loud, whooping laugh. She held her stomach as she threw her head back. "Did you print that out just now? You are a fucking *psycho*."

"And you love it." Dylan offered the bat to her with a smirk.

A wicked grin split across her face, taking the bat from him. As she rolled it in her hands, getting a feel for its weight, she tried to remember what she'd learned from times playing together as a kid. She was never that into it, but she'd played occasionally with Erin and Dylan on the field after games and at their house. "It's been a while since I've tried to hit a ball."

"Muscle memory is your friend. Just lock your eyes on the target and let your instincts do the rest," he said casually, closing the door behind her.

"Easy for a pro to say. Especially one not wearing heels." Lennon got into a stance, digging her shoes into the clay dirt and wrapping her hands around the base of the bat.

"Ready?"

She gave him a nod. A moment later, the machine whirred to life ahead of her. Lennon's heartbeat increased, the anticipation of a ball flying toward her at any moment instinctively waking up her system. When the ball finally shot out and raced toward her, she swung and missed. It plunked into the dirt an embarrassing distance from the cage wall. She realigned herself. A few seconds later, another ball went out. She missed again. On the third try, she clipped the side and it went foul, colliding with the side of the cage. "*Damnit.*"

"Keep your right arm close to your body," Dylan instructed, "and keep it bent at a ninety-degree angle as you follow through."

Lennon corrected herself and aggressively swung again when the ball came at her. The next few were all either complete misses or foul balls. She wanted to see *one* of those things hit Kelsey's photo straight in the center. She needed something to go her way.

Frustration coursed through her as she wondered why she couldn't even hit a damn ball once.

She was batting zero in life and in this stupid cage.

The machine powered down, and the door squeaked open behind her. She let out an exasperated sigh as she let the tip of the bat drop to the ground, the base hanging from her grip. "It'd be easier if I just walked down to the target and hit her in the face."

"We already agreed murder was off the table," Dylan reminded her. "Here, let me show you." The light touch of his hand on her elbow sent sparks fanning across her skin. The frustration in her evaporated. His presence at her back made every nerve in her light up, rooting her into an intense state of awareness. She followed his nudge to pick up the bat, then allowed him to adjust her hips, legs, and torso to stand correctly. His arms encircled her, the length of his body lightly pressing against hers. Gentle hands positioned her arms in the proper hold before settling atop her grip on the bat to shift her hold on it.

"You want to stand like a triangle, with your head in the center of your feet. Keep your front leg firm and back foot on your toes so you can easily rotate," Dylan explained, his voice slightly deeper and quieter than before, the vibration of it tickling her ear. Butterflies chased each other up her spine. Layering over the sea and freshly cut grass, she smelled his cologne again, and it took everything in her not to lean into him. "Got it?"

Lennon realized she'd been distracted, her eyelids fluttering as her gaze refocused. She nodded tightly. "Mmhmm."

The corner of his mouth nudged upward. He'd noticed. "Good. Now, focus on your target—envision the ball hitting it. See it like it's already happened." The slow, focused way he spoke and the way his tongue rounded over certain words from his comfortably familiar accent made her legs feel like they were about to melt into the dirt. That certainly wouldn't help with her batting average. "Take a deep breath, then exhale it all out. Watch the ball."

Dylan let go, stepping away from her. For a moment, she felt his absence so profoundly that she almost instinctively dropped the bat to go after him as if she were magnetized to him. She managed to keep her feet planted and reminded herself to focus on the target.

Lennon followed his instructions. She zeroed in on the picture of Kelsey. Imagined the power in her swing, the crack of it hitting the ball, sending it soaring through the cage, square between Kelsey's smug eyes.

The machine whirred back to life.

She took a deep breath and let the exhale take the tension with it. When the ball came, she swung with force and precision and sent the ball into the right-hand corner of the photo.

"Hell yeah—that's it!" Dylan shouted over the buzz of the machine.

The next several balls were all pretty good, hitting somewhere around the target. When she finally hit it square in the middle, she screamed in delight, shooting her hands up over her head. "I GOT IT!"

The machine clicked off, and the chain-link door screeched open. She dropped the bat before jumping into his arms, and he spun her around. When she landed back on the ground, she said breathlessly, "I want to do it again."

Dylan laughed as she picked up the bat and went for several more cathartic rounds.

Once she'd tired out her arms, they stretched out on the lawn as her heart rate came down, her dress clinging to the sweat on her skin. Lennon discarded her heels so her bare feet could sink into the cool grass, and he'd done the same with his socks and shoes. They stared up at the full moon hanging in the clear night sky peppered with stars.

"Remind me never to piss you off if there's a bat nearby," Dylan mused.

Lennon smiled as she looked over at the battered photo of Kelsey. She'd drawn devil horns and a mustache on it, and Dylan pinned it to a palm tree to celebrate her victory. "Well, if this whole reality show thing doesn't end up giving my music career the boost I was hoping for, at least I have a backup plan now."

"I hear the Tidebreakers are looking for new players," he remarked wryly.

Lennon's stomach tightened with the reminder. She played with the grass between her fingertips. "You haven't told me what's happening with that since you left."

Dylan kept his eyes on the sky and took a deep, slow breath. "This past week, Carmichael Enterprises' stock took a big hit. The company's been struggling, but now everyone knows. Add that to everything that's been going on with the team …. They're pushing him to sell it. Soon."

"They?"

"The board. They want the commissioner to force the sale if Eddie doesn't decide to do it himself."

"Well, what's he going to do?"

A muscle in his jaw pulsed. "Eddie and my dad want to put me back on the team." Dylan turned to her. "Now."

The air around them grew thick, sticking in Lennon's lungs. "You mean, *now* now? To play this season?" she asked. He gave a curt nod. "How do you feel about it?"

"I have a meeting with the board tomorrow to plead my case. If they approve it, I'll be back on the field as soon as next week."

Lennon searched his eyes for the answer to her actual question. Whatever it was, he was hiding it from her. Or from himself. "Is that what you want?"

Dylan rolled his head back to the sky, his hands clasped and thumbs fidgeting around each other on his abdomen. "I want to help the team. I'm just worried it'll have the opposite effect. Especially if what happened at the party gets out."

"Aren't your lawyers working on that?"

"Trying to, but the studio's calling our bluff," Dylan answered with a tight exhalation. "They told us to move forward with an investigation if I want to do anything about it. My lawyers are looking for an alternative."

"I know you'd rather this not get out to the public, but I think you should consider filing a police report if they can't figure something else out. Or sue the fucking show."

"We signed waivers."

"I feel like being drugged against your will should be an exception."

A sharp divot formed along his jaw. He stared at the sky without answering, but he didn't have to. She nearly reeled back when she realized what it was she saw there. "You blame yourself," Lennon surmised.

"I should've been more careful."

"Stop with the victim-blaming, Dylan. This isn't your fault. *You* were the one taken advantage of." Her voice shook a little, her lungs straining around the shallow breaths she took.

"I don't even know if I was singled out," Dylan reasoned, becoming exasperated. "Look—I'm not saying it's not fucked up, it is. It's extremely fucked up. I'm trying to do something about it, I'm just—" He pushed out a sigh as he scrubbed a hand across his face. The subsequent admission came with a timbre of defeat. "I'm tempering my expectations. My lawyers said I can expect the studio to put up a formidable fight if I pursue this and probably leak the footage before we even get to it. They're confident we'll eventually win, but not without it going public first. At that point, the league may decide it's better to cut their losses than be involved in the circus."

A deep pit formed in her gut, threatening to swallow her whole. They *would* do something like that.

Lennon tried to find a steady breath through the despair creeping through her. A breeze swept through the palm trees, their shadowed fronds briefly blocking the stars as they rustled. "I don't know how things have gotten so out of control," she wondered aloud. "Whenever I think I'm finally getting a handle on life, something goes wrong, and I realize I don't know anything. I'm sick of feeling powerless." She paused, her voice softening to almost a whisper. "I'm sick of failing."

"Me too." Dylan shifted beside her, raising an arm to shove it behind his head, the fabric of his white dress shirt stretching across his bicep. "Even when I achieve something in my career, I can't shake the feeling of being a failure. There's always another goal, another level to reach. Someone who's done it better. Usually, someone I'm related to. I feel like I'm always chasing something and falling short, like … I'm running after a moving train I can never catch up to."

Lennon's body—her soul—went heavy from the exhaustion. She could practically sink through the earth. "I keep wondering how long it will take to be able to relax and finally just … be."

Dylan fell quiet for a few moments, the murmur of cicadas and the distant hum of the ocean filling the space between them. "Maybe we're the ones who have to give ourselves permission to do that."

Lennon considered it for a moment. "I'm not sure I can."

His chest deflated with a soft release of air through his nose. "Me either." A beat passed before he added, "But the closest I feel to that is when I'm with you."

The admission caught her by surprise. She felt an expansion in her chest as she turned to look at him. He was already watching her. "How can you say that when I'm the one who got you into this mess?"

"You mean the show? I got myself into this mess because I wanted to," Dylan said with conviction. "And I'd do it again to have all this time with you."

The intimate, vulnerable look in his eyes sent a rush of warmth through her. His hand brushed hers in the grass. Her heart skipped. She reached back, softly nudging a finger between two of his.

His eyes fell to her lips, then rose back up, questioning.

Lennon thought of how he'd stood up for her that evening, accepting responsibility for their failed marriage in front of everyone. Even the way he looked at her now—open, raw—was different from the past when he'd been distant and unreachable.

Her fear begged her to play it safe, but her heart nudged her forward.

She leaned in closer, answering.

Their lips brushed together as tentatively and tenderly as their fingers, like the ocean breeze dusting across her neck. It was a sweet, somewhat hesitant kiss, like they were teenagers again, exploring each other for the first time. The tip of his tongue grazed her lower lip, and she met it the next time with hers. The kiss slowly deepened. His other hand came around to cup her face as he rolled onto his side. She swept hers up his neck so she could dive into his soft, thick hair, fulfilling the fantasy she'd had while dancing at the party, watching him across the room. Her fingers curled and tugged him deeper into her, eliciting a soft moan that poured onto her tongue.

Blades of grass tickled her back as his hand traveled up her hip, pushing her dress away and baring her skin. The coolness of the earth contrasted with the heat radiating from her. From him. As his thumb grazed her waist, electricity exploded in its wake. Her skin was hypersensitive, every molecule intensely alive. She couldn't help how her muscles contracted, and her hips rose slightly at his touch. As she pressed against his groin, she felt the intensity of his desire for her straining against his pants. Lennon caught his lower lip between her teeth, biting gently, and the tension against her torso grew harder.

Under the canopy of stars with the languid roll of the ocean and soft earth beneath her, the moment was a perfect collision of sweet-tasting elements, a pocket of time separated from reality, like a dream. Only the best parts of themselves were there, sharing that moment.

Lennon sank into it, ignoring everything outside of it as they kissed—slow, steady, deep.

Dylan's body molded to hers like a well-worn glove, warm and familiar. But there was also something new there, the people they'd both grown into in the last six years bringing an extra edge of excitement. A rush. There were slight differences in the way he kissed, the way his hands moved along her body with more confidence and control. And in the way she received it. A teenager's inexperience and insecurities replaced with a woman's assurance. She knew what she liked and how she wanted to be touched.

And how she wanted to touch him.

Lennon's fingers loosened their grip and slid down his neck, stopping to let her thumb trace his jawline before landing on his chest to apply gentle pressure and slow down. He followed her lead, tapering off with a few soft touches to the corners of her lips, jawline, neck, and finally, her forehead.

Dylan then loosed a sigh like he was barely holding himself together, touching his forehead to hers. Their chests briskly rose and fell, coming together, drawing apart as he hovered over her.

He pulled back just enough to meet her eyes. She was struck by the apprehension she saw in his—the fragility of his heart resting in the deep pools of brown. Was he worried she'd change her mind? That he'd lose her again? The same fears, among others, bubbled within her. She saw the shift in his eyes as he noticed what must have been a shift in hers. They stared at each other with their hearts open, saying nothing and everything.

She realized her hand was still against his chest, holding him back. He wasn't fighting it. He was giving her the chance to change her mind. Despite how he felt, he was willing to let her go if it was what she wanted. She could feel it. His gaze searched hers, asking. Waiting, patient.

With a soft nudge, Lennon guided him away. Disappointment briefly flickered across Dylan's face before he hid it with a swallow and rolled back onto the grass beside her. He stretched out, staring up at the sky, hands on his stomach as he worked on coming down from the high.

Lennon waited a few seconds for him to settle in before saying, "Race you to the house." She shot up from the ground and made a mad dash across the lawn.

"What the—"

As she'd hoped, the element of surprise gave her a slight

advantage. By the time his brain caught up to what was happening, she was already halfway to the sprawling patio, holding up her gown to give her legs more freedom to move. However, her lead didn't last long. His long, baseball player legs quickly closed the gap. He yelled after her, and she was startled at how close the sound was. Looking over her shoulder, she yelped as her adrenaline spiked, her primal need to avoid being captured kicking in.

Grinning, Dylan reached out and narrowly missed her as she snaked around the patio furniture. He gracefully jumped over the back of the sofa, causing her to let out another shriek, which evolved into a fit of giggles as he cornered her, a large fire pit between them. She teetered left and right, but whichever way she went, his long arms and limbs had the advantage.

"It's cute you thought you could get away," Dylan remarked with a smirk. That smirk—it sent a wave of fire through her.

Lennon reached behind and grabbed the pillow from the chair, tossing it across the fire pit. As it flew toward his head, she bolted for the pool.

Dylan caught it midair and laughed. "Really?" He was behind her again in a flash as she rounded one end of the long, infinity-edge pool. His fingers brushed her back, eliciting a scream/laugh from her, and then his arm hooked around her waist. She tried to tug away, but his strong arms held her against him. They were danger-ously close to the edge of the pool.

Physics defied them, and they were a ball of laughter as their weight began to topple toward the water. She held her breath, brac-ing for impact. He twisted their bodies as they plunged in so he would fall first into the water on his back, softening her landing.

When Lennon resurfaced, she sucked in a sharp breath. She kicked her legs as her pink gown floated around her. He was up a second later, shaking his wet hair. Looking at each other made them burst out laughing again. After a few moments, it tapered off, and they silently bobbed in the water, staring across the short stretch of space between them.

Warm lights illuminated the pool from within, glinting off the dark blue waves undulating around them. The water's reflection danced across his face, the light occasionally catching one of the droplets clinging to his skin. Her attention went to his mouth, to the water dripping from his lower lip. She tasted the salt water on her own.

"I wanted to be caught," Lennon said. She dragged her gaze back to his, letting the heat she felt blaze in it.

In a swift, fluid movement, Dylan crossed the space and pulled her into him, crashing his mouth against hers. Lennon wrapped her legs around his waist as his fingers splayed across her back, his other hand cradling the back of her head, digging into her wet hair. She cupped his face, both pulling each other deeper in, needing to be closer, closer, closer.

Lennon clawed at the muscles in his shoulders, wanting to rip off the white dress shirt that clung to him. Her legs gripped him tightly, pressing the heat between her legs into his torso. He took the message, carrying her up the pool steps and across the patio as their mouths remained greedily attached.

Dylan fumbled to push open the large sliding glass door without breaking the kiss. When he finally had to turn away for a second, she went for his ear, nipping and licking. He moaned, cursing under his breath at the door. As soon as he finally got it open, he carried her to the massive dining room table a short distance away and carefully lowered her onto it. They both immediately tore at the hem of his shirt. Lennon helped him rip it off and then stilled for a moment as she took in the glistening muscles sculpting his long, lean torso.

Dylan stopped, too, chest heaving as he looked down at her. As he watched, she reached behind and unzipped her dress, slowly lowering the straps and letting the bustier fall to her waist. He helped her pull it down her hips as she lifted them from the table, the dress dropping to the floor, leaving her in a lacy thong and matching strapless bra.

The yearning admiration that flooded him made her limbs feel like the water pooling on the table. "Wow," Dylan breathed, taking her in. "You're so beautiful, Lennon." His having that reaction, even after all these years, made her heart swell and liquify. He brushed his thumb along the small tattoo on her ribcage beneath one of her breasts, leaving goosebumps in its wake. A line drawing of waves interrupted by a crescent moon—a break in the tide. Dylan lowered his lips to it to place a soft kiss there. He then moved to the tattoo on her upper thigh, palming the inner swell to hold her leg steady as he reverently traced the words with his tongue, a soft moan humming against her skin. Lennon dropped her head back, shivering and yet on fire.

Tearing himself away from her thigh, Dylan took her face in his hands, kissing her slow and deep. Her fingertips slipped along his body's firm lines and ridges, starting at his chest and traveling down until she grazed the trail of hair below his navel. She felt him lightly shudder beneath her. She went lower, gripping the button of his pants.

Dylan released her from the kiss. "Are you sure?" She unlatched the button with a sharp tug as her answer. The corner of his mouth tilted up. "I need to get a—"

"I'm on the pill." Lennon yanked down the zipper. "Now, take off your pants and fuck me on this table."

She practically felt the heat that ignited in his eyes, Dylan's gaze turning primal.

They collided again, tearing off the rest of each other's clothes. His hands explored her, one cupping her breast as the other went between her legs. Dylan parted her, his long fingers teasing, eliciting a soft moan from her. Lennon arched her back, propping herself up with one hand behind her as the other squeezed the nape of his neck. Her core throbbed mercilessly. When he pulled away, she waited for him to fill her, but instead, he dropped to his knees. With ease, Dylan slid her to the edge of the table and spread her legs further, resting them up on his shoulders as his hands braced her hips.

When his tongue brushed against her, Lennon's entire body

shuddered. She threw her head back, fingernails searching for purchase on the smooth wood as the other hand buried itself in his hair. It wasn't long before she was near the edge of exploding.

Fuck, he'd learned some new things.

"Dylan—get up here. I'm—I need you inside me," Lennon begged, struggling to form coherent words. He kept going, moaning into her and tightening his grip on her hips as if made hungrier by her pleas. She felt hollow, *aching* for him to fill her. "Please. Oh, God." She bit down on her lower lip so hard she was surprised she didn't draw blood. "*Dylan—*"

Dylan let go and rose slowly, his impressive silhouette—broad, lean, sculpted—bathed in the soft moonlight pouring through the wall of glass behind him. Dark, wet hair tousled around his face. Swollen, pink lips. Eyes heavy with passion. He was so beautiful, it hurt.

Dylan crawled over her, taking his time, caging her between his arms. He parted her lips with his, devouring her slowly. As his narrow hips lowered against hers, Lennon felt him brush against her center, and her body erupted with intense need all over again. She wanted to be impossibly close to him. Feel every inch of him against her and inside her. She lay back against the table, wrapping her legs around his waist to pull him closer.

Dylan took it slow at first, both exhaling the moment they connected. But they were both so eager for release, so hungry for each other after years apart, that soon he was picking up the pace, and she was encouraging him to go harder, her nails digging into his back and her cries ringing out as he groaned into her neck. Sweat mixed with the saltwater from the pool, making her cling tighter to him so he wouldn't slip away.

"Don't worry. I got you, baby," Dylan rasped, his breath hot on the shell of her ear, then groaned as she internally tightened around him. "*F-fuck… you're so perfect.*"

He breathed her name, warning her when he was on the

precipice, barely holding off until she was ready, and they both came apart together.

Dylan released his body weight onto her, and Lennon rested her arms around his shoulders, legs holding him to her, his face nuzzling into her neck. His breath warmed her skin as the length of their bodies pressed closer with every gasp for air. Lennon didn't want to move. She enjoyed the feeling of his skin against hers. Of him filling her.

She hadn't realized how empty she'd been.

"I can't believe that just happened," Dylan rasped in her ear, still breathless. Blissful. Sounding the way she felt.

"Me either."

Dylan stiffened slightly against her, pulling back to look at her. She met his gaze, finding a shadow of concern in it. "You don't … regret it, do you?"

A soft smile formed on her lips, her eyelids heavy. Lennon shook her head. He relaxed again, happiness radiating from him. Dylan placed a gentle kiss on her lips, then returned to his spot in the crook of her neck, tickling her with his facial hair.

They stayed like that until their breaths calmed to a stable rate, and she reluctantly released her grip around him, allowing him to slide away. Dylan peppered kisses down her neck, chest, abdomen, thighs. Lennon lay there, enjoying his delicate worshipping of her body.

He offered her something to drink, and she followed him into the massive kitchen. After hydrating, she ended up bent over the sprawling island for round two.

CHAPTER 33

ylan gave Lennon a tour of the house—on the living room floor, against one of the walls in a hallway, in the shower, and finally, in his actual bed.

By the time they got there, they were both exhausted and hungry. While Dylan ran downstairs to retrieve the pizza delivery, Lennon helped herself to a soft, faded t-shirt she found in his closet and crawled back into his massive bed. She buried her face into one of his pillows and pulled his shirt up to her nose, taking deep breaths of Dylan's earthy musk mixed with fresh linens. Sunshine spread through her.

She already missed him, and he'd only run downstairs for a minute. What was she, fifteen?

When Dylan walked back into the room, two flat cardboard boxes balanced on one hand and sweatpants slung low on his hips below his bare torso, he stopped inside the doorway, staring at her.

"What?" Lennon asked, lying on her side. She had her top knee bent with the other stretched out long. His t-shirt gathered around her waist, exposing her bare hip.

"You're just …" Dylan's eyes softened, and a small, self-conscious laugh trickled from his throat as he dipped his head. Was he blushing? He lifted his head with a wistful smile. "I can't stop looking at you."

Butterflies exploded in her chest.

Lennon sat up, resting her weight on one hand. Her hair was air-drying, creating a halo of frizzy, messy waves around her face, and her makeup had mostly melted off between the pool and the shower, but the way he looked at her made her feel the most beautiful she'd ever felt.

Now, she was the one blushing.

"I can't stop looking at that pizza," Lennon joked with a bite of her lip, though she was really looking at him. If her stomach weren't growling, she'd have opted to devour him again instead. She needed her strength so she could.

Dylan crawled in bed beside her, and they dug into the deliciously cheesy, greasy slices as they watched a *Golden Girls* rerun. After a stressful day, the four women gathered around the kitchen table late at night to commiserate. Both she and Dylan perked up, exchanging a glance, knowing one of them was about to be proven right from the argument they'd had during their phone call on the train.

When Sophia grabbed a cheesecake from the refrigerator, Lennon jabbed a finger at the screen in victory while the other hand gripped her third slice of pizza. "See! I told you it wasn't wine."

"What? No—that has to be this one time. I swear, it's usually wine."

"It's never wine. It's cheesecake."

"OK, wait, wait, wait—but you said *pie*, not cheesecake."

"What?" Lennon feigned ignorance.

"You said they ate pie together. Cheesecake is not pie."

She rolled her eyes. "Close enough."

"But not the same."

"It's closer than wine!"

"What about dessert wine? Or, *or*—" Dylan pointed his half-eaten breadstick at her. "Wine pie."

Lennon gave him a look as if he were insane. "What the fuck is *wine pie*? That's not a thing."

"Yes, it is. It's French."

"You're making shit up now."

"I swear! Google it."

Lennon shot him a playful glare. She didn't want to be proven wrong again, so she said, "I don't know where my phone is, and I'm eating. I'll do it later."

"I look forward to your apology." Dylan ripped off another bite of his breadstick as he rested his head against the padded headboard, returning his attention to the flat-screen television that had lowered from a hidden spot in the ceiling.

Lennon smiled into her pizza slice despite herself. His hand rested on her thigh as she sat cross-legged beside him. She watched him laugh at something snarky Sophia said to Rose, and her heart grew so wide in her chest that she wondered if there was enough space to hold it.

She prayed he wouldn't break it again.

Lennon slept so soundly, she didn't even dream. She didn't need to. Last night had been enough of one.

A decadent, sugary scent coaxed her awake early the next morning. She stretched her arms overhead, arching her bare back, and reached beside her. Soft sunlight poured in through the open balcony doors, along with the relaxing sound of the waves and swaying palm trees. She frowned at the empty space until she found a note on the pillow.

> *Come downstairs for your favorite.*
> *P.S. You're really cute when you sleep.*

Lennon scrunched up her nose in a smile as her cheeks flushed. Her heart stretched now, too, wide awake and *thump, thump, thumping* in her chest.

She slipped on his oversized shirt, which they'd tossed to the floor at some point after finishing off the pizza, then wandered into the large en suite. It looked like it belonged in a luxury hotel. Lennon approached the long vanity to the right, where his personal items were arranged a little haphazardly but not in the cluttered way they had been when they lived together. She ran her fingers along the beautiful watch Rhett had gifted Dylan after he signed his contract with the Tidebreakers, his shaving kit, cologne. She picked up the bottle and removed the top, waving it under her nose. The spicy, earthy scent woke up every molecule in her body.

Suddenly, she couldn't get to him fast enough.

Glancing up at the mirror, Lennon caught the other vanity in the reflection. She turned to look at the fresh toothbrush and toothpaste sitting on the counter. He'd also plugged her phone in to charge, placed her shoes at the base, and hung her clothes to dry.

Dylan's thoughtfulness—and the fact that he'd already settled her into her own vanity—surprised her with a rush of emotion. Tears pricked her eyes. Lennon smiled, overwhelmed.

Lennon ignored her phone, uninterested in the outside world for now, and freshened up before following the sweet scent downstairs. She found him standing in the kitchen, shirtless, grey sweatpants hanging below the dimples in his lower back and the muscles in his shoulders flexing as he scrambled eggs over a sizzling pan. The island was filled with a spread of freshly cut fruit—strawberries, blueberries, and bananas—and a stack of pancakes.

"You did not cook a whole freakin' breakfast," Lennon said, her morning voice scratchy.

Dylan glanced over his shoulder, a smile stretching across his face under a mess of bedhead. "Oh, I did."

Lennon felt like a giddy five-year-old, and a heartsick fifteen-year-old, and a deeply in love twenty-five-year-old all at once.

Dylan turned with the pan and spatula in his hands. "Hope you're hungry," he said, his voice a little hoarse, too. It was deeper. Even sexier somehow, which was quite a feat.

"Starving." She slid onto one of the cushioned barstools at the island, where one of two place settings had already been arranged beside each other. As she dangled her feet, he carefully scooped the steaming eggs onto her plate, then a pancake.

"Help yourself," Dylan said, gesturing to the butter on a serving dish and a glass syrup carafe. Beside them were pitchers of ice water and orange juice to fill her crystal glass.

Lennon stared at the spread, wide-eyed and gaping. It smelled as incredible as it looked. It wasn't plated quite like a magazine, but she could tell he *tried* to make it look that way, and that made it all the more adorable. "When did you become Martha Stewart?"

"My therapist suggested I take up a low-pressure hobby while I was stuck at home. To help with the anxiety." Dylan turned to the stove, his back to her again, as he cracked a few more eggs into the pan to make them over-easy for himself. Quietly, he added, "And I wanted you to feel at home."

There it went again, Lennon's insides melting like the butter she'd spread over the pancake. She stopped for a moment, watching him as he cooked over the stove. He'd barely been able to boil pasta when they were married. Whatever he ate had to be pre-cooked or delivered. Now, here he was, taking care of a house, cooking breakfast, and setting her clothes out to dry.

Being open about his struggles.

Acting like a man, not the boy she'd divorced.

In that split second, Lennon saw herself at home there. Waking up next to him every morning, brushing their teeth at his and her vanities, cooking breakfast together, planning out their day. She imagined shopping at the local farmer's market and getting to know their neighbors, strolling along the beach, writing music by the pool while he hit balls in the batting cage. Living in their little pocket of heaven.

Fear nipped at the heels of that beautiful vision. That had been her dream when they were first married, as misguided as it was. Back then, there was no evidence to support that he could be that to her, but her teenage mind had assumed that once someone got married, it just *flipped a switch,* and marital bliss was activated. He would stop partying, grow up, and everything would work out. They would have their happily ever after. They hated people telling them they were too young, but their warnings had been valid.

They were the ones who had been wrong. Just like with the dessert on *The Golden Girls.*

What if Lennon was wrong again? What if the timing still wasn't right for either of them? Her heart curled inside her chest, fearful of being shattered again. Her love for him was growing deeper, expanding beyond what it was before.

It would hurt even worse this time.

Dylan slipped onto the stool beside her, and they ate in comfortable silence, their shoulders and knees brushing to maintain steady contact. As he reached for the pitcher of orange juice to fill his glass, the pinkish, jagged scar on his shoulder flexed. Lennon's heart panged at the reminder of what he'd been through. And how much worse it could have been.

When Dylan put the pitcher back down, she reached out and lightly traced the scar with her fingertips. He seemed to shiver a little under her touch but didn't pull away.

"It looks worse than it is," Dylan reassured her.

Lennon frowned. "I wish I'd been here."

"You were."

She looked at him questioningly. He gently took her hand, kissing her knuckles, then pressed it against his chest where his heart beat against her skin. Hers felt like it may completely burst inside her.

"You have some new ones, too," Dylan commented, turning her hand over to expose the small butterfly tattoo on her wrist she'd gotten her first year in New York. A symbol for leaving the safety of what she knew to grow into something better. A little cheesy, but she loved it anyway. Dylan rubbed his calloused thumb over it.

"Guess we both missed a lot."

"I want to hear all about it," Dylan told her, still holding her hand. "From you, not secondhand from Erin. Girl code or whatever kept her from giving me too many details."

Lennon smiled. "Pretty sure she did the same with you. Sister code." She admired their joined hands. "I want to hear about yours, too."

The muscle in his jaw twitched slightly, but he gave a slight nod. "Whenever you're ready."

They needed to have that conversation, but not now. As he released her hand, she read the clock on the stove. "What time is your meeting with the board?"

Dylan scraped his fork across the plate, shoving some of his eggs onto a thick piece of pancake. "Not 'til later this afternoon."

"My offer stands to start that riot if they don't agree to take you back."

He smiled, but it was weak. Doubt weighed it down.

Lennon gently bumped his shoulder with hers. "Hey. You've done everything you can. What is it you told me? If they can't see the good thing they have in front of them, that's on them, not you."

His brow lowered. "I don't remember that. It was early, I was busy absolutely killing it at a golf tournament, and some girl on a train interrupted me …"

Lennon shoved her shoulder into his harder this time and he laughed.

As she reached the last few bites of food on her plate, she realized her eyes had been bigger than her stomach. Lennon held one of the strawberry slices up to his mouth to pawn it off on him. Dylan parted his lips, and she gently placed it between his teeth. His tongue scooped it into his mouth, making something stir low in her torso, awakening a different kind of hunger. Her hand remained poised at his lips, red juice slowly sliding down her fingers as she watched him, her eyes glazing over with desire.

Dylan noticed, his own darkening.

Placing his fork down, he gently caught her hand in his, then leaned forward. He took her thumb in his mouth, his warm tongue rolling over the pad of her finger, sending a shot of heat straight up between her legs. After a moment, he dragged his lips away, then did the same thing to her index finger. When he finished, he pressed a soft kiss to her palm.

Lennon swallowed, nearly swaying on the stool. Voice low, she asked, "Are there any other rooms you haven't shown me yet?"

Following a tour of the movie room, home gym, and game room—Lennon particularly loved the pool table—they ended up in his spacious shower again. That was quickly becoming one of her favorite spots, the water reminding her of the way this had all started in the pool the night before.

They would have to go back there at some point.

When she stepped out, Dylan wrapped her in a warm towel, closing his arms around her from behind. "How are these always so warm?" she asked. "Like they're fresh out of the dryer."

"Towel warmers," Dylan answered, gesturing to the metal racks on the wall. He placed a kiss on her damp shoulder before grabbing a towel for himself.

As she tightened the towel around her, Lennon padded over to where her dress hung from one of the racks. Sure enough, it was dry and toasty. "This is amazing."

"I know, right?" Dylan wiggled his eyebrows. "You think that's amazing—" He walked over to a small tablet hanging on the wall beside his vanity. He tapped something, but nothing seemed to happen. "Wait for it."

After a few seconds, warmth began to radiate under her bare feet. Lennon gasped, looking down at the floor, then back up at him, his face lighting up like an excited child. "The floors are *heated*?"

"The floors are heated."

"Get the fuck out of here. Who needs that in Florida?"

"No one but it's awesome."

"It's amazing."

Lennon flexed her toes against the warm tile, and he chuckled as he began to dry his hair. She caught sight of the clock embedded in the mirror. A quarter to twelve. She opened her mouth to ask if he wanted moral support at the meeting later when the realization kicked her in the stomach. "Shit."

Dylan tugged the towel back, peering at her through the sides hanging around his face. "What?"

"I forgot I have a job interview today. In a couple of hours. I need to run back to my apartment and get ready. *Shit.*" Lennon quickly patted herself dry, then let the towel drop to the floor. She grabbed her bra and panties from the heated towel rack. The warmth was soothing as she pressed the fabric to her skin.

"What's the job?" Dylan asked as he continued to towel off.

"Cocktail waitress at some fancy schmancy rooftop bar. I hear the tips are pretty good. I'm going to need them after that throw-down at the wedding airs. I doubt anyone is going to want to give me a record deal, and I'm not holding my breath for an invitation back for season two." As Lennon reached for her dress, her fingertips barely missed it as Dylan tugged at her other hand, holding her back. She turned, looking up at his mischievous smile and damp, disheveled hair, the towel now hanging loose on his hips. And dangerously low.

"Hey. You'll get a record deal. No matter what happens with the show, it won't erase your talent or how amazing you are." He intertwined his fingers with hers. Her knees melted.

"You're only saying that because you want to sleep with me," Lennon joked.

"Are you calling me a liar?" Dylan pulled her around to face him, snaking the fingers of his other hand through hers, too. His thumbs caressed her skin as his bare chest pressed against hers. Her willpower to leave was rapidly melting.

"Just questioning your motives," she said, eying his lips.

"That's fair. I am morally corrupt by the league's standards," Dylan pointed out in a low, rasping tone. It reverberated in her core.

"Exactly. How can I—" Lennon lost track of her sentence when his mouth dipped to her neck. "Trust someone like that," she finally muttered after a moment. A stupid smile bloomed on her lips as she leaned into him. He smelled of fresh soap. He made her heart flutter, even when her life was seemingly falling apart around her. She wanted to curl up with him for the rest of the day.

Why did the interview for a job she didn't even want, have to be *today*?

"Does that mean you *wouldn't* like to have dinner with me later, then?" Dylan whispered in her ear, his breath tickling her. "I know someone who's gotten pretty good at cooking." She felt his lopsided grin against her cheek.

"Who?" Lennon questioned, and he squeezed her hands.

"The guy who made you pancakes."

Lennon waited a beat. "You'll have to be more specific." Dylan nipped at her earlobe, eliciting a string of giggles from her throat. He went back to sucking on her neck. "Careful. I can't show up to an interview with a giant hickey on my neck." He began sucking harder, and she laughed, pulling at his hold on her as she tried to escape. "Stop it!"

Through their laughter and her attempt to wriggle away from him, a soft chime rang in the background. It took a few seconds for it to register. "Hold on—what is that?"

Dylan raised his head, listening. When it chimed again, he said, "Someone's at the gate." He planted a kiss on her lips, then released her hands as he walked back over to the wall-mounted tablet. He tapped open the notification to a surveillance shot of a red convertible. He turned to Lennon, his expression hard. "It's Kelsey."

All the joy drained from her body. "What the hell does she want? How did she even know where you live?"

Dylan shook his head. "I don't know. I'll tell her to leave."

"Wait—" Lennon said, and his finger froze over the touch-screen. "Let's find out what she wants first."

Reluctantly, Dylan tapped the button to speak to her. "What are you doing here, Kelsey?"

"Dylan, hi—" Kelsey lifted her sunglasses, perching them in her blonde hair, and leaned into her forearm across the window. She smiled directly into the camera. "I was hoping we could talk."

"About what?"

"You know, to clear the air. Plus, I have something to ask you."

"I'm busy right now—"

"It'll just take a sec. I think you're *really* going to want to hear this."

Now, her interest was piqued. Lennon waved at Dylan to get his attention. When he looked at her, she mouthed, "Let her in."

Dylan didn't seem as curious, his brow crinkling in a "why" fashion, but when she urged him again, he sighed. "I'll be down in a few." He pressed another button to open the gate.

Lennon watched Kelsey smile with satisfaction and then punch the gas on her two-seater convertible.

"I don't know what she could ask that would be worth our time," Dylan said.

"Me either. If she has something up her sleeve, we should find out what it is, even if it's just a clue to her next move or the narrative she's planning to spin on this whole thing."

Dylan released another sigh, leaning back against the vanity. He stretched his long, bare legs out in front of him as he folded his arms. "Why did we sign up for this show again?"

"Because we thought it would help us get our lives back on track," Lennon said sardonically. "It's going *great* so far."

His eyes softened. "At least it brought you back to me."

Lennon's heart cartwheeled. "There's that." As she stepped closer, Dylan opened his arms and Lennon folded into them. She laid her cheek against his damp chest as he kissed the top of her head, stealing a few more moments in their peaceful bubble.

CHAPTER 34

Lennon

Dylan slipped on a dark pair of jeans and a t-shirt before heading downstairs to answer the door. Lennon decided to hang back so Kelsey wouldn't know she was there. She wanted to see what she would say without the awareness of an audience.

Lennon quickly squeezed more water from her hair with a towel and threw on her dress, then tiptoed barefoot to the edge of one of the archways overlooking the living room. From there, she could hear the echo of Dylan and Kelsey's voices perfectly.

"Beautiful home. I looked in this neighborhood but decided it's a bit too remote for me. I prefer to be in the city where there's more culture and vibe," Kelsey remarked.

"I prefer peace and privacy wherever I can get it," Dylan replied blankly.

Peeking around the corner through the wrought iron railing, she watched Kelsey take a seat on the sofa. Dylan took the armchair adjacent to it, resting his elbows on his knees as if he was ready to spring up and lead her back to the door.

Kelsey, on the other hand, settled in, sitting back and crossing one smooth leg over the other. The hem of her short sundress snaked upward as she angled her body, exposing the side of her thigh. She rested an elbow on the arm of the sofa as she placed the other hand on her knee, pushing against the curve of her cleavage through the deep-cut neckline.

Lennon stifled a laugh at how painfully obvious she was, feeling a tad smug knowing none of it was going to work. She sat down on the wood floor, pressing her back against the wall, her side just beyond the edge of the railing so she could duck out of sight if Kelsey happened to look up.

"So. What is it you wanted to ask me?" Dylan asked, clasping his hands together.

"I heard you think your drink was spiked the night of the party," Kelsey said. Lennon's stomach clenched. Why would she come all this way to bring that up? He nodded, and she blew air through her lips. "Wow. I'm sure it was an accident, but like, obviously, that doesn't make it OK. Especially since that's going to affect your career when it comes out, right?"

The tension in Dylan's jaw carved a shadow across his face as he wrung his hands. "Yeah. Pretty much guarantees my career is over. At least for now."

"Can't you be drafted to another team?"

"The league's making the decision, not the team."

"What if they didn't find out about it?"

Dylan released a humorless laugh. "Yeah, I just have to hope they don't watch reality shows or read the news."

Lennon furrowed her brow, wondering where Kelsey was going with this. She tilted closer, listening.

"You know my dad's one of the producers?" Kelsey asked. Lennon's brows lifted, eyes widening.

What?

"Uh … no. No, I didn't know that."

"Huey Donaldson. I'm technically Kelsey McCroy-Donaldson, but I go by McCroy, my mom's maiden name. I don't like people knowing I'm a nepo baby. There's *so* much prejudice against us. Well, you know."

Oh, my God.

Lennon's head swam with all the potential implications of Kelsey being Huey's daughter. The main being—Lennon was fucked.

"So, what are you saying? You can ask him not to air the footage?" Dylan asked.

"I already did after Avery told me what happened. At the time, I figured you were just shit-faced like the rest of us. I barely even remember anything from that night. But he said no," Kelsey explained. Dylan audibly sighed. "Obviously, what happened at the party will probably be one of the most explosive moments of the season. He doesn't have a good argument for taking it out to tell the rest of the studio, especially when they want to make sure it gets picked up for a second season. They want to keep the streaming platform happy. The new owner of Versal is cutting projects left and right. It doesn't make sense from a business perspective, y'know? He said you can clear the air in your confessionals."

Dylan slumped back in the chair. "Yeah, no one's going to believe me without proof. I'm already the party boy in people's minds. The damage will be done regardless."

"Which is why I got creative and asked him if he'd be down for something else."

A beat passed. Dylan said, "I'm listening."

Kelsey's lips gently curved. "This is show business. Their goal is to get as many people watching the show and talking about it as possible. They invited you to the cast because people are interested in your story. They *want* to root for you. You messing up again—or them thinking you've messed up—will get people talking for a little bit, but what will get people talking even more, for longer … is a love story."

"Lennon and I—"

"I'm not talking about you and Lennon. I'm talking about you and me."

Lennon's head shot to the side. Was she fucking *serious*?

"I'm … not following here," Dylan said, breathing out another humorless laugh. "You understand there's nothing between you and me, right?"

"*Obviously*," Kelsey remarked, as though the question were ridiculous. As though she *hadn't* thrown him in Lennon's face the night prior. "If I'd known you were actually drugged and not just drunk, I never would've crawled into bed with you. I was too fucked up that night to know the difference. Maybe I got a little of whatever you got, too." She leaned forward. "I'm talking about a mutually beneficial PR relationship. We say we've been hanging out off-camera and hooked up at the party. It turned into something real and now we're together. There's your cliffhanger for season two. It secures us both lead spots, gets you back on the team, and everyone gets what they want."

"You want us to *pretend* we're in a relationship? How's that going to help?"

"You rebelling at the party will definitely be explosive, sure, but people love a love triangle even more. It'll last longer. They'll get invested. They're going to eat up Lennon's reactions, her jealousy, the so-called beef between us that she's already laid the groundwork for. It can go back and forth for a while, all the way into the next season. Then, down the line, she can give us her blessing, and boom—people will feel sorry for her, you've got your career back, I've got a boost for mine. Everyone's happy. We can quietly break up once it's no longer beneficial."

Dylan went quiet for several seconds. "This is … a *lot* to take in."

That was a fucking understatement.

"I get it. I grew up around this stuff, but it must sound a bit crazy to an outsider."

Dylan uttered a small, clipped laugh. "A *bit*." He stood up and began to pace in front of the fireplace.

"This is how the game works, though. You've got to learn to play it, or it'll play you."

"I don't know that I want to be a part of a game like that."

"You already are," Kelsey said. "You're a famous baseball star with a major PR problem who went on a reality show. This *is* your game. It's all of ours. Lennon's, too, if she's really serious about a music career. Villains are some of the biggest stars in reality TV and she's already got the victim thing down to a T. They're going to hate her and then fall in love with her, and record labels will be clamoring to give her a deal. It's actually going to work out well for her if she sticks with it. Trust me, I've been doing her a favor playing into it."

"I don't think Lennon sees it that way."

Kelsey shrugged, arching an eyebrow. "She will."

Dylan stopped, facing her. "You said a love story trumps everything. Why not Lennon, then? That's why they asked us on the show in the first place. They were hoping we'd get back together."

Kelsey pulled a doubtful expression. "Honestly … Lennon isn't going to really *help* your case. I know how these things work. She's *definitely* panning out to be the villain of the show."

"Lennon isn't a villain—"

"Right now, she seems like a two-faced, opportunistic gold digger. It's not a good look."

"That's not true," Dylan shot back, voice sharp. "She's not like that."

"It doesn't matter what the truth is. It's what the public *perceives* to be the truth. Like how they'll perceive you as an entitled nepo baby party boy who's never going to learn his lesson if the footage airs exactly as it happened."

"It hasn't aired yet," he reminded her. "They can edit this all differently, so Lennon doesn't come off the way you're saying—which you pushed her into, by the way—and keep what happened at the party out of it."

"But then there's nothing in it for me," Kelsey stated simply. And there it was. "I'm the one brokering this deal for you. Dating a baseball player with your level of fame will catapult *me* into a whole new level. I'll get better acting opportunities and sponsorships. And look, you getting back with your ex-wife is cute, but it isn't as interesting as a love triangle. My dad won't trade a relapse for a rom-com. An interesting lie always sells better than a boring truth."

Dylan narrowed his eyes, jaw a little slack in disbelief. "You're so callous and nonchalant about this."

Kelsey shrugged again. "It's business."

"It's our lives," he corrected.

"You could say that about any job. We're all selling pieces of ourselves for something." Kelsey lounged back, casually picking at her nails as though she hadn't stated something profoundly disconcerting. "You get what you need out of it. I get what I need out of it. It's a business transaction. Everyone in showbiz does it. Most of the relationships between celebrities aren't real."

"And what if the truth comes out? A lot of people were there that night."

"Everyone signs an NDA when filming. They can't talk about anything that happened on the show without express permission. They'll edit it so it looks like we were hooking up and Lennon walked in on us. The truth will be buried. All the public—and your team—will know is that you went to the party and got laid. End of story."

Dylan shook his head. "I can't do that to Lennon."

"If she really cares about you, she'll understand," Kelsey said. "And if you want to fuck her or anyone else off-camera, go for it. I don't care what you do behind closed doors. That's the beauty of it. We're only together in the public eye. Outside of that, we're totally free to do whatever we want. Just keep it quiet. NDAs are our best friends." She winked.

Dylan went quiet again, a stunned look etched on his face as he processed everything she said.

Kelsey glanced at her phone, then stood. She slung her small bag over her shoulder. "I've got to go. Think about it. But don't take too long—we need to act fast to film some extra scenes before the first season airs."

Dylan didn't say anything as he walked her to the door. It wasn't until it was open that he posed a question to Kelsey. "You said Versal has a new owner. Do you know who it is?"

"Nolan Pierce."

The air stilled around Lennon—no, evaporated—as if the hall had suddenly turned into a vacuum.

"Apparently, he's some tech billionaire-genius-entrepreneur-dickhead. He bought controlling shares in Versal recently and everyone's scared their show will be on the chopping block." Kelsey pulled her keys from her bag. "That's why we have to make sure ours isn't." After a brief pause, she said, "Call me when you're ready to discuss the details of my offer."

Once she heard the front door shut, Lennon expelled a jagged breath.

What. The. Fuck.

CHAPTER 35

Dylan

SIX YEARS AGO

Amber streetlights throwing shadows on the slick
pavement. Wet soil and car fumes heavy in the air.
Distance sirens punctuating heavy footfalls on
metal stairs.

Dylan hadn't intended to stay more than an hour at Craig's party. Just long enough to make an appearance, congratulate him on getting called up to the Tidebreakers' major league team, and then dip out. Every Tidebreaker—minor and major—was there. He heard his father's voice echoing in his head. *"The best team building happens off the field. You want in, then you show up. Show 'em you care."*

Even Dylan's downtime was about baseball.

It was only supposed to be an hour, but time had a way of disappearing at Craig's parties. Especially after Dylan had a shitty day, and the first drink took the edge off. Anything serious, anything important, was criminal in those walls. They were all blowing off steam. Blocking out the real world for a night.

And it felt good.

He'd figured out the drinks that quickly numbed him and let him coast through the evening. The guilt when he came home to her was the one thing it couldn't numb.

It gnawed at him, ripping through the fog. Dylan wanted to be home with Lennon. He ached for it. But he couldn't sit still, and he couldn't talk to her about what was bothering him.

To complain about it would be too fucking selfish.

Lennon was grinding—with school, work, her music. She'd turned down NYU to stay in Arden Beach with him so he could play on the Tidebreakers. How could he complain about the pressures of his job while she was fighting to pursue her own dreams?

Dylan had no clue how to be around her unless they were making love or playing video games or keeping busy some other way— all of which they rarely had time for anymore. The quiet moments, which used to be his favorite, were the ones he now dreaded. He sensed her waiting for him to open up when they lay together in bed. Ate takeout. Walked along the beach.

It was easier to hide from Erin. She didn't live with him. He could tell her to leave him alone, and she'd put up a fight and call him an idiot, but she'd eventually relent. But with Lennon … he'd bared his soul to her in ways he never had with another person. It was what she expected from him.

But Dylan couldn't give it to her now. Just thinking about it made his body lock up. Like he couldn't breathe. He needed to push on.

4:00 a.m. and a cab was finally dropping him off at their apartment complex. A night owl, Lennon was likely awake or had just gone to bed. The alcohol was wearing off, the memories of the day steadily crowding him again. With every step, his legs grew heavier, dreading the silence of a dark room for hours of fighting off his demons and losing the battle.

When Dylan walked into the apartment, the light was on that she always left for him, but she wasn't on the sofa next to it. The television was off. The coffee table was clear. He sighed with both relief and disappointment.

Mouth dry and foul with the taste of liquor, he tossed his keys on the table by the door and headed toward the kitchen. A suitcase standing upright at the end of the counter stopped him dead in his tracks.

Lennon's suitcase.

A figure appeared in his peripheral. He looked up at his wife standing between the threshold of their bedroom, dressed in ripped jeans and a sweatshirt. And sneakers.

She crossed her arms, staring at Dylan with a coldness that sucked the air from his lungs.

"Where are you going?" was the only question his sluggish brain could come up with. They'd barely seen each other that week, but he would've remembered her telling him something like that.

"Erin's."

"Oh. Why? Is she OK?"

A small sound exited her nose, almost a laugh. "She's fine." The words were quiet but thick with contempt.

Dylan wasn't drunk enough to miss that she was pissed off—at him. Not that he could really blame her. "Look, I'm sorry," he told her with sincerity. He grabbed the back of one of the bar stools, leaning into it to steady himself. "I wasn't planning on staying, but the whole team was there. Time got away from me. I had a rough day and I needed to forget about it for a while."

"You do that a lot," Lennon noted, emotionless.

Dylan clenched his jaw. "Yeah, well. I have a lot of rough days."

Lennon pulled in her lower lip, dropping her gaze to the floor. She didn't say anything. Instead, she walked back into the bedroom, returning a few seconds later with a manila folder. She dropped it on the counter with a loud *thud*.

Dylan went deathly still. "What is this?"

"Divorce papers."

His heart stopped—suddenly painfully sober. "Are y—" He stared at her. "You're serious?"

Lennon tightly folded her arms again, staring at the folder. Tears glistened in the corners of her eyes. "We shouldn't have gotten married," she said. She sounded like it was a realization that had come too late, now frustrated with herself for the mistake.

Dylan's brain moved too fast and too slow, like a hummingbird beating its wings through mud. A million thoughts crashed into him while his body buckled from the shock. The first thing he felt as he regained sensation was a stabbing in his chest.

"We weren't ready," Lennon continued. "I think we need … time apart."

"Then, why don't we try that? Why are you serving me papers already?" He couldn't believe she'd actually gone to a lawyer. Had actual *divorce papers* drawn up. She was so fucking impulsive.

Lennon's eyelashes shuddered as she pressed her lips together, lowering her chin. She took a moment to answer. "Because I don't think this is something that will just go away," she said, her voice unsteady. "I'm not part of your life anymore, Dylan. Not really. And I don't think you want me to be."

"Lennon, that's *not* true—"

She fixed a sharp gaze on him. "Are you going to stop getting drunk and partying with your friends every night? Are you going to actually fucking talk to me?"

An answer died in his throat, Dylan's voice cracking and dissolving into a strangled sigh. Lennon shook her head as she looked away from him. "It's not—it's not that simple. I have to spend time with the guys off the field. And it's how I unwind. I don't get much downtime. When I do, I just want to shut off. I don't want to talk. I don't want to think about anything. I just need—I need to escape." His voice had risen, defensive.

Lennon's brow sunk in, fresh tears rising in her eyes. *Fuck.* "It's not you," Dylan reiterated, lowering his tone. "It has *nothing* to do with you. I've … got a lot on my mind."

He knew it wasn't enough. He was frustrated with himself, but he had no idea what else to say. He needed her to let it go.

Lennon turned away from him. He waited with bated breath until she reached for the suitcase and rolled it to her side, facing the door. "Erin will come get the papers from you."

Dylan's lips parted, air temporarily gone from his lungs once again. He let go of the chair, running both hands through his hair. They slid down his neck, hanging there as he tried to process what was happening. "So, it's just … over? Just like that?" He watched her in disbelief. "Is this what you want?"

A tear finally slipped down her cheek as her chin trembled a little. "I can't keep living like this," Lennon answered, sounding small. "I'm not happy."

Those three words crushed him. Grief swept through him, her pain and his failure gutting him.

Dylan's knee-jerk instinct was to try to fix it. Ask her what he could do—what she needed to make it right. But as quickly as the promise rose, the realization that he couldn't fulfill it smothered it.

He was already barely keeping his head above water.

The truth cut him at the knees. Lennon deserved better, and he couldn't give it to her.

Dylan's chest strained against each breath he took. He pressed his eyes shut. He had no right to ask her to stay, but how the hell could he let her leave?

"Lennon …" He swallowed against a dry throat, looking at her. For the first time in a while, he *really* looked at her, and what he saw broke him. The light was gone from her eyes.

And he hadn't noticed it until now.

He'd never forgive himself for being the one who took it.

"I'm sorry."

Lennon's jaw tensed, another tear falling. Dylan dropped his hands and fisted them at his sides, stopping himself from reaching for her. "Me too," she said softly, sounding as broken as he felt. She swiped a hand across her cheeks, tilting her luggage forward onto the wheels. Dylan dug his teeth into his lower lip as she quickly passed him for the door.

Her name burned in his throat.

The door creaked open, but the wheels and footsteps didn't continue. For a split second, hope surged that she'd changed her mind. Dylan looked over his shoulder.

"I'm sorry I wasn't enough," she said, taking another piece of his heart. Lennon pulled the suitcase over the threshold and let the door swing shut behind her.

CHAPTER 36

Lennon

Lennon met Dylan in the foyer in her wrinkled bridesmaid dress, shoes on and clutch in hand. He stood there with his hands on his hips, dazed. He didn't look up at her right away. "That was—"

"You should take her offer," Lennon said numbly, cutting him off.

He almost laughed. "What?"

She dropped a halfhearted shoulder. "It makes sense. I mean, she's evil, but it wouldn't be forever, and it would save you from ruining your career over nothing. At this point, it'd probably be stupid *not* to do it."

Dylan still teetered on the edge of laughter, but confusion set in when she didn't laugh with him. "I don't—are you serious?"

Somewhere, under a thin layer of ice, her heart beat painfully. On the surface, she'd kicked into survival mode.

"Yes. I'm serious." So serious, it made her sick. "It's the whole reason you went on the show: To fix your image and get back on the team. You can't let it end up being the thing that destroys everything." Guilt came in a hot, sickening wave. He wouldn't have even been *on* the show if it hadn't been for her. She was partially responsible for getting him into this mess. The least she could do was not get in the way of his one chance to avoid the fallout.

Dylan simply gaped at her for a while, sounds of confusion crackling in his throat as words seemed to evaporate as quickly as they formed. "I … I don't know what to say. This isn't what I expected you to say."

"What did you expect me to say?"

"Not this!" He waved his open palms in a circling gesture, huffing an ironic laugh.

"Nolan bought Versal, Dylan," Lennon said. The vitality drained from his body, his expression dropping and leaving only anger flaring in his eyes. "What if your drink *was* spiked on purpose?" Her voice trembled slightly as she posed the question, the first sign of emotion she'd let slip through. "You think his father was behind Rhett's injury. What if—" Lennon couldn't believe they were in a situation where this was a possibility. She hadn't wanted to believe he was right about Nolan sabotaging his father, but now, the timing was horrifyingly convenient.

She hoped she was wrong. The idea that Dylan was in actual physical danger, that someone would hurt him on purpose … .

A wave of panic swept through her. Who knew what else Nolan's ownership of the studio could mean for them? The game had changed yet again, and they had to be smart about it.

Lennon loathed Kelsey, but she was Huey's daughter. Huey controlled the show. And Huey answered to Nolan. Their hands were tied unless they played along.

The more that realization sunk in, the sicker she felt. Like a black hole had opened up inside her and was sucking her into it, ripping her apart piece by piece. She had to stay together right now— long enough to get through this conversation.

Lennon found Dylan studying her. It took her a moment to

realize what he was probably looking for. He needed more than her permission.

He needed to know he wouldn't break her again if he accepted Kelsey's deal.

He would, but she wouldn't let him know it.

They'd had fun together, which is all it could be for now. A familiar, comfortable escape from all the shit they'd been dealing with. Dylan hadn't told her he loved her or wanted to recommit to each other in any long-term capacity. His recovery and the mounting pressure of his career still hung over them. She couldn't expect him to sabotage his career to be with her if she wasn't OK with Kelsey's proposition.

Dylan had made his priorities very clear, as had she.

If he didn't accept Kelsey's offer to leverage her connections, his career with the Tidebreakers was as good as dead—and by extension, so was his father's. That was his legacy. What he'd been working tirelessly to salvage. It was everything to him.

She'd rather walk away on her own again before it all blew up in their faces.

"This was a nice distraction, but we've both got a lot we're trying to accomplish," Lennon said, stiffening her spine to show strength she didn't feel. "We can't let it pull us off course. Maybe one day, the timing will be right for us. For now, we have to stay focused on what's important."

Dylan gaze wavered to the side, stunned. "What's important," he repeated quietly.

"Yeah. Our careers. Getting our lives together. Speaking of which … I need to get to that interview. And you need to prepare for your meeting."

Dylan's eyes were glassy and vacant. "Right." He cradled his jaw in his hand, absently rubbing it. "I can drive you home," he offered.

"You don't have to. I'll order a car. You've chauffeured me around enough lately and I'm sure you have better things to do."

"I don't mind," Dylan said earnestly. "But if you'd prefer I didn't, at least take one of my cars. They're just sitting in the garage anyway."

Lennon's pride bristled at the idea of accepting yet another favor from him, but a glance at the clock on her phone revealed she had a tight window to get back to her apartment, make herself presentable, and arrive at her interview on time. Waiting on a car would make that window even tighter.

This was the last favor she'd accept from him.

"Sure. Thanks."

Dylan walked off to grab a set of keys, giving her a moment to suck in a deep breath through the pain and stabilize herself before he returned with a sleek fob sporting the Porsche logo. As it passed between their hands, he asked, "Are we still on for dinner later?"

Shit. Dinner. How the hell was she going to manage that?

"Yeah," Lennon said, forcing a smile. "I mean, we can see how the day goes. I have to bring the car back, anyway. But it'd be good to talk about everything. Figure out all the details so we're on the same page moving forward. Like we did when we started the show."

The corner of his mouth briefly lifted in faint, grim smile before he tightly nodded. He dropped his hand. Dylan's energy shifted, suddenly distant, like there were a million miles of space between them rather than an arm's length. A chill rushed through her at the stark contrast from what she'd felt wrapped in his arms less than an hour ago.

Lennon knew this was the probable outcome, and yet she'd opened her heart again, anyway. Her chest felt like it was crumbling into sand and pouring into her gut, through her arms, and down her legs, making her body impossibly heavy.

"I need to go," she pushed out. She had approximately sixty seconds, give or take, before she collapsed under the weight of it.

Dylan led her to the vehicle—a small, sleek SUV—and made her aware of all the important buttons to get her back to her apartment without blowing anything up. Her main priority was finding a good radio station she could crank up and lose herself in.

"Good luck with the interview," Dylan told her, a hand resting on the door. He blocked the afternoon sun, the light of which gleamed through his messy hair and the white of his shirt, revealing the outline of the body she'd spent all night curled against.

"Good luck with the meeting," Lennon said back.

His lips barely curved into a smile. He waited a beat before tapping the roof and stepping back to shut the door.

Once Lennon had pulled away from his house and the gate had shrunk to a dot in the rearview mirror, she turned the music up to full blast and released the dam.

Lennon gave herself the space of her commute to her apartment to let it all out—cry, shout, bang her hands against the steering wheel, admonish herself for being so stupid, curse the universe for being so unfair—and then she'd have to go back to survival mode. She had an interview to prepare for. One she'd have to nail in case Kelsey turned the tables on her and *didn't* help her tag along for season two.

Or if Lennon decided she didn't have the strength, after all, to keep up the charade.

CHAPTER 37

Lennon

SIX YEARS AGO

```
Blurred lights. The scent of his favorite laundry
detergent on her sweatshirt. His weak apology
repeating over and over in her head, instead of a
plea for her to stay.
```

Erin was already standing outside the door to her condo, waiting for her in her silk robe. Lennon dragged her luggage from the elevator across the carpeted hallway. When she joined Erin at the door, they simply looked at each other, having a wordless conversation. Erin's compassion wrapped around her like a hug.

"I left him. I left Dyl—" Lennon choked on the rest of his name. Her face cracked open around a silent cry as Erin reached for her.

Lennon collapsed in her arms, dragging them both down to the floor outside the door. Erin held her, leaning against the threshold and rubbing Lennon's back as painful sobs wrenched from her lungs.

CHAPTER 38

Lennon

Lennon pulled the SUV to a stop in front of her apartment building, parking parallel to the quiet street under a row of palm trees. They swayed peacefully against a crisp blue sky with a few wispy white clouds. A beautiful day. By all other measures.

She glanced in the rearview mirror at her red, puffy eyes stained with day-old mascara and groaned. Snot slowly slipped from her nose as she searched for something to wipe it with. She had to settle on her hand to clean herself up. At least she did find hand sanitizer tucked in the door.

Lennon stepped out on the pavement, locking the vehicle with the fob before checking the time on her phone. She needed to be presentable and back behind the wheel in less than an hour. As she walked toward the building, she struggled with the lock on her clutch again to access her keys, cursing under her breath.

"Lennon?"

She froze, fingers gripping the bag. Every molecule within her turned in on itself at the sound of the female voice Lennon hadn't heard in nearly a year. Lennon slowly looked up. "Mom?" Her voice came out hollow around the word.

Katherine, an almost spitting image of Lennon twenty years in the future except for the sensible outfit of khaki capri pants, a white scoop-neck t-shirt, and sandals, stepped away from the building's management office, her hand slipping from the handle as it shut behind her. As Katherine closed the gap between them, she scanned Lennon's appearance—her frizzy hair, ruddy face, wrinkled dress. Lennon wanted to disappear into that black hole expanding inside her. "What the hell is going on? What are you wearing?"

"I … I went to a wedding," Lennon answered weakly, her throat tight. The hot, humid air hung heavy around her.

"Like that?"

Her brain sluggishly reoriented to the situation. She shook her head, shaking off the stunned fog with it. "What are you doing here?"

Katherine's expression of confusion morphed into one of hurt and reproof. She gripped the tote over her shoulder, shifting her weight to one leg. "I should be the one asking that question. When were you planning to tell me that you were back in Florida?"

"How did you even find me?"

"One of my neighbors said they saw you and Dylan on some gossip website. Do you know how *embarrassing* it was to have to learn about my daughter's whereabouts from someone else? I called your old landlord in New York, and they said you'd had your stuff mailed to this address."

"Wow, so much for privacy laws," Lennon mumbled to herself.

"I'm your mother, and I had no idea what was going on with you because you haven't called me in almost a year."

"Well, the phone works both ways."

Katherine's eyes went cold, her nostrils flaring—the first sign Lennon had struck a nerve and was heading into dangerous territory. As a kid, she knew to back off when she saw that warning, and even now, her body sent off alarm bells. "I was giving you space. You weren't exactly happy with my honesty the last time we spoke." She ignored Lennon's eye roll and derisive laugh. "I was worried about you, but I figured you'd reach out to me once you calmed down and came to your senses. I see now that you've dug in your heels again, like you do." She surveyed the building and the street, her brow pinching in disapproval.

"When I called you and told you I'd finally gotten a record deal, you told me they were going to turn me into another 'pop-star whore,'" Lennon reminded her, the biting pain of the memory as fresh as if it'd happened yesterday. "I was excited and wanted to celebrate this huge milestone with my mom, and *that's* what you chose to say."

Katherine set her attention on Lennon again. "I was worried. You're my daughter. It's my job to protect you. Everyone knows how dangerous the music business is—how unreliable it is—how it treats people like products and spits them out when they're done with them. Why would I want that for you?"

"Because it's what *I* want."

"And how's that working out for you?"

Shame rose up in a hot, blistering wave. Lennon's grip tightened around the clutch, her lashes flickering slightly.

"I assume because you're living here in Arden Beach and not New York that things aren't going so well," Katherine added, shamelessly condescending.

The distant sound of traffic from the main boulevard and the occasional pedestrian across the street reminded Lennon how public their conversation was, making her feel disgustingly exposed. Drawing in a deep breath, she gathered what strength she could find to push out the words—and not cry as she said them. "The record deal didn't end up working out. I found another opportunity here, so I took it."

The look of self-righteous satisfaction on her mother's face twisted the ball of knives in her stomach. Katherine's gaze flitted past her to the SUV. "Whose car is that?"

"Dylan's. He let me borrow it," Lennon answered calmly, though her jaw was tight.

"Ah." Her mother nodded once and smiled as though something finally made sense. "So, he's taking care of you?"

At this point, she shouldn't have been surprised by anything her mother said, but her words echoing Kelsey's cut particularly deep. Tears stung the back of her eyes. "You really think I came back to Arden Beach for my ex-husband's money?"

"I don't know what you'd do in a desperate situation, Lennon," Katherine said with a sigh, exasperated. "I tried to warn you not to make the same mistake I did and marry your high school boyfriend, but you didn't listen. You never do. Then, I warned you pursuing a career in music would end badly and, well." She flipped her palm, shrugging a shoulder before letting her hand drop to her thigh. "I worked my ass off to get you that scholarship—"

"For a dental program. I told you countless times that I wasn't interested in that career path. I don't want the same things as you—"

"Now that you've had a taste of how bad it can get, I can see how you'd look for an easy way out," she continued as if Lennon hadn't even spoken.

Lennon curled her lower lip, biting down on it to keep herself from crying. She shook her head. "Nothing about this has been easy."

"I read about his troubles. He may be well-off, but he's a mess. Why would you want to get involved with someone like that, Lennon? He already abandoned you once. Surely, you're smart enough to know he'll do it again."

Lennon nearly lost her breath at that gut punch. "We're not getting back together," she gritted out. "He just let me borrow his car." It felt like all the blood in her body was slowly draining out onto the pavement. "I need to go. I have an appointment to get to." She started toward the building, passing her mother.

"Appointment for what?"

"That's none of your business."

"What is all this hostility for? You know … I don't get it,

Lennon," Katherine said to her daughter's retreating back. "I sacrificed so much for you. I raised you as a single parent while I was working and going to dental school full-time. I did everything in my power to set you up for success, and you don't seem to care about any of it. You just want to fool around instead of putting in the work to actually make something of your life."

Lennon stopped halfway between her mother and the building's entrance. The frustration that had been mounting within her hit critical mass. She fisted her empty hand, swinging back around. "No, *you* don't get it. I have sacrificed everything to make my life something that means something to *me*," she said, jabbing her forefinger into her chest. "It's not about you or Dylan or anyone else. It's about me being able to live with myself."

A breeze lifted Lennon's hair, blowing it across her face. Some pieces stuck to a thin layer of sweat. She didn't move to peel them away as she watched her mother's expression slowly devolve into disappointment.

And pity.

"So, there's nothing I can say to make you change your mind?" Katherine asked. Lennon gave a small shake of her head in response. Her mother dropped her head as her eyes fell shut, her thumb absently brushing along the strap of her tote. She released a sigh. "I'm so scared for you, Lennon."

The rawness of her mother's voice surprised her. "I'm scared for me, too," Lennon admitted. "But I'd be more scared if I accepted a life I knew would chip away at my soul until there was nothing left of me but a shell of who I am. At least this way, I have a shot at real happiness."

Katherine frowned, her eyes glassy as she raised her head. Lennon's heart sat suspended in her chest, waiting. Hoping.

"I hope you understand that I can't watch you live like this. It's too hard for me," Katherine said sorrowfully. "And I can't condone it."

Lennon blinked back the tears welling in her own, her chin

faintly quivering. She tightened her jaw to freeze it in place. "It's hard for me not having my mom support me."

Katherine smiled sadly. She softly canted her head. "That's what I'm doing, just not in the way you'd like."

Lennon's bruised heart sank, taking with it the last shred of hope she'd carried that things would someday be different between them. For a moment, she stared at the concrete, unable to speak.

"All I've ever wanted is for you to see me for me and to like what you see," Lennon finally said, her voice shaking slightly. She lifted her gaze to her mother. "I'm sorry we're both such a disappointment to each other."

Katherine's expression didn't budge, and she made no move to argue or come toward her. Lennon had her answer. She just had to accept it.

"Goodbye, Mom."

Lennon turned back to the building, pushing onward to her apartment. She hoped her mother would call out to her, that she'd hear her sandals slapping against the concrete as she ran to stop her, but Lennon continued up the stairs in silence.

When she made it to her apartment and looked out the window, Katherine was gone.

CHAPTER 39

Dylan

The machine methodically spat out baseballs and Dylan methodically swung at them, hitting each one with enough force to send them crashing against the opposite end of the cage. He only paused to lift up the hem of his shirt and wipe the sweat from his brow, then swung again.

Less than twenty-four hours ago, Lennon was standing where he was. Dylan had his arms wrapped around her, guiding her swing as he fought against the distractions of what he really wanted to do to her. Everything had fallen back into place. He'd held her tight in bed that night, determined not to lose her again.

Yet somehow, he had.

Dylan was reeling from how quickly it had all fallen apart, and not even entirely sure what—or how—it had happened. The whole thing was a blur. He hadn't fully processed all the bombs Kelsey had dropped before Lennon's detonated. He was still picking out the shrapnel, trying to make sense of it.

"This was a nice distraction, but we've both got a lot we're trying

to accomplish. Maybe one day, the timing will be right for us. For now, we have to stay focused on what's important."

Dylan winced. *What's important.* As if what they had wasn't.

He swung at the next ball with more aggression, the crack of the bat mimicking the feeling in his chest when she'd said it. It hadn't been just a distraction to him, and he had a hard time believing it had been to her, either. He could feel it in her kiss. Her touch. The way she'd responded to him.

Had she changed her mind, and Kelsey had given her an out, or was she doing what she thought *he* wanted?

The machine stopped shooting balls, going empty. Dylan dropped the bat with a heavy exhale. His phone chimed from the bench outside the batting cage to alert him that someone was at the gate. He swung open the door and rushed to grab it, hoping it was Lennon.

The smug face smiling at the camera stoked the fire burning through him. Dylan smacked the button to activate the microphone as he squinted toward the sky. "What the hell do you want, Pierce?"

"Afternoon. Free for a chat?" Nolan answered with mock-friendliness, brandishing a smirk beneath a pair of wayfarer sunglasses.

"If you want a meeting with me, call my manager. I think I have some openings in a couple of years."

"You think Lennon can wait that long?"

Dylan clenched his jaw at her name in his mouth. "What does this have to do with her?

"Open the gate and I'll tell you."

Dylan almost told him to go fuck himself, like he wished he'd done with Kelsey, but he didn't want to risk Nolan going straight to Lennon if he turned him away. He opened the gate without another word, then took his time heading inside.

After Dylan toweled off, downed some water, and changed out of his sweat-soaked shirt, he finally answered the door. Nolan stood a few steps from the threshold, his body angled between the door and the steps. Despite the heat, he wore a navy blue, three-piece suit. Always trying so damn hard. He regarded Dylan with a knowing, slightly perturbed look, which gave him a sliver of satisfaction.

"You know, I came here to make you a pretty generous offer," Nolan remarked, one hand resting casually in a pocket of his dress pants. His driver waited by the vehicle parked in the motor court behind him. "But maybe I should let you hang."

Dylan lifted his arm, leaning it on the doorframe. "There's nothing I need from you."

The corner of Nolan's mouth curved slightly. He removed his sunglasses. "By now, you're probably aware of my deal with Versal." His eyes sharpened on Dylan like he was unsheathing a blade. "I know what happened at the party, and that you've called a meeting with the board later today to make a case for a mid-season return." Dylan curled his hand into a fist as a weight settled in his gut. Lennon had been right—Nolan's hands were all over it. "If it works, it buys Eddie some time, and you get to slip back on the team before that damning episode airs." Nolan glanced toward one of the stone statues in the courtyard of a female figure holding a pot under one arm, pouring water into a basin. "Cancel the meeting."

"Sure, I'll call them right now," Dylan slung back, heavy with sarcasm.

Nolan directed his gaze back to Dylan. "You do, and I'll guarantee that footage never sees the light of day."

Dylan laughed humorlessly. "So, I have to fake-date Kelsey *and* help you get the Tidebreakers?"

Nolan's eyes marginally narrowed. "I don't know anything about Kelsey. This is between you and me."

"You already tried to hire a journalist to take me down. For all I know, you're the one who had someone drug me so you could use it for blackmail."

"For all I know, you got fucked up and you're scrambling to hide it with some fake story about being a victim because you have no proof. I could leak the footage right now and get what I want, but I'm coming to you as a gesture of good faith."

Dylan scrutinized him, not sure what to make of this. What game was he playing?

"What really happened is irrelevant," Nolan continued, shrugging it off. "If you agree to leave the team for good and back my bid for it—or at the very least, not get in the way—I'll not only bury the footage from the party, but I'll make sure Lennon gets a favorable edit on the show, something the showrunners currently have no intention of doing." He paused, letting the implications hang between them for a moment. "I'll also throw in a record deal, one that won't drop her. You know I have the connections to make it happen."

Nolan successfully landed a blow to Dylan's resolve.

It would solve all of their problems—Lennon's especially—at the cost of being a traitor to his father and Eddie. But something about the deal didn't sit right with him from Nolan's side. Even with Dylan's support, it wouldn't guarantee him the team, and if he wanted to hurt Dylan, the footage was enough to do damage. It didn't make sense. "Why are you doing this?"

"I'm trying to make a deal that benefits us both. It's business."

"Then, why does it feel like a trap?"

Nolan chuckled, the sound dry and patronizing. He scratched an eyebrow with his thumb. "You know the difference between us, Strickland?"

"A soul."

"I don't hate you and your father based on a lie," he answered.

"Your father hired someone to injure mine, so he'd lose the championship, then spent the next few decades trying to ruin his career."

"You got any proof of that?"

"We know Lan did business with the player who did it. And anyone who knows anything about baseball can tell it wasn't an accident."

"So, in other words … no."

Dylan stared blankly at him, his patience wearing thin. "Your father let jealousy get between them. It killed my dad. Lan was still a brother to him."

Nolan swiped his tongue through his lips and looked away, appearing to recede into thought. The fountain's gentle trickle of water and the breeze rustling the palm trees filled his brief silence. "Did you know my father knew your mother in college, before she met Rhett?" Dylan's eyebrows drew together, a flicker of doubt skimming his gut. His father had never mentioned it. "He told me she was a dancer who wanted to be on Broadway after graduation, but she married your father instead and gave up her dreams to support his." Nolan turned back to him, cold and hard. "That's why I don't respect you and your father—you self-righteously act like family is important to you, but you prove time and time again that your so-called *legacy* trumps everything. He put it ahead of his friendship with my father and his marriage to your mother."

Anger and defensiveness coiled tightly in Dylan's throat, along with something else he couldn't quite place but that left him uneasy.

"You can give Lennon what your father couldn't give your mother, or you can follow in his footsteps and put that legacy ahead of her best interest," Nolan continued. "Your choice."

His words sliced a nerve, slowly seeping in.

That's what that other feeling was.

Shame.

"My offer expires tonight." Nolan reached into his jacket's inner pocket, producing a business card on thick cardstock. He propped it in the hand of the statue, glancing at Dylan one last time before strolling down the steps as his driver opened one of the vehicle's rear doors. He slipped inside, not looking back.

CHAPTER 40

Lennon

As it turned out, Lennon could still nail an interview, even when her life was falling apart.

After everything she'd been through that day, convincing someone she could wait tables at a snazzy cocktail bar was a walk in the park. They hired her on the spot and scheduled her to start training in two weeks, although her hours would be limited until a full-time position became available. At least it took some financial pressure off and gave her time to decide what to do about the show.

Whenever Lennon tried to think about it, a rush of anxiety spilled out and she pushed it away.

A conference of some kind had let out as she was leaving the hotel, putting Lennon behind a large group of women, at least fifty or so, in heavy makeup and brightly colored athleisure waiting to hand in their tickets to the valet. Lennon pulled her phone out as she waited, toggling the "Do Not Disturb" mode off to check any messages she had missed while in the interview. Two missed calls from Carol Anne loomed at the top of her notifications. Her stomach knotted. She'd call her back later—

The phone rang in her hand. Carol Anne.

Sighing, Lennon accepted the call to get it over with. "Hey, Carol Anne. What's up?"

"What are you playing at, Lennon? Did you think we weren't going to find out?"

"I'm sorry, what?" Lennon pressed the button to turn up the volume on her phone, assuming she hadn't heard her correctly through all the noise from the crowd. She plugged her other ear with her finger.

"Your contract with Goldrush," Carol Anne explained, her tone clipped. "You should've told us everything."

"I did …"

"What about the exclusivity clause?"

"What are you talking about?"

"The one that prohibits you from recording anything without Goldrush's permission. We can't release the song you recorded without paying them an exorbitant fee. Thank God we cut it from the show, otherwise, we would've been fucked."

The blood rushed in Lennon's ears. For a moment, the world around her stopped, pressing into an unimaginably small point. "That can't be right," she said. "The contract was terminated. It was all terminated."

"Not everything. Didn't your lawyer tell you anything?"

"I … don't have a lawyer."

Carol Anne released a short, humorless laugh. "Well, you might want to get one. We're taking the money for that day at the studio out of your paycheck. Is there anything else we need to know?"

Lennon held her stomach, fighting back the urge to vomit. "No."

The line went silent. Lennon glanced at her phone screen and saw the call had ended. She stood immobile among the chattering, lively crowd, her heart banging a hollow drum in her chest as the ground seemed to sway beneath her feet.

Lennon stood reeling in the valet line long enough for all fifty women to disperse. But by the time it was her turn, she decided not to turn in her valet ticket yet.

She needed to take a walk.

And she needed some advice.

A few blocks later, Lennon stood in front of the Alonsos' imposing doors, pressing the call button below the camera. They'd given her the code to the gate in case she ever wanted to stop by. She'd never expected to use it, but here she was. It wasn't until that moment, between her finger pushing the button and watching Agueda's shadow approach through the glass, that panic spiked. Lennon wondered if she'd just made another mistake in the heat of distress.

Before Lennon could run back down the stairs, Agueda opened the door and greeted her with a smile as she dried her hands on a dish towel. She wore an apron over a bright, floral maxi dress. "Lennon! What a nice surprise."

"Hi, Agueda. I hope I'm not overstepping or imposing," she said apologetically. "I was just … in the area and wondered if I could talk to Mr. Alonso for a minute. If he's free. I realize I should've called first." Lennon's eyes fluttered shut, inwardly admonishing herself for not thinking this through more. She probably looked like a desperate fangirl with boundary issues showing up at their door. "You know what, I'm sorry. Nevermi—"

"Come in," Agueda said, waving a hand as she held the door open.

Lennon's brain lagged for a second before she fully comprehended that she was actually being invited inside.

"Last I checked, he was with Bebe. I'll see if he's available to see anyone," Agueda said as she led her to the living room. "Wait here, darling."

As Agueda disappeared down one of the corridors, nerves skittered all around Lennon's organs. Who was Bebe? He wasn't married and didn't have any kids. Another artist? A girlfriend? Someone who knew how to make appointments with him rather than randomly dropping by his home?

Agueda popped around the corner a minute later and Lennon straightened, preparing to graciously exit.

"This way," Agueda said, waving her hand.

She led Lennon to one of the outdoor spaces. Not the one they'd dined on with Raquel Rosas—Lennon still couldn't believe *that* had happened—but another with a lap pool and a cozy seating area. Oscar sat on the edge of a chaise in a guayabera shirt and shorts, a dark-haired teacup Chihuahua sitting alert at his feet on the polished stone floor, sporting a tiny diamond collar. Her large, round eyes focused intently on the treat between Oscar's thick fingers. He said something in Spanish and the dog suddenly hopped up on her tiny hind legs, spinning in a circle. His gravelly laugh drifted through the open French doors as they approached.

"Can I get you anything? Water, tea, coffee. Oh, I made fresh lemonade this morning," Agueda offered.

"Lemonade sounds nice. Thank you." Lennon's walk from the hotel in the hot, afternoon sun had left her mouth feeling like sandpaper.

Agueda warmly touched her on the shoulder and then went on her way.

Lennon stepped out onto the large terrace. "Hi, Mr. Alonso."

"*Buenas tardes, bonita.* Watch this." Oscar told the dog to sit again, and she plopped herself down in front of him. He gave her another instruction in Spanish, and she responded with a lift of her front paws, sitting back on her hind legs. She then put her tiny front paws together and began to lift them up and down in a waving motion. A deep, joyous belly laugh poured out of Oscar as his freckled face lit up with pride. "So smart, isn't she?" he mused as he rewarded the dog with a treat. Her ears folded back against her apple-shaped head as she took the treat, her little tail wagging rapidly. "Her name is Bebe. I trained her myself."

A smile touched Lennon as she watched the two of them. It almost made her forget about the pit in her stomach.

"So, to what do I owe this unexpected pleasure?" Oscar asked, stroking Bebe's back as she lapped up water from the bowl beside his feet.

"Thank you for agreeing to see me. I'm sorry for showing up without warning like some kind of stalker. I promise, I won't take up much of your time—" Lennon stopped as he waved her off.

"I told you, my door is always open," Oscar insisted in earnest, putting her at ease. He studied her. "You look troubled."

"That's an understatement." The breath she took pulled tight across her chest, shame sitting cold in her belly. "I did something really, really stupid. I didn't have a lawyer look over my contract before I signed with Goldrush, or when it was terminated. Honestly, I couldn't afford one, and I stupidly trusted them because they're such a big label and … I was excited to have a deal. Which, looking back—" Lennon shook her head in disgust. "I should've known better. They had an exclusivity clause in the contract that's still active."

Oscar briefly closed his eyes, a barely perceptible nod following. "For how long?"

Lennon pushed past the lump in her throat. "My original contract was for ten years from the date signed."

"Those vultures," he said with a sigh.

She blinked back the tears framing her vision, maintaining her composure. "Is there anything I can do or am I completely screwed?"

Agueda returned, delivering a glass of lemonade to Lennon and an iced tea to Oscar. She then excused herself.

Oscar squeezed a lime wedge into his drink, stirred it, and moved to the larger armchair adjacent to Lennon's spot on the sofa. He relaxed back, considering her question. "Goldrush is a huge label, like you said. Their lawyers will have done everything they can to make that contract ironclad." A rush of panic raced up Lennon's sternum. "But in my experience, every contract has a loophole. And if it doesn't, one can usually be negotiated. It's finding the right buttons to press. Everybody has some."

"How do I do that?"

"You'll need to start by getting your own lawyers, ones big enough to take on theirs."

Lennon sighed with her whole body, deflating. "I don't have the money for that. I don't know what I'm going to do. Ten years, I—I can't imagine putting my dreams on hold for *ten years*."

"Then, you have to find a way to fight for them."

Lennon stared out across the balcony to the endless stretch of blue. She'd *been* fighting for years. She didn't know how much was left in her.

The show was painting her as a villain to the public. Goldrush owned all her music. To fight this, she would *have* to agree to the show's second season if it was picked up so she could afford the legal fees. The thought of being stuck under Nolan's, Huey's, and Kelsey's thumbs any longer—going along with their game—made her want to hurl herself off that balcony.

And what if she went through all that, only to end up losing the legal battle against Goldrush?

Maybe this was the universe's way of telling her this wasn't the path for her.

Lennon squared her shoulders to Oscar. "I'd like you to be real with me. Don't worry about hurting my feelings. I can take it. Do you genuinely think I have the potential to make it as a recording artist—*really* make it—or were you only saying that because of Dylan? Because if I'm just OK, I need to know before I take on this fight. I need to know if I actually have a chance of making it in this industry, or if my music will remain something I make solely for myself."

Oscar steepled his fingers, pressing the tips to his lips. The man was never in a rush, even as she waited with her heart in her stomach. "Listen—I like Dylan, he's a great guy. A real one," he finally said after a few agonizing seconds. "But I don't like anyone enough to put my integrity on the line to make someone's girlfriend happy.

I'm not in the business of stroking egos, even though my artists wish I were." He tilted his fingers toward her, pointing. "If I say you're good, you're good. And you genuinely have the magic, Lennon."

Lennon's organs had become so tightly coiled that it took a moment for what he said to sink in and her body to relax into it. "Thank you," she said on an exhale.

"Now, you be real with me. Were you going to let this stop you?"

A soft lift tugged at her lips. Lennon felt pretty shitty and defeated right now, but no—probably not. She was too fucking stubborn for that.

The look on her face seemed to be enough of an answer for him as a small, self-satisfied smile found its way to his. "Can I give you some advice?"

"Please."

"Fame, money, awards—they're nice, but they aren't what we do it for. You can do anything for money. Money is everywhere. You can be a waitress and make whatever music you want to make for the rest of your life and be happy as a pig in shit because you have everything you need. It doesn't matter if anyone else hears it let alone likes it. Don't get caught up in all this." Oscar gestured to the wealth surrounding them. "I know that's annoying to hear from someone who has a lot. I used to hate it when I was playing on street corners in Havana and people said shit like that to me. But it's true. No one can take away your dream if your dream is to make music. So, if that's how it ends up going, it's not a loss. But you should always fight for what you want."

Bebe had been exploring the balcony as they spoke. She took a few dainty steps over to Lennon and sniffed her nude pumps. Reaching down, Lennon let the dog evaluate her fingers before she gently buried them in the weightless fluff of her neck and gave her a little scratch.

"You want to know the secret to a good life?" Oscar asked as Bebe sat against her shoe, leaning into Lennon's hand.

"Being a spoiled Chihuahua?" Lennon answered with a half-smile.

The deep grooves around his mouth lifted as Bebe squinted, nearly falling asleep against Lennon's palm. "Not letting anyone tell you what a good life is." The words settled over her, warm and liberating. "You gotta know what happiness means to you. It isn't the same for everyone, but the world will try to tell you it is because they have a stake in making you believe it."

Though she hadn't even begun to untangle what his advice meant to her, that poignant truth reverberated through Lennon's bones, striking a chord deep within.

"The song I played for you the other night … I wrote it to impress a label, and it did," Lennon admitted. "But it never felt fully like me. Could I play you something that does?"

"It'd be my pleasure."

Oscar led her to his office, which was attached to the same long, winding terrace. She sat down at the white grand piano while he perched himself on the edge of his desk again, grabbing a cigar from the polished wooden box. It must have been a ritual for him—a cigar and music. She glanced to the side, missing Dylan's presence.

But in a sense, he was there.

He always was.

"I was supposed to play this at my friend's wedding," Lennon said. Taking in a deep breath, she began to play the first notes. They flowed to her not in conscious words or thoughts, but in feeling, her fingers moving to the song she'd begun writing the day of her first visit to this house. Unlike the other song she'd performed for him, this one felt real. Raw. True to her.

When Lennon finished, she quickly swiped a tear that had pooled in the corner of her eye before spinning around on the bench to face Oscar. Like last time, he was a picture of stoicism. Unlike last time, she wasn't nervously awaiting his praise or criticism. Instead, she regarded him with grounded curiosity.

"How'd you feel while you were playing?" Oscar asked, the unlit cigar perched between his fingers and Bebe tucked in the other against his chest.

Lennon considered her answer for a moment. "Alive."

A smile lifted his face. "Money helps us survive. Music, art, love … they're what makes life worth living. For that feeling, right there." He tapped the left side of his chest. "That was beautiful, Lennon. You got anything else?"

For the next hour, Lennon played a few other songs she'd been working on in various stages of completion. Agueda joined them, and they snacked on *coquetas* she'd made. They offered her advice at the piano as they worked on them, even though there was a chance no one outside that room would ever hear them. Where working with the record label had been draining, dehumanizing, and disheartening, working with the Alonsos gave Lennon an example of what true collaboration could be like, and what it felt like to have people appreciate the art she was creating without trying to force her into a box that suited them.

Lennon thanked them for their help as they walked her to the front door. She had to reluctantly turn down their offer to stay for dinner since she had to return Dylan's car to him.

"Feel free to drop by whenever you're in the neighborhood," Oscar told her. "Like I said, our door's always open to friends."

"Even friends of friends?" Lennon asked.

"You and I are friends now. Let Dylan know he's been replaced."

"Will do." They hugged, and as Lennon pulled away, she said, "By the way, I'm not actually Dylan's girlfriend."

"Could've fooled me."

"He's my ex-husband." She stepped outside, taking in a deep breath of plumeria and sea salt. It layered over the sadness settling in her heart at the thought of him probably forever carrying that title.

"I produced love songs for a living," Oscar remarked as she met his gaze over her shoulder. "I know a man in love when I see one."

CHAPTER 41

Lennon

With the press of a button above her head, the wrought iron gates glided open. Lennon had texted Dylan when she was on her way, and he told her to let herself in.

It felt a little too much like coming home.

Her heart squeezed at the sight of him already waiting at the front steps, leaning against one of the pillars with his hands in the pockets of his dark jeans, feet bare on the polished stone. Since that morning, he'd styled his hair and changed into a fitted button-down shirt. The fractures in her heart deepened.

This would need to be quick.

"Thanks for letting me borrow your car," Lennon said as she stepped out onto the paved driveway, tugging her tote over her shoulder. She squinted against the sun, cursing herself for leaving her sunglasses on her kitchen counter in her rush to get to the interview. The heavily tinted windows in his car had helped, but now, she wished she had something to help her hide the pain she felt while looking at him.

"Any time. How'd the interview go?"

Lennon pushed the door shut with a sigh. "I start in two weeks."

"That's great," he said, pride glowing in his smile. "Congratulations."

"Thanks." Lennon stopped between the steps and the car, smoothing a hand down the front of her pencil skirt. "It's been a … busy day. I'm exhausted, so is it OK if I take a rain check on dinner? You probably should focus on preparing for your meeting, anyway."

Dylan's smile faded a little, disappointment flickering across his expression. "Yeah. Sure. I can drive you home—"

"No, it's OK. You've already done enough for me." And she couldn't bear to sit that close to him. It was hard enough coming back, seeing him with that invisible barrier resurrected between them. Knowing what was going to happen next. Part of her wished last night had never happened. It made losing him again feel like she was carving out a piece of herself right after it had scabbed over.

Lennon slipped her phone from her bag, checking on the status of the car she'd ordered. Six minutes out. She could manage six minutes. She could check her email, say she has to take care of something for the new job—

"I'm not taking Kelsey's deal."

Lennon's head shot up. She couldn't have heard him correctly. "What?"

"I'm not taking her deal," Dylan repeated more firmly.

Lennon's stomach briefly lifted in relief, but then quickly dropped back to cold, hard reality. "You have to."

"No, I don't. It's not worth losing everything over a lie."

"Are you kidding? That's exactly what's going to happen. You'll lose your career, your reputation, the team—"

"You. I mean you, Lennon."

Lennon blinked, shell-shocked. The palm trees swayed in a breeze that swept across the motor court. She nearly swayed with them.

"I was never going to take her deal," Dylan continued. He

pushed away from the pillar, straightening. "I don't want to be with her, real or fake. Especially after how she treated you."

It took her a moment to find her voice. "What about the team?"

Remorse surfaced in Dylan's eyes. His neck flexed through whatever inner turmoil he was fighting. "Either I move forward with things the way I'd originally planned, or—" He glanced at the statue of a female figure holding a tipped pot, watching the water trickle into a small fountain. "I take Nolan's deal instead." His gaze returned to her, sharpening. "He came by earlier. He wants me to stay off the team this season and help him get the Tidebreakers in exchange for burying the footage of me at the party."

Lennon's eyebrows nearly disappeared into her hairline. "So, you've basically been blackmailed twice in one day," she deduced, disgusted. His mouth twisted in a "basically, yeah" kind of way. "Did you tell him to go fuck himself?"

"I've been waiting to talk to you. He also promised to give you a good edit on the show." Dylan paused, watching her. "And a record deal."

The surprises kept on coming.

"Are you serious?" Lennon almost asked if Nolan even had the power to do that or if it was a manipulation tactic, but then she remembered who they were talking about. He had the connections, the money, the influence. And most of all, the audacity.

But it didn't matter.

Lennon's shoulders caved, shame and grief squeezing between her bones. "Even if he could get me a deal, I couldn't take it," she said, her throat tightening around the words. "I didn't realize the exclusivity clause wasn't voided when my contract with Goldrush was terminated. I can't record any music without their permission for ten years." Saying it out loud still felt wrong, like it wasn't real.

Dylan's expression went from shock to sorrow to anger all in a matter of seconds. He set his jaw. "We'll fight it. We'll get you out of it," he promised, his voice deepening.

"It's not important right now. Don't take Nolan's deal because of me. If it will cost you the Tidebreakers, it's not worth it."

"You're worth more than the team."

Lennon's heart expanded and ached at once. It was exactly what she had waited for years to hear him say. But the funny thing about getting what you want is that sometimes it comes too late, and the cost of accepting it becomes too great.

How would Dylan feel down the road when he realized what he'd given up? How could his family ever look at him—or her—again after he threw it all away over a mess she'd gotten them both into?

She had to dig herself out of this and live with the consequences.

"I'll be fine. I can take care of myself," Lennon declared. "What about Eddie and Rhett? You're making that decision for them, too. You'd force them to sacrifice something we both know they wouldn't agree to."

"They'll get over it. Eddie's a billionaire, and my dad's a decorated player. He's won championships. He's in the Hall of Fame. The only thing he's missing is winning one with me, and that's a small disappointment in the grand scheme of things." Dylan's eyes were clear, his voice unwavering. "Yeah, it'll hurt like hell if they lose the team, especially to someone like Nolan. But it's not the end of the world."

Though his reasoning was sound—their problems were absolutely of the champagne variety—Lennon knew the heart rarely cared about logic. This was his family's legacy. Maybe he'd eventually get over the loss, but would his father? Would that put an even bigger rift between them? She knew the pain of losing a parent who was still alive, of having them look at you like you'd ruined their life. She wouldn't be the reason that happened to Dylan.

And she wouldn't be the reason he gave up his own dreams.

Dylan's gaze drifted somewhere past her shoulder, unfocusing, as he seemed to recede into thought. A tiny divot formed between his brows. "I've always put them and the team first. I've spent my whole life trying to live up to the idea of someone else. My grandfather. My father. The perfect baseball player. Meanwhile, I've failed at being the things that matter—a brother. A friend. A husband." His dark eyes softened on her. Every part of her ached in response. "Of all my mistakes, my biggest regret is not being there for you when you needed me."

The world turned blurry as tears surfaced. Lennon shook her head. "I can't let you throw away everything for me. I *won't*."

"I'm not throwing anything away. I'm making a choice." Dylan came down the steps—the pressure building in her eyes, throat, everywhere as he moved closer—and stopped a foot away. The way he looked at her with such determination nearly made her come apart. She took an uneven, steadying breath. "I should've chosen you every time because you were and are the best thing that's ever happened to me. I'll happily spend the rest of my life choosing you, Lennon. If you let me."

Lennon turned her head to the side, needing not to look at him so she could get a hold of her emotions and think straight. She was suspended between everything she wanted and everything at stake if she gave in to it, ripping her in half.

"The only team I care about is this one—" Dylan took her hand and gently cradled her fingers in his. His touch made her release a jagged breath. "But if you don't want this—us—tell me," he said. "I'll understand. I just want you to be happy. With or without me."

Lennon closed her eyes. Happiness felt as elusive as any other dream, always slipping through her fingers when she thought she'd finally grasped it. It seemed like her only option at this point was not to make a bigger mess of things. "I can't let you bail me out, Dylan, especially not at the expense of you and your family. I have to do this myself."

"Why?"

"Because," Lennon said, voice rising in frustration. She whipped her head forward. "I have to live with the consequences of *my* choices."

A wrinkle formed between his brows. "Did you talk to your mom?"

The truth cut deep. She clenched her jaw to keep from crying, unable to answer.

Dylan hissed a sigh through his teeth. "I don't know what she said, but whatever it was, I feel pretty safe saying it was bullshit." He barely reeled in his anger, his voice softening around the edges. "You deserve to have everything you want, Lennon. Let me help you."

Her mouth dragged into a frown. She shook her head. "I won't take it at your expense."

"It wouldn't be—"

"It would. You fucking know it would."

"Well, I don't fucking care."

Lennon's heart pumped fast, staccato beats. A tear slid down her cheek as she stared in his eyes—looking back at her with fire and desperation. Pleading with her. She waved her head again in denial but before she could argue again, he pulled her to him and crashed his lips against hers. She sunk against him. His hands framed her face as he kissed her like he was fighting for his life. Her fingers grazed his ribs, curling around shirt to wrench him closer.

"I just want you," Dylan breathed against her lips. "I don't care about anything else."

Lennon wanted to say fuck it all. To take what he was offering and run with it.

But where would that leave them once reality caught up to them? When he'd lost everything he loved, so he wouldn't lose her.

She couldn't live with him resenting her, too.

"I can't, Dylan," Lennon said with finality, her edges fraying. His expression twisted with frustration. "Please—go to that meeting. Fight for your spot on the team. If you don't want to take Kelsey's or Nolan's deal, fine. But don't do it for me. Do what's right for you." She fixed him with a steady look, so he knew how serious she was. He watched her with a scrunched brow over pained eyes. Her voice cracked as she said, "I need you to be happy, too."

Her phone dinged.

"That's my ride." Lennon sucked in a sharp sniffle. "Let me know how it goes tonight, OK?" She could tell he was fighting against honoring her decision and arguing with her further. She gave him a look that pleaded with him to let her go, then peeled herself away from him.

Dylan reluctantly released her.

And she reluctantly walked away.

CHAPTER 42

Dylan

Dylan considered jumping in the Porsche to go after her. It's what he should have done when she served him divorce papers.

He could call Nolan—accept the deal, anyway. But she would never forgive him for that.

He would never forgive himself for losing her again.

The car rolled away, disappearing down the drive, and Dylan's chest felt like it was splitting open.

He didn't know how long he stood outside. Dragging himself into the house, Dylan let out a roar of frustration as he threw the car key at the sofa. Running his hands through his hair, he paced before the fireplace.

The photograph hooked his attention—the one of him, Lennon, and Erin as kids at the ballpark the first summer they met. A year after his mom died. Lennon had helped a grieving kid feel like himself again.

A photograph of his mother sat next to it. He braced his palm on the mantel's edge, leaning his weight into it. God, he wished she were here. In moments like this the most.

"What do I do, Mom?" he asked quietly. "How do I fix this?"

CHAPTER 43

Lennon

Boats silently sailed the harbor, passing under the bridge to the city. Lennon watched through the car window as bittersweet memories floated between the clouds.

When they became too much to bear, she started cleaning out her email inbox on her phone to have something to do. Anything to keep her from having a breakdown in a stranger's blue sedan where a faded palm tree-shaped air freshener hung from the rearview mirror and a little plastic hula dancer's hips bobbed on the dashboard with every jostle of the vehicle.

Lennon tapped on an email from her apartment complex. A reminder that her lease was up in three weeks. She had a week to renew it before it went to someone on the waitlist. Without the studio's help and only part-time hours at her new job, she wouldn't be able to swing it. She'd have to find someplace else to live.

And she had to decide if that someplace would be in Arden Beach.

Lennon's heart felt like it was being torn in two—ripped into jagged, mangled halves. On one side, her pride and fear. On the other, a deeply rooted love tightly threaded through her DNA. She couldn't remember when she wasn't in love with Dylan Strickland. It was as much a part of her as her love for music.

The two halves of her heart were like sound waves out of phase—one pushing, one pulling—creating destructive interference. They canceled each other out, leaving her stuck in a silent void. To hear music again, she'd have to choose one wavelength and release the other.

Right now, the choice felt impossible.

Or maybe there wasn't a choice—not if she loved him. Being together put Dylan at too steep a disadvantage. And Lennon wasn't sure she had the strength to be in the same city where she would be reminded of him around every corner.

She opened her text message thread with Erin, her most recently received message a response to Lennon and Dylan's photo at the wedding with the tier of cheese:

> Erin: My two favorite cheeseballs.

Lennon stared at the photo, her heart breaking and mending in a loop.

She couldn't bear it if Dylan ever looked at her the way her mother had. Katherine's disappointment echoed in her mind, cutting a fresh wound. *"I sacrificed so much for you."*

Lennon never wanted Dylan to resent her like that. It would tear her apart.

But so would walking away from him. Again.

The driver dropped her off in front of her building. Lennon dragged her aching body upstairs to her temporary home. The late afternoon sun slanted through the windows over the space that wasn't hers. It felt more temporary now than the entire time she'd lived there, as if she were letting herself into someone else's apartment. So much had transpired since the day she moved in. She'd been full of hope, optimism, ambition. She believed she'd turned a corner, launched herself into a new chapter.

Now, it was a reminder of all she'd lost in the process. She was back at square one, if not further behind than where she started.

Lennon deposited her bag on the sofa, kicked off her heels, and slipped off the tight skirt, leaving on only the long, silk shirt. Her stomach gurgled, reminding her she hadn't eaten since breakfast. She drifted into the kitchen to hunt through the fridge and pantry, but they were practically empty because she hadn't gone grocery shopping in a week. She yanked open the drawer beside the sink, and several packets of soy sauce and folded takeout menus slid forward.

With them came Dylan's laugh as they played "Name That Tune" on her living room floor. The mischief in his eyes as they flicked their noses at each other on the beach to secretly communicate. His out-of-tune singing during karaoke. A brush of his finger against hers after he'd bared his heart to her late at night on the dock. Another brush of his fingers in the grass under a blanket of stars. An electrifying kiss—on the ground, in the pool, on the table, in his bed.

"It's not worth losing everything over a lie. This is the only team I care about."

Lennon slammed the drawer shut. Sliding to the floor, she sagged against the cabinet and tucked her knees to her chest, like she had in New York a few short months ago when she felt just as lost and confused.

Everything was the same, yet it wasn't.

Lennon couldn't pretend she hadn't fallen back in love with Dylan. She couldn't pretend he hadn't asked her to spend her life with him again. She couldn't pretend that she didn't want to. Gone were the days she could put her feelings for him in a drawer, run away to another city, and pretend a piece of her heart wasn't left behind in Arden Beach.

In a drawer.

The impulse hit her hard and swift.

Lennon pushed herself up and strode to the bedroom, dropping to her knees before the dresser. Under her sweaters in one of the bottom drawers, she removed a shoe box filled with miscellaneous keepsakes—ticket stubs, guitar picks, lyrics scribbled on napkins. She dug through it until a white envelope with her name written in familiar handwriting stared back at her. She sat on the carpet, tucking her legs to the side, and took in a deep, shaky breath.

Lennon turned the envelope over, running her thumb under the seal to finally break it.

As she carefully unfolded the paper, his handwriting, messy and imperfect, made her smile. The same as all the notes he'd written her when they were kids and teenagers. He would slip them into her backpack at the ballpark, so she'd find them when she got home. Something his mother used to do for him.

But this one wasn't a sweet love letter detailing his dreams of a future with her—this one was about the pain of their past, something she hadn't been ready to revisit through his perspective. Until now.

Bracing herself, Lennon began to read:

Lennon, I've started and trashed this letter at least 20 times. Nothing I wrote felt right. I realized it was because I was still holding back on the things I've been struggling to admit to myself. It's hard enough to say them out loud, let alone put them on paper. But you deserve the truth, not just an apology, so here it is.

I let you go.

Lennon squeezed her eyes shut at his admission, the truth tearing through her. She paused a beat before continuing.

I pushed you away because I couldn't face the truth that I was afraid of the life I felt obligated to. A life living up to my family's legacy. You were right about my heart not being in it. You always saw through my bullshit. You saw what I couldn't admit to myself. And if I had admitted it, I would've disappointed you because I wasn't strong enough to walk away from the game. The irony is that I ended up losing something even more important to me.

You.

At first, I lied to myself and figured you were better off without me. And maybe it wasn't a lie—you <u>were</u> better off without me as I was. I was a coward. I was scared to let down my dad and the Carmichaels and the fans, but I was also too afraid to quit. I didn't know who I'd be without baseball, and I was terrified of that unknown. Honestly, I still am.

It was easier to stuff it all down, pretend it wasn't there. Stick to the game plan while self-sabotaging. You always had a way of stripping me bare. In a way, I became scared of you, too. I could never lie to you, but I wasn't being honest with myself, so my only option was to avoid you. To shut you out.

When I got signed, shit got real. I realized how scared I was of disappointing everyone—of being the Strickland who fails and ruins the legacy. I felt trapped. I was in too deep, I couldn't turn back, I couldn't admit that I <u>wanted</u> to turn back, so I numbed myself instead. I wanted to clear the noise in my head. Nothing mattered in those pockets of time. I wasn't me. Baseball didn't exist. I was free.

But obviously, that was a lie, too.

I've done so much lying to myself, Lennon. You fought like hell to be there for me, but you were fighting a losing battle because I couldn't— or wouldn't—let you in. And the worst thing is, I abandoned you in the process. We were supposed to be a team. We made vows to go through life together, and I broke them immediately. You needed me and I wasn't there for you.

Our last conversation before you left haunts me, especially when you said you wish you could be enough for me. Lennon, you were <u>everything</u>.

You are more than I deserve. I was the one who wasn't enough— brave enough, strong enough, honest enough.

I hope you'll let me be part of your life again someday, but I'll respect it if you don't.

Thank you for trying to love me. I wish I'd been strong enough to let you.

I hope you have a beautiful life, Lynx.

Lennon aggressively swiped the tears from her face, then clutched the letter to her chest as if it were the man who wrote it. She tilted her head back, staring up at the ceiling.

"Fuck."

CHAPTER 44

Dylan

A secretary walked Dylan to a conference room on the executive floor of the Carmichael Enterprises tower. Through the glass wall separating it from the hall, he saw his father already waiting inside, a disposable coffee cup in hand and a pensive expression on his rugged face. Behind him, more skyscrapers carved the horizon. Rhett looked up from the long, sleek table as they approached.

"Can I get you anything, Mr. Strickland?" the secretary asked as she held open the door for Dylan.

"No, thank you." Despite the situation he was walking into, he felt surprisingly calm.

"Mr. Carmichael's finishing another meeting. He'll be with you in a moment."

As the secretary shut the glass door, Dylan came around the table to greet his father with a hug, then took a seat across from him. A tray with a pitcher of water and paper cups sat between them. "How are things on the road?"

"Won against Colorado. We play Houston tomorrow," Rhett said as he settled back into his chair.

"Hopefully, they'll carry that energy into the next one."

"We'll see."

Eddie swept through the door, a clean-cut young man with a tablet and leather folio following close behind. "Always a good day when I have two Stricklands in my office," he said with an amiable smile. He shook their hands, then introduced his colleague. "This is my new assistant, Gabe. He'll be taking notes, so we don't miss anything." Eddie pulled out the chair at the head of the table, unbuttoning his jacket before sitting down. Gabe sat to his right and handed him a stack of papers from the folio. "The commissioner's plane lands in about an hour, and he's coming straight to the meeting, so let's quickly recap everything one last time."

As Eddie thumbed through the papers, the cold air shifted from refreshing to uncomfortable. Dylan's muscles and joints began to stiffen. He remembered Eddie telling him that he always kept their offices cold because it was scientifically proven to make thinking and decision-making easier. Probably because you were too fucking cold to sit there for long.

"We've got statements from your doctors clearing you for the game," Eddie said, organizing the papers before him. "I got some of my contacts at a couple of big media outlets to run positive stories about you this week and get the buzz going, so I'll bring those up in the meeting, too. Show the tides turning in your favor." His phone lit up with a notification. He read it, then quickly punched out a text. "Have you been practicing the pitch we wrote?" The question was met with silence. As the text message whooshed off, he glanced up. "Dylan?"

Dylan stared at his interlaced fingers on the table. He didn't know if the cold air was actually helping, but he felt more clear-headed than he had in a long time. "I need to tell you both something." He faced his father and Eddie. "Something that happened while filming the show."

Eddie studied him briefly before something shifted in his eyes. "Gabe, can you give us some privacy?" His assistant stood, exiting the room to wait in the hall. Eddie carefully put down his phone, waiting until the door was shut. "How bad is it?"

Dylan recounted the situation at the party and how his lawyers were negotiating with the studio about burying the footage. As it stood now, it would air on the show in a few months, and his word was the only proof he hadn't taken it willingly.

"Jesus Christ, Dylan," Rhett mumbled, hanging his head. He wiped a hand down his face.

"When did this happen?" Eddie asked, his expression tight. Voice eerily calm.

"Two weeks ago."

Rhett looked up. "You were at the boot camp two weeks ago."

"It was the night before I left," Dylan explained. "Dr. Callow did a house call. He ran a drug test, hooked me up to an IV. Thankfully, it wasn't a huge dose. Just enough to disorient me for a little while."

"Why am I only now hearing about this?" Rhett's tone teetered between anger and disappointment.

"Because I've been handling it." Though his father's disapproval stung, Dylan didn't waver. "My lawyers are working on it. Everyone there signed an NDA, so I was hoping we'd come to an agreement before the public knew anything about it."

"The fact that they haven't been able to strong-arm the studio yet is concerning," Eddie pointed out. "They've probably conveniently lost any evidence that would come up in an investigation by now." He ran the edge of his thumb over his lips as he seemed to go into thought, calculating everything. "When does the show air?"

"January."

Eddie nodded curtly. "Good. That buys us time. It won't affect the game this season while we figure out how to deal with the show—"

"I've decided not to come back to the team this season."

Eddie gaped at him, stunned, while Rhett shook his head,

laughing humorlessly. His father stood and began pacing along the windows, hands on his hips.

"And why the hell is that?" Eddie asked.

Dylan assessed the two men he respected most, burdened with remorse for the impossible choice he had to make. There was no perfect option. No way to meet the needs of everyone he cared about without hurting someone else.

So, he had to take a page out of Lennon's book and do what felt right. In his heart.

Dylan drew a steadying breath, filling his chest and setting his shoulders. "Because I'm not ready," he answered Eddie. "My shoulder's not where it needs to be. I was going to push through because I want to get back out there, but I'm going to do more damage in the long run if I do. I need more time."

"How much more?" Eddie questioned.

"At least until next season. I'll see where I'm at then." Dylan glanced at his father, who had stopped at the window with his back to the table. His organs felt like sandbags pressing on his ribs.

"What if you changed hands? Pitched with the right," Eddie suggested.

"I've never trained with the other," Dylan said. "And it would still affect my left shoulder."

"But not as much?" Eddie deferred to Rhett for confirmation.

Loosing a sigh, Dylan dropped his gaze to the dark, polished wood. "It's not easy for me to walk away. I want you both to know that. Baseball—the Tidebreakers—is my life. But that's also part of the problem. I've been working since I could hold a bat. My doctors and therapists think the constant push has affected my recovery. And I've finally realized … finally accepted that they're right. If I want to recover and have a long career ahead of me, I need a break. A real one."

Eddie analyzed him, the hard line of his brow and coldness in his eyes making his displeasure clear. Even as their silent disapproval burned a hole in his chest, Dylan remained steadfast.

"And honestly—I don't think I'm the answer for bringing up the team's morale," Dylan added. "I think they lost faith that they had any worth to the team when you didn't back Diego, but you backed me."

A harsh, exasperated breath was expelled across the table. "It's not favoritism—"

"It is," Dylan asserted, surprising Eddie with his bluntness. "He deserved a second chance as much as I did. Diego's young and made a mistake getting on that boat, like I did. He tried to stop Craig from taking it out—"

"We don't know that for sure—"

"I believe him. And I think you do, too. You just didn't think it was worth fighting two PR battles, so you threw him under the bus to get rid of some of the heat. If I'd been the one with the black eye, you would've believed me and still fought for me. Wouldn't you?"

Eddie pressed his mouth into a line and inclined his head slightly. His silence was enough to confirm Dylan's assumption.

"Use the meeting to advocate for Diego." Dylan maintained eye contact with Eddie across the table, challenging him. "At the very least, make it known to the board and the public that you stand behind him. I don't know if it will help you keep the team. I don't even know if it will help us win this season. But winning's not always the point."

Eddie's gaze lowered to the table as he tapped a forefinger on it. The corners of his mouth lifted slightly, but his eyes held no light in them behind his black-rimmed glasses. "None of us in this room would have the lives we've had without winning. We owe everything to it," he said, voice measured, edges sharp. "I don't need some rookie who hasn't even played a major league game yet. I need you. It's time for you to do your part, and you're telling me you'd rather let us down when we need you most."

That sliced deep. Dylan clenched his jaw, pushing through the razor-sharp guilt. "I'm sorry that's how you see it."

"Your father recovered quickly from his injury and had a long career—"

"Well, I'm not him."

"No, apparently not." The room went silent, letting the accusation ripple through the cold, fraught air. Dylan knew Eddie would be pissed, but that didn't make the blows land any less painfully. "Let's see if you still care about not winning when everything your family worked for is gone after you finally decide to come back from your 'break.'" Eddie rose from his chair, buttoning his jacket. "I'll give you ten minutes to talk to your father and come to your senses. Then, we need to get back on track."

Dylan shook his head. "I'm not changing my mind, Eddie."

Eddie stopped gathering the papers in front of him. He studied Dylan for a beat. "And I'm not changing mine," he declared. Dylan's brow tightened at the threatening edge in Eddie's tone. "You've been medically cleared. That means you have to play if I want you to."

Dylan couldn't believe he was pulling that card. The betrayal stung—a slap in the face to a relationship he'd thought was built on mutual trust and respect. But apparently, at the end of the day, Dylan was just another asset to him.

Dylan's expression hardened. "Then, I'll file for a mental health leave." Eddie huffed a quiet, patronizing laugh, but Dylan didn't flinch. "My psychologist will sign off on it. They've been seeing me for panic attacks. Per the league's rules, you'll have no choice but to put me on the injured list for anxiety."

Eddie stared at him in disbelief. Like he was looking at a stranger. They both seemed to be—or maybe they were truly seeing each other for the first time.

"Then, I guess we're done here," Eddie said, devoid of warmth. He piled the papers into the folio and snapped it shut, then strode out of the room. He dropped the folio in Gabe's hands as he blew past him, who proceeded to rush after his boss.

Dylan fisted a hand, releasing a long breath through his nostrils. Despite knowing he was making the right choice—or at least, he hoped he was—it killed him to let down someone he cared about, and for that person to likely think differently of him for it.

His father continued staring out the window. Silent.

"Are you going to say anything, or did Eddie already say it all for you?" Dylan asked. He braced himself for the next blow. It would cut even deeper coming from Rhett. He'd feared a moment like this his whole life, but now, he was prepared to deal with the fallout.

Rhett turned, hands still on his hips, and fixed his stern glare on Dylan. As always, his expression was stoic, but the disapproval emanated from him like a force of its own, disturbing the air around them. Something about how he held his shoulders, and his mouth pinched at the corners. Dylan had seen it on the field when players messed up a play, or the umpire made a bad call, or Dylan was struggling to execute his technique correctly on an off day.

Dylan kept his head up and spine straight, bracing himself.

"I believe in doing everything it takes to win," Rhett finally said, his voice like a crunch of gravel. "I wouldn't have gotten where I am today if I didn't. But you can't win this game if your heart isn't in it." He paused, and Dylan's brow slowly drew together, watching his father with uncertainty. "I can't say I understand where you're coming from, son, because I don't. It's not how I operate. But you're your own man. I respect your right to make your own decision."

Dylan stared at him, waiting for the other shoe to drop.

"Eddie's wrong. It's not on you," Rhett continued. Some of the tension eased in Dylan's chest. "If the team falls apart without one player, then something else is broken."

It was hard to tell with his father, but he sensed his disappointment didn't extend solely toward him. It pointed inward, too.

"If anyone can fix it, it's you. But I think you have to start by listening to the team," Dylan said, hoping he'd take his suggestion about Diego seriously. "They need to know they're supported, too."

Rhett didn't say anything. Only gave a slight, almost imperceptible nod. Dylan wasn't sure if it was approval, disapproval, or somewhere in between. "I need to talk to Eddie, see what the game plan is now." He crossed the room to the door. As he set a hand on the long, metal handle, he stopped. Dylan turned to look at him, waiting.

After a long pause, Rhett looked back, his expression unusually pensive. "You're a lot like your mom. She'd be proud."

With that, Rhett left the room.

Dylan sat in the parking garage, staring at his sunroof. Any feelings he'd kept at bay during the meeting surfaced in the dark, quiet privacy of his vehicle. Relief and guilt came tightly intertwined.

The burden he'd put on others saddled him with a weight he couldn't shed. He wouldn't be able to numb it. Wouldn't be able to outrun it. But what he could do was make peace with it.

Little by little, he would make peace with it.

His phone chimed with a text message. Dread snaked through him until he saw the name attached to it.

Lennon: Are you still free for dinner?

A surprised smile pulled at his lips, some of the tension in his body evaporating.

Dylan: I am

Dylan: In fact, I'm free all evening. I'm not going to the meeting with the board

Lennon: Why?

Lennon: Tell me you aren't taking Nolan's deal

Dylan: I'm not. I'm not taking anyone's deal. I need to prioritize other things for a while

Nothing came through for several seconds. He waited, staring at the screen until three dots signaled her typing.

Lennon: I know that couldn't have been easy to
do. I'm proud of you

Pressure mounted behind his eyes. He swallowed it back.

Dylan: That means more to me than you know

He hadn't realized how much he needed that. And how much it would mean coming from her. It didn't eliminate the weight, but it made it a little easier to carry. He rested his head back, releasing a full-body sigh.

A soft ping brought his attention back to his phone.

Lennon: Meet me at our secret place

A sly grin spread across his face. Three dots appeared, then another message a second later.

Lennon: See you soon (if you remember it…)

CHAPTER 45

Lennon

The only people better at finding hiding places than criminals and secret agents are teenagers sneaking around with their lovers.

When Dylan and Lennon reached adolescence and began craving privacy, they found the perfect spot at the local baseball field where Dylan had played before going pro. The bonus of it being a little bit dangerous—and *definitely* off-limits—made it that much more appealing.

Though the field was empty and had closed in recent years due to lack of funding, Lennon still felt a rush of rebellion as she climbed over the rusted "Employees Only" sign to the metal ladder leading up to the back of the electronic scoreboard.

At the top, she hoisted herself onto the narrow walkway. A fresh, salty breeze mixed with pine swept across her face as she peered through the trees to the ocean churning silently in the distance. The wind rustled through the woods, birds singing among them. Lennon simply listened to nature's chorus for a while, letting it soothe her tired soul.

"Wow."

The sound of his voice rustled her heart awake. She looked to the ladder where Dylan stood, leaning against the last few rungs, watching her with a lovesick look on his face.

"I'm glad you remembered," Lennon said with a small, teasing smile.

Dylan climbed the rest of the way, joining her on the ledge. His forehead creased a bit. "What would you have done if I hadn't?"

"Found another baseball player to invite up here."

Dylan sank his teeth into his lower lip, tilting his head back. "I guess I would've deserved that." He smiled softly as his gaze settled on her. "We said 'I love you' for the first time up here. There's no way I could forget."

Butterflies flitted through her like they had all those years ago. It felt like it had happened both yesterday and in another lifetime. Life hadn't been perfect then either, but she'd believed it would all eventually work out exactly the way they'd imagined. She no longer possessed that blind faith, but something new had emerged in its place.

"I read your letter. The one you sent me after the accident." Lennon angled her body to his as the muscles in his face slackened. He suddenly appeared strikingly vulnerable, and her heart squeezed in response. "Thank you for being honest with me. I meant what I said. I really am proud of you, Dylan." The corner of his mouth twitched upward, his brow stitching together over glassy eyes. Her own filled along the rims. "I'm sorry for how I left earlier. For running again. I was scared you'd resent me, like I thought you did when we were married. I never want you to regret choosing me—"

Dylan took one long stride toward her, and in a second, his hands cradled her face, and his lips pressed against hers. She grabbed his forearms to steady herself, then sank into the deep, slow kiss. It wasn't hesitant or exploratory, or lustful and passionate as the others had been. This one was an expression of something too deep for language. It had to be *felt*. He held onto her like she was something precious. She curled her fingers into his forearms as their mouths melded to each other's in steady ministrations, the last barriers between them gone.

"I love you, Lennon," he declared quietly. "The only thing I could regret is *not* choosing you."

Her lips curled into a smile against his as his thumb wiped a tear from her cheek, affectionately stroking her skin. Gone was the destructive interference. Her heart committed to one wavelength, falling in step with his. "I love you, too. I'm ready to be a team with you again. Cheese and all."

The breath from his laugh tickled her chin before he kissed her again. She hooked her arms around his neck as he circled her torso, pulling her close. They stayed like that for a while until she slid her hands around his waist and laid her head against the hard planes of his chest, nuzzling into his warmth.

Lennon didn't want to ruin the moment, but she knew he probably needed to talk about it. "So, how did Rhett and Eddie take the news?"

"You mean, you didn't hear the celebration all the way across town?" Dylan's chest deflated under her cheek with a sigh. He tightened his arms around her. "Neither of them are happy. Eddie especially. My dad took it better than I expected, though. He actually … complimented me, I think."

"Really?"

"Yeah. Said my mom would be proud." He spoke hesitantly, like he was both overwhelmed and confused by it.

Lennon lifted her head to look up at him. "She would be. But I think that was his way of telling you he is, too."

The edges of his mouth formed a faint smile, but his eyes held a trace of sorrow. "I know I made the right choice. I just wish it felt better."

Lennon knew what he meant. Intimately. She pulled away slightly, keeping her arms around him. "My mom found my apartment. Today." Compassion flickered in the depth of his gaze. His thumb began drawing comforting circles on her back. "We got into an argument about my life choices—like we always do. I told her I didn't want to speak to her anymore if she wasn't going to respect what I want. And … she left. And I let her."

Dylan briefly shut his eyes, the line of his jaw hardening. He dipped his forehead to touch hers. "I'm so sorry, baby," he said quietly.

"Me too." The wound ached, as she knew it would for a long, long time. Probably forever. But one good thing had come from it; Lennon was more aware and appreciative of the unwavering support she did have. "Thank you for always believing in me and loving me for who I am, Dylan. Especially lately, when I've had trouble seeing it myself."

His hands gave her back a gentle squeeze. "Ditto."

Lennon lifted onto her toes and pressed her mouth to his. Love for him radiated through her unrestrained. The spaces left empty in his absence were filled with warmth, finally alive again.

They held the kiss until she needed a breath. She swept her hands around his torso and up the solid planes of his chest to cradle his face. Her thumbs brushed his scruff as she looked into his soulful, deep brown eyes, watching her with a sense of peace only found in one place.

Home.

They were both still in the middle of a storm, but they no longer had to bear it alone.

Lennon slid her hands back to his chest, resting them there. Feeling his heartbeat. "The wrap party's tomorrow night. You planning on going?" she asked, cocking an eyebrow. His answer would probably be the same as hers.

"I'd love to, but it was between that and setting myself on fire, and I figured I'd been to enough parties lately. What about you?"

"Wow, that *was* a tough choice. Unfortunately, I'm going to be busy at the Kelsey McCroy-*Donaldson* Fan Club meeting. By the way, can we borrow your batting cage?"

Dylan's chest rumbled against hers with a deep laugh. "Only if I get the first swing."

Lennon smiled, but the reality of the situation pulled her back down. "What are we doing to do about the show? We're on our way to total character assassination when this thing streams."

"I could take Nolan's deal," Dylan offered, his tone reluctant but willing. "One of the conditions was for me not to go back this season, which I decided not to do, anyway."

"Yeah, but he also wants you to back his bid for the team, which you can't do."

"He only said I have to not get in the way of it."

"What does that even mean, though? There's no telling what he could end up asking for once you agree."

"Well, I'm sure as hell not taking Kelsey's deal, so what other choice do we have? I'd flesh out the details and have it all put in writing. Get my lawyers in on it before anything's set in stone so he can't throw any surprises at us."

The fact that they even had to entertain the idea of getting into bed with Nolan made Lennon's skin crawl. But she couldn't see another way out. Letting them edit the show the way they planned to only benefited Kelsey and the studio at Lennon and Dylan's expense. At least with Nolan's deal, they got something out of it.

"If he asks for too much and expects you to betray the team completely, then don't do it," Lennon said. "We'll find another way to deal with the show, or if worse comes to worst, we'll deal with the fallout." She ran her thumbs over the unbuttoned edges of his shirt, slipping them beneath the fabric to touch the smooth skin along his sternum. "I'm not afraid."

A soft smile touched his lips. "Me either."

"Let's deal with this later. It's been a long day, and I want to go back to our bubble for a while."

"Deal." Dylan's fingers brushed along her spine, leaving an electric charge in their wake, coming to rest in the curve of her neck.

He guided her mouth open with his, sinking his tongue inside and making her melt against him.

When they finally parted, they simply breathed each other in for a moment. Savoring it.

"So, now that we're officially back together," Lennon asked after a few seconds, "does that mean I get to keep the Porsche?"

Dylan bit his lower lip, seemingly fighting back a smile. "On second thought, I don't know if I can be with someone who only wants me for my money."

Lennon's eyebrows jumped up. "Well, I don't know if I can be with someone who can't win a single game of 'Name That Tune.'"

"Oh, really?"

"Yeah."

Dylan's hands slid to her torso, tickling her sides. She yelped, but she couldn't escape his grasp in the tight space, so all she could do was laugh and curl her body against his. He buried his face in her neck, peppering it with kisses.

"Dylan, I'm going to fall off this thing."

"Don't worry, I've got you," he said quietly, his breath brushing her ear as he stopped, circling his strong arms around her. "I'm never letting you go again."

Lennon's phone buzzed in her pocket, interrupting them. She almost ignored it, but something told her to look. Bruno. She smiled to herself.

"Hey, Charon," Lennon answered. "Finally taking a day off?"

"I wish. I'm on my way home, though. Darius told me what happened at the wedding—that *pendeja*. How are you, *mija*?"

Lennon looked up at Dylan. "Actually, having a pretty good day." He gave her a gentle squeeze.

"Well, I'm about to make it even better—or worse—depending on how you look at it," Bruno said. "You free to come over?"

CHAPTER 46

Lennon

Massive, old oak trees shaded a charming 1950s conch-style house with a white picket fence. Some kids played basketball on the street, layering over the sound of a neighbor mowing their lawn a few houses away. The black Escalade, in which she'd been shuttled to and from set, sat in the driveway. Bruno met Lennon and Dylan at the door in a Hawaiian shirt and shorts—the first time Lennon had ever seen him in casual attire.

"Did you see the piping hot tea that dropped this morning?" Bruno asked after Lennon introduced him to Dylan, leading them further inside. The walls were a happy, vibrant orange, and the air smelled of old wood and citrus.

"About what?" Lennon popped an eyebrow.

Bruno stopped in the hallway between a staircase and a gallery wall filled with framed photos of him, Darius, and a little girl growing from infancy to childhood. He pulled his phone from his pocket and briefly tapped around before turning it to Lennon. The headline on the screen read "Fashion Conglomerate Files for Chapter 11 Bankruptcy." She skimmed the article, which included a photo of Candace and her husband, the CEO of the conglomerate. They explained how the companies they had invested in, including Candace's boutiques, looked successful on the outside but were revealed to have been floundering financially behind closed doors. They got into hot water with investors they'd been hiding the truth from.

The abashed look on Candace's face at the wedding after she'd aligned with Kelsey and thrown Lennon under the bus now made sense. That's what Candace had meant at the party when she said they were there for the same reason—they both needed the exposure *and* the paycheck.

"Wow. I guess we were all pawns on that show, huh?" Lennon mused, disappointed but no longer surprised.

"Some more than others," Bruno remarked with an arched brow. He glanced at Dylan, who was reading the article over Lennon's shoulder. "I'm sorry everything went down the way it did. You both deserved better."

Dylan smiled somberly. "Lesson learned. Don't try to put out a fire by throwing a reality show on it."

"We're enjoying the calm before the storm," Lennon said as she handed the phone back to Bruno. "When the show drops, things will get ... interesting." She released a sigh. They still hadn't made a decision about Nolan's deal, but she was already coming to terms with the show moving ahead as planned in case they weren't able to stop it.

"Or maybe not," Bruno said. The expression on his face suggested he knew something.

The back door slid open, carrying in the sound of a young girl's laughter followed by Darius's smooth baritone. Bare feet slapped along the tile floor and a moment later, a twelve-year-old girl with wet, curly hair and a towel draped over her hot pink bathing suit came running into the hallway.

"Hey, hey, hey—careful! You'll slip," Bruno told her.

"Are you the musician my dad drives around?" Rosie asked Lennon with a wide-eyed grin.

"I am. Are you the piano prodigy he's been telling me about?"

Rosie rolled her eyes at her father. "He exaggerates. But I do play the piano."

Lennon stifled a laugh at the exasperated expression Bruno gave her and the Spanish he mumbled under his breath. "I hear you got a record player for your birthday," she said, and the little girl lit up again, nodding her head enthusiastically. "I know a great record store in town. Want to go sometime?"

"Yes! Oh, my gosh. Can I, Papa?" Rosie looked at Bruno expectantly as Darius came up behind her with swim shorts on and a towel around his neck. He warmly greeted Lennon and Dylan.

"If you go upstairs and take a bath right now, Miss Prodigy," Bruno answered.

Rosie gave him an annoyed look but then smiled brightly at Lennon. "I can't wait!" She ran up the stairs to the chorus of Bruno and Darius both reminding her to be careful.

"I'm going to make sure she's got everything ready for tomorrow," Bruno told them. He eyed his husband. "You want to show them what you found?"

Darius regarded Dylan and Lennon with a heavy look, directing them to follow him upstairs.

After grabbing a shirt and slipping it on, Darius led them to an A-frame attic that had been converted to an additional bedroom. It was jam-packed with instruments and sound equipment Lennon could easily spend hours exploring. He closed the door, blocking out the sounds of the party downstairs thanks to the black acoustic foam panels lining the walls, then crossed the room to the L-shaped desk in the corner.

"I was reviewing the hours and hours of sound footage from the party recently. The one at the mansion," Darius said, opening one of his laptops. Cold trickled into Lennon's stomach just thinking about that night. She watched a muscle in Dylan's jaw pulse. "You catch all kinds of crazy shit with productions like that, especially when there's alcohol involved. People forget about the mic packs." He tapped around on the keyboard and opened a file, then pressed play.

Ambient noise from the mansion party—music, chatter, bodies shuffling—filtered through the speakers, a mostly unintelligible cacophony. Gooseflesh rose on Lennon's arms and neck as the memories of that night surfaced with vivid clarity. A voice triggered her rage with its nasally, languid tone.

Kelsey.

"It's showtime."

"I can't believe you're actually doing this," another female voice said, the words slurring together a bit. A faucet turned on—they must have been in the bathroom. *"You're fucking crazy. I love it."*

"It's getting a little boring. I'm just … spicing things up," Kelsey remarked casually. Unlike the other, her voice sounded eerily sober. The two of them giggled wolfishly.

"I can't believe he's so fucked up. You think he got one of the spiked ones?" The more she spoke, the more familiar the second voice became, too. Tana, Lennon realized. Shuffling of a bag, the click of a lipstick lid coming off.

"I don't know, but when opportunity presents itself, you take it."

"You're not gonna, like … you know?" Tana asked tentatively.

"Ew no, of course not. I just need to get Dylan in a compromising position. All that matters is how it looks on camera. No way he won't take my deal after that."

"What about Lennon?"

"Oh, she won't be a problem. She's so hung up on him, she'll be out of her mind when she finds him with me. The trash will take itself out."

"You've got Avery losing her shit over Steph and now you're about to nab yourself a baseball player. You're an evil fucking genius, Kelsey McCroy. I've got so much to learn from you."

Someone knocked on the bathroom door, interrupting them, and their conversation veered off into Tana asking Kelsey for a tampon. Darius tapped a button to stop the audio.

Silence stretched through the office except for the hum of the electronics.

"That fucking bitch," Lennon hissed, the gooseflesh on her skin melting in her fury. It had never occurred to her that Kelsey *knew* he was drugged—but now, she wondered how she *hadn't* thought of it.

Kelsey had even planted the story about Steph and Chad having an affair.

The rest of the cast hadn't just been pawns. They'd been puppets.

"I can't believe she set me up," Dylan rasped, dazed. "She tried to fucking blackmail me."

"Huey asked the sound department for all the files," Darius said, his grave expression confirming what they had been thinking: The studio did intend to bury the evidence. "We turned them over, but I made copies first. I found this part last night." He reached into a drawer and retrieved a small USB drive. He held it out to Dylan. "I'm leaving High Wave. All I ask is that you don't name me because I'll be in breach of contract, and their lawyers will eat me alive. I can't risk this coming back on my family."

Dylan accepted the USB drive, looking Darius in the eyes. "I won't. But if they do come for you, call me. I've got your back." He extended his other hand. "Thank you."

Darius took his hand, shaking it. "Be careful. Their lawyers are sharks."

Dylan clenched the USB drive in his fist. "So are mine. They've just been waiting for me to throw them something good."

The equalizer for the audio file filled the laptop screen, its jagged peaks and valleys holding the smoking gun they'd been looking for. The game had shifted again. They had a chance to turn things around; they just had to make sure they played their cards right and didn't fumble it.

They needed to get a step ahead.

"I have an idea," Lennon said.

CHAPTER 47

A champagne corked popped, a bartender in a white jacket pouring the contents into a group of flutes arranged on a tray. Glass balustrades offered a nearly seamless view of downtown Arden Beach, the buildings and streets lit up like their own star systems against a clear night sky, surrounding at least a hundred people packed onto the hotel roof in cocktail attire. House music played as they drank and mingled under string lights.

Lennon and Dylan arrived half an hour into the celebration, arms linked and clad in black. A few heads turned toward them, then others, surprise rippling through the crowd.

The pounding of Lennon's heart reverberated through her body. But unlike at the brunch, or the party, or the wedding, it pounded against steel. They were no longer passengers on this ride.

They finally had their hands on the wheel. And she was ready to drive it off a cliff.

"*Heyyyyy.*"

Cold snaked through Lennon's veins at the sight of Tana as she slinked toward them. She clenched against Dylan as Tana's surprised gaze roved over Lennon's black faux-leather mini dress. Lennon's dark hair hung wild and messy around her bare shoulders, her eyes smoky and lips painted a nude brown. Dylan matched her with black dress pants and a deep V-neck, slim-fit, button-down.

Tana clocked their linked arms. Her fake smile faltered. "Hold up—are you guys back together?" She waved a finger at them, a near-empty martini clasped in the other hand.

"We are." Dylan enveloped Lennon's hand nestled in the crook of his arm.

The model's sharp eyebrows pulled together slightly, clearly thrown by this development. Tana knew Kelsey's plan—and she'd probably been as confident as Kelsey that he would take her deal. "Wow. That's … amazing. I'm so happy for you guys." A laugh tumbled out of her. It sounded hollow and forced, like her smile. "Hey, umm—I hope there's no hard feelings about what happened at the wedding. Emotions were high. Everyone was a little tipsy from the open bar," Tana said, tugging her lip to the side as she rocked her head dismissively. "Glad we can put all that behind us now that the show's over. At least until next season." She tilted forward, winking.

The urge to call her on her bullshit burned for release, but Lennon didn't want to tip her off that they knew anything. Yet. "We're not doing another season," she settled on instead.

That part didn't seem to come as a surprise to Tana. "I think we all feel that way right now, but once the series streams and the opportunities start pouring in, we'll be ready for round two." She tossed back the remainder of her drink, dropping it on a tray as a server passed by. Before he walked away, she snatched the speared olive from it. "You heard about Candace? So sad. She's obviously not coming tonight." Tana dragged the olive off the toothpick with her teeth. "Crazy. Just goes to show you never really know someone."

"The truth always has a way of coming out," Lennon said, not bothering to hide the bite in her voice.

Tana paused chewing the olive, her catlike eyes narrowing as she studied Lennon.

The music stopped and Kelsey's voice grated through the speakers, addressing the audience from the stage. "Hey, gorgeous people. Can I steal your attention for a sec?"

Lennon's attention flicked to the stage where Kelsey held a microphone, wearing a skintight, red, mini dress. The blonde waited a moment as chatter across the roof ceased and a sea of heads turned her way.

"I'm going to get something to drink. You want anything, babe?" Lennon asked Dylan.

"Lead the way." Dylan's glare lingered on Tana, disdain simmering in it.

They worked their way through the dense crowd to the bar at the opposite end of the roof, parallel to the stage.

"Let's give it up again for the two geniuses behind the show—Huey Donaldson and Maeve Greenberg," Kelsey said, leading the crowd into applause. "They're amazing, right?"

Huey stood at one of the high-top tables with Maeve, acknowledging those around him, while Maeve did a little wave of her fork as she ate a piece of cake. Her signature red lipstick was flawless as ever. Lennon caught Avery's eye at a table near theirs. They waved at each other while Chad nodded to Dylan.

Avery appeared tense, like she wished to be anywhere else. Lennon could relate.

Lennon and Dylan stopped at the bar, ordering sparkling water before turning to face the stage. Anticipation buzzed under Lennon's skin.

"How ya doing, *mija*?"

Bruno leaned on the bar beside Lennon, while Darius flanked Dylan.

"Feels like I'm back in the Underworld," Lennon answered. "Only this time, *I'm* Charon."

"Well, we know one thing. This party won't be boring." Darius raised his champagne flute, passing them a look of solidarity.

Kelsey babbled on about how the show was about to "change all of their lives." For once, Lennon and Kelsey agreed on something. Dylan pressed his shoulder against hers. When Lennon looked up at him, he gently flicked his nose. *All good. It'll be OK.* Her lips stretched into a smile, melting some of the chill inside her.

Whatever happened, she knew they would be.

A tall, slender man in a suit carved a path through the crowd, making a beeline to Huey. His stern, purposeful energy clashed with the relaxed audience.

Adrenaline spiked in her chest.

"Here we go," Lennon whispered, directing their attention with her sightline.

The man stopped beside Huey, whispering something in his ear. Gradually, the producer's face fell, turning ashen. He snapped his head to the side, saying something back, and then dragged his wide-eyed gaze to his daughter on stage.

Though Lennon couldn't hear it, the next thing out of Huey's mouth was perfectly clear. "*Fuck.*"

Huey dipped his head to say something to the other man, the latter of whom gave a curt nod before making his way back through the crowd while Huey cut toward the stage. He moved with purpose yet restraint, evidently trying not to draw attention to himself.

"People like to make fun of reality shows, but they can't stop watching them," Kelsey continued, completely unaware of what was unfolding.

As Huey tried to get around people, excusing himself and

clamping down on his frustration as they got in his way, Lennon glanced across the crowd. A few recorded Kelsey's speech with their phones, while some others scrolled and texted.

Lennon's pulse quickened.

"We couldn't have done this without all of y—" Kelsey's voice cut out with a high-pitched interference, no longer projecting through the speakers. Confused, she tested the microphone. Her lips moved silently. She gestured to someone off-stage to fix it.

"*It's showtime,*" Kelsey's voice returned through the sound system.

But her mouth wasn't moving on stage.

"*I can't believe you're actually doing this,*" came Tana's voice. Lennon watched her eyes widen in the crowd as a hush fell over them, wondering what was happening. "*You're fucking crazy. I love it.*"

"*It's getting a little boring. I'm just … spicing things up.*" Kelsey's face slowly fell as she recognized her own voice.

Confused murmurs bubbled across the roof.

"Oh, my God," Tana breathed, the blood draining from her face as the recording continued. Beside her, Joel regarded her with confusion.

"Shut it off!" Huey yelled to the audio team near the stage.

"We're trying. Someone's hijacked the system," a frenzied crew member explained.

"Then, unplug the goddamn speakers!"

"Oh, shit," someone muttered in the audience, looking at their phone. "It's on *Star Pulse.*"

Others immediately dug out their phones, gasps and quiet chatter spreading like wildfire, all while Kelsey stood frozen in the middle of the stage, gripping the microphone. Her father raced up the stairs, grabbing her by the arm and dragging her off it.

"*You've got Avery losing her shit over a fake affair and now you're about to nab yourself a baseball player. You're an evil fucking genius, Kelsey McCroy. I've got so much to learn from you.*"

Tana quickly slipped away, eyes following her as she rushed toward the exit. Her husband hesitated a moment before joining her.

Huey tried to follow the same path with Kelsey, but Dylan stepped in front of them, making them stop short.

"I can't believe you knew and tried to blackmail me. For a fucking TV show." Dylan glared down at her with contempt. "What kind of pathetic person does something like that?"

Kelsey stared at him, stunned.

"Kelsey, don't say *anything*," Huey ordered. "Move out of our way."

"How does it feel," Dylan asked her, solid as a rock, "being the one who's not in control anymore?"

"Don't worry, Kelsey," Lennon remarked, standing beside him. "Villains are some of the biggest stars. Right?"

Huey tugged on Kelsey's arm, about to circumvent Dylan and Lennon, but a large figure blocked his path. Chad towered over them with a searing glare, his torso nearly the width of the two Donaldsons side by side. Avery came around him, planting herself in front of Kelsey. A tremor of panic rippled across the blonde's expression.

"How *dare* you." Tears pooled in Avery's eyes, anger and grief closely intertwined. "I can't believe you're the one who started the rumor about Steph and Chad. Why would you do that to me? You were my *maid of honor*."

"It's not personal," Kelsey snapped back, finally finding her voice, though it was shaky. "I was making sure the show wouldn't be so boring that it got canceled after one season. It's business—"

"Kelsey, shut up," Huey demanded.

"I trusted you," Avery said, her voice breaking. "I thought you were my friend."

"I am—"

"Friends don't use each other and try to ruin their wedding."

"You mean the wedding the studio paid for? Why do you

think they did that?" Kelsey's blue eyes turned sharp as a blade. "You don't get how this business works, Avery. This isn't just influencing people to buy shit on social media. I was helping make this thing a success. A pretty face and designer clothes only get you so far. You need drama to keep people hooked. Without me, no one would end up watching this fucking show."

Avery drew back like she'd been physically slapped. "You could've at least told me what you were planning to do."

"Come on, you know you never would've gone for it. And you wouldn't have been believable even if you tried." Kelsey expelled a hollow, condescending laugh. "I was doing you a favor. It's not like anything *actually* happened; it was all fake. Everyone needs to calm down." She scanned the crowd, directing the message to all the eavesdroppers.

"You assaulted Dylan," Lennon reminded her. "That wasn't fake."

"Oh, please." Kelsey pulled a "give me a fucking break" expression. Dylan's arm clasped around Lennon's waist, holding her back from doing something she'd later regret.

"You have no proof of that," Huey interjected. His face was as red as Maeve's fingernails. "That audio was tampered with, and we'll prove it. Whoever pulled this stunt will pay. We're done here." He made to step forward, but Chad remained a statue. Huffing, Huey raised his chin to the ex-quarterback, trying for a show of strength even as fear flickered in his eyes.

"You did all this for what—fame? To boost your career?" Avery surmised. Her voice was pitched low. "I hope everything you ended up losing in the process was worth it."

Something flashed in Kelsey's eyes—something that looked dangerously close to pain—but it quickly vanished. Stone-faced, she replied, "That's what we were *all* here for. I just had the balls to make the most of it." A bitter smile shaped her lips. "What do they say? Hate the game, not the player."

Avery shook her head, her expression hardening into disgust.

She glanced up at Chad, sending him a small nod. He finally stepped aside to let Kelsey and Huey pass. Huey wasted no time dragging his daughter toward the exit.

"You'll all thank me when this show blows up and you're making bank," Kelsey threw over her shoulder. Lennon wondered if she was trying to convince herself as much as everyone else.

One of the guests the Donaldsons passed by recorded them with their phone. Huey slapped it out of their hand. Looking around, Huey proclaimed, "If any of you taking videos ever want another job in this industry, you'll delete them—*now*."

As they stormed off, the stunned crowd remained suspended in silence for a while, unsure what to do.

"OK, well. I think it's time to call it a night," Maeve announced loudly, her upbeat mood jarring with the tense atmosphere. "Thank you all for coming. Feel free to take advantage of the open bar once more before you leave." Under her breath she added, "God knows I will." Turning on her heels, her attention landed on Lennon and the others. Her expression went solemn as she approached the group. "I swear—I didn't know anything about what was on that recording. I'm all for shaking things up, but that crossed a line."

Though she seemed earnest and as disturbed as they were, Lennon didn't feel particularly trusting in that moment. The others remained quiet, too.

Maeve didn't press it. Her chest rose and fell with an inward sigh before heading back into the crowd, probably to make her best attempt to put out this raging fire before it took her down with it.

Chad wrapped an arm around Avery, who looked as ill as Lennon felt. "You OK, baby?"

"No." Avery shook her head, her cheeks stained with tears. "I'm sorry, Lennon. I didn't want to believe she was like this. She was always so good to me. Or at least, I thought she was." She squeezed the bridge of her nose. "I feel so stupid."

Lennon sighed. "You're not stupid, Avery. You just wanted to see the best in someone you care about."

Avery frowned. "The person I care about apparently doesn't exist. And while I was defending her, I wasn't a good friend to you."

"Well, we're trauma-bonded now, so you have time to make up for it." The corner of Lennon's mouth quirked up.

Avery's twitched a little, too, but then her eyes fluttered shut with another small, quick shake of her head. Her voice cracked. "I'm sorry … I'm so embarrassed. I need to go."

"Let's go home." Chad lovingly stroked her arm. "I'll call you later, man," he told Dylan, who nodded. Avery hid her teary face in Chad's chest as he escorted her away, the crowd parting like the Red Sea around them.

"You ready to get out of here, too?" Dylan asked Lennon, giving her hand a gentle squeeze.

"So fucking ready."

CHAPTER 48

Lennon

**SUSPECT FOUND GUILTY OF DRUGGING
BASEBALL STAR DYLAN STRICKLAND**

Last month, Star Surge obtained an EXPLOSIVE audio clip from an anonymous source of socialite Kelsey McCroy and supermodel Tana Cordova allegedly talking about baseball star Dylan Strickland's drink getting spiked at a party. They were both filming a reality show in Arden Beach, Florida, that's streaming this winter on Versal.

An investigation led to the arrest of Jeremy Miller, a model working at the party as a "host" going by the name Alexei, who was found guilty this morning on drug charges.

In the audio, Kelsey can be heard bragging about taking advantage of the opportunity to make the Tidebreakers pitcher's ex-wife, Lennon Young (also present at the party), jealous, and coercing him into taking some "deal." Yikes.

Kelsey McCroy is the daughter of Huey Donaldson, one of the producers of Arden Elite at High Wave Productions. After the audio leak, she was dropped *by her management company and her first feature film role was cut from a movie slated for release next summer. Since the leak went viral, she hasn't been seen in public, except for a court appearance as a witness in Jeremy's case. Can't say we blame her. Social media has been rallying behind Dylan and crucifying Kelsey, especially after he recently took medical leave from the Tidebreakers and publicly opened up about his mental health struggles.*

Tana has also been off the radar after she was forced to sell her stake in her popular skincare and beauty line when consumers called for a boycott of the company in response to the audio leak.

All parties involved have declined to comment on the scandal. Guess we'll have to wait and see what happens when Arden Elite premieres in January. We know we'll be glued to our TVs!

"So, they're taking the silent approach and using it to stoke interest in the show," Harold mused, reading the article on his phone. The journalist glanced across the table at Lennon and Dylan over the rim of his glasses. "'Any press is good press,' or so the saying goes."

They sat in a secluded booth at Merritt's Steakhouse, black and white photographs of Dylan's grandfather watching over the table.

"When you know how to spin it," Lennon said as she lifted a cup of cappuccino to her lips.

Harold hummed a sound of agreement. He studied them both. Putting down his phone, Harold's expression grew serious under the dim light. "I'm sorry this happened to you," he told Dylan. "I'll be honest, though, I'm surprised you finally called me. What made you decide to let me tell your story?"

"That's not why we called. We're done letting other people tell our story. But we know you're open to suggestions," Dylan remarked, alluding to Harold that they knew about his connection with Nolan. The journalist's mouth quirked up in the corner, a guilty but remorseless glimmer in his eyes. Dylan's gaze shifted darkly. "I hear you're not a big fan of Huey Donaldson."

Harold raised a wiry eyebrow at Lennon, seemingly impressed she'd picked up on that at the gala. "We go back a bit. I've … heard things, but I've never been able to get people to talk on the record because of his ironclad NDAs. He hands them out like candy. Scares people off." He measured them, as if noticing a missing puzzle piece. "Which I'd imagine you signed, as well."

Lennon lowered her cup to the table. The soft music from a Spanish guitar drifted between them as the energy in the air shifted, taut like the instrument's strings.

"I had an off-camera conversation with Kelsey—after the wedding," Dylan said. "My lawyers said it would be hard to prove a blackmail case. It'd be easier to fight the defamation clause in my NDA."

Harold's eyes sharpened, more with intrigue than surprise. "The 'deal' she spoke about in the recording?" Harold clarified, to which Dylan gave an affirmative nod. "One I'll bet she wasn't planning to facilitate by herself?"

Dylan didn't directly answer, but he didn't need to. His eyes said enough. Harold blew a gust of air through his lips, sitting back. The gears turned. They were offering him a *much* bigger fish.

"If I give you enough to build a story from, do you think you could get others to come forward with their experiences?" Dylan questioned.

Harold rocked his head, tapping a finger on the table. "Depends. Sometimes, it only takes one to open the floodgates. But they still may be too afraid of the repercussions. Most don't have the resources you have."

"They may be protected under loopholes and not be aware of it. Especially if anything illegal occurred," Dylan pointed out.

"With your story bolstering its credibility, I can probably get away with some of the others remaining anonymous." Harold rolled his forefinger and thumb together beside his plate of half-eaten crab cakes, his gaze lost somewhere in the table's dark, polished wood as he appeared to contemplate it.

Dylan released a humorous breath. "Nice to be thought of as credible again."

It was wild how quickly the tides of public opinion had turned back in his favor. Everyone was rallying around him. It was a nice change of pace, but they knew not to get too comfortable. The show hadn't come out yet, and they had no idea how Huey was planning to spin things in the edit.

Lennon dropped her head to the side, watching Harold. "Don't you think it's strange one of the employees at the party is the person who spiked some of the drinks, even knowing it was all on camera? Almost like he knew he'd be protected. Alexei … or Jeremy, whatever the hell his name is, had a pretty expensive lawyer who miraculously helped him avoid a lot of jail time. And now, his mugshot's gone viral because of how good he looks in it. Who wants to bet he ends up with his own reality show?"

"You'd think the public would be condemning him as much as Kelsey," Dylan remarked with disgust.

"People are always more enthusiastic about hating a woman." Harold casually tossed out the observation, but it stuck with Lennon.

With the audio leak, the public was firmly on Dylan's and Lennon's side, but would that all be forgotten once the show aired? Their goodwill was fickle. It all hinged on the edit the show gave her. Huey would be working overtime to sway viewers back in Kelsey's favor, so Lennon didn't imagine their plan to give Lennon the "villain edit" had been abandoned. In fact, it would probably be worse now.

Their only hope was to expose the entire corrupt operation, so the public *didn't* forget so easily.

The weight of Dylan's hand came to rest on her thigh under the table. She found him watching her with some concern, apparently sensing the tension in her body. She sent him a soft smile of reassurance, placing her hand on his. He spread his fingers so she could thread hers between them.

"You said you care about the truth," Lennon reminded Harold, turning back to him. "Time to put on your big boy investigative journalist pants and figure out a way to expose this asshole."

The corner of Harold's mouth gently arched before a genuine laugh rumbled out of him. "Man, they didn't know what they were in for when they cast you."

Lennon smiled. "When we're done here, I hope they rue the day they did."

Harold pulled a crumpled notepad from his tweed jacket, clicking the tip of the ballpoint pen he'd unhooked from the spiral binding. "You've finally learned how the game works."

"We know it's not over yet," Lennon said. "We're going to hit them with all we've got in this last inning."

Dylan's brows raised slightly. "Good baseball metaphor, baby. Perfect cheese to symbolism ratio."

"Thank you."

Harold glanced at the two of them before gently shaking his head, dropping his attention back to the notepad as he scribbled something in it. "Oh, to be young and in love," he mumbled. "Hope you guys are ready for what's coming. They're not going down without a fight."

Dylan squeezed Lennon's fingers, and she met his steadfast gaze. The message in his deep brown eyes was clear: *I'm with you. Completely.*

For the first time, she felt a strange sense of calm instead of a charge of anxiety over what the future held. A storm was coming, but they were prepared now. And they'd face the aftermath. Together.

Lennon squeezed his hand back. "Neither are we."

EPILOGUE

Lennon

THREE MONTHS LATER

Warm, amber hues of a setting sun glinted off the end of her pen as ink glided along the lined pages of a notebook. Notes filled the margin, various lines scratched out and notated, the beginnings of musical notes scribbled alongside the lyrics. Under her breath, Lennon hummed a melody repeatedly between fragments of lyrics, making small changes, exploring different arrangements.

Boisterous sounds of excitement called her attention up from her spot on the bleachers behind a black net separating her from the field. One of the kids, a nine-year-old girl, booked it for home plate. Dylan cheered her on from the sidelines along with her friends on the field—a mix of boys and girls around her age—and a group of parents on the bleachers. Lennon watched the girl's tiny sneakers carry her across the clay mounds, the opposing team trying desperately to wrangle the ball from the outfield and send it back before she completed a home run.

She made it just in time, sending everyone into a frenzy.

Dylan whooped the loudest, as though they'd won the National Series. He ran out to the field and cheered with the players like a kid himself, praising the girl and everyone else for their teamwork. They tackled him to the ground, covering his white t-shirt and jeans in orange clay.

Lennon laughed, enjoying the sight of Dylan in a genuine state of joy. Her heart radiated warmth through her body like the afternoon sun beaming down on the field, comforting her against the crisp chill in the air.

When he finally stood, he went to the other team and praised them for playing such a great, competitive game. Instead of looking dejected, they looked proud, motivated, and pumped for the next match. Dylan had discovered he had a gift for striking that balance—seeing the beauty of both winning and losing and playing the game on your own terms.

Lennon's hand drifted across the pages of the notebook again as an idea popped into her head. She then grabbed her phone, opening a text thread with the name Raquel at the top.

Lennon: What do you think of this for the bridge?

She then recorded a voice memo with some alterations to the lyrics and melody they'd been working on together. It joined the long thread of texts and voice memos they had been sending back and forth for weeks, the last being Lennon's text to Raquel a week ago letting her know she was beginning her tech blackout at a cabin in the mountains with Dylan. They'd finally turned their phones back on that morning, but the terrible cell service in the area had kept them disconnected from the outside world for a few extra hours.

After the recording from the party leaked, Dylan and Lennon found themselves thrust back into the limelight and Lennon's new serving job called to rescind their offer, stating that her publicity would be "disruptive" to their clientele. But the saying was true— when one door closes, another opens. Not twenty-four hours later, she received a call from Oscar about a songwriting opportunity.

She'd nearly burst when she showed up at his house the next day and Raquel was there, wanting to hear the other songs Lennon had played for Oscar and any others she was working on.

And she'd loved them.

Raquel hadn't officially announced it yet, but she was producing a new album and looking for something fresh. She asked Lennon to be one of the songwriters on it. Though Lennon was grieving her ability to record her own music—and actively working with Dylan's lawyers to fight it—it was another dream come true to have one of her idols sing *her* words.

Because they could work on things remotely, Lennon also said yes to Dylan when he asked her if she'd like to take the road trip they'd always dreamt about.

For the last month, they'd been driving across the country, stopping at small ball parks along the way. While Lennon worked on her music, Dylan spent a day at each one volunteering with the kids, teaching them how to improve their baseball skills and drumming up interest in youth programs to keep them funded after he left. His love of baseball had transformed when he shared it with others, seeing the game through their young eyes.

It helped him cope with the powerlessness he felt over the fate of the Tidebreakers.

With Diego back on the team, they made it to the postseason but lost the series match-up that took them out of the running for the championship. Though disappointing to come so close, it infused some confidence back in the team's future. Eddie was able to leverage their late-season comeback to convince the Commissioner to hold off on forcing a sale of the team, but its fate still hung in the balance. A lot was riding on the next season.

But that was a problem for later. Right now, they were enjoying their break from it all.

They'd made it to California to a small mountain town in the desert the day before the show premiered, spending the past week in a secluded cabin with their phones off. Only Rhett and Erin had the number to the landline to reach them in case of an emergency. Erin was in the second week of her own tech-free mindfulness retreat in Florida, on break from work and school. They'd timed them to avoid the inevitable media circus when the show premiered.

The dry air was a change from the humid climate Lennon was used to in Florida, as was the desert landscape and mountains cutting across the horizon beyond the baseball field. All the different cities and geography they'd traveled through had served as rich nourishment for Lennon's creativity.

Making love to Dylan in a different place every night hadn't hurt, either.

A memory of their time in Arizona brought a smile to Lennon's lips and a flush to her cheeks as it flashed through her mind. They'd stopped at a drive-in movie theater to watch *Grease* and were nearly kicked out when things got a little too heated between them in the back of his SUV. They stopped and finished the movie, then pulled over on an empty road on the way to their next hotel to finish what they'd started. She bit down on her pen, hiding her smile as she tucked in her chin.

"What were you thinking about?" Dylan asked with a grin as he approached the net.

"Sedona."

His smile grew as he dug his teeth into his lower lip, eyes sparkling mischievously. Dylan's face was already flushed from playing on the field, but she swore the color in his cheeks deepened a bit. He raised his arms, hooking his fingers through a couple of holes in the mesh, and she stood up to meet him. The underside of his arms, bronzed and corded with taut muscle, glistened with sweat. Lennon's hands latched onto the loops under his, and he curled his long fingers over hers. Pressing her body against the fence, their noses brushed through one of the holes. Fireworks exploded in her chest.

"We could see if they have a drive-in somewhere around here, too," he whispered.

"It's worth looking into," she agreed. They kissed through an opening, restricted by the limited diameter to do anything more than a simple peck and a careful flick of the tongue. It made her even hungrier for him. "Are you finishing up here soon?"

"Yeah. I just need to shower off, and we can go," Dylan said, his voice low and laced with need.

"Too bad this is a family place. Otherwise, I'd join you."

Dylan released a strained sigh from deep in his throat. "I'll probably need another one when we get back to the hotel."

"You are *really* sweaty."

"Really, really sweaty."

"And dirty," Lennon added, glancing at the clay marks on his chin, down the front of his tight white t-shirt, along his biceps.

Dylan bit his lip as he hung his head. "Lennon, there are still some kids around, and my pants are too tight for you to talk like that."

"Then, you'd better hurry up."

He dropped another peck on her lips, nudging her fingers with his before pressing off the fence, a stupidly happy grin on his face as he turned around. She whistled. "Man, I do like those tight pants." He laughed, shaking his head as he jogged off.

Lennon's phone pinged with a notification. Her message to Raquel had been unable to be delivered, and there were still no bars on her phone.

Good.

Their hands rested intertwined on the center console as music from a mixed hits station played low in the background. Dylan's fingers absentmindedly drummed the steering wheel while Lennon looked out the passenger window, taking in the unfamiliar sights as they passed.

"You know how the Arden Beach Ballpark has been closed for a while? Just sitting there, overgrown and empty," Dylan said. "I was thinking … what if I got some investors to go in with me, maybe some buddies of mine from the team, to rehab it and get some youth programs involved again? Maybe even start one of my own. I think it'd be good for the community. Give them a place to play and have fun."

"Dylan, I love that."

"Really?"

"Yeah."

His smile grew as he faced forward, eyes on the road, but she could tell his mind was venturing into the possibilities.

As they drove further into town, their phones began to buzz and *ding* rapidly.

"Well, we've got cell service back," Lennon remarked grudgingly. Unlocking her phone, it opened to Raquel's text thread where Lennon's message to her from earlier finally zipped through and the progress bar on the voice memo inched forward. A couple of texts from Raquel popped up after it.

Raquel: Lennon!!!

Raquel: YOU'RE A STAR BABY

Lennon smiled at the message, confused by its context. Probably something to do with the music they'd been working on before her break—maybe a voice memo hadn't come through yet. Dozens of other texts poured in, too fast for her to read them all. Amid the chaos, she tapped Erin's thread to read messages she must have sent last night or that morning after returning from her retreat.

Erin: Call me as soon as you get this!

Erin: Not an emergency but WE NEED TO TALK ASAP!

"I'm gonna call Erin," Lennon said, but as she went to tap on the button, her phone began ringing. "Ugh. Maeve."

After Harold's bombshell article was published three weeks before *Arden Elite's* planned release date, three separate lawsuits were filed against Huey Donaldson, and an investigation was opened into his potential involvement with the spiked drinks at the party. He was promptly fired from High Wave Productions, putting Maeve in charge and leaving a big question mark over whether the show would still air. Versal ultimately chose to move forward with it. But instead of the weekly drip they'd planned, they decided to dump all eight episodes at once last week.

It had been easy to avoid all the media chatter leading up to the show's release while on the road, driving in and out of cellular service. They could mostly forget about it and live in their little bubble. Staying in a quiet, secluded cabin with no access to the internet or cellular service had been even more blissful.

Of course, they knew they couldn't stay there forever. Bubble, officially burst.

"I'm just gonna get it over with," Lennon said. She reluctantly tapped the green button and put the call on speakerphone. "Hey, Maeve."

"Lennon, dear! How are you doing?"

"Great. Here with Dylan, you're on speakerphone."

"Hey, Maeve."

"Hi, handsome," she cooed back. "I'm *so* glad I got you two on the phone. None of my calls have been going through all week."

"We've been traveling," Lennon explained. "We're going in and out of dead zones, so we may lose you." She mimicked to Dylan how she could accidentally press the "end call" button with a silent *"oops!"* He stifled a laugh, shaking his head.

"Oh, no! OK, I'll make this quick, then. People are going *nuts* over the show. It's all over social media."

"It's only been out for a week," Lennon said.

"People are binging it," Maeve explained. "Everyone's been waiting for it. It's all anyone can talk about."

Lennon gave Dylan a wary look. "I don't know if that's a good thing …"

"It is. Everyone's obsessed with your love story. I want to talk to you about doing another—"

"Maeve, we already told you, that was it for us," Lennon said. "We're not doing another season."

"No, a *different* show—about you and Dylan." Maeve spoke fast, pausing for half a beat. "We want to follow your music career. You'd have complete control over the narrative. We could even put it in your contract that you have to sign off on all the editing, any other cast members, or whatever you want. I'll do whatever it takes to make it happen. I know lightning in a bottle like this doesn't happen often, and I don't want to waste any time not taking full advantage of it."

"We're not working under Nolan," Dylan stated firmly.

"You wouldn't be. I'm going to pitch the show to other networks. I've already put out some feelers, and there is a *lot* of interest." Maeve lowered her voice, almost conspiratorially, like she was about to say something she shouldn't. "*Arden Elite* will likely be dead without you two signing on, and Versal knows it. If you sign with a different network with a new show … that's going to sting. A lot."

Lennon looked at Dylan, unsure how to respond. They'd agreed to close that chapter. They didn't regard the reality show as a success or failure, simply an experience. One they were done with. But the idea of having complete control over a wide-reaching platform was enticing. And sticking it to Nolan? That would be a nice little bonus.

By the look Dylan gave her, he was thinking the same thing.

One mistake she wouldn't repeat—jumping in without thinking about *every* possible angle first.

"We need to talk about it," Lennon told her. "We'll get back to you."

"Yes, yes, talk about it! I'll stand by for any questions. Enjoy your trip. Oh—and if you haven't yet, check out the show. I think you'll be pleasantly surprised by the final product."

After they hung up, Lennon and Dylan exchanged a "what the hell was that" look.

"Are we seriously entertaining this?" Lennon watched him, the wind blowing through his hair as shops and restaurants passed in a blur of color beyond the open window.

"I don't know, are we?"

Lennon snorted, shaking her head. "The last one was such a clusterfuck."

"We survived it, though. I'd say it turned out pretty OK." Dylan lifted her hand to his lips, planting a kiss on her knuckles. She smiled.

"I'm scared to look at the comments online." Lennon grimaced.

"May as well rip off the bandage."

Lennon heaved a jagged sigh, her stomach coiling in knots. Still gripping his hand, she maneuvered her phone with the other to see what people were saying about the show. The top comments and articles about *Arden Elite* popped up on the first page of her search. First, she flipped through some of the social media comments, reading them aloud over the wind.

"Watching the downfall of Evil Incarnate, Kelsey McCroy, is satisfying to my core."

"The socialites on Arden Elite *made me want to move to Arden Beach, if only I were social and elite."*

"Who isn't in love with Dylan Strickland after watching Arden Elite? *The guy's comeback is an inspiration. And he's hot."*

Then, Lennon tapped on the most recent article from the pop culture news website *PopSphere* titled "Why Everyone in Your Office is Crying Today (You Can Blame a Reality Show)." She read the article to him.

After two big scandals this year involving Dylan Strickland, everyone has been waiting to watch Arden Elite, *and boy, it did not disappoint. It's packed with all the juicy drama you'd hope for from a reality show with a bunch of hot people, but it's the relationship between baseball star Dylan Strickland and his ex-wife, Lennon Young, that has everyone talking. The will-they-won't-they back and forth has us in a chokehold. We're all Dylennon shippers now, wondering if (read: hoping) they'll get back together. Judging by the way he stood up for her at the wedding, we're thinking yes. And we're also still sobbing over his speech defending her to the show's resident villain, Kelsey McCroy.*

> *We've reached out for a comment from their teams. No word yet to confirm, but sources say they've been spotted together since then.*

Lennon glanced at Dylan, her lips lifting in a smirk. "Guess we'll have to tell them at some point." Then, she went back to reading the article and nearly stumbled over the next part.

> *We're all wondering when we're going to get an album from Lennon Young, the aspiring, down-on-her-luck musician.*

She loosed a small exhale, that pit in her stomach twisting every time she thought about it.

> *Everyone has been invested in her journey, wondering when we'd get to hear a song from her, and the finale finally gifted us with an original song over the credits that has us all in tears.*

Lennon stopped and stared at the article, assuming she'd read it wrong. "Wait—" She reread it, this time more slowly. "That doesn't make any sense. Carol Anne said they couldn't use it because the record company had to sign off on it and it'd cost a fortune."

Dylan's attention jumped between the road and her. She continued scrolling through the article, which included other people's comments embedded from social media:

"*I need an entire album from Lennon Young like, yesterday.*"

"*Told my boss I can't come into work today because of emotional damage from* Reality With You.*"*

"*My therapist and I cried over* Reality With You *together and I think we both consider Lennon OUR therapist now.*"

She could barely breathe.

"Lennon …" Dylan's voice practically hummed with excitement; his lips parted in a surprised smile.

"I don't understand. That's impossible—"

"Ask Maeve. Call her."

Lennon's hands shook as she called Maeve back, who answered before the first ring even finished.

"Thought I'd hear back from you pretty quick," Maeve answered through what sounded like a grin.

"What are they talking about with the song?" Lennon asked.

"That was my little surprise. It cost me an arm and a leg to get Goldrush to sign off on it because they're a bunch of dicks, but I *knew* people would love it. Consider it my peace offering."

"Holy shit. Maeve …" Lennon's heart hammered against her ribcage. She couldn't think straight. "I—I don't know what to say. Thank you."

After they hung up, Lennon read through more social media comments, trying to process them. She wiped the moisture from her cheeks, sniffling, and finally put her phone down, needing a moment to soak it all in. To process the feeling of another dream turning into reality.

Dylan caressed her hand, beaming with pride beside her. She looked out the window as the crisp autumn air blew through her hair, her chin pressed into her palm, overwhelmed.

"Wait, is that?" Dylan turned up the volume on the radio.

"—so here it is again," a radio DJ said, "the most requested song today and the viral hit everyone on the internet is talking about, *Reality With You* by Lennon Young."

Lennon dropped her hand, her mouth falling open as her song began to play on the radio.

The actual fucking radio.

"Oh, my God. *Oh, my God!*"

"Lennon, you're on the radio!"

"OH, MY GOD."

Dylan cranked it up as loud as it would go and opened the rest of the windows as they both shouted in excitement. He honked the horn at passersby, screaming, "Hey, her song is on the radio!"

The moment wasn't exactly how she'd envisioned it, but it was somehow better—because it was real.

"This melody isn't the one I imagined.
But if I have to live in reality,
I want reality with you."
—LENNON YOUNG, *Reality With You*

Want to see what happened the night of Lennon and Dylan's first wedding? Head to lemcquinn.com/rwybonus or scan the code below to read a special bonus flashback not included in the book. You're welcome. ;)

If you enjoyed this book, please leave a review on any platform (Amazon, GoodReads, etc) to help other readers discover it, too. Reviews are the quickest, easiest way to support both the author and the book community as a whole and are greatly appreciated!

ACKNOWLEDGEMENTS

The people who helped me bring this book across the finish line and a dream to fruition are dear to me in ways I could never fully express. For as long as I can remember, I've dreamed about publishing my debut novel, and it wouldn't have been possible without some very special people helping me see it through.

To my parents: This is the hardest one to write because my feelings and gratitude are too big for words. Just know that your unending support, love, encouragement, sacrifices, and belief in me has had a profound effect on my life, my work, and who I am as a person. Thank you for everything. You are the greatest blessing.

To Kristine and Jessica: Thank you for all the hours-long voice memos, late-night chats about anything and everything, Disney trips, laughing so hard it hurts, dancing to 90s boy bands, and most of all, the unwavering support and cheerleading you've both given me throughout our friendship. You've always made me feel seen, loved, and supported. You're more than my best friends, you're my sisters. LYLAS and FSUL energy for life.

To Sarah and Michelle: My TSBM fam. The Blossom and Bubbles to my Buttercup. My Australian twin and soupmate. I know soulmates exist because the three of us are. You both constantly inspire me—as humans, as artists, and as friends. I cherish you so deeply, and I wouldn't want to do this without you.

To Sarah of Wildflower and Main Editorial: Thank you for being such an incredible friend, critique partner, and developmental editor. You helped me make this book stronger with your wisdom and helped me stay sane with your support.

To Davona and Christina: Thank you for all the deliciously wicked conversations to match your equally wicked talent and senses of humor, and for not only helping me grow as a writer, but also for being such incredible cheerleaders. (And Davona, I promise—you'll see Gordon again.)

To my beta readers: Thank you for taking the time to read my book and patiently answer my questions about it. You may have not felt like you were being helpful, but trust me, you were.

To my line editor, Erika of ELA Editorial Co. and my proofreader, Sharon of Prose Polish: Thank you both for your magnificent expertise, kindness, and professionalism in helping me make this book as polished as possible. I'm so grateful we connected and to have you on my team.

To my interior formatter/designer, Stacey of Champagne Book Design, and my cover illustrator, Alina: Thank you both for making this into the book of my dreams. Stacey, you did a stunning job on the interior. Alina, you *captured* Lennon and my vision for the cover art perfectly; I'm still in awe every time I look at it.

To everyone else who helped make this book a reality: Thank you for every word of encouragement, kind gesture (big or small), piece of advice, like, comment, follow, and show of support so many people have given me over the years. Every single one of them has had an impact on me. Seriously.

Thank you, dear reader, for reading (and finishing) this book. I sincerely hope you enjoyed it. If not, I hope it makes good kindling for a warm, cozy fire.

And finally, I want to thank myself. There were (many) times I questioned if I'd actually get to this point after so many delays and false-starts. I'm grateful to my past self for staying committed, even when I wanted to chuck my laptop off a very tall bridge. *in Elle Woods's voice* We did it!

ABOUT THE AUTHOR

L.E. McQuinn is a Floridian fantasy and contemporary romance author who grew up obsessed with love stories, from fairytales to soap operas. When she's not writing or engaging in some other form of fiction-fueled escapism, she's probably at a theme park, cuddling with her fur-babies, or stargazing while listening to an astronomy podcast.

Connect with her, read free short stories, dive into bonus content, receive updates and announcements on future projects, and more at www.lemcquinn.com.